REALMS OF EDENOCHT

The Timeless Plains

Realms of Edenocht

Realms of Edenocht Timeless Plains

D.S. JOHNSON

A Young Adult Fantasy Fiction Action Adventure Novel

DS JOHNSON

2020

First Printing: 2020 B&N

ISBN 978-1-7352859-4-8

Illustrator -DS Johnson

Rosecrest Printing
Herriman, Utah 84096

www.dsjohnsonbooks.com

Realms of Edenocht

Dedication

To my family! To my husband Don, who loves the stories as much as I do and supports me through each one, (with the gentle pushes to get it done so he can read it). To my kids who keep the family dinner table make-believe sessions alive.

To my fans and all those who will come across this book at some future time and fall in love with it as I have.

Contents

Prologue- I Am Jaduuk'ai

They once lived a vibrant life dedicated to caring for the land and animals. They harnessed the elements and with their supernatural abilities devoted themselves to the world of Edenocht. Their traditions were deep in the laws of conduct, and they valued their rights and responsibilities. But times changed. The shadow crept into their hearts and madness ripped across the land. Father and son fought against father and son and mothers were left desolate.

"Alisdair are you sure you want to do this?" a man asked.

His medium-length white hair was pulled back into a knot at the back of his head as was most of the warriors.

"We either die by fighting or we just die," Alisdair said looking into his friend's sky-blue eyes.

"Then we fight to the end," the man said with a slight grin, but Alisdair knew his guts ached too.

Alisdair wanted to puke, the fear for his people ripped through his guts as he examined their finely chiseled features, high cheekbones, and strong jaws.

"You have been my best friend and loyal supporter Onen," Alisdair said.

Onen studied Alisdair's strong features, pale blonde hair and deep-blue eyes that reflected the high-sun's rays with intensity. It was a face he had looked up to his entire life.

"You have been more than that since before the time I can remember," Onen said.

Alisdair smiled and nodded, but his heart ached for his people. They didn't start this war, and it wasn't their fault, but they had to finish it, or die trying. Overwhelming dread sank into his chest. He searched the distance and found nothing but a ruined world. Death, and destruction brought on by anger, jealousy, and greed. He examined the horizon, and his fear was confirmed. It was just him and his army now.

Alisdair sucked in a deep breath and nodded to his commanding officers, shoved his heel into the side of his horse and it lurched forward. He gripped the reins and relaxed them but slapped the leather straps against the animal to give it permission to run. The horse complied and gained a fast pace quickly. The officers followed suit and then the rest of the army. It wasn't long before the powerful thudding of the horses' hooves hitting the dusty ground surged through the atmosphere.

Alisdair's horse gripped the terrain with fierceness. The hundreds of horses followed with diligence as did their riders. The army of the Tooatha De Dannon was strong, fierce, and loyal, but they had been fighting this war for so many rotations and the creatures just wouldn't stop coming. Every time they wiped out the hordes, more hordes returned. The wind whipped through their hair as they raced toward the mountain and the growing stench of death and decay sank into their senses.

The Tooatha De Dannon were a fair-complexioned people with hair colors ranging from blonde to white with blue and gray eyes. Remarkably different from their brothers the Fir Bolg in likeness and in every other way. The Fir delighted in bloodshed and fierce cruelty. They were the first to succumb to the shadows enticing, all because of Baltair the fourth born to the God of Glory. As the fourth son, he was always overlooked by the brothers and sister. Especially the oldest, Alisdair. Baltair hated him, he was fair, blonde, blue-eyed, strong, powerful, and the *chosen* one. Despite Alisdair's attempts at loving his younger brother, Baltair embraced the darkness.

Heavy thuds pelted his ears and Alisdair turned to find another army on horseback led by his sister, Malita, and on the other, his brother Todan. Alisdair wasn't sure they were going to come as they had had their differences, but his heart swelled with gratitude, but then a fear sank into his being. He was leading them all to their deaths. The wind rushed by with a loudness that left the pit in his stomach deep and Malita nodded with her beautiful smile. Her long warm golden-brown hair flowed off the back of her delicate features and her deep green eyes twinkled as she gave him her silent support.

Todan was a vibrant individual with a love for life and fun, but had a serious side that was often misunderstood for a hot temper that matched his red hair. His soft brown eyes nodded and also gave Alisdair his silent support. The three leaders of their people moved into ranks as the horses barreled over the now barren wasteland. Baltair's evil pact with the Shadow had left its mark on the world as well as his people, most of which had been killed and or replaced with his underworld beasts.

Alisdair pointed and the siblings looked. The underworld creatures came into view still several lengths ahead, but they could see them running on all fours. The Jaduuk were a mix of an orc-like wolf hunter that walked upright, and ran on all fours with clawed hooves. Their long-pointed fangs that went upward to the crest of their eyebrows reflected the sun and drool dripped from their wolves snout.

Alisdair pulled his longbow and settled into the saddle squeezing his legs tightly against the horse. He loaded an arrow and the others in the front few lines followed. He sucked in a deep breath and released the arrow as he breathed out. With intense speed, he released every arrow in his quiver and every one hit their marks into the beasts. The arrows sank deep into the Jaduuk's bluish hides that were covered in patches of bristly and ragged fur, and they roared as they fell backward.

The oncoming beasts leaped over their fallen and embraced for the oncoming hit. They rose onto their hind legs and pulled their battle-ax's as Alisdair and the others neared. Alisdair gripped the hilt of the Honor Blade and listened as the hum it constantly made sounded in his ears. The comfort the blade brought gave him the last bit of nerves he needed, and he let out a war-cry. His army replied with their own and the Jaduuk roared in return.

Alisdair gripped the fire element he controlled and sent a billowing inferno that drenched and consumed the Jaduuk. Malita whipped her hand around her head and let go of a blast of wind-blades. The invisible force thrashed their thick blue hides and sent a spray of rancid blood into the atmosphere. Todan slammed his hands together and a blast of kinetic energy emerged from the earth and shot the beasts across the distance, liquefying their insides as they melted to the ground. Blasts of elements from the warriors careened over the landscape as the three forces united.

Blades slashed, fire billowed, earth opened and swallowed the beasts, and the wind tore through their flesh. Over and over, the

Tooatha De Dannon, Lavari, and Bair Tiornecht defeated their at-
tackers, but the day became night and day again and the beasts just
kept coming. Alisdair had pushed hard to get as close to the mountain as he could and when he thought they were close enough he
signaled to his officers.

They broke away from the battle and made their way toward
the entrance of the mountainous hole, Baltair called home. The rancid smell intensified, and they were certain their nose hairs had been
singed with its stink. The heat radiated around the jagged black-
stone of the immense cavern. An eerie silence gripped their senses
and they slowly made their way past the gurgling acid as it made its
way down the sides of the walkway.

Steam wafted over their heads and large egg-like nodules,
the size of twice that of a man, sat on a nest-like structure that was
being fed with the heat of lava. They could now tell where the acid
was coming from as it dripped off the rough egg.

"Is that egg-thing breathing?" Todan asked.

"It certainly looks like it," Onen said.

"This is just gross," Malita said.

"Did you think it was going to be pretty, sis?" Todan asked.

Malita gave him a sideways glare, and he snickered, then she
rolled her eyes, and he snickered again.

"He's close," Alisdair said.

Alisdair held out his hands and Malita and Todan joined him
in the center and took hands.

"Shido'ah, chada'rrha la tenta no somalla. Shento tere.
Anotay re nada' chento ma'ha vi say na marri she'late. Narata
noshari sanate'. Shatyoha marra mevina charlata moha latenta no
mevina somella nome tere," Alisdair said in the language of his father.

His voice was raspy and dry from the hours of battle but
there was a strength that emerged from within him.

"What do you think you are doing? Coming into my home and thinking you can banish me?" Baltair boomed.

The crew looked around but didn't see anyone. Alisdair sent his search magic out and found Baltair's essence around the corner and sitting on a throne of ebony. Alisdair led the group of soldiers around the next bend, and Malita gasped.

"You are displeased with my looks big sister?" Baltair asked.

Baltair now resembled the Jaduuk, except his face and head were still more human but his eyes had shifted to look more like the wolves'. His frame was also exceptionally larger than that of his once human frame.

"Baltair what have you done to yourself?" Malita asked.

"I am not Baltair anymore, I am Jaduuk'ai. I have become what I want to be, not what you or big brother here wants me to be," Baltair said through the fangs at the sides of his mouth giving his sounds a soft lisp.

"And what is that, a slave to the Shadow. You're not free, you can't do what you want, you have to serve *it* and do *its* bidding," Alisdair said.

"I thought you would appreciate the sentry I chose. The great orc-wolf-hunters from the shadow realm. Though long thought to be extinct, created to hunt only the heirs of the Tooatha De, during the Crimson Tide crusades. Some improvements have been made," Baltair laughed a throaty gurgling laugh and the irritation of the shadow magic ate at their nerves.

The heat in the cavern intensified and Malita, Todan, and the others wriggled with the discomfort. Alisdair took Malita's hand, and she joined his voice.

"Ano tere nara shay'nto," Baltair lifted his hands and sent a blast of green lightning toward them. Onen blocked the onslaught with the shield of his water magic and the others threw out their shields around them. "Mey'ha te ah'mi stay' la marri. Shayla'tah narata nochar ri somatay te la narrato," they said as they struggled against the force of Baltair's earth and shadow magic. Todan then brought his magical force to the casting and joined in the spell.

"Ma'rray machina ma no ha, notenta ray mevina anoto te tere tay're nar'rah shento stayna marri. Shayla'tay nochari, somatay te narrato," they managed under the pressure of the shadow magic. Alisdair added his shield to his warriors and closed his eyes. He focused on the light inside him and the powers of the cosmos. The earth magic of his brother Todan, the wind magic of his sister Malita, and his fire and light magic emerged from the emptiness and wrapped around them. Baltair stood and with pure anger and rage began to suck the elements toward him. Alisdair jerked at the force and pulled back holding onto the powers, but Baltair was stronger. Onen put his hand on Alisdair's shoulder and Alisdair felt the surge of Onen's life force encompass his frame. He turned to see his lifelong friend give up his life's essence, and he shouted.

The pain of his sacrifice ripped his heart in two and a sudden pain hit the back of his head. Another soldier, and then another until all of his officers touched Alisdair's shoulders and gave up their life force. Alistair stared in utter shock. Malita put her hand on his shoulder and then Todan. Alisdair's pain and anguish was overloading his frame, and he struggled with his heartfire's pain. The wicked laugh of his possessed brother seeped into his mind, and he choked back the huge lump in his throat.

He found it both a relief and a burden that he had asked so much of them, and they lived up to it, all them. To their very last breath.

"Do it," Onen whispered as his body faded into dust and disappeared.

Alisdair opened his heart and absorbed their energies. His body shook as it became too much for himself to bear. He arched backward with the force and the ringing in his ears consumed his thoughts.

"Tarren menin shelt, la noshari tere mea'aha. Tay nada' no'halla toma nosh vi say na moha," Alisdair managed.

A power so intense careened across the land with the cosmic forces and radiated every living thing as it pelted the distance and the boom it made as it split the atmosphere in half deafened the land. Baltair screeched as his powers were ripped from his body. Rancid blood oozed from his skin and his eyes went black. Alisdair took out the time tablet and read the last of the incantation.

"Kina nara sto'mae'ah'ha potenta nome ha'la'tay," Alisdair said.

An enormous pillar of cosmic light shot from the blackened sky and Alisdair gritted his teeth with the anticipation. Pain ate at every corner of Alisdair's body as the conduit from the universe shot through him and into the ground below his now floating body. A wall of blackness erupted from the ground around the cavern and encompassed Baltair. His shrieks of agony and rage thundered across the sky and into the universe and then disappeared behind the tomb of magic. Alisdair's body sagged with the extreme weight of what had just happened, and he drifted to the ground. The pain eased but his limbs were numb, and his lungs were still on fire. Blackness encompassed the cavern, and he couldn't see anything. He laid on the warm stone for what seemed like hours until he regained the function of his body. He managed to find the path. A dim light lifted the darkness at the end of the tunnel, and he made his way to the exit.

Tears escaped without his consent as he beheld his lost and broken world. Bodies of his people mixed with the beasts plastered the landscape, and he fell to his knees and sobbed.

1-He Still Has A Pulse

The starry sky-like atmosphere of the time shift was becoming more comfortable and Shaz was starting to like the tingle it left on his skin. The misty fuzz that signaled the end of the portal came into view and Shaz stuck his hand through the shimmer. Shaz stepped to the other side and braced for the sudden shift in motion as he came to a stop. Shaz took a quick inventory of the portal room as he stepped through the last bit of the energy field. The dimness decreased as the lights in the ceiling lit and Shaz stepped out of the way as Serin came through. The eagerness to return to the castle eased from his chest, and he breathed in a sigh of comfort. Riddick and Amirra stepped through and then the Minca and Jag. The tingle of energy faded as they moved away and Shaz put his hand on the runes along the side of the portal and read the glyphs that illuminated.

"Don't be too long," Serin said.

"Aye," Shaz said.

Serin kissed him and took his satchel and followed the others out of the room. He read the marks and pulled the notebook from his lower back. The shadow magic tingled his skin, he was starting to get used to it, and he wondered if that was a good or bad thing. The more he used it the stronger he became, but the stronger it became, and it was a constant tug at his emotions to keep his own thoughts from the shadows.

He flipped through the pages and stopped on the one he had made note of. There were several marks that he hadn't seen before, but they resembled the marks on the walls around the portals, so he wanted to compare them and see if he could figure it out. The notebook on Gavin Rhill he had found in Isot's lair, had Gavin's personal notes on his finding of the script that evoked the opening of the underworld, but it wasn't complete and Shaz couldn't make out some of the marks because of the wear over the rotations. Shaz closed his eyes and tried to think of what the meanings were but nothing came.

Shaz tried to stay focused on the notebook but a twinge at the side of his eye kept pricking his awareness. He shut the book and stuck it on the shelf inside the secret book-box and started toward the door. A heavy thud hit his core as he passed the portal that had been active for quite a while. Shaz stopped and peered into the disturbed energy. There was a faint image of a person on the other side and Shaz's heart thudded, but he took a step closer. Shaz felt the draw of the portal entice his understanding, and he tried to pull away, but the person on the other side came into view. The thud in his chest ripped open a sense of panic and pain he wasn't ready for, and he gasped.

Shaz crossed the last few lengths and ripped open the shimmering mist. Motavo's battered and bleeding body fell through the opening and Shaz caught him as he went down. Motavo's lifeless frame was cold and rigid and Shaz checked for a pulse. To his surprise, there was still a slight beating in his chest and Shaz rested him onto the floor.

"Serin!" Shaz yelled.

Serin's heart leaped from her chest as the sudden sensation of dread, and the prick at her mind hit her with intensity. Serin grabbed the handrail of the staircase tightly to keep from falling. She sucked in a deep breath and Shaz's cry pummeled her ears. A burst of adrenaline spiked, and she raced back toward the portal room.

"Motavo, can you hear me? What happened?" Shaz asked with panic in his tone.

"Riddick!" Serin yelled at the top of her lungs.

Riddick dropped is pack and shot out of his bedchamber and down the stairs nearly flying over them. He rounded the large lobby-like entrance tightly and raced down the hallway. Amirra and the Minca ran from their rooms and followed. Serin peeled around the corner into the portal room and sudden tears released as she internalized Motavo's body lying in Shaz's arms.

"What happened?" Serin cried.

"I don't know, he was standing in the portal and I barely saw him, and he just fell out when I opened it," Shaz said.

Serin raced across the vast room and ripped open Motavo's shirt. His skin was cold, and her heart thumped harder. She put her hand on his chest, closed her eyes, and sent her magic into his body. Riddick rounded the corner and cleared the room in a few long strides and stopped next to Serin. The blue hues encompassed Motavo's frame and her eyes shifted under her eyelids as she interpreted the information she was receiving.

"What happened?" Riddick asked.

"I don't know," Shaz said.

"Is he," Riddick started.

Shaz shook his head.

"He still has a pulse," Shaz said.

Amirra and the Minca peeled into the room followed by Jagwynn. Riddick motioned for them to stop and not say anything.

"He's alive, but there is a toxin of some kind that has paralyzed his body," Serin said.

"Can you reverse the toxin?" Shaz asked.

Serin called her healing magic from her core and sent the blue mist into his body again. The energy rolled around his frame but didn't sink in like it usually did and Serin scowled. She tried again but the magic drifted off his being and a surge of angry panic raced to her to brain. The portal wiggled again, and Riddick stepped toward it.

"Shaz, is that what it looks like?" Riddick asked.

Shaz turned to see the portal was wiggling and his heartfire raced. Amirra hurried to where Shaz was and took his place holding Motavo's head. Shaz stepped next to Riddick and peered into the mist. The large frame of a man came into view and Shaz recognized it to be Asher.

"Aye, that's Asher," Shaz said.

Serin looked up and around his legs and tried to see into the portal, but nothing stood out.

"Is he?" Riddick asked.

"Aye," Shaz said.

"What is it?" Serin demanded.

Serin pulled the new hydro-light magic and sent a boost into Motavo's frame which sank into his body and his rigid frame softened, but he still didn't move. Serin did it again and his frame relaxed a little more.

"Serin," Motavo barely managed.

His mouth hardly moved at all and his voice was raspy and weak.

"I'm here Yappa, what happened," Serin asked.

"Asher," Motavo said.

Serin turned to find Shaz had a struggled scrunch on his brows.

"What is it?" Serin asked.

"Asher is in trouble and needs our help," Shaz said.

"Go!" Serin said.

Shaz drew his blade as he leaped into the portal and Riddick and the Minca were close behind.

"What is happening?" Amirra asked.

"He has been poisoned with some kind of toxin and it's not responding to my magic, I don't know what to do," Serin said.

Tears flowed off her cheeks, and she tried to wipe them with her shoulder. She didn't dare take her hands off his body as she didn't know what would happen.

"Is there a book or anything I can find," Amirra asked.

"Find Inelius," Serin said.

Amirra nodded, but as she was about to stand up, she found his old frame coming around the doorway.

"Oh good, we need your help," Amirra said.

Serin turned to see Inelius making his way as quickly as his old frame would let him.

"Oh goodness, what happened?" Inelius asked.

"He has been poisoned with some kind of toxin that is not responding to my magic," Serin said.

****

The tingle on Shaz's skin turned to pulsating irritation as the dread of what could be on the other side of the portal ripped through his being. The time-shift movement added to his worry and the stars that whizzed by gave him a seasick feeling he didn't usually have.

Shaz raced toward Asher, but a nagging sensation pummeled his attention, and he ducked in time to avoid a surge of a white gooey substance. Shaz threw up his shield and turned to find a tremendous spider with long skinny pincers. The eight-legged critters' black shiny eyes, all six of them, penetrated Shaz's energy and he shivered.

"Riddick through up your shield," Shaz called.

Riddick shielded himself and Turkill and Ladtwig hid behind it. Shaz allowed his shield to encompass his whole frame and slashed the long square-like pincers. The blade slid through the insect's tentacle easily and it reared back and screeched as its gooey blood oozed from the wound.

"Get Asher out of here," Shaz called.

Riddick rounded Shaz and moved toward Asher's stiff form. Shaz parried and tried to look around to see where the spider was. A pit in his stomach anchored itself deep as he found numberless more coming from what looked like a hole in the starry sky. Shaz sent a torrent of flames and squelched the insects. Riddick tried to move Asher's large frame but found it harder than he expected. He rubbed his hands together and called the earth element and sent a pulsing wave that encompassed his frame and Riddick instructed it to carry him back through the portal. The magic obeyed and Riddick quickly pushed Asher's floating body back toward the opening.

Turkill gripped his dart gun between his teeth and shot a rapid-fire toward a spider that was coming from the other side. The spider squealed and fell onto its belly and jerked and writhed and then hissed and faded into the blackness. Ladtwig scurried in front of Asher and gripped the portal's fabric like exit and held it open.

****

"Oh dear, there is a book, in the library, but I fear it will take me so long to find it," Inelius said.

"Send your magic search spell and Amirra will follow it," Serin said.

Inelius looked a little surprised but smiled with the remembrance of his magic search spell. Inelius snapped his fingers and a red sparkle emerged into existence.

"Take Miss Amirra here, to the book on toxins," Inelius said.

The magic started across the room and Amirra stood and hurried after the sparkles. Amirra was soon running down the hall to catch up to the magic and barreled into the library. The sparkles hovered for a minute as though it was taking an inventory of the materials and then shot into the upper levels. Amirra cursed and ran to the rounded staircase and examined each of the isles until she found the glitters pointing to a book. Amirra heaved the heavy book off the shelf and started back to the portal.

Amirra set the book down and Inelius started combing through the pages but his shaky hands couldn't keep a good grip and was getting frustrated.

"I'm sorry, I'm just not fast anymore," Inelius said.

Serin looked up and found frustration and panic all over his frame. Serin breathed in a slow and steady breath and tried to picture what she needed. A soft breeze picked up the pages and sifted through them. The pages settled and rested peacefully and Inelius smiled and started to scan the page. He pointed to the text he was looking for and showed Amirra.

"Alright, it says, that there are over eight hundred types of toxins, two hundred of which can cause paralysis," Amirra said.

"How am I going to figure all that out?" Serin asked.

"I seem to remember Helios being quite good at all this sort of stuff," Inelius said.

"You're going to have to go get Helios," Serin said.

"Alright, how do I do that?" Amirra asked.

"That's the portal there," Serin said.

Serin pointed to the portal that took her and Shaz to the witches cave and gave a little shudder with the memory. Amirra's heart started to race.

"Am I going to be alright?" Amirra asked.

"Yes, Helios has secured it and it should take you straight to the fortress," Serin closed her eyes and tried to remember how to give her directions but Amirra could tell she was having a hard time.

"Don't' worry, I'll figure it out," Amirra said.

Amirra hurried to the portal and made sure she still had her piece of the time tablet and stepped into the misty energy field.

****

Shaz started toward the trove of arachnids and had a hard time not cringing. He didn't realize until now that he really didn't care for spiders and especially ones that came up to his knees. He let the blade carry itself with ease and sliced through the middle of its head and then moved quickly to the next spider and Turkill sent another blast.

"Get out of here," Shaz said.

"No way, not without you," Turkill grunted through the bamboo shoot between his teeth.

He let go of another blast and rolled his head letting a series of multiple darts fly, each hitting several of the spiders. Shaz parried and blocked the arm-like pincer and rolled his wrist, pulling the blade up through it and then down taking off both the pincers of the spider on the other side of him. Shaz checked to find Riddick had already made it out and threw out a blast of fire and waved it over the oncoming spiders. They pulled back and screeched. Shaz's nerves twinged at the sound, and he shivered.

"Tarren shelt la noshari tere menin mea'aha Tay nada' no'halla toma nosh vi say na moha," Shaz said.

The hole in the time shift's fabric sealed shut and Shaz wondered if that was part of the underground. Riddick set Asher on the floor next to Serin, and she put her hand on him. She sent a boost of her light magic, but it barely did any good. Shaz came through the portal and sheathed his sword and found a frantic Serin. He knelt in front of her and sent a boost of his magic into her core and put a hand on each of hers that was resting on their bodies and focused on giving his magic to her.

Serin's body absorbed the energy, her breathing steadied, and she became still as she sorted out her thoughts. The new mix of energy eased into Motavo and Asher and their color started to fade back into their skin. Motavo's eyes blinked, and he sighed into the floor as his body relaxed from the rigid paralysis. Motavo rested his hand on theirs and watched their focus. He had seen it before, but it still amazed him how perfect they were together. Asher blinked and his body eased from the stiffness. Shaz opened his eyes and found Serin full of relief.

"Are you alright?" Shaz asked.

"I think so," Motavo said.

"What happened?" Serin asked.

Motavo started to sit up and Serin helped him while Shaz and Riddick helped Asher.

"Those blasted Ruin Silk Spiders. There seems to be more holes in the underground and the old tunnels are crawling with them, but we didn't find out until they had started to block us in," Asher said.

"Where do they come from?" Shaz asked.

"They are usually in the Realm of Yinavion, and we haven't ever seen them in the tunnels, something must be driving them out," Motavo said.

Shaz ran through what he remembered from the books he read on the realms.

"I bet I know," Shaz said.

"What?" Riddick asked.

"Jaduuk, that realm is where the Timeless Plains are," Shaz said.

"That would make sense," Riddick said.

"Let's get you upstairs, so I can take a proper look at you," Serin said.

Serin cast her air spell on Motavo and Asher and started to help them to the bedchambers. Shaz and Riddick helped, and they made their way up the stairs and into a bed. Their bodies were still very stiff, and they struggled to do anything.

"Where is Amirra?" Riddick asked.

"She's gone for Helios," Serin said.

"Helios, why?" Shaz asked.

"He is an expert on toxins, and we didn't know what this was, and she left before you returned," Inelius said.

Shaz, they are still affected, our magic didn't cure them, it just put off the effects for a time, and the toxin is quite complex, I don't know if I can figure it out myself, Serin said in her head.

Shaz nodded and motioned for Riddick to follow him, and they hurried back to the portal room.

"What is the time difference between the realms?" Riddick asked.

Shaz thought about it for a minute.

"She should be back anytime now actually, that's if she found Helios right away," Shaz said.

2-I Suggest You Figure That Out

Amirra shivered as the energy prickled her skin, it was a sensation she didn't care for and was glad it didn't last long. The energy field wiggled and a pale-yellow gryphtoness jumped. The gryphtoness hesitated and then took a few steps toward the portal. Amirra hurried to the other side of the tunnel of time and put her hand through the shimmering mist at the end.

The blackness shifted to a warm purple and the gryphtoness' heart skipped as the small human hand breach the surface. The gryphtoness swallowed hard and took a step back as Amirra's frame emerged. Amirra blinked a few times adjusting to the bright light around the room.

Amirra jumped and gave a little squawk when she internalized the big bird-eyes of the massive lion-like-eagle-human creature staring at her. She swallowed hard and tried to put on a mix of her stern Velshari face mixed with her regular Amirra face. The surge of adrenaline raced through her body, and she was sure she was going to be sick.

"I need to speak with Helios," Amirra said.

"And who might you be?" the gryphtoness asked.

"I'm Amirra, and I'm with Shaz and Serin and I really need to find Helios and fast, who are you?" Amirra blurted. The gryphtoness scrunched her face, as much as a beak could and studied her. "Please, I really need him and fast," Amirra said.

"I am afraid I don't know where he is at the moment, but Ralti may, let me send for him," the gryphtoness said.

"No, you need to take me to him, we have to hurry," Amirra said.

"May I ask why?" the gryphtoness asked.

"Someone has been poisoned and Helios is the only one that can help, now you either take me to him or I will find him myself," Amirra said sharply.

"I see, please follow me," the gryphtoness said.

The gryphtoness started out of the magnificent portal room and Amirra suddenly felt very small. Her long strides were hard to keep up with, as Amirra was nearly running. The gryphtoness led her through a series of hallways and corridors and into the ginormous courtyard inside the fortress. Amirra's heart leaped with both shock and awe as she internalized all the gryphton's that were both flying and mingling around the courtyard. She tried to keep up with the gryphtoness, but she lost her. The other gryphton's started to stare at her, and the tingle of embarrassment etched at her cheeks. The gryphtoness returned and grabbed her hand and lowered to the ground.

"Here, get on," the gryphtoness said.

Amirra climbed onto her back and tried to find a decent grip but found that the best way was to partially lay between her incredible wings. The gryphtoness maneuvered the crowd and made her way to the main fortress doors.

"Halt, who goes there," a gryphton soldier asked.

"It's me Leeta, I must speak to Ralti immediately," Leeta said.

"Why?" the gryphton asked.

Leeta gripped Amirra's behind, so she wouldn't fall off as she stood onto her hind legs.

"It is no concern of yours, now let me in so that I can speak to my father," Leeta said sharply.

The gryphton cringed and nodded and pulled the heavy solid-wood doors open. Leeta returned to all fours as they were faster that way and hurried through the Fortress halls. She skidded around a corner and barreled into a sizable meeting room coming to her full height.

"Father, I have a pressing matter you must see," Leeta blurted.

The gryphton's around the long table jumped and turned and stared at her. Ralti blushed and started toward Leeta with a surprised but stern look. Leeta let Amirra off her back, and she came around in front of Leeta. The room gasped. Half of the gryphtons stood quickly with instant concern on their brows.

"A pretty one," the big bulky gryphton said.

Amirra's heart raced, and she almost felt like she was about to become the afternoon snack. She swallowed hard and took a few steps toward them.

"Where is Helios, I need Helios," Amirra said.

"He is not here, may I ask who you are and what is going on?" the fire-red gryphton at the end of the table asked in a kind voice.

"I'm Amirra, and Serin's grandfather and uncle have been poisoned with a toxin that won't respond to her magic and they're at Shaz's castle and if I don't find Helios, because he is the expert on toxins, then they'll die, and I have no idea how much time has already passed and if they're already dead, or if they 're going to be permanently paralyzed or," Amirra blurted.

"Where is Helios," the red gryphton asked.

"He's at the academy sir," Ralti said.

"Who is our fastest and strongest flyer," the red gryphton asked.

"Phanes is, but Azrack, he's under watch," Ralti said.

"Remind me why?" Azrack asked.

"He has, um, well," Ralti stammered.

Leeta blushed and slunk onto her haunches. Azrack nodded, and understood it was a personal matter and wondered how long the cubs had been having their secret relationship and tried to keep the tiny grin from the corner of his beaked lips.

"I suggest you figure that out and fast, *he* will be the one to fetch Helios," Azrack said.

"Yes sir," Ralti said.

Ralti left the room with Leeta and Amirra heard him bark orders to another soldier and then returned. Amirra wrung her hands together nervously and Azrack motioned for her to come toward him.

"This is Brigdon, Jaxton, Pontos and Ralti, and these are new to our command, Shar, and Cluck. Please, tell us everything," Azrack said.

"It's a pleasure to meet you all, I have heard so many stories, I mean not stories, events, things that actually happened, I didn't mean," Amirra stammered.

The gryphton's chuckled and Amirra's face scrunched with uneasy fear.

"You don't have to be afraid, you are welcome here, but without Helios, I'm afraid I don't remember what to offer you," Azrack said.

"Thank you, but I'm fine, I'm just supper nervous for Serin right now," Amirra said.

"Tell us what happened," Azrack said.

"Oh, goodness where to start, well I suppose, after Shaz and Serin left here, they made their way to the crystal catacombs in the Minca realm where they were bonded by Synmagic, dealt with spitting hot earth that melted everything it touched, saved the Minca people, found the earth sage, found the Runecaster," Amirra held up her hand, "fought a war against the Jaduuk, battled a fire demon and got the sheath, closed the torn rip in the fabric of time, got engaged, stopped a hundred-rotation flood, battled *your* shadow Selket, met the Ukari and gave them back their voice to the moons, traveled to Ebassia and battled more Jaduuk, evaded an army, freed his family from the dungeons of Ebassia, absorbed the Binding of the Crypt spell, stopped a necromancer who was about to murder thousands of people, umm what else, oh yeah, Serin's grandfather is a Teorran Traveler, the secret, secret group of the Dodjen, and has been in charge of moving the Sev-Rin-Ac-Lavah around through the realms and was going to be traveling through the underground, which is the secret, secret portals of the portals but there is trouble there too, and he was poisoned with some kind of toxin that paralyzed him and Serin's magic couldn't reverse the effects so Inelius sent me here to find Helios," Amirra said as she inhaled a deep breath.

The new gryphton's stared at her with curious skepticism, and Azrack nodded with a tight beak.

"Sounds like Shaz and Serin alright, they sure know how to make a stir in the world don't they," Pontos said.

Brigdon grunted and Jaxton nodded and rubbed his chin and Shar and Cluck looked around at everyone to determine how serious they all were and finding the matter to be of concern they turned to eager curiosity.

"What does 'engaged' mean?" Shar asked.

"Oh, that means they are going to get married, after Shaz sacrifices himself of course," Amirra said.

"Won't that be kind of hard to do?" Jaxton asked.

"Yeah, that's a bit of a concern for them, so I hope we can figure things out first, I think they would make some really cute war wizard babies," Amirra said.

Amirra blushed as she realized what she had said.

"Sir," Phanes said as he came around the corner and saluted. Ralti stood quickly and Azrack rose and saluted.

"You must fly to the academy and fetch Helios, give him these exact words, 'I'm not here for an afternoon of tea'," Ralti said.

Phanes lifted one eyebrow and Azrack blurted a hearty ga-fa, Pontos and Jaxton snickered and Brigdon chuckled. Ralti tried to keep the humor from overcoming his face and Phanes' heart thudded.

"Sir," Phanes said in a salute.

Azrack controlled himself and cleared his throat.

"Tell him he needs to bring his can of whoop-ass too," Jaxton said.

Ralti couldn't help it and blurted a ga-fa and Shar and Cluck were dumb-struck at their high-commanders acting like this. Amirra watched them all and could now see what Shaz and Serin had described them to be and smiled. Phanes wasn't sure what to do and tried to remain serious.

"Dismissed," Ralti managed.

Phanes ended his salute and spun on his paw and hurried from the room. He wasn't sure what was going on, but he made his way quickly toward the fortress doors.

"Ssspp," Leeta said.

Phanes stopped and scooted backward and looked down the dark corridor he had just passed. Leeta waved him to come to her, and he turned the corner.

"You're going to get me in trouble, I am already being scrutinized by your father," Phanes said.

Leeta looked into his soft gray eyes and smiled. He was handsome, and she liked how serious and grown-up he tried to be. They had been close since they were cubs but Ralti had only recently found out about their growing intensions.

"I just wanted to tell you good luck," Leeta said.

"On what, completing this task or not getting pummeled by your father?" Phanes asked.

"I guess both," Leeta said.

Phanes smiled and gripped her paw and gave it a squeeze.

"I'll be back soon, and I'll meet you at our spot," Phanes said.

Phanes hurried back out of the hallway and left the fortress. He ran on all fours to the ledge at the far side of the courtyard and shoved off with his hind legs and propelled his body into the air. He threw out his wings and caught the updraft that came from the shear drop off of the cliffs. The bright mid-day sun reflected off his ice-blue feathers as he banked toward the east.

Jaxton rose from his chair and offered it to Amirra who smiled and tried to figure out how she was going to climb onto the large chair.

"What I want to know is what you mean by 'your shadow Selket'," Ralti asked.

Brigdon grunted. Jaxton helped Amirra onto the chair, and she found herself feeling like when she was a child and the grown-ups table and tried to keep her focus.

"Well, that orb, the one that Shaz got from you, turned out to be a Shadow Selket. A Selket warrior that was transformed into a servitor of the sorcerer Rhoefeus, well it got loose in the castle portal room, and we had to fight it and put it back into the orb, Shaz never takes it off now, turns out a little Gray Tailix was under the instruction of the Velshari to find all the shiny's from the castle, and he accidentally let it loose," Amirra said.

"Not that thing again!" Brigdon grunted.

Everyone grimaced.

"Oh, don't worry, Shaz won't let it out of his sight ever again," Amirra said.

"Shiny's?" Shar asked.

"Yeah, you know things that are shiny, like gems, jewels, or gold and silver, stuff like that, he really likes shiny things too," Amirra said.

"Oh," Shar said with raised brows.

Shar still wasn't sure what to think of all of it.

"Tell us about the underground and the portals," Azrack said.

Amirra recounted the details and explained the Velshari and the dealings with Isot and filled them in on the rest of the details of the time in the Minca realm and Semias and her being the Runecaster and Nitida and the Sev-Rin-Ac-Lavah and everything she could think of. Azrack was aware of the Velshari. After Shaz and Serin left, Helios spent a great deal of time getting them caught up on the events of the world, but they were still dealing with the Kronos. Even after defeating Kronos himself and Groargoth, the hordes of the Kronos were determined even more to take their revenge. And being that Helios had returned to the academy to help there, Azrack hadn't been filled in on the latest details.

"I'm sorry to ask, but how long will it take for them to return?" Amirra asked.

"I would think it won't be long now," Ralti said.

Amirra yawned and her stomach grumbled.

"What can we get for you?" Azrack asked.

"I like bread," Amirra said.

"Bread we can do," Pontos said.

Pontos hurried from the room and returned a few minutes later with the biggest loaf of bread Amirra had ever seen.

"Azrack, I'm concerned about this underground, what does that mean for our portal?" Ralti asked.

"As am I, when Helios arrives, we'll make sure we ask him," Azrack said.

****

Phanes pulled in deep steady breaths as he pushed his wings through the strong winds. The academy was shielded with a barrier of clouds that had been enchanted to keep the academy hidden and only those who had permissions could enter, but only after they proved themselves by being able to press through them. He gripped the wind with his wings and thrust them close to his body to narrow the resistance and then pushed again. Phanes broke through the last bit of resistance and soared into the cold sky above. He threw out his wings to snag the air and bent at the waist and leveled out. He flew over the smaller building on the edge and toward the center.

He had never been to the academy before and wasn't sure where he was supposed to go. Phanes rounded the next building and found a few gryphtons walking along a stone pathway. He dipped toward them and landed in front of them a few lengths away.

"Sorry to trouble you, but I am in need of Helios, where would I find him?" Phanes asked.

Phanes lowered his head in a slight bow instead of a salute.

"He is in the main building, but he can't be disturbed right now," one gryphton said pointing to the tallest building.

"Thank you," Phanes said.

Phanes leaped into the air again and made his way to the tallest building on the campus. He landed on the front steps, pulled his wings in tightly and pulled open the door. The academy was nothing like the fortress and Phanes took in the light-colored stone and brightness of the sky-lights that were strategically placed around the building.

"May I help you," a sun-yellow gryphton asked.

"I must speak to Helios right away," Phanes said.

"May I ask for what reason?" the old gryphton asked.

"My message is for Helios, Sir," Phanes said.

"I am sorry to say, but he is unavailable right now," the old gryphton said.

"I must speak with him immediately," Phanes said.

"You will have to come back tomorrow," the gryphton said.

"Is that the message you would like me to give Azrack the King, Sir?" Phanes asked.

The old gryphton's brows raised.

"Azrack you say?" the gryphton said.

Phanes wasn't sure what to say, of course that's what he said.

"Where can I find him? Sir," Phanes said.

The old gryphton pointed to a set of doors and Phanes made his way around several lounge chairs. He threw the doors open and a classroom full of gryphtons jumped. Helios looked up from his book and peered at Phanes.

"Helios Sir, I have an urgent message," Phanes said.

Helios set his book down.

"Go on," Helios said.

"I am not here for an afternoon of tea and you need to bring your can of whoop-ass, Sir," Phanes said.

The classroom broke into a roar of laughter, but Helios' brows tightened, and he took off his instructors cloak and hurried out of the room. The class hushed as the military training in their instructor overcame his frame. Phanes followed Helios out of the room and closed the doors.

"You're Grace, it would seem that there is an urgent matter I have to attend to," Helios said.

"What is it?" Mazark asked.

Phanes' face drained of color when he learned who the old gryphton was.

"The War Wizard," Helios said.

Mazark nodded and Helios turned to Phanes.

"What else did they say?" Helios asked.

Helios started toward the doors and Phanes followed him.

"Something about a toxin and humans," Phanes said.

"Let me fetch my things, I will be right back," Helios said.

Helios leaped into the air and banked around the building and a few minutes later Phanes met him in the sky, and they flew back to the fortress.

Azrack, Ralti, Jaxton, Brigdon, and Cluck stood near the edge and Amirra sat on a large stone bench several lengths away. She gazed into the sky and found the magnificent creatures breathtaking as they came and went, flying like an eagle and then running like lions. Her stomach did somersaults each time they dipped down and wondered if that was what her mother felt when she rode her wyvern. She remembered her dream of Ada and smiled and found herself really wanting to fly. Leeta came up next to her and sat on her haunches.

"What is it like to fly?" Amirra asked.

Leeta looked at her with a questioning glance and tried to think of what to say.

"Ummm, I guess it feels like a sense of being free, being alone to think your own thoughts, able to do whatever you want," Leeta said.

"Sounds amazing," Amirra said.

"I can take you for a ride if you like," Leeta said.

Amirra turned with the widest but most terrified eyes ever and Leeta chuckled.

"Here they come," Ralti said.

"I guess that will have to wait," Leeta said.

Amirra found Leeta's expression shift when Phanes came into view, and she was certain there was something going on, at least on her part. Amirra noticed Phanes' tight expression flash a quick smile at Leeta as he started to descend and understood it to be mutual. Amirra turned to Leeta, but she wasn't there and smiled to herself. Phanes landed in front of Ralti and saluted and Ralti returned the salute.

"Did you have any trouble?" Ralti asked.

"Sir, no Sir, except having to fly with an old gryphton, Sir," Phanes blushed and regretted the words as he realized what he had just indicated.

Azrack snickered and Jaxton coughed to keep from saying anything. Ralti gave them both the stink eye. Helios landed on the platform next to Azrack.

"What is going on?" Helios asked.

"This is Amirra, she will be taking you to the realm of Ebassia where you will help Serin find a cure for the toxin her family has been afflicted with," Azrack said.

Azrack motioned to Amirra who smiled and gave a little wave.

"Good to see you all," Helios said to everyone. Jaxton slapped his back and Ralti gripped his paw. They started toward the cave that led to the portal and Amirra had to jog-run to keep up.

"Your new protégé?" Helios asked Ralti.

"And soon to be kin," blurted Jaxton with a huge grin.

Ralti shot him a glare and he busted up laughing.

"Oh, fun for you," Helios said.

Brigdon knelt down and offered Amirra a ride with a wink which she agreed and climbed onto his back.

"What do we know about this toxin?" Helios asked.

"Nothing, except they're paralyzed, and kinda have a bluish tint to their skin," Amirra said.

"I'm going to need some things and will need someone to fetch them for me, but it will be hard to do, I will need the venom from the Saraswati insects," Helios said.

"Not those," Azrack said and rubbed the back of his neck.

"I'll send Phanes," Ralti said.

"I won't know the complete list until I get there, he will have to come with me," Helios said.

Ralti nodded and turned on his paw to fetch Phanes. They made their way back to the portal and Brigdon let Amirra down.

"I'll send word as soon as I know what's going on," Helios said.

Azrack nodded and Amirra parted the misty wall that was now glimmering the purple sheen. Phanes came through the entrance and Amirra was impressed at how fast he actually was. Amirra held the curtain-like energy field open for the two gryphtons and then followed.

3-Jaduuk'ai Temple

Heavy thunder rippled through the land sending a shudder over the landscape. The short stalky trees swayed back and forth, and the earth released its fresh scent of rain that was quickly turned into the stench of rancid plants. The darkness that consumed the prison lifted and an eerie pitch of green wafted toward him. He struggled to open his eyes as the hot air hit his black pupils. The blackness he was accustomed to drifted away but his eyes couldn't focus on the surroundings.

His limbs were heavy, and an irritating itch coursed through his tough bluish hide. The signals to his brain came and went and he wasn't sure what was happening. The hot air filled his lungs, and the tightness gripped his chest as he tried to stifle the burning. He lifted his fingers that were now barely moveable and found the sting of being stuck in one position bit at his nerves. His head pounded and the sharp pain at the back of his head slammed into the back of his eyes. He sucked in a heavy breath to stop the pain but sputtered as his lungs couldn't fill completely.

Images of his family entombing him in this eternal prison sifted in and out of his mind as the pain he was once used to feeling ate at his being. Anger lit in his chest and grew as he remembered how his brother Alisdair ruined his life and stole everything from him. The pain began to ease as the shadow crept back into his heart and soul. The energy eased the discomfort of the itch and sting in his body and he slowly stood up.

His large head was the defined features of the orcish-wolf hunter of the Jaduuk mixed with his once human features. His large rippling muscles and bits of scraggly fur in patches over his now animal-like frame heaved as his own magic ignited his chest and filled his being with strength. He blinked several more times and found his vision return. He looked around and examined his once wonderful lair now in total shambles.

Anger bit again and surged through him. He tried his legs and found they had the strength to move his sizable body. He took inventory of what was left and picked up his old helmet. This was where he had made his transformation to the Jaduuk'ai, where he finally found his purpose, where he was going to ruin his brother and destroy all of his descendants. But that didn't happen. He didn't know what had happened. Jaduuk'ai didn't understand the language his brother had spoken, or how it encapsulated him. How long had it been, why did it end? The questions rolled around his mind as he smashed the helmet and kicked the breastplate out of his way.

I am Fir, I am a son of the God of Glory too, he thought.

But he was never allowed to do what he wanted. Alisdair ruled over him, Alisdair told him what to do.

"I hate you Alisdair," he sneered breaking the silence in his ears.

Baltair hated Alisdair with more than angry passion. He needed to find out what happened, why he had been released, and by whom. He searched the cavern and found that there was a small opening that led to what was once his personal quarters, but the opening was meant for his human size. He stepped back and ran into the side of the cave a few times until the rocks crumbled.

Jaduuk'ai heaved the stones out of the way and ducked under the new opening. Everything was still there, but it was so much smaller than he remembered. He made note of the items and searched for the time-teller but at first glance it wasn't there. He rummaged through the books and scrolls he'd used to become the Jaduuk'ai and set them into their holders on a shelf at the far side of the room. Baltair kicked an object that went clanging across the stone and he recognized it as the time-turner.

Jaduuk'ai picked it up and the small object twisted open under his grip. Several small discs inside spun rapidly until they caught up with the current time and Jaduuk'ai observed the numbers. His heart sank and a heavy dread coursed over his body. He shook the time-teller, but the disc remained on the time. Four millennium, there was no way his family would still be alive, even with being part-gods they would have been gone a long time ago. His ability for revenge was ruined, he would never be able to watch Alisdair's face as he sucked the life from Malita and Todan.

A faint heartbeat emerged through the darkness and he turned to see the yellow-green light of a pod illuminate his outer lair. He set the time-teller on the shelf next to the books and made his way out of the room. The yellow-green light brightened the closer he came, and he put his hand on the egg-like pod. The heartbeat inside thudded heavily and the ground underneath it opened letting in the lava needed to bring life to the capsule.

The egg started to grow, and a thick slime formed on the outer layer. The lava pooled underneath it and moved in the same motions as the heartbeats. Thick yellowish veins bulged from the underneath side of the egg as it became as tall as a man. The veins wriggled and searched for the earth and when they found it they dug into the gritty surface and took hold. The egg finished growing to its full size and Jaduuk'ai soaked in the putrid odor. Another heartbeat emerged and then another and Jaduuk'ai knew he needed to find the exit soon so that his beasts would be able to grow and mature.

Nothing had changed, he would still search out and destroy every living descendant of Alisdair's and anyone who gets in the way. He rounded the egg shaped Jaduuk-spawner and stepped over the new veins and continued to search for the way out. He rounded several tunnels and found the entrance at the back of the mountain lair was open. He carefully made his way to the end and examined the scene before him. The sun was a small yellow disc in the sky and the light was not nearly as bright as he had remembered it to be. He stood on the edge of the cliff and gazed out over the landscape. It looked nothing like it used to and he wondered what had happened.

A memory surfaced and he returned to the lair. Another yellow-green light emerged from another cavern and he turned to find another egg-spawner growing and he smiled. He made his way through the maze of tunnels and stopped when he reached the one he wanted. He had to duck nearly in half in order to enter but he didn't want to disturb the egg in the nearby cavern, so he didn't widen the opening. Jaduuk'ai panned his hand across the darkness and the sconces around the room lit. He put his hand on the wall and a string of glyphs illuminated. Jaduuk'ai touched the glyphs and a black mist wobbled at the edge of the room.

The dark mist sifted and wafted around into an evenly flowing circular pattern in the center of the wall and the more it twisted the stronger the energy became. Jaduuk'ai touched the mist and a string of gooey green emerged and began to circle around with the mist. The green string soon consumed the opening and the swirling stopped. Jaduuk'ai put his hand into the mist and it pricked his skin and he shuddered. He stepped into the portal and felt the draw of the power pull his large frame toward the other side.

Heavy thuds echoed as the pounding of the drum-like vibrations hit the edge of the large rocks that speckled the distance. A gripping stench of rancid ore wafted into his nostrils and he puckered with the stink. The Shadow Empire was riddled with pockets of seeping gasses that wafted into the atmosphere and left a mirage sitting at the back of his mind. A bitter cold emerged and bit at his skin and he shivered. The cavern was gone, and a barren wasteland encased in a gooey green substance consumed the distance.

The clapping of his clawed-hoofed feet bounced off the cold jagged-stone walkway as he moved toward the enormous iron doors. Shadow figures wafted in and out of the jagged boulders and gave him the impression they were stalking him. He understood them to be the chosen souls the shadow hadn't consumed. The latch was cold and stung his skin as he gripped the long lever and heaved the door open, but he was glad for the feelings because that meant he was alive.

A cascading chandelier draped from the ceiling to the floor and gave a soft green hue to the iron and black-stone walls. Glyphs etched into the walls drifted in and out of green and gray as he walked by. Jaduuk'ai pulled the heavy handle of the double doors on the far side of the reception hall. A grand entertaining room opened with smaller but similar chandeliers that hung around the room. There was a certain appeal to the Shadow Temple, one that he wouldn't have anticipated from the evil of evil's.

An elaborately carved iron and gem-encrusted throne sat at the far side of the room in front of enormous windows. Heavy fabric framed the windows in a manner which made the windows have a feel of them being alive. Jaduuk'ai made his way to the throne and admired the details. He ran his finger along the top edge of the thick strands of carved iron details along the back of the chair and remembered the first time he sat in it, when he created it for himself. He turned around and sat into the throne and found it was just as he remembered, and he sank into the comfort it gave him.

There was a power in it, a sense of accomplishment and control. He smiled at the idea of his being the ruler of the underworld and sucked in a deep breath. The air was stale but there was a hint of pleasure in it and he leaned his head against the tall-back of the throne. The cold iron tickled his leathery hide and he looked around the vast room.

Darkness crept into the corners of the room and emerged from the floor and he watched as the numbers grew and made their way closer to him. The shadow at the front was in the likeness of large man and the one next to him was that of a woman but he couldn't make out any details from their previous life. The darkness of the man sifted in and out of a more solid state and mist as he bent to one knee before him. The woman followed as did the rest of the shadow's in the great room.

Jaduuk'ai's heart swelled with joyous heat and he gripped the bulky armrests and the sting of the shadow magic bit at his emotions. Black smoke eased from the floor and wrapped around his hooves and legs and a shot of panic crossed his mind. The blackness wound itself around his legs and torso and then arms. The top of the misty smoke stopped at his chest and arranged itself into a sharp point and then shot into the very center of his chest.

Jaduuk'ai roared with pain as the shadow consumed his flesh and soul. The red-hot searing consumed every inch of his being and he found his body wouldn't respond to his commands. The heat dissipated and was replaced with ice cold. His sharp fang-like teeth chattered, and his breath steamed in front of him as it escaped his lungs. The blue of his skin deepened and took on a dark-purple hue as the cold brought his blood to the outer edges of his limbs to keep him warm.

He closed his eyes and tried to control the pain, but his mind was full of the agony and sorrow that all he felt was the enormous weight of the worst kind on his being. He pulled in several long deep breaths and the pain began to ease. The blackness crawled along the inside of his skin and wrapped around his limbs and chest embedding itself into his skin leaving a new set of tattoos over his body. The mist then unraveled from his being and returned to the floor and the shadows dispersed.

"Now let's get to work," a strong but raspy voice echoed in his ears.

4-I Think We Should Go Investigate

Dark clouds sifted in, covering half of the landscape in a dark shadow. A flock of white long-legged birds splashed in the nearby marshes and the coolness of the new shade left a heavy thickness in the air. The herd of eight elk-like human warriors stood silent under the acacia shrub-trees. The leader of the Forrne was the largest bull of the trapper-herd and had led successful raids throughout the warm season, but they were still short several of the heavily furred turtlepotomous.

The farming Forrne used the hardened shells and armor-like plating for tools and the trappers used them for armor and coverings. The trappers had found the hunt difficult the longer the season progressed, and uncertainty began to sink into their beings. One of the trappers lowered the net into the watery marsh and waited until the rocks, tied to the edges, pulled it into the water and secured the ties to the poles, that had been pounded into the soft murky mud, and blended in with the tall swampreeds. The tall elk-like man flicked his long ears at the side of his head back and forth and listened and then made his way out of the slushy surface. His movements were nearly undetectable as he trotted to the trees. Another trapper stopped and examined the distance but when he couldn't make out what he thought he had heard he continued around the other side of the marsh. He dropped his net and secured the ties and then signaled to the others and trotted toward the brush.

"Now we wait," the leader said.

The trappers found places to lay down and rested on their hooves. Their sizable antlers were the only thing that poked out from the tall wildgrass leaving an unsettling image from the distance. The leader stood and kept guard and his ears flicked back and forth as he internalized the new sounds coming from the distance.

"Modez, what do you think it is?" one of the trappers asked.

"I am not sure," Modez said.

"I think we should investigate," another said.

"No, we keep our distance," Modez said.

"But what if" the trapper started.

"Antorn, we are not going to leave our nets to go traipsing after *something*," Modez said.

Antorn lowered his ears and nodded but the ripple in his guts increased, and he was certain there was something wrong. The other trapper gave a cynical smirk and Antorn rolled his eyes.

"Just because you think you are the smartest one here, doesn't make you even close to being in charge," another said.

"Nor, do I want to be, that's your issue Efren, not mine," Antorn said.

Efren rolled his eyes and sneered and Antorn walked to the edge of the tree cover and searched the surroundings. A flash of something reflecting off the mid-day sun caught his eye, and he took a few steps out from under the tree.

"Modez," Antorn whispered.

Modez turned to see Antorn nod toward a cluster of trees several lengths away. Modez moved slowly toward Antorn and he searched the distance.

"Look," Antorn said.

Efren noted their stoic stances and carefully walked up next to Modez.

"What are they?" Efren asked.

"I have no idea," Modez said.

"What do you want to do?" Efren asked.

"Stand still, maybe they won't see us," Modez said.

One of the traps tripped and a large turtlepotomous splashed in the water and started to scream its awkward billow. One of the beasts stopped and turned toward the ruckus and the Forrne stood still, and studied the creature. The creatures long snout rolled upward and let out a howl that made the Forrne flinch. Several more beasts emerged from the tall wildgrass and the Forrne could see they were a canine-like beast with long pointed ears with tufts of fur at the tip. The long sharp fangs curved upward and crested their eyebrows which hovered over black glassy eyes. The Forrne's hearts thudded in their chests, and they took a step back under the shadow of the tree.

The beast at the front of the pack's eyes met with Modezs', and he was now certain they were going to attack, but he found his legs didn't want to obey his commands. The beasts' snarl gurgled from their throat and Modez finally gave the signal to run. The

Forrne shot out from the tree and the beasts lunged into a dead run. The Forrne leaped over the smaller bushes as they darted across the flatlands.

Modez looked back to find the beasts hot on their trail and veered off to one side. The herd followed each taking their own way as they rounded. Antorn noted they had what looked like weapons strapped to their backs and wondered why the canine would have them. Antorn rounded a small marsh and darted the other way and a few of the beasts followed him and the rest went after the others. Antorn pulled a spear from the sheath on his back and moved his hand to the right spot that offered the best balance for a long throw and searched for the beast closest to him.

He located the animal and steadied his breathing as he kept a steady gate and examined the distance and arc he would need. He took his shot and the spear sizzled through the air with a slight whip of the long wooden pole. The sharpened bone tip sank into the creature's side and the beast howled in pain as the life force drained from the wound. The rest of the pack heard the howl and shifted their weight to move toward Antorn.

Modez, Efren, and the others took the chance and launched their spears. Each spear hit its mark but only a few of the beasts fell. Modez pulled another spear and rounded a tree and skidded to a stop and fired. Efren too sent another spear toward the beasts hitting its mark and the beast flew through the air and fell into the ground plowing into the dirt.

One of the beasts stood onto its hind legs and was now a few lengths taller than the Forrne. It gripped its battle-ax and Antorn could see the bluish hide speckled with patches of mangy black fur and his heart skipped a beat. He pulled his sling from his side belt and loaded a small, sharpened piece of bone into the pouch, whipped the long laces over his head and released one of the straps sending the shard careening into the creatures head. The beast tumbled backward dizzily but it didn't fall. Antorn released another shard and the beast again stumbled.

Modez released another spear and it hit a beast in the side. The beast yelped as the blade of bone sank into its flesh and the creature stumbled to the ground. Efren leaped over another shrub in time to make the beast plow right into it. The sharpened barbs embedded into the beast's skin and it hollered. Efren rounded as sharply as his four-legged body allowed, and he pulled his hand blade from his belt and shoved the long narrow blade into the beast's chest.

The blade didn't sink as deep as he had expected, and Efren shoved harder. The wreak of the oily blood that sprayed his face made his guts lurch, and he nearly hurled. The beast lashed out with its clawed hooves and Efren saw it coming but didn't quite move in time and the tip of the outer claw slashed his shoulder. Efren cursed and lifted onto his hind legs and slammed his front hooves into the beasts head. The creature fell silent and Efren pulled his blade and spear from the dead body.

Modez slowed slightly and waited for the beast to catch up to him and as the beast launched itself toward him, Modez lifted his hind legs and plowed his hefty hooves into the beasts head. The creature recoiled and flew several lengths and hit the ground hard. Modez pulled his blade and ran toward the beast and shoved it through the beast's heart. Modez too had a hard time with the stench and pulled his blade from the lifeless body.

The other Forrne grouped together and led the beasts back around toward Efren, Antorn, and Modez who made ready to attack. With a few more well-placed spears and a few slings the last beast fell.

"Let's get out of here," Modez said.

"We're days away from the nearest village, what about the traps?" Efren asked.

"I think there is a bigger issue here, but Antorn can stay here and watch the traps while we return to the village," Antorn shot him a surprised glare and noted the slight flicker of glee in Modez's eyes. There was no surprise Modez didn't care for him, but to suggest him leave the herd was nearly unthinkable, "And Tobis can stay here with him since Antorn has so much to offer, the new recruit would love to learn it all," Modez said.

Antorn nodded but his chest heaved with angry heat, and he wanted to take his spear and stab it through Modez's thigh. He didn't want to kill him, just maim him good. Modez gave Antorn a sly grin and motioned for the rest to head out. Antorn and Tobis watched the dust settle as the herd disappeared into the distance and Antorn turned to the beasts.

"What do you think these are?" Tobis asked.

"I have no clue," Antorn said.

"They really stink," Tobis said.

Antorn nodded and stepped over one of the beasts. He made his way over the fallen bodies and made note of their long ears with tufts of fur at the tip, long snouts, and thick heads. They had clawed hooves and Antorn now understood why there was so much noise when they ran. Their hind legs were shaped as to be able to run both standing upright as well as on all fours, and he found it interesting that they had a mangy mane similar to the wild canines from the far side of the savanna.

He picked up the battle-ax and inspected it. He had never seen such a weapon, and he gauged how heavy the blade was and measured the length of the staff and rolled the ax around in his hand. There was an odd comfort to it, and he swung it around a few times. Tobis walked to another beast and pulled the ax from its clutches and mimicked Antorn. Antorn wasn't sure what to think, he almost wanted to keep them, but it wasn't something that their kind had ever seen or had. He rolled the creature over and unlatched the belt that held the holster and fitted the straps on himself, then slid the battle-ax into the sheath at his back.

The blade was so comfortable that he decided he was going to keep it and figure out how to use it. Tobis also picked one up and latched the belt to himself.

"We need to bury these things, so they don't bring the scavengers," Antorn said.

"How, we don't have any earth scoops," Tobis said.

"With this," Antorn said.

He motioned to the hard shell of the turtlepotomous that was stuck in the net. Antorn pulled the bulky, squat, and slimy body by its large fur-covered hard shell out of the water. The bulbous head drooped and Antorn set the heavy frame on the ground and began to skin the shell off while Tobis checked the other net and reset the first one. They spent the next several lengths digging a large enough hole that they could shove the bodies of the beasts into. It took the rest of the day and after fashioning a new net they heaved and dragged the bodies into the hole and covered them up.

They pulled all the battle-ax's and gear off the animals and broke off a few of their fangs that they would fasten to a leather strap to wear around their necks. The night sank into existence, and they found shelter under the trees near the marsh after checking the traps again. They found another turtlepotomous, and they cleaned and prepared it to return when they had caught the few more they needed, that or when Modez returned whichever came first.

It took a few days for them to catch all the turtlepotomous they needed and decided that if Modez didn't return by morning they would head out for home. Antorn rested his head on his hooves and closed his eyes. His rust-tanned skin sat on his well-defined features and accentuated his human face giving him a serious but friendly look. The darkening sky began to lift as the sun pushed from the corner of the misty atmosphere. A soft warm breeze passed over the savanna with a hint of diligence. Heavy thudding pounded the earth from a distance, but the faint echo resonated in their bodies.

"Antorn do you hear that?" Tobis asked.

"Yes," Antorn said.

"It sounds like there could more of those beasts," Tobis said.

Antorn nodded and the pit in his stomach grew. The distant rumble sank into his guts, and he struggled with whether they should go and find out what was happening. Tobis scooted under the heavier section of the thicket but kept a steady eye on the distance. Tobis' smaller more-slender frame sparkled as the moon's rays that trickled through the brush illuminating his tribal markings which were a sharp and jagged-edged pattern as it wrapped around his fair human-like torso before descending onto his stag body and rounding down his long lean legs and tail.

"Antorn, something isn't right, I can feel it, it's been too long since Modez left," Tobis said.

Antorn lifted his head and the moon's rays ignited his tribal marks too. The illuminated pattern gave Antorn the appearance of a mix between a tiger and a zebra around his muscular torso and front shoulders and half-way down his thick elk-trunk. Small specs that resembled a cheetah's spots sat deeper under his rust-red fur and gave a gentle hint of illuminated color to his frame.

"Me too," Antorn said.

"What if they need help," Tobis said.

"I agree, but we are just two of the herd, what can we do?" Antorn asked.

"Fight," Tobis said.

Tobis' thin but strong hands gripped his weapon, patted the new battle-ax, and he motioned toward the distance. Antorn sucked in a deep breath and nodded, then grabbed his own spear and crawled out from under the brush. Tobis' narrow dark eyes smiled but the knot in his guts shot to the surface, and he swallowed hard. The two Forrne Stags maneuvered quietly through the thickets of the savanna toward the rumbling until the open landscape came into view. They slowed even more and flicked their narrow ears back and forth as they examined the noises that were now mixed with howls that penetrated the early day.

A sharp clapping hit the ground and Antorn recognized it as the hooves of a herd, and he moved to where he could see them running at an incredibly fast rate. He looked behind them and found a small pack of the beasts chasing them. He gripped the staff of his spear and leaped out of the bush and hurled the long straight weapon. The tip of the sharpened-bone blade sank into the upper chest of the lead beast and Tobis responded with the same exactness taking out the beast behind it. The small group of Forrne Stags peeled off to the side sending a tuft of dusty earth into the air.

One of the stags leaped over a small bush and skidded around and pulled his slingshot, but he had no more bone shards. The stag took a quick inventory of the distance from the last beast and whipped the slingshot toward the creature and let it soar into the air. The straps rotated through the air and hit its mark and wrapped around the thick bluish skin of the beast's neck. The impact spun the tightening rope around the neck and cinched tight. The creature grappled the string but couldn't get it unraveled before he lost consciousness and fell with a thud.

The stags rounded the last beast and Antorn pulled his slingshot. He loaded a smooth narrow piece of bone into the center pouch and whipped over his head. With a flick of his wrist, the piece of bone ripped across the dust and embedded into the side of the creature's face cracking it's skull. The beast recoiled and fell to the ground and skidded backward several lengths. The stags turned to find Antorn and Tobis coming out of the trees and ran to meet up with them.

"Pillip, is everyone alright?" Antorn asked.

"Those of us that are left," Pillip said.

Antorn's deep-tanned skin wrinkled as his brows sank into the center of his pained expression as he inspected the four of his fellow stags.

"What are these?" Pillip asked.

"I don't know. What happened?" Antorn asked.

"We were trapping the farside and came across some blackened earth. We followed it for a bit to find out what it was, but then were attacked by these things," Pillip said.

"Where were you when they attacked?" Antorn asked.

"On the edge of the bush, just before the mountain range," Pillip said.

"Black earth?" Antorn asked.

"There are veins of scorched earth, and we wondered if it was what was causing the shortage of water, we haven't been able to trap anything for over half a moon," Pillip said.

"This isn't looking good," Antorn said.

"We need to get back and report our findings," Pillip said.

"That's what Modez was supposed to do," Tobis said.

"You have seen these things before?" Pillip asked.

"Yes, a few days ago, we were attacked and Modez and the others went back to report it to the Herd-Lord," Tobis said.

"And he left you out here without a herd?" Pillip said.

"Yes, in fact he ordered us to keep watch on the traps," Tobis said.

Pillip studied Antorn's face and found him to be truthful and a flare of anger sat in his chest.

"That's not our way, no one gets kicked out of a herd," Pillip said.

"I guess Modez has become one of Tage's pets," Antorn said.

Pillip wasn't sure what that meant exactly but he inferred it meant Modez had sided with Tage and his 'new society' of nonsense. Antorn looked out over the fresh day's light on the wildgrass. The morning breeze brought with it the stench of the beasts, and he crinkled his nose. Antorn found his spear and yanked it from the dead carcass and returned to the others.

"Come on, we need to get back to the Herd-Lord and report this," Antorn said.

5-I Guess I'm Going For The Spit

The portal wriggled and Amirra emerged followed by a jade-green gryphton and then an ice-blue one.

"Helios, so good to see you," Shaz said.

"Shaz, I'm honored to be here, but we must move quickly if this is the toxin I fear this is, we have a big task ahead of us," Helios said.

"Of course, this way," Shaz said.

Helios and Phanes followed them through the castle at a quick pace and Phanes tried not to let his sudden feeling of small spaces overwhelm him as he examined the castle, which wasn't actually small, even for a gryphton. Shaz hurried into the room with Helios right behind.

"Helios!" Serin blurted.

Helios crossed the room quickly and wrapped Serin in a tight squeeze. Helios's eagle-eyes shifted quickly around the details of Motavo and Asher's bodies.

"They're going to be alright, but tell me everything," Helios said gently.

"They were attacked by Ruin Silk Spiders," Serin said.

"I thought so," Helios moved to Motavo and Motavo's expression seemed to stop on a friendly 'hello' as the toxin resurfaced. Serin's panic surged and Shaz pulled her into a tight hug.

"Give him a minute to examine them," Shaz said softly.

Serin nodded but Shaz could feel her intense need to do something and kept her tight. Amirra tried to keep the tears from forming and Riddick took her out into the hallway where they found the Minca, the Whispmother, Inelius, and Jagwynn.

"I think some food may be helpful," Riddick said.

"Yes, Master Riddick, I will begin right away, Inelius will you please help instruct on what to prepare for our gryphton friends," the Whispmother sang.

Inelius nodded and they made their way down the hallway.

"Are they going to be alright?" Turkill asked.

"Aye, but I think there's going to be some things we might have to find to make an antidote," Riddick said.

"That's why Phanes is here, Helios said he was going to need the venom from some kind of insect," Amirra said.

Helios pulled out his notes and scanned the pages and set the book on the side-table. The toxin had taken over again, and he tried to move their rigid forms to gain an idea of how many bite marks were on their bodies. Serin's worry started to worry Shaz, and he struggled with his inability to help her.

"I think it will be best to give them a tonic to put them into a deep sleep, so the pain of the muscle stiffness doesn't continue to wear them down. They can hear everything we say, but can't respond, which can be quite difficult to deal with, this way they can sleep while we secure the things we need," Helios said.

Shaz let Serin go, and she stood next to the bed. She understood Motavo's energy agreed, and he needed the rest and Asher too was tired of dealing with the pain, and she nodded. Helios took out a jar and Serin helped him open their lips and drop the slippery substance into their mouths. The medicine took a minute but Serin could sense them drift to sleep and their energies fell to a smooth pulsing and a comforting dread overcame her. Shaz's heart broke as he understood her emotions. Phanes stood at full attention and kept his eyes straight forward but found it oddly perplexing as the exchange gave him a sense of sadness he had never had.

"They will sleep until we are able to make the antidote and bring them back out of the sleep, but we have a lot to do," Helios said.

"What do we need to do?" Shaz asked.

"Phanes, you will return home and secure the Saraswati Insects and bring them back, but they have to be alive, and they are poisonous to us so you will have to use extreme caution," Helios said.

"Sir," Phanes said.

"Are they poisonous to humans?" Shaz asked.

"No, but they are hard to catch," Helios said.

"How many do I need?" Phanes asked.

"Six or seven should do it," Helios said.

"I can go," Riddick said stepping through the doorway.

"Aye, good idea," Shaz said.

"I'll go too," Amirra said.

"You are the earth sage?" Helios asked. Riddick nodded. "I think you would be better suited to secure the nectar of the Sable Cy'ad Tree, but the Minca can go with Phanes," Helios said.

Ladtwig and Turkill stepped around the corner at full attention but Ladtwig couldn't contain himself and scurried over to Helios who swallowed him in a big hug. Phanes shook his head at the prospect of having to deal with the tiny humans and Shaz chuckled. He knew it wouldn't take long for them to change his mind and gave them a nod. Turkill grunted but gave Helios a quick grin, and they hurried after their things.

"Where is this Sable Cy'ad tree?" Riddick asked.

"It's found in a very remote place in the Realm of Atamar, called the Turbulent Reef," Helios said.

"That's our homeland, I know just about every island in the reef," Riddick said.

Helios cocked his head sideways with curiosity.

"I suppose that would be an excellent place to hide you," Helios said.

"You've heard about us?" Riddick asked.

"I have, it is part of our responsibility at the academy to know the histories and legends of the world, but it wasn't until we met Shaz some time ago that the rest of my kind learned of your history," Helios said.

"You can think of Helios here like an earth portal," Shaz said.

Helios chuckled.

"Maybe not quite," Helios said.

"Alright, but we'll have to sail through the barrier, which will take moons to get to the islands," Riddick said.

"It won't take you long to get there, but it might take a bit of time getting back. There is a portal here at the castle that goes to Turob, but since we have no idea where it is on the other side, that will be the problem," Shaz said. The childhood cave he and Riddick used to play in flashed across his mind, "But I have an idea as to where it might be."

"Where?" Riddick asked.

"In the cave," Shaz said.

"Of course, where you could see all the glyphs and I couldn't, I've been meaning to check that place out again, but we will still have to sail through the reef to find the tree," Riddick said.

"I'm sure Yerild can take you," Shaz said.

Serin could tell Shaz secretly wanted to go too, he missed his island and a pang of homesickness hit his chest.

"Aye, do you happen to have an idea which island it's on?" Riddick asked.

Helios picked up his book and scanned the text.

"It's known to be on the Island of Hissing Sirens," Helios said.

"Of course, the only island that's a myth," Riddick said before catching himself with the realization it was in fact real. "Never mind, I know where it is said to be," Riddick said. "It's still going to take some time to sail there, and the time goes slower there than here," Riddick said.

"Aye," Shaz said.

"Then we best be getting on," Riddick said.

Riddick turned and left the room and Amirra followed. The Minca returned with their things.

"You will have to let the Minca ride on your back," Helios said.

"No, we will ride on Jagwynn," Turkill said.

Phanes started to object but nodded when he saw how large of a cat she was, which wasn't too much smaller than the gryphtons when on all fours. The group hurried back to the portal room and

Shaz followed behind.

"Be careful," Shaz said.

"Who do you think you are talking to," Turkill grunted.

"I was talking to Phanes," Shaz said with a smirk and Phanes gave him a half-glare.

Shaz instructed the portal to allow the party to enter and return and then watched them fade into the purple haze. Shaz started toward the door but Riddick and Amirra entered the room.

"Are you going to be alright?" Shaz asked.

"Aye why?" Riddick asked.

"Don't forget what the islands' myth is about," Shaz said.

"The Hissing Sirens, I know, but Amirra here has an idea for that," Riddick said.

"Alright, be safe," Shaz said.

Riddick slapped his shoulder and Shaz opened the portal.

"So, if you think the return portal is in the cave, where will we come out of," Riddick asked.

"I'm hoping it will be in the same place, but if not, I have no idea," Shaz said.

"How comforting," Riddick said.

Shaz chuckled and Riddick took Amirra's hand, and they stepped into the mist. A tinge of jealousy and guilt hit Shaz's guts, but he shoved it aside and hurried back upstairs. Helios had pulled out several glass jars and a contraption which connected them all and was setting it up on a table across the room.

"I can tell there's more needed, what else do we need?" Shaz asked.

Helios turned and took in a deep breath.

"We need a mushroom found here in Ebassia, and the Ruin Silk Spiders' spit," Helios said.

Shaz ran his hands through his hair and was glad he saved that for when Serin wasn't in the room.

"What about the mushroom?" Shaz asked.

"I'll go find it, it shouldn't take too long, I don't believe it's too far from here and Inelius can care for Motavo and Asher in the meantime," Helios said.

"So, I guess I'm going for the spit," Shaz said.

"That means I'm going too," Serin said. Shaz turned to Serin at the entrance and started toward her, "Shaz, don't you dare say it, I am going, and you know it," Serin said.

Shaz kissed her.

"I know love," Shaz said with a curious tone and then passed through the entrance to make the arrangements with Inelius and the Whispmother.

Helios smiled, he knew things would play out this way, but it was good to see it. He was one of those who believed their love would make them stronger.

"Once we have all the ingredients, how long will it take to make the antidote?" Serin asked.

"I'll begin the process as soon as I have the mushroom being it's here and not far from the castle and then it won't take too long once we have everything else," Helios said.

"Thank you," Serin said.

Helios looked up and nodded at Serin, and she hurried to find Shaz. She found him in the armory rummaging through a box near the back corner.

"What are you looking for?" Serin asked.

"I thought I saw something that might help in here," Shaz said.

"You don't want me to come do you?" Serin asked.

Shaz looked up from the box and turned to see her confused brows tight on her face.

"Of course I do, I just really don't like spiders in general, little ones, big ones, brown ones, ones with six eyes, ones with eight legs, ones with spots on them, ones with no spots," Serin smirked at his 'hee-bee-gee-bees' shudder, "and especially not paralyzing spit throwing ones," Shaz said.

"I'm sorry I mistook your intentions, I guess I'm just worried," Serin said.

"It's not your fault, and you have every right to be, so let's put that energy to use and figure this out, alright," Shaz pulled her into a squeeze, and she slumped into his grip as she let his energy realign hers for a minute. "Are you good," Shaz asked.

Serin nodded.

"Is there anything in Amirra's closet of stuff that could help," Serin asked, her brows softened.

"Maybe, let's go take a look," Shaz said.

6-Did You Figure Out Where We Are

Riddick took the last step toward the end of the portal and tried to determine what was on the other side before opening the misty curtain of safety. He was able to make out a few trees and what might be a setting sun, but nothing more.

"You ready?" Riddick asked.

"I guess, but for what I have no idea," Amirra said.

"Me either, so I guess we find out," Riddick said.

Amirra nodded, and Riddick slipped his hand through the portal and peeked his head out. The cool mist of the ocean filled Riddick's nose and his heart rejoiced with its comfort. This was definitely an island in the reef, but which one he couldn't tell yet. He moved all the way through and Amirra emerged behind him. He looked back for the portal, but the mist was gone, and his heart sank.

"Well, looks like we were right, we'll have to find the portal which goes back the other way," Riddick said.

"Well, like you say, let's have an adventure, yah," Amirra said.

Riddick chuckled, but he could tell she had more fear running through her than usual.

The sun was setting over the top side of the island and Riddick picked up a rock and chucked it. He listened for sound, but it didn't offer anything, so he sent out his magic and got a general picture in his mind.

"Well, we are on one of the larger of the small islands and as soon as the stars come out, I'll be able to tell which one for sure, so let's take a walk around and see what we can find and make a shelter," Riddick said.

They started around the island and the terrain was uneven but tolerable. The waves started to move further up the shore and Riddick moved them away from the water's edge.

"I've never seen an island before," Amirra said.

"Yah," Riddick half-stated-half-asked.

"I spent most of my life in a Velshari temple inside a mountain," Amirra said.

Riddick helped Amirra up a jagged rock and started toward the higher peak of the island. The rocky shore started to even out and the trees thickened. Amirra looked around as she took in the surrounding details. She studied the green lichen which covered much of the bigger rocks and cringed when the stink wafted into her senses. Amirra avoided the strange little black worm-like things burrowing into the gritty sand and hurried around the big slimy red and brown toad staring at her. She was convinced it was making a diabolical plan to eat her, and she glared at it. The wind picked up and brought a tightness to her chest and a sudden feeling the sky was going to crash on top of her stifled her breathing. Riddick turned around and found the panic on her face and hurried back toward her.

"What's wrong?" Riddick asked.

"I can't breathe," Amirra said.

Riddick looked around for anything she might have touched, but nothing on the islands would do this kind of thing.

"Why, did you touch something?" Riddick asked.

"The sky is squishing me," Amirra managed.

Riddick understood and quickly moved her under the trees and tried to help her focus on the feelings of being safe. A few minutes past, and she was able to calm herself, but she struggled to keep the lump from her throat.

"I can't believe I'm such a mess," Amirra said.

"No, you're not, I've seen it before, and it makes perfect sense being you were raised with things higher than you. Your sense of up and down just needs to adjust and the sky is very big if nothing holds it up," Riddick said.

"Exactly, how does the sky not squish you?" Amirra ask-stated.

Riddick chuckled.

"I never thought about it, but let's figure out a shelter, speaking of the sky, it's very unpredictable and could rain on us at any moment," Riddick said.

"Can I stay under the trees?" Amirra asked.

"Of course, and tomorrow we can work on getting you used to the sky, we have a lot of it to travel under," Riddick said.

"Do you know where we are then?" Amirra asked.

Riddick touched the trunk of a tree and the branches started to move into a tight canopy.

"I have an idea, but I will be certain here shortly, as soon as the stars come out," Riddick said.

Amirra tried to make herself useful and gathered some wood and cleared a spot for them to make camp. Riddick continued to organize the trees into a shelter which included walls around it. He knew if the weather decided to, it would thrash around the island, and he didn't want to get caught. Riddick inspected the weaved branches and figured they would work alright but the leaves on these trees were small and after a few attempts to make them bigger, he decided they weren't capable of getting big enough to do any good.

"I'm going to go look around a bit," Riddick said.

"Alright," Amirra said.

Riddick started back toward the ocean and surveyed the landscape. He closed his eyes and reached out to the earth's energy and learned what size the island was and how it was connected to the archipelago. The archipelago was the tips of mountainous peaks deep under the waters, and some had sand barges connecting them, while others were divided by sharp and jagged peaks, which made for difficulty to sail around. Most people didn't sail to the end, being nothing was out there anyway.

Riddick and Shaz started sailing with Merrick when they were small and as the Territory Warden, Merrick would sail around the Turbulent Reef, as it was called, a few times a rotation. Merrick would take them to the different islands, and they would explore them for anything new, animals, formations, plant life, and keep a record of what they found. Now standing here remembering their adventures, he understood Merrick was actually searching for the portal. The truth hit his core, and he looked for the marks they had left signaling they had inspected the island.

Riddick jogged up the beach a bit to one of the larger rocks sitting in the sand and looked around, but he found nothing. He climbed onto the top and sat and looked out over the horizon. The sun was now below the sea, and he studied the first few stars to show up. He was both relieved and not, as he confirmed they were in the lower half of the reef and not too far from the Hissing Siren island, that wasn't really there, except now that the new islands were now visible, he was certain it would be also, which also meant it would take some time to travel back to Turob once they made it to the is-land.

Riddick climbed down and made his way back to the shelter and found Amirra had started a fire and was waiting nervously for him.

"Sorry, did I take too long?" Riddick asked.

"No, I'm just not sure what all the sounds are and there's a lot of bugs and things," Amirra said.

Riddick noticed the fire had drawn a swarm of gnats buzzing around the smoke and tried not to chuckle.

"Ah, these are just gnats, they like smoke, they'll go away when the smoke dies down," Riddick said.

Amirra nodded but she still didn't like them.

"Did you figure out where we are?" Amirra asked.

"Aye, and good news, we aren't too far from where we need to go, which means we will have a long trek back to Turob," Riddick said.

"At least we don't have to go all the way just to go all the way back," Amirra said.

"Aye,"

"So, what is the legend about this Island?" Amirra asked.

"One thing to understand about sailors, when you spend a long time on a ship with the same people, you start to get bored and the imagination takes over and before too long the tales from last season are bigger and better than before. So, as the stories go from the fish was this big," Riddick held out his hands in front of him about a foot in length, "next season the fish was this big," he held out his arms wide. Amirra chuckled. "They call those 'fish tales' but a legend stays the same each time it's told. Over time, they can change especially if the sailors are the ones telling it, but this one was told by Grandfather, which means it's completely true," Riddick said.

"I take it that's bad," Amirra said.

"Aye, like I said before the hissing sirens are a creature with a soft and soothing sound that is both curious and intriguing. The sound makes you want to check it out, move close enough to find out what is making the noise, but then the hissing starts and you're too far into its clutches and suddenly your dead," Riddick said.

"So, what kind of creature is it?" Amirra asked.

"Grandfather said it's not a creature at all, but the island itself, that the *island* is the creature," Riddick said.

"So, the island eats you," Amirra asked.

"Pretty much," Riddick said.

"How lovely," Amirra said.

Riddick chuckled.

"But Grandfather also told us the island is actually a being with an intelligence, it understands what your intent is, and I'm counting on that," Riddick said.

"I'll start first thing in the morning enchanting some ear protection, so we don't hear the islands' song," Amirra said.

"Aye, and I'll build a boat," Riddick said.

Amirra cringed, she didn't realize she was going to feel this way about the ocean and struggled with the panic in her chest. Riddick sensed her uneasiness.

"You'll be alright, I'll help you," Riddick said.

Amirra nodded, but she wasn't sure how things were going to work out. They organized their bedding and let the fire die out as they drifted to sleep.

The wind picked up sometime in the night and Amirra woke with a start. She looked around and found a tiny red glow from the coals in the fire, so she could make out Riddick wasn't there. Panic shot to her brain, and she tried to calm her nerves. She slipped out of her bedroll and opened the door and the cold wind hit her face. Her pale skin instantly reddened with the blast, and she shivered. She climbed out and found Riddick standing near the waves and made her way to where he was.

"Is everything alright?" Amirra asked.

Riddick turned and pulled her into a hug.

"Aye, no, not really," Riddick said.

"What's wrong?" Amirra asked.

Riddick pointed to the north-west part of the horizon and Amirra squinted but shrugged.

"I don't see anything," Amirra said. A bright flash ripped across the sky and Amirra jumped. "Oh, you mean that," Amirra said.

"Aye, this is the direction we need to go and I'm guessing the storm is going to last several days," Riddick said.

"What are we going to do?" Amirra asked.

"I'm at a loss, it's already going to take us much longer than the others because of the time shift, and with this delaying us, I haven't a clue how long this will take," Riddick said.

"How long till the storm gets to us?" Amirra asked.

"Won't be but a few more hours, the wind is getting colder and a heavy mist is sitting just over the top of us," Riddick said.

"Will the shelter hold up?" Amirra asked.

"I hope so, but these winds can become pretty strong, enough to take the trees with it," Riddick said.

"Well aren't you full of optimism," Amirra said.

Riddick laughed and they returned to the shelter. Riddick inspected the roots of the trees and tried to make them grow deeper into the earths depths, but there was only so much length before the solid rock was too dense, so he organized them to wrap around each other deep under the ground.

Amirra scooted her bedroll closer to Riddick and tried to sleep but the wind grew stronger and the treetops bent as the wind brought the pelting rain. Riddick wrapped his arm around her and pulled her close and propped his head on his bent elbow and listened to the storm. They talked quietly about things that made them happy in an attempt to calm their nerves, but it was harder than they expected.

Riddick didn't know what time of the seasons they would arrive and feared they had arrived during the storm seasons. Riddick explained to Amirra how the islands were set up, how Turob was one of the largest and sat in the middle of another smaller reef which meant the storms were much less making it possible to inhabit, not to mention the trees were much larger and withstood the winds better. He described the tree buildings and the mountain on the island which of course was small now compared to the rest of the world. Amirra started to daydream about the island and hoped she would be able to see it. Sleep finally overcame them as the storm raged.

7- Things Are About To Get Weird

The small herd hurried over the flatlands and navigated the speckled stumpy trees and shrubs for a good part of the day. The sun was warm but there was heat sitting in Antorn's chest that he hadn't experienced before. He found himself angry, and sad, but most of all angry. One, because he didn't go sooner like Tobis had wanted, and two, because he had listened to Modez in the first place. But he had no choice, he was the outfit leader and that was the line of command. Antorn struggled with his thoughts and didn't realize they were nearing the edge of the prairie lands.

Tobis veered around a large bush and Antorn nearly ran into it but leaped over it and barely kept his footing on the other side. Tobis tried not to be obvious but he had been sensing Antorn's odd behavior for days. It wasn't like him to be scattered but something was different and Tobis was certain it wasn't only the new beasts causing it.

Several fawn Forrne scurried out of the way of the larger stags and shouted as they barreled passed them. The Forrne were a group of people that included a smaller fawn-like people and the larger stags. The stags were usually adept at the hunting, trapping, and bone working. They made things such as the spear tips and building and farming tools. The smaller fawns were adept, and usually kept their interests, in the prairies growing grain and farming the needs of the people.

Antorn leaped over a pile of bushelled grains and Tobis rounded it with the other stags and caught an earful from an angry fawn woman who was shaking her rake. Antorn did feel bad about startling everyone, but they had no idea what was out there, and a sudden thought hit his mind. The fawn are nowhere close to being able to protect themselves from the beasts and because their towns or villages were spread out from other family groups it would be so easy for them to get picked off.

The stags raced around another small settlement and into Kambu, the largest village where the main trades were made. The majority of the structures were large one level buildings that allowed for the Forrne to conduct business without stairs, but the building the Herd-Lord used to manage the affairs had three levels in which were accessed by a series of ramps. Antorn slowed as they came into the main square, but his fast pace was still more than the towns liking and the turtlepotomous-smith held out his fire poker and yelled as did the bakers and meat carvers. The dread of the situation sat deep in Antorn's chest and he tried to smile at least with a 'I'm truly sorry' kind of smile but he knew it wouldn't matter much.

The Fawns were not more intelligent, but they were more crafty and cunning, with a flair for engaging in conversations the stags thought were nonsense and useless. Stags had a more direct sense of duty and obligation and preferred the quiet side of their own thoughts. In general, the two groups lived peacefully under the Herd-Lord who was elected every ten rotations and most of the time it was a stag.

Antorn slowed to a trot and examined the entrance. He ran through a few scenarios as to how long it would take for the guards to catch him if he didn't check in and gain access first. He found three fawn and one stag at the entrance and decided he would make it pretty far, so he picked up his speed and the rest followed.

The first guard saw them coming and gripped his spear and took a few steps out from the overhang the building offered. His deep-set eyes widened as he interpreted the fact that Antorn was not slowing down. His palms instantly went sweaty and his heart raced. His mind filled with panic and he struggled to figure out what to do. Antorn took inventory and noted the other guards didn't even move.

"Halt!" the fawn yelled.

Antorn's large hooves hit the ground with sharpness as the softer dirt was now replaced with tighter compacted earth. Antorn reached the fawn and moved close enough to brush against the man to knock him off balance but not plow him over and barreled into the main lobby. The rest of the stags followed and a left a plume of dust. The fawn guards coughed and sputtered and tried to follow them in while yelling the commands to stop. On one side were the upward ramps and the other the downward. Antorn dug his front hoof into the dirt and turned to the side where the ramps went up.

The ruckus sounded the alarm and the two stags at the personal office of the Herd-Lord stepped in front of the door with their spears at the ready.

Antorn rounded the corner and made his way to the second level. He moved quickly and came to a stop at the door. Tobis came up behind Antorn breathing heavily.

"I must speak to the Herd-Lord right now," Antorn said.

"I don't think so, you have to have a schedule," one of the stags said.

"I don't think you understand what is at stake here, now let me in," Antorn said.

"No," the second said.

Their gruff expressions were determined and Antorn understood that they meant well and a small part of him felt bad for what he was about to do. Antorn gripped the spear of the first and yanked it upward smacking the man in the face and placed the staff into the stags throat. Pillip did the same to the second stag and their faces drained of color.

"I will speak to the Herd-Lord now," Antorn said.

The stags squirmed under the pressure of the sticks shoving into their throats and Tobis stepped closer to indicate he would also fight as did a fourth. The stag guards nodded and stepped aside from the door and Antorn handed Tobis the spear. Antorn pulled the latch and shoved the door open and the Herd-Lord looked up from his papers.

"So, you think you can barge into my office now do you? Just because you think you're so smart and that the rest of us are dumber than posts doesn't mean you have the right to do whatever you want," the Herd-Lord said.

"You think that is what this about? Then that certainly makes you dumber than a post," Antorn said.

The Herd-Lord's long ears twitched and Antorn was certain he had just made things worse for himself.

"Alright, since you're such a smart guy and I am not, then why am I in this position and you are not?" the Herd-Lord asked.

Antorn rolled his eyes and shook his head, as if he even cared about the stupid position.

"We have much more pressing issues than your stupid game of brawns over brains. Everyone knows that your intellect is that of a bat. But why they chose you, I guess that's a mystery for the cosmos to figure out," Antorn said.

"No, it's because I have repour with the people and they clearly favor me over you," the Herd-Lord said not understanding the direct insult.

Pillip and Tobis tried not to snicker.

"I never ran for this office, so your point is mute, but fine you win, you're so remarkable. The masses just love that amazing hair, and you are superior to everyone, especially with that amazing physique of yours. Now, can we actually do something to deal with our new problem, or are you going to keep staring at your stunning self all day," Antorn said.

Tobis and Pillip's eyes widened and they smirked with the insult, but they weren't sure how things were going to play out being that that was a serious offense to insult the Herd-Lord. Not that they didn't agree. Antorn's glare bit at Tage's nerves and he swallowed.

"Fine, tell me what is so important that you should have to have the-" Tage began.

"The beasts have killed half Pillip's outfit, hasn't Modez reported this yet?" Antorn said.

"He came to see me, I offered him a promotion if he kept his mouth shut, the last thing I need is for rumors to start spreading," Tage said.

Antorn's blood boiled and he wanted to shove his spear in his heart, but since he didn't have a heart, it wouldn't do any good.

"It's true, we were attacked. Only four of us survived, but if weren't for Antorn and Tobis we wouldn't have made it either," Pillip said his voice tight with anger.

Tage studied Pillip. He was a younger stag, but he was of large stature and always eager to get involved and came from good stalk, at least according to Tage. Tage could see the seriousness of the situation in his expression and tone and examined the rest of the men.

"The whole herd?" Tage asked.

Antorn wanted to roll his eyes, more and more he was convinced that the bigger your muscles were the smaller your brain was. He knew that wasn't completely true, being that he himself was of a fair stature and smart, unlike a good chunk of his people. Pillip too wasn't sure if he had asked the question with the intent of getting an answer or just to clarify what he had just now processed.

"What do you want us to do?" Antorn asked.

"You, nothing. I will send Pillip here to gather a herd and send them back out to kill the beasts," Tage said.

"I'm sorry Sir, but I won't go without Antorn and Tobis," Pillip said.

Tage's lip twitched with the indication and he narrowed his dark brown eyes. Pillip held out his chest and stared him in the eye. The other stag held out his chest also and Tage's blood boiled under his skin.

"Alright, if you want to get caught up in all of his nonsense then you go right ahead, but Pillip with be the outfit leader," Tage said.

"Sir, I respectfully defer to Antorn," Pillip said.

Tage shot him a surprised glare and Pillip held his ground.

"You don't get to decide that, I do," Tage said.

"Actually he, does, you made him outfit leader and he deferred to me, that *is* our law," Antorn said.

Tage's lip peeled harder but it was true and before he could make another argument, Antorn turned and started to the door with Pillip and Tobis behind him. Pillip pulled the door shut with a stronger than needed pull and it felt good. Antorn stopped at the corner of the descending ramp.

"Why did you defer to me, I'm the weird one that everyone

makes fun of," Antorn asked.

"Not everyone, those that don't know you maybe, and I don't know, my gut just tells me you're the one," Pillip said.

"And I second it," one of the stags said.

"And I too," Tobis said.

Antorn wasn't sure what to do, but he nodded and continued from the building. The sun was bright overhead and they blinked to adjust to the discomfort it gave. Antorn lead them through the markets and into the outer edges of the village. Antorn stopped at a huge stack of grain and turned to the group.

"Alright, each of you go gather as many stags as you can and meet at the bridge by sunset," Antorn said.

"What are you going to do?" Tobis asked.

"See about supplies," Antorn said.

"How long will we be gone?" Pillip asked.

"I'm not sure, but plan on it being a while, I have a feeling things are about to get weird," Antorn said.

The stags weren't sure what that meant exactly but they saluted and hurried away. Antorn crossed the field that led to his small home on the northern side of the village. The soft breeze brought the aroma of fresh cut grains and herbs from the nearby farms and the meat roasting in the fire of the modest dwelling he was passing, and he sucked in a deep breath. As Forrne, being part human and part deer or elk, they had a mixture of tastes such as cooked meat and raw grains. At this moment smelling the food was probably all that he was going to be able to do.

He pulled the thatched door open and the sun shot across the dingy dirt floor. It wasn't much but he didn't spend a lot of time there anyway and had no mate or children, so he didn't see the need to keep fancy things. His sleeping quarters consisted of, well nothing, it had been so long since he slept there. He sighed and rummaged through a cupboard and found, also nothing. He decided he would get something to eat at the local eatery and closed the door behind him. He made his way through the few buildings and found the eatery near the last half of the village square.

Antorn's stomach lurched excitedly as he realized he hadn't eaten for some time, but the ache that was now a permanent fixture reminded him that he didn't want to eat leaving him confused. The eatery was large with tall round tables scattered around. A long bar ran along the back side of the arena and Antorn made his way. He was thankful it wasn't busy as he stepped up to the counter. A woman stag set a mug on the hooks on the back wall and gave him a gentle smile and tossed her towel over her animal skin covered shoulder. Antorn nodded, and admired her slender face with delicate amber eyes and long wavy sun-kissed honey hair.

"How are you Antorn, it's been awhile," the woman stag said.

"I'm alright Mazen, how are you?" Antorn asked.

"Can't complain, but I've heard rumors," Mazen said.

"Rumors?" Antorn asked.

Antorn swatted a fly that was buzzing around his face and flicked his ear as his nose twitched. Mazen smiled and Antorn's cheeks warmed.

"Yeah, rumors about some kind of beasts in the trappers lands," Mazen said.

Antorn nodded, he knew she was too smart and wouldn't allow him to evade her questions. She had been the most persistent and annoying little sister there could be, except she wasn't his little sister. He never understood why she always picked on him or made his business her business but as he got older, he found he didn't mind as much.

"There are beasts, I have never seen such things and unfortunately they have already killed more than half Pillip's outfit,"

Antorn said.

Mazen looked at him with intense brows and studied his face. He gave her the 'I wish I were kidding' look and she scowled.

"How?" Mazen asked quietly.

Antorn shook his head.

"I don't know exactly, I wasn't there, but Tobis and I saved Pillip and three others from them. They had already taken out several they said, and they are fast and ruthless," Antorn said.

Mazen bit her lip and jumped as another stag slammed his empty mug on the counter.

"More ale Mazen," he staggered.

"I think you have had enough, it's time you go home Brandtzen," Mazen said.

"No, more now," Brandtzen said.

Mazen took the mug and shook her head and he began to beg but she refused. Several minutes later he gave up and staggered out of the eatery.

"I'm sorry," Antorn shrugged it off. "What can I get for you?" Mazen asked.

"Anything hot," Antorn said.

He didn't know what he wanted, nothing sounded good and it was a weird feeling to be starving but not hungry at all. Mazen nodded and went into the kitchen area and brought back a plate of roasted meat and vegetables and set in front of him. He smiled thankfully and she made herself busy while he ate. Antorn struggled to get it all down, but he knew he needed to because he might not have another good meal in a long time, if ever. He finished off the mug of brewed grains and pushed the plate to the other side of the counter.

The fang hanging around his neck brushed his arm as he ran his hands over his face, and he picked it up and examined it. The images of the beasts came to mind and he started to assess the different aspects. Mazen returned and cleared the dishes and served a couple of fawn Forrne before returning.

"I get off in about twenty minutes, do you want to meet up and you can tell me all about the beasts," Mazen said.

"I would like that, I don't have long though, we are leaving tonight," Antorn said.

"Then let me try and get out of here now," Mazen said.

Antorn smiled and she indicated that she would meet him at the back. He made his way through the growing crowd and out of the eatery. The day was bright, and he was thankful that he still had some time before he needed to get his gear and meet up with the others. Mazen slammed the door behind her as she finished yelling at her boss and Antorn smiled.

"He didn't want you to leave?" Antorn asked.

"He never wants me to leave, he's such a clackerback," Mazen said.

Antorn's brows raised, he didn't know exactly what a clackerback was, but the way she said it indicated that it wasn't a good thing.

"I'll have to take your word on that," Antorn said.

Antorn knew she didn't keep her thoughts to herself and sometimes used colorful expressions, especially when she was energized about those said opinions, and often used sarcasm with her feminine flair tossed in. It was quite confusing at times.

"Come on let's get out of here," Mazen said.

Mazen grabbed his hand and practically dragged him into the distance and it felt good. It had been a long time since he had anyone but the trappers to talk to and a sudden fear crept in his mind. Mazen rounded the largest acacia tree at the edge of the village and stopped next to the now low stream. She bent down and settled into the tall grasses and Antorn sat next to her.

"So, tell me what's going on?" Mazen asked.

Antorn took in a deep breath.

"I don't know what is happening, but while trapping half a moon ago, we came across these beasts. They were like the wild canines from the farside, but had a different kind of head and fangs that went upward. Their skin is a blueish color with ragged tufts of black and brown fur. They snarled like the canines and howled but growled too. They were able to stand on their hind legs and they fought with these," Antorn pulled the battle-ax off his back and handed it to Mazen who took it with wide eyes, "they were fast and large, as big as us when they stood on their hind legs. Modez made Tobis and I stay behind to keep the traps and he returned to talk to the Herd-Lord, which ended up getting him a promotion and silence," Antorn rolled his eyes and Mazen snickered, "but a few days later we heard commotion and went to check it out, that's when we came across the beasts chasing Pillip and the others," Antorn said.

"But you killed them all, yes, so we won't have to worry about them now?" Mazen asked.

"I have no idea, but we killed the first pack and then there was a second pack, so there might be more," Antorn said.

Mazen scowled.

"I don't like the sound of that," Mazen said.

"Me either, we are leaving tonight to go and find out what we can about them. Another weird thing is, there is this burnt ground too, Pillip said they came across it just before they encountered the beasts, so we are going to go back and check it out. I have no idea what we'll find or what it will mean, but I have a feeling things are about to change in a big way," Antorn said.

"What does the Herd-Lord have to say," Mazen asked.

"He's the dumbest stag on the planet, he doesn't have anything to say unless it's about how amazing he is at nothing. He just likes to hear himself talk as if anyone actually cares about what he has to say. Everyone knows it's the rest of the herd counselors that actually do anything," Antorn said.

Mazen laughed.

"Antorn, I can't believe you just said that about our dearly beloved Herd-Lord, his grace, his majestic-ness," Mazen mocked.

Antorn chuckled.

"Yeah, I guess I have gotten a little sassier in my older age," Antorn said.

"Oh, what, all of twenty-five, you are," Mazen teased. Antorn smiled but he caught a glimpse of the late afternoon sun that was now peeking around the top of the tree and a pit returned to his guts. Mazen noted the shift in his face and put her hand on his arm. Antorn gazed at her and appreciated her friendship. "Things will be alright," Mazen said.

"I hope so, but do me a favor and go to you nama's and make sure she's alright, and then stay there," Antorn said.

Mazen studied his face and found he was as serious as she had ever seen him and nodded. A pit formed in her guts and she looked out over the distance.

8-You're A Tiny Human!

Leeta jumped as the shimmer rippled across the portal and her heart spiked as Phanes emerged from the mist. He shook off the tingles with his feathers on the top of his head as they ruffled down his neck and onto his chest. His ice-blue feathers were pale against the more tanned skin of his human chest and his lion fur was a darker tan that stood out against the feathery tufts of the ice-blue on his tail. He caught her eye and stopped but moved out of the way as Jagwynn and the Minca came through.

Leeta's eyes popped and she took a step back as the ginormous black jaguar's eyes quickly scanned the room. Then her eyes got bigger when she noticed the two tiny dark-skinned humans on her back. Turkill rolled his eyes and waited for the remark about their being so small.

"Where's your father," Phanes asked.

"There are tiny humans," Leeta said.

Yep, Turkill knew it and shook his head. Ladtwig snickered at his brother and Turkill elbowed him.

"Come on, he's probably in the war room," Phanes said.

"Hey that's what we call it too," Ladtwig said.

Turkill shook his head and Jagwynn followed Phanes out of the portal room. They made quick time through the tunnels and into the courtyard and Phanes leaped into the air to fly over the crowded plaza. Jagwynn snarled and Turkill and Ladtwig laid low and hung on as she maneuvered quickly around the mass amounts of gryphton's. Most of the gryphton's moved quickly if they saw her coming, all with shocked expressions, as much as their eagle faces could give. Phanes landed on his hind legs in front of the main doors and Jagwynn leaped up the stairs right behind him. Phanes was surprised she was already there and decided that maybe it wasn't going to be too bad.

"Let me pass," Phanes growled.

The soldier unlatched the sizable steel handle and pushed the door open and Leeta made her way in behind Jagwynn as she followed Phanes. The soldier couldn't help but take a second look at the Minca but Turkill had already changed his focus. They made their way to the room and Phanes stopped.

"Leeta, you need to stay here, this is Armada business," Phanes said.

"But," Leeta started.

Leeta saw the intensity in his eyes and nodded. She didn't like it, but if she wanted to keep seeing him, she needed to respect the way things were. Phanes smiled at her to reassure her of his feelings, and pushed the door open.

"Sir, I have my mission," Phanes said.

The room stood and Ralti moved around the table.

"How is Serin's family," Azrack asked.

"They have been paralyzed by the Ruin Silk Spiders. Helios put them into a deep sleep while we secure the needed items for the antidote," Turkill said.

"Ah, Turkill, Ladtwig, and Jagwynn so good to see you, welcome," Azrack said.

"You too, you have been well?" Ladtwig asked.

Azrack nodded. Jagwynn nodded and purred.

"We hear you have been busy," Ralti said.

"Well, you know, it's always a day with Shaz and Serin," Turkill said.

The gryphton's that knew them laughed and Shar and Cluck smiled but hadn't yet had the pleasure. It was clear to them, however, that Shaz and Serin were important to them, and so they took that to heart.

"What is the mission?" Ralti asked.

"We need to secure the Saraswati Insects, Sir," Phanes said.

"Those are poisonous to us," Jaxton said.

"They are not to us," Turkill said.

"Where will I find them?" Phanes asked.

Brigdon pulled out a map from a shelf under the table and placed it on the surface. He unrolled it and held it for Azrack who pointed with his clawed paw.

"This is where I ran into them, but Helios said they weren't there when he went to study them, so I am afraid you will have to search for them, and that area has been retaken by the Kronos," Azrack said.

"That could lead to another invasion if they find them there," Ralti said.

Azrack nodded.

"We can go in on our own, that way you won't have to start anything," Turkill said.

"But-" Phanes started.

"There are too many, you'll never make it through without being spotted," Cluck said.

"They don't know us yet, do they," Ladtwig said to Turkill who smiled and shook his head.

Cluck's eyes widened, and he looked at Azrack who had a slight grin at the corner of his beak. A sudden rock hit the bottom of his stomach and lurched, and he felt a pang of worried intrigue.

"What do we know about them?" Turkill asked.

Phanes was about to ask but Turkill had beat him to it and found the little man to be interestingly trustworthy. It wasn't that he didn't trust people, but he had never dealt with humans, and small ones for that matter.

"Did Helios ever find them?" Ralti asked.

"Not that I'm aware of. Only that they expel a venom and live in hives in the trees. According to Helios, they used to be in our realm until the End of the Realms and only returned when Shaz went through the barrier. Did Helios give you any instructions?" Azrack said.

Phanes shook his head and Turkill pulled out a paper in his pocket and handed it to Ralti. Ralti unfolded the piece of parchment and read the scribbles and handed it to Azrack. Azrack read the note and nodded and tucked the paper under a stack on the desk. Phanes looked between them and wondered if they had some kind of language they were speaking, and a pang of anger mixed with jealousy hit his guts. He didn't like being in the dark and it felt like there was something going on, but he wasn't in the ranks just yet and kept on task.

"Cluck and Shar will go with you," Ralti said.

Phanes nodded.

"You will need to be very stealthy and go in from this point here," Jaxton said.

"We have been told by some scouts that they are planning another attack, see if you can find out any more information while the Minca get the Saraswati Insects," Azrack said.

"Phanes will take point," Ralti said.

Shar and Cluck nodded and saluted. Shar's mint-green feathers ruffled against her fair human skin and lioness fur under her leather chest armor and Cluck's dark brown feathers complimented his warm eyes.

"It is a few days journey on paw, so we better be going," Phanes said.

Phanes started to the door and Jag let the Minca climb on and followed with Shar and Cluck right behind. They made their way from the inner sections of the fortress and out through the armory. The gryphton's loaded a supply of weapons and garbed their lightweight battle gear and then headed toward the forest. Phanes lead the crew down the backside of the fortress's mountain pass, but Turkill could tell he wasn't going as fast as he could and was getting annoyed. The mountain leveled off and the landscape evened as the trees encompassed the land.

"Which way?" Turkill grunted.

Phanes indicated the direction and Jagwynn lunged forward. She was also not impressed with how slow they were moving and needed to show them they were capable of moving faster. Jagwynn's long thick hind legs powered her forward and the gryphton's were surprised at her speed, but were thankful and lunged to catch up. Phanes regained the lead, and they padded through the thick forest with a soothing silence. At this speed, it wouldn't take more than a day's travel, but they hadn't had a chance to figure out what they were going to do about the Kronos.

The sun dipped below the tree line and a chill hit their faces. The Minca were glad for Amirra's uniquely charmed cloaks that kept them warmer or cooler whichever was needed. Jagwynn's strides had lengthened over the last several moon's as they had done so much running, that she had developed an unusual endurance for it. Jaguars were excellent runners but as a Sakura, an intelligent and exceptionally large jaguar, her size usually limited how far she would normally run. Jagwynn understood her collar she had received from Mathieu was a part of the Synergybond, which gave her access to Shaz's magic and aided her in being able to handle his needs.

Her slick movements also allowed the Minca to ride for long periods of time, and they had grown quite close to her, and she to them. It wasn't a situation any of them would have ever imagined, but it was more natural than they would have guessed.

The moon's shown through the leaves of the brightly colored trees giving them an eerie beauty and the Minca mused at the colors as they swayed through the cool breeze. Phanes slowed his pace and moved toward the large pine trees.

"We'll stop here for the night, so we can reach the Kronos territory by nightfall tomorrow," Phanes said.

Shar and Cluck agreed and climbed under the heavy branches that draped downward leaving a warm nook between the bottom branches and the ground. Turkill and Ladtwig climbed off Jag and held up the lower branch for her and climbed in after. It didn't take long for the sleep to overcome them and soon the sun was hitting them in the face. Ladtwig woke and started rummaging through his satchel for his morning meal and Turkill popped his into his mouth.

Ladtwig unwrapped a sizable piece of dried meat for Jagwynn who gripped it with her sharp teeth. It wasn't her preferred food, but she appreciated the Whispmother's attempts at her comfort. They climbed out of the tree and found Shar and Phanes near a little stream.

"So, what are your plans for a distraction?" Turkill asked.

Shar gave him a glare and Turkill gave her his extra grumpy harrumph look which made Phanes snicker and then cough to keep from laughing.

"What is your problem?" Turkill barked.

"Shar here, is just a bit skeptical about this whole mission," Cluck said.

Cluck flapped his wings gently as he glided from a nearby branch.

"Well, so am I, what makes you think that you are going to be able to get this done any better than us?" Turkill asked.

"Are you for real? You're a tiny human!" Shar shot back.

"And you are an overgrown lion with the head of an eagle and a body and brain of a human, so what does that make you, some kind of amazing?" Turkill barked.

"And a girl," Ladtwig chimed in.

Phanes and Cluck busted up laughing and Ladtwig snickered from where he was peacefully eating his white cheese. Jagwynn even looked up from cleaning her fur. Shar looked around and tried to hide the blushing anger in her chest.

"Alright, we need to gain some intel on what the Kronos are up to as well as get the Minca close enough to get to the Saraswati bugs. They are poisonous to us anyway, so what is your plan to catch the bugs?" Phanes asked.

"We have a plan," Turkill said.

"They are going to have lookouts probably around here, so we need to be careful as we approach," Phanes said.

"Shar and I will go east and north, and you can take the center," Cluck said.

"Alright, we go here, and then regroup," Phanes said and pointed to the sections of the map. "Jagwynn and the Minca will go with me," Phanes said.

The gryphton's nodded and the Minca climbed onto Jagwynn. They started out at a quick pace and half-way through the day Phanes slowed his pace and searched the distance and waited for Shar and Cluck to make their way to where they were.

"Shar, Cluck, you take a quick inventory of the sky and I'll make a sweep down here," Phanes said.

Shar and Cluck nodded and leaped into a tree and disappeared into the sky and Phanes headed left. Jagwynn lowered to the ground and Turkill and Ladtwig pulled their dart guns.

"Turkill, three gryphton's ahead on your right," Jagwynn said.

"How can you tell?" Turkill asked.

"Because, lion's stink," Jagwynn said.

Turkill gave a quick snort but wasn't sure if she was serious or not and cleared his throat. Turkill motioned for Ladtwig to move to the side, and he took the other. Turkill hurried to a tree and Ladtwig found a big rock. Jagwynn crawled under a pine tree and waited for the all-clear. Turkill crept from one tree to the next and made his way until the gryphtons came into view. He made a bird call and Ladtwig found him pointing.

The gryphton's deep tan skin emerged and then the feathers on his head and tail. They were the same color as the intense amber-orange of the leaves of the trees and Ladtwig and Turkill now understood how they blended in. Turkill searched the trees and found the other two and motioned to Ladtwig. Turkill pulled his dart gun and loaded it with his newly formed sleeping toxin that they had created at Serin's request. He figured one put a human to sleep for days so two or three should be enough for the large felines.

Shar and Cluck landed behind them and Phanes came from around a large tree and watched as Turkill sucked in a deep breath and blew hard and fast sending a blast of his rapid-fire. The darts shot out at great speed with a tiny hum and embedded into the neck of the orange gryphton as Ladtwig launched his at the deep-red gryphton. Turkill stepped out and let go of another burst and his darts seated into the chest and neck of the third gryphton. Shar looked in the directions they had pointed and waited for the gryphton's to fall from the tree perches and hit the ground with a thud.

"How did you see them?" Shar asked her tone full of surprise.

"Jagwynn said lion's stink," Turkill said.

Shar wasn't sure what to think but Cluck chuckled. Jagwynn came up behind them and Turkill and Ladtwig climbed on.

"Are they dead?" Phanes asked.

"No, but they will sleep for some time, now let's go," Turkill said.

9-One Spider Is Too Many In My Book

Shaz ran into the kitchen where he found Inelius helping the Whispmother and grabbed their packs they had just finished packing.

"Inelius what do you know about the Ruin Spiders?" Shaz asked.

"Not much I'm afraid, other than they live in the Timeless Plains and are usually not aggressive, unless provoked," Inelius said.

"Timeless Plains huh?" Shaz asked.

"What is the matter?" Inelius asked.

"That's where the bird told me Gavin Rhill is creating an army of Jaduuk," Shaz said.

"That could explain their aggression," Inelius said.

"Aye, we'll be back soon," Shaz said.

Shaz hurried from the room and met Serin at the stairs.

"You ready?" Shaz asked.

"Yes, where are we going?" Serin asked.

"The Timeless Plains," Shaz said.

"Do you think this has to do with what the bird told you?" Serin asked.

"Aye, so we will probably run into other things happening as well," Shaz said.

"And we don't know where the portal is to return, do we?" Shaz shook his head. "Do we have an idea as to how to find it?" Shaz shook his head. "Well, your full of answers," Serin said.

"Hey, maybe the earth portal might have an answer," Shaz said.

Serin followed Shaz to the earth portal, and he brought a ball of energy from his core, asked permission, and sent his magic into the rock's surface. The portal's eyes opened, and the rock formation illuminated the face of the portal.

"Shaz, how may I help?" the portal asked.

"I need to know if you can tell me the locations of the portals from the other side of the barriers back to the castle," Shaz said.

"Which realm are you seeking?" the portal asked.

"All them, but in particular The Timeless Plains," Shaz said.

"Let me see," the portal said.

"Oh, and where will the portal take us," Shaz asked.

"I have your information,"

Illuminated images flowed from the earth portal and Shaz allowed the energy to form the images in his mind. He was getting better at organizing new information, but he was always scattered for a time after receiving this amount, and he still hadn't processed everything from the scroll and grandfather's loss. Serin gave him a boost of her light magic that helped illuminate the needed space in his mind, and he blinked as the magic faded away.

"Thank you," Shaz said.

The portal faded back into its solid state, and they hurried back to the portal room. Shaz pulled a book from the shelf at the back of the room and thumbed through the pages until he found what he was looking for. He calculated on his fingers as he worked out the new information and put the book back.

"Alright, I have a pretty good idea of what happened when the time shifts were moved," Shaz said.

"Am I going to like the answer?" Serin asked with a hint of tease in her tone.

Shaz smiled and noted her attempt at making the best of things, grabbed her hand, and they stepped into the misty purple wall of the portal. Shaz hesitated at the end of the time shift and examined what he could make out on the other side and put his hand into the mist. The heat surged, and he stuck his head out and looked around. The daylight was sitting at dusk and the moons were in the far sky which offered a bit of light, but the sun hadn't dropped all the way yet, which left a dimmed vision on the landscape.

Shaz stepped out and Serin behind him. The heat hit her in the lungs with a pounding, and she struggled to breathe. Shaz was certain this was going to be hard for her as she needed more moisture to keep her water magic up and a sudden panic hit the back of his mind. He pulled the map from his satchel and examined the floating colored spheres.

"I hope this isn't going to be like the Desert of Trials," Serin said.

"Aye, we're going to need to figure out how to rejuvenate your water magic when it's hot," Shaz said.

"So, you think we're going to have to be here a while?" Serin asked.

"If I have done my calculations correctly then we will have a ways to travel to find the portal back home," Shaz said.

"Let's hope your calculations are not correct," Serin said.

Shaz chuckled.

"Come on, this way," Shaz said.

Serin buffed them with wind-walk, and they hurried across the dry grasslands. Short stalky trees speckled the landscape and the gently rolling hills blended into the current version of the hill they were on. They moved quickly but had to avoid a heard of large gray animals that neither of them had ever seen before. They had long snouts that they could pick things up with, and extensive floppy ears that sat at the side of huge gray leathery skinned frames. Rounded horns sat on the top of their heads and faded as they ran down their spines. They had short hair on the backsides of their legs and on their short tails that had a mix of blacks and whites giving a striped appearance. They were majestic in their own way and Serin felt a peaceful power that came from them.

They traveled for what seemed like half the night, but the sky only decreased in darkness a small degree, and they marveled as the soft beige of the straw-like grass began to glow a luminescent shadow of its form. The underneath side of the trees opened, and a glowing flower-pod exposed a brightly colored pedal like structure.

The reflection of the intense colors added to the stars that were now visible showing a vast sky covered intensely with the brilliant colors of the universe. The stars gave the appearance that they were shining brighter than any other sky they had seen. They passed small patches of water and several animal dens and Serin rebuffed a couple of times before they reached the area they were suspecting the spiders to be, but as they came to the location, there was nothing, not even grass.

"This is where the map indicated they were last known to be," Shaz said.

"Well, we do know that the map isn't completely accurate," Serin said.

"Aye, let's get some sleep and see what we can figure out in the morning," Shaz said.

Serin agreed and yawned and stretched. She hadn't realized how tired she was, and it was hard to tell how much time passed in this realm.

"What is the time difference here?" Serin asked.

Shaz pulled out the map and ran the calculations through his head.

"The time moves about the same as the castle. I wonder why the sun hasn't come up yet," Shaz said.

"Hopefully, we can be quick and make it back before we disturb things here," Serin said.

Serin unrolled her bedroll and flattened the sparse grass with her feet and then laid the bedding on the ground.

"Aye, but we have to come back anyway," Shaz said.

Serin scrunched her nose but nodded. Shaz could tell she wasn't in the mood to take on an army of Jaduuk, or whatever was going on here, but quite frankly neither was he. She pulled out a wrapped package and popped the dried food into her mouth. She was at least thankful for the Whispmother's flavorful food, and she sighed as the morsels filled her stomach. Shaz too enjoyed the food. The heat of the night eased, and he felt the pit in his stomach move into his mind thinking about how hot it was going to be, come the sunrise.

"It is beautiful here," Serin said.

"Aye," Shaz said.

"Do you think we will run into any Jaduuk?" Serin asked.

"Probably," Shaz said.

Shaz laid onto his bed and Serin laid down next to him with her head on his chest. He wrapped his arm around her, and she closed her eyes. Shaz gazed into the sky and examined the constellations and the new stars he couldn't see from Turob and his mind again raced around how big the universe was but his mind settled on the memory of watching his grandfather step into the green pillar to become the ultimate sacrifice and a lump formed in his throat. His death was so much harder than Shaz had ever expected. Things were worse knowing how much he had sacrificed to teach him everything he could without using magic, and what it must have been like to harness Shaz's uncontrolled war wizard magic as he grew, until he was old enough to harness the magic himself, which proved difficult at first and even now still caused some turmoil. Serin hadn't fallen asleep yet and listened to his feelings and was now facing her own set of fears.

Serin had never thought about what losing her family would be like and seeing others suffer grief was one thing, but now that it was hers, and Shaz's, her heart was filled with turmoil. The one thing she couldn't heal, was a broken heart, and both of them had one. Shaz gripped her tighter, and she realized he was listening to her thoughts too. The next few hours followed with unrestful sleep, and they decided to get up and keep moving. The sky had lightened some and Shaz guessed there was still several more hours until sunrise.

The brightly glowing trees eased to soft pastel colors and the beige grasses returned as they searched the surroundings for any indications of the spiders.

"I am not finding any forms of life," Shaz said.

"What do you think happened to them then?" Serin asked.

"The only thing I can think of is, if the Jaduuk are here, they have forced them to leave, which could explain why they were in the underground," Shaz said.

"Maybe that's where we will find them then," Serin said.

"Except I closed the holes," Shaz said.

"Do you know where the underground is in this realm, maybe if we go in that direction we will find them," Serin said.

"I don't, but I have an idea," Shaz said.

"Sorry, there's no high points to stand on and yell to see if they come out and eat you," Serin said.

Shaz blurted a ga-fa and Serin smiled. Shaz took a quick inventory of the sky and noted the moon's had faded to be barely visible and the sky had lightened to the degree of dusk back home and wondered if the sun only came up to near the horizon here but didn't cross the sky as usual.

"What is that?" Serin asked.

Shaz searched the distance.

"It looks like the ground has been burned," Shaz said.

"That's what I thought too, I wonder what would cause that," Serin asked.

"Jaduuk," Shaz said.

"Really?" Serin said with a hint of dread.

"Aye, and I smell them too, so let's get out of here," Shaz said.

Serin boosted them with her wink-walk and they hurried away from the scorched earth. The further they traveled the more the animal life came out and the sky lightened. The bright yellow disc they were used to seeing, was a softer orange and only gained a few lengths into the atmosphere before declining again. Shaz wondered why it was so warm when there was little sun to heat up the world, but was glad it wasn't as hot as he had expected it to be.

"Look, there," Shaz said.

Shaz pointed to a dark hole near a group of the short stalky trees and Serin veered toward them. She stuck her foot into the air padding underneath her and came to a quick stop. Shaz sent out his energy and nodded.

"How many are we talking?" Serin asked.

"Well, one spider is too many in my book, but there are quite a few," Shaz said.

"Do you have a plan?" Serin asked.

"Kind of," Shaz half-stated. Serin scrunched her brows with a scowl and Shaz snickered. "They aren't usually aggressive unless provoked, but with what has happened here, they may already be on the alert, so we need to be careful. I think we should start with shields on, can you wrap yours around your whole body instead of just in front of yourself?" Shaz asked. Serin searched her brain and then called her shield and told it to encompass her frame and it did. She gave him a thumbs up, and he armed his shield. "Alright, I'm going to try to get one to come out and you lift in the air," Shaz said.

Serin nodded and Shaz crept to the hole. He searched with his energy and picked up a rock the size of his head and dropped it into the hole. The rock free-fell for a few lengths and then hit the ground with a thump. Shaz back away and waited but nothing happened. He found another rock and dropped it down the hole and this time a hissing rippled from the hole and Shaz pulled his blade and took several steps away from the opening.

A furry leg gripped the top and then another and another and six glassy black eyes emerged from the darkness. Shaz noted the spider was smaller than the ones in the time shift and this one had no fangs like the others. Serin grabbed with her air and lifted it out of the hole and cringed at the size. The black eyes frantically moved about trying to figure out what was going on and it started to flail around. Shaz rounded the spider and could see markings on the underbelly which began to radiate the iridescent glow the savanna showed the night before.

"I don't think this one is going to have any spit," Shaz said.

"What do you mean?" Serin asked.

"This one isn't the same as the ones in the shift, the others had very long and skinny pincers that looked like a set of arms with spikes on them," Shaz said wriggling his fingers over his mouth like Serin does when referring to the critters they have fought with fangs.

"You're not funny," Serin said. She kept her lips tight, but she did find him cute and that he got the hee-bee-gee-bee's from the spiders. "So, now what do we do, as soon as I let this one go, it's going to come after us," Serin said.

"Aye, can you knock it out, take just enough air that it passes out but doesn't die," Shaz asked.

"I'll try," Serin said as she shrugged. She gripped her hand tightly and focused on the air inside the bubble it was now in and the spider frantically struggled as the air dissipated. A minute passed, and the spider passed out and Serin moved it away from the hole. "Now, what?" Serin asked.

Shaz dropped another rock and moved back. Another spider emerged and this time it was the bigger one with the fang-like arms that came out from the sides of the furry face. Serin gripped the air element again and lifted it out of the hole. Shaz grabbed an iron jar from his pack and stepped in front of the spider and lunged forward with the sword. The spider's black eyes flashed, and its long pincers flung out. The spiders spit shot from the tips of the spikes and Shaz flinched as the liquid hit his shield and sizzled from the fire elements heat. Shaz lunged again but this time he held out the jug. The spider pulled back but spit again and Shaz caught most of the white liquid in the jug. He wasn't sure how much they needed, so he lunged again and the spider again spit. Shaz capped the jug and nodded to Serin who restricted the breath and rested it back into the hole as it passed out.

"Let's go," Shaz said as he met up with Serin.

They hurried back the way they came being careful to avoid a pack of prairie animals and the herd of the large gray animals.

"Where will we find the other portal?" Serin asked.

"It will take a day or so, I think, whatever a day is here," Shaz said.

Serin nodded but a pit in her stomach formed, and she could tell he wasn't telling her something, *yet*. She understood that he didn't always tell her things right away because he believed he was trying to keep her safe, or him safe from her frustration, which only made her angry, but she understood his intentions were good, and tried to push the irritation out of her mind. Maybe if she thought about ways to inflict pain without leaving marks he might get the hint. She chuckled at herself and found Shaz too was trying to hide the smile. She was right! He *was* listening to her thoughts, and she glared at him in her mind. Shaz laughed and gave her a sideways smile.

10-We Have An Enemy To Crush

A strong odor wafted around the cave as the ooze dripped off the egg and into the small, chiseled trench that flowed away from the spawner. The gurgles and spurts of the ooze as it hit the hot-rocks surface echoed off the unevenness of the cave. Jaduuk'ai rounded the corner and inhaled a full breath of the odor. He found it oddly pleasing now and remembered at first when he couldn't stand the stench and puked every time. Jaduuk'ai stepped over one of the eggs roots and circled the oval sphere. His large, clawed hooves both scratched and clopped on the black stone floor sending another echo through the surroundings. He studied the glowing heartbeats inside and counted them. Thirty-two of his creatures were currently growing inside the egg and he smiled.

He pulled out the time-ticker and examined the details and then frowned as he realized how long it took to breed only thirty-two. He put the ticker back and walked around the egg again. There were several eggs now in production, but he feared it wouldn't be enough. He needed to figure out a way to make them grow faster. If he was going to start his invasion on Edenocht by the time the comet came around, he needed to speed things up. It had been his plan before he was entombed, and after checking the time-ticker and the revolutions of the Sariandi Comet, he found he was just in time for the next rotation.

He understood that the force that pulled the comet close to the planet also brought the planets magic closer to the surface making it stronger and more apt to be harnessed. Jaduuk'ai reached out to touch the egg but hesitated. He didn't want to disturb the peacefulness of the heartbeats but his curiosity of what the egg felt like drew him in. He hesitated but then lightly touched the sphere with his pointed finger. The egg was firm but soft at the same time and a ripple of energy moved outward from his touch. The energy rippled back to the center point and Jaduuk'ai touched it again.

This time he placed his hand on the slick exterior and he felt the many heartbeats inside thump against his skin. A tingle of excitement coursed through his body and he felt a kind of love for them. He put his other hand on the egg and closed his eyes and allowed the forces to radiate through his being. It was a sensation he hadn't experienced, and he liked it. The power to create, to create something powerful, dreadful, feared, carnal, fierce, savage, destructive...what else, oh yes, don't forget pure evil. Jaduuk'ai laughed to himself, of course to himself, there was no one else there.

Jaduuk'ai pulled his hands off the egg and frowned. He hadn't realized being the only one would be lonely. Not that he wanted anyone there to tell him what he should or shouldn't do. He hated the 'shoulds' and 'shouldn'ts'. His face contorted through a series of eye rolls and sticking his tongue out as though he were saying 'blah, blah, blah' to himself. That was it, he needed to make a better Jaduuk. Not only a magnificent creature but a smart, magnificent creature, but not too smart. He was going to have to think about that for a bit.

Maybe the old books might have some information on what to do. A quickening in his blood-pressure sent tingles through his body with the excitement of a new challenge. He traipsed with a heavy foot through the corridor just to make noise so that he could explore the new idea of having extra sounds around. If he was going to have companions, he needed to be ready for it. A child-like glee formed in his chest and he giggled. Yes, giggled. He was so pleased with himself for coming up with his own ideas. Just because one was evil, didn't mean they couldn't have a little fun, even enjoyment in their successes.

Jaduuk'ai scooted several of the rocks that had fallen from his widening of the doorway to his old quarters and pulled the little book from the shelf. He tried to be careful with the pages and was finding it a bit harder to navigate the delicate parchments with his clawed fingers. They were useful for only one thing, slashing through the flesh of other creatures, and as much as he loved that idea, he was now perplexed as how he was going to do this. He set the book on a table and found there was no chair. Jaduuk'ai snarled under his breath, glared around the room, and slammed his clenched fist into the wall. The pain pulled him from his frustration, and he examined the cut now on his knuckles. He licked the drip of oily blood and tasted the mixture of his human blood and the Jaduuk's blood. It was an odd flavor, one he couldn't exactly describe, but it gave him an idea.

He made his way back to the egg and crossed the veins and roots. He clenched his sharpened fingernail-like claws into his tough skin until they broke through and blood seeped out. He waited until there was a descent sized puddle in his palm and then dripped it onto the egg. The reddish-purple liquid absorbed into the outer finish and the egg jumped. He put his dripping palms on the warm soft shell and hissed as the egg sucked his life force. Jaduuk'ai struggled against the force and started to feel lightheaded. He yanked hard and nearly fell over as he was released with a loud suction sound that reverberated around his head.

He regained his footing and examined his hands. The puncture marks were puffy and irritated, but a satisfying notion sat at the back of his mind. He wiped the small bead of sweat from his brow and started out of the cavern, but the egg shifted and wobbled as it grew brighter. He examined the structure and found over fifty heartbeats and he smiled. He would have to wait until they were ready to find out if he had done what he wanted to, but now he needed to stay and watch so when the beasts emerged he would be able to examine them. It didn't take as long as he thought it might as the egg started to wobble. Small movements pushed against the rubbery shell and Jaduuk'ai took a step back. The green glowing rubber thinned and wrapped around the form of a large Jaduuk until the creature broke free and the thick layer of protective ooze dripped over its body. It wiped the ooze from its eyes and blinked several times and then sucked in a deep breath.

The hot air was a new sensation to the beast, and it coughed as it's lungs dried out. Jaduuk'ai watched with wonder as it licked itself clean of the goo and then the egg wobbled again. Another creature emerged from the egg as did several more.

"Welcome my pets," Jaduuk'ai said.

The beasts turned and examined Jaduuk'ai and lowered onto their haunches and bowed.

"How may we serve you?" a beast said.

Jaduuk'ai's heart jumped. The giddy excitement crested his emotions, but he kept his lips tight.

"We have a world to destroy," Jaduuk'ai said. The words heated up his chest with his own truth and he chuckled a deep and raspy sound. For an instant he didn't recognize it, but then understood it to be the shadow that was now a part of him. "Come follow me, we have an enemy to crush," Jaduuk'ai said.

11- I Guess We'll Learn Quickly

The day quickly faded, and Antorn finished loading his satchel. He slung the heavy pack over his shoulder and adjusted it so that it would rest on the elk's side of his back. He would normally live off the land and he was still planning on it, so the bag was mostly filled with a sizable amount of bone shards and a few extra slings. He added some dried rations incase things got dire with the food sources. Even though they could eat the grasses of the plains, it was his least favorite dish, but in a pinch at least he wouldn't die of starvation. Unless the scorched earth made for difficult situations.

He galloped quickly to the bridge and noted Pillip and Tobis coming from the side with their crews. The group slowed to a soft trot until they made it to the bridge and greeted Antorn with a salute. It wasn't the usual greeting for a trapping expedition, and they didn't have an official military because they never needed one, but it was the formal greeting that was used during the elections, so he supposed it seemed fitting. He returned the gesture, and another group of stags came up behind them.

"We're just waiting for Soren's outfit," Pillip said.

"What's the plan?" Tobis asked.

"Pillip will take us to where he and the others were attacked and we will start from there," Antorn said.

Hooves thudded the ground as Soren's outfit rounded the bend and Antorn nodded to Pillip who lurched into a fast gallop. Each of the stags fell into place as he led them into the fading sun. It was a bright night as the numerous stars in the sky took over the atmosphere. The bright colors wafted in a wave-like pattern and spanned the majority of the sky. Antorn never got tired of staring at them which was one of the reasons the other stags had always thought he was weird. He was certain there was something big out there, something more to life and the universe, the world, or whatever it was, but he could never explain what he felt, and the rest of the stags were more interested in being the fastest and strongest.

A herd of black rhino-mowa covered the wallows that they were partially bathing in and Pillip rounded them keeping a fair distance as they were not exactly the friendliest of savanna creatures. It would take all night and part of the morning to reach their destination and Antorn needed to come up with a plan. He really had no idea what he was doing and now there was over fifty stags under his command, and he was supposed to know what to do.

Antorn pulled in a deep breath as his lungs were starting to sag and the hint of pitch etched at his senses. He flicked his ears and listened to the distant night, but nothing stood out. He searched the distant trees and shrubs, and a tiny glint caught his eye and his heart thumped. He held up his closed fist and came to a quick stop. The company followed quickly and stood still. It was one their best features, the ability to stop and stand nearly still at a moment's notice.

Antorn took a step toward the trees and squinted. Two figures flashed and he took another few steps. The figures came out from the trees and he could tell that they were partially like him, but had only two legs and no rump. He blinked and looked again but they were gone. He waited a few minutes but didn't find anything more and returned to the company. He wasn't sure if his mind was playing tricks on him, so he shook it off.

"What was it?" Tobis asked.

"Nothing, but I think we should go slower from here," Antorn said.

Pillip nodded and continued over the landscape with a more cautious gate. Small strings of black dirt began to emerge under their hooves and the smell of burnt grasses eased into the air. The new morning sun was now nearing the horizon and the stars were fading.

"We're nearly there, it's just over that ridge," Pillip said.

"Alright, let's make camp here, then we'll break into smaller groups and start to make a sweep around the area," Antorn said.

Pillip nodded and gave instructions to the rest of the group. The stags quietly set up a meager camp. They didn't usually have shelters unless they were going to be in one area for a while during trapping season, so most of the gear was canteens and traveling dishes for food and traps and nets and such. They really had no idea what they were up against and Antorn watched one of the stags organize his spears. A thought came to mind and he signaled to Tobis.

"I was thinking we should go back to where we buried the beasts' weapons and outfit everyone with them," Antorn said.

"We don't even know how to use them," Tobis said.

"I guess we'll learn quickly then," Antorn said.

Tobis nodded, but Antorn could see the doubt in his expression.

"Take your outfit and gather the weapons and meet us back here, I'm going to send Pillip around that way, and Soren's crew over there," Antorn said.

Tobis nodded and returned to his men and they quietly slipped over the ridge back the other way. Pillip filled Antorn and the others in on the course they took last time and rehearsed the events. Antorn made as much of a mental picture as he could but there was something that ate at the details, but he couldn't tell what it was. Things were changing rapidly, Antorn could feel it, but he still had no idea what he was doing. He did know that he needed to start thinking differently than they ever had, and for him it wasn't that hard, but he wondered how the rest of the stags were going to be able to adapt.

"I want to divide into small recon groups but staying close to each other. Who here knows mapping well?" Antorn asked.

A bulky stag in the center raised his hand slowly. It wasn't usual for the Forrne to keep maps, they usually used landmarks to interpret their surroundings. Antorn nodded to the stag who's deep set eyes flashed a hint of fear that his secret was now out, and the others would think he was weak and brainy. Antorn puffed out his chest to indicate that no one in the company was to question anything, and the group accepted the terms without saying a word. It wasn't their usual way, but nothing was usual about this and for some reason they liked the acceptance that Antorn gave them.

"What is your name?" Antorn asked.

"Gabe, Sir," Gabe said.

"I want you to start mapping everything, the landscape, the scorched earth, if and where we find the beasts. I also want you to note things like, scratches in the ground, trees, whatever. I want a complete assessment of these things," Antorn said.

"Yes, Sir," Gabe said.

"I'll help," a stag said.

The man gave Antorn a 'please' look and Antorn got the feeling that there were so much more to these stags than even they knew about themselves and a warm heat emerged in his chest. Antorn nodded and the two stags gathered the needed supplies and started their process.

"Who here is adept at spear fighting?" Antorn asked. The stags weren't sure what 'adept' meant and tried not to look around at the others but had no answer. "Who is really good at spear fighting?" Antorn asked. Several arms went up and Antorn took the battle-ax off his back and handed it to one of them. "This is the weapon the beasts have, we are going to learn how to use them and fight against them, organize yourselves and start figuring this thing out," Antorn said.

"Sir," the stags said.

The group left the rest and began to examine the weapon excitedly. Antorn noted a difference in their vibes and smiled to himself.

"What do you want us to do?" Pillip asked.

"Take your outfit and start a sweep around that way," Antorn pointed in the direction he saw the other humanoid-things, "But don't go far, I just want you to pay attention to the landscape, the ground, what it feels like, the trees, water-plants, animals, everything. Then report it to the mappers," Antorn said.

"Yes, sir. May I ask why?" Pillip asked.

"I want to learn as much as possible about what is happing both in and out of the earth. These beasts are fast, cunning, we've seen them hunt, but we don't know how they live, we need to be better trappers, so we have a chance to play at their same game," Pillip understood and a hint of curious excitement etched at his being and he saluted Antorn who saluted in return. "Soren, you take your outfit and do the same, that way. Stay in echolocation distance," Antorn said.

"Sir, but we haven't used echolocation for generations, I'm not sure any of us are going to be any good at it, it's not even taught anymore," Soren said.

Antorn studied the stag. He was right, it was lost to the new ages, the times of plenty. Antorn had forgotten that he was the weird one and loved to study the history's and old ways. Antorn ran his hands over his face and took in a deep breath. He took out a small slender stone stick and tapped it on one of the horns on his large and wide antlers. A soft vibration rippled across the atmosphere and all the stags internalized the sounds. The two mappers looked up and stared at Antorn who hit the stick against his antler again. The stags in the distance working on the weapons stopped and turned sharply to see Antorn strike his antler again.

This time the sound was a little sharper and the stags internalized it. The vibe the energy gave their beings gave them a 'hurry' feeling and Antorn struck it again. The new vibe 'sounded' gentle and soothing, but had a directness about it and the stags began to understand. Antorn handed the stick to Soren and nodded for him to do what he had done. Soren struck the bone stick against his antler and the sound emanated from his antlers in the same way but different.

The stags could tell the difference and understood what Soren's 'sound' sounded like as opposed to Antorn's. They moved through the outfit each taking a turn until everyone had 'heard' their brothers' sound and then Soren went out to the stags working with the weapons to teach them. There was an excited new energy about the group and Soren nodded and the two groups readied for their first sweep. Antorn's nerves settled a little with a calmness he was glad to have, if only for a little bit.

12-Keep An Eye On The Water

Riddick stirred to the sounds of the barking of the animals that live on the beaches and quietly slipped out his bedroll. He opened the door a tiny bit and found the sun was out, and he slipped outside. He sighed as he did an inspection and found the trees were all there and the storm was gone. The sparkling sun rays hit him in the face, and he estimated it was late in the morning. He searched the sky and found the last bit of clouds parting in the south-east and understood the storm had only just now cleared. Amirra stirred and made her way out of the shelter.

"Looks, like the storm is gone," Amirra said.

"Aye, let's get to work yah," Riddick said.

Riddick smiled at Amirra giving her his bright expression. She smiled, and he kissed her and then quickly started toward the trees. Amirra got to work enchanting her ear coverings she had found at the castle. They reminded her of the furry blanket she had at Nitida's, and she hoped they would be strong enough. Riddick bent and twisted the new planks he had 'grown' into the shape of the hull of a moderate boat. He didn't need the vessel to be too big for them to fit in, but he needed the vessel to be big enough to handle the larger waves that they would encounter.

After he had organized the shape and length of the planks Amirra helped him find the small black stones in the sandy shore while Riddick rolled them through his fingers making them bend into the sharp points of a nail. They would need quite a few and Amirra used her cloak as a bag to carry them all. The chores kept Amirra busy enough that she had hardly paid attention to the sky and before too long, she didn't feel like it was going to squish her. Riddick fashioned a flat rock onto a handle and began hammering the nails into the planks while Amirra secured the sticky brown goo from the sun-dried seaweed.

Riddick explained it would be needed to seal the gaps in the planks and keep the wood from becoming waterlogged. The sun passed over the soft blue sky and had started to sink into the horizon as Riddick finished the last bit of goo. He pushed the boat into the water keeping a tight grip to check its buoyancy and finding the hull was good, began to secure the seats, and the mast pole to hoist the sail he had taken from the castle.

"I think that should do it," Riddick said.

Riddick finished the knot of the rope he had also brought and tested the sail a few times. The pole wasn't as smooth as he would have liked but it would do, and he was getting tired. Amirra smiled big and gave him her 'you're amazing' smile, and he jumped out of the boat. Amirra handed him a package of dried meat, and they sat on a rock nearby.

"How long do you think it will take?" Amirra asked.

"I'm hoping not more than a day, but since I only know of its suspected location, we may still have to search a bit," Riddick said. Amirra nodded. "You seem to be doing pretty good with the sky, yah?" Riddick asked.

Amirra nodded.

"I started to think, and the idea that the sky is just a big blanket keeping me warm and tight, made me feel better," Amirra said.

"Atta girl," Riddick said.

Amirra smiled. She loved it when he said that, she felt like he was proud of her and that he knew she would figure it out. It was a feeling she never received from Semias and the longer it had been the easier it was to begin allowing herself the chance to learn and grow, which she learned was also to make some mistakes too.

"So, we leave in the morning?" Amirra asked.

"No, we'll leave in an hour or so, when the tide goes out, the stars will be the easiest to sail by, and the surface is usually calm at night," Riddick said.

"Really? I didn't think you could sail at night," Amirra stated.

Riddick chuckled.

"It's actually fairly easy, most ships sail all day and night, and I spent days sailing the Mirabella, without a sail mind you, a few rotations ago after the hurricane," Riddick said.

Amirra finished her bite and pulled her cloak around her. The chilly evening breeze sank into her bones, and she shivered. Riddick popped the last bite into his mouth, and they started to pack their things into the boat. The wind was constant, and Riddick understood it would make for good sailing and wanted to get into the water quickly. Amirra climbed in and situated herself at the back and Riddick shoved and heaved the boat from the last bit of sandy shore and hopped in.

He pulled the ketch line and allowed the sail to drop from

the top and the heavy cloth billowed with a pop. The noise startled Amirra, and she tried to keep her breathing steady. Riddick shoved his foot against the notch he had made knowing that would be where he would be standing to steer the sail. Before the hurricane, he had only sailed a ship with a full rudder system and a helm, but after making the makeshift mast that was three times too small for the large vessel, and hand steering with Batovi, he was an expert with the small ship.

The wind ate at the sail and the ship quickly made her way out to sea. Amirra paid attention with eagerness to learn as much as possible and asked a ton of questions as to what he was doing. Riddick didn't mind because he liked that she was interested in him. Riddick struggled not to let his growing feelings for her confuse things, and he tried to keep his tasks at the forefront of his mind. He taught Amirra how to find the constellations and how to determine which way they were going by placing his hand out in front of him and lining up the stars with different parts of his hand.

This was one thing he was really good at, memorizing the stars in the sky, it was the one thing that lead them to the Kar-ka-dannon. He hadn't stopped thinking about how that worked out, and wondered if it was safe. Riddick had no reason to believe otherwise, but he ended up soaring through the earth itself for who knows how long and ended up in the realm with Shaz and the others. He didn't even know how different the time shift was from the Realm of Yune and found his thoughts going around in circles. He had been so busy that he hadn't realized Amirra had fallen asleep. He checked his directions again and shifted the degree two notches and the ship started to veer to the left. The three moons were bright and shining the brilliant purple haze that was also constant between the realms.

He heard a splash and found a pod of the large sea animals off to one side.

"Amirra, wake up," Riddick said.

Amirra stirred.

"Is everything alright," Amirra asked.

"Aye, but look," Riddick pointed and Amirra sat up.

Amirra gasped at the incredible site and watched with the biggest eyes ever.

"What are those?" Amirra asked in a whisper.

She didn't want to disturb them and their beauty.

"Whales, and look there's a couple babies," Riddick said.

"They're magnificent," Amirra said.

Amirra stared in amazement and took in all the details her brain would hold and Riddick smiled at the child-like glee she had. It was one of the things he liked about her the most. Riddick checked the sky again and again adjusted the sail. His hands were starting to ache with the constant tug against the wind and his arms had been burning for some time, but the wind was so constant he didn't dare relax the sail. Amirra gazed at the whales as they started to veer away from them and rested her chin on the edge of the boat. Riddick noted the whales start to change course and studied the surface of the water. He observed a slight change in the color about twenty lengths or so deep and checked the sky again.

He decided to shift the sail and follow the whales. The majority of the night had passed, and the blackness of the sky was beginning to lessen, and Riddick found a reef to the other side, which was a good thing he had followed the whales, or they would have ended up on the wrong side and who knows if they would have been able to cross. Riddick pulled the line and the sail swung to the other side as the wind shifted and the boat eased in speed. Riddick saw a tiny dark spot on top of the water and was guessing it was going to be their hissing island.

"Amirra, you awake?" Riddick asked.

Amirra stirred and sat up and rubbed her eyes.

"I'm sorry I fell asleep again," Amirra said.

"It's alright, but look," Riddick pointed.

"Is that it?" Amirra asked.

"I think so, so let's get ready, I have no idea what we will find the closer we get," Riddick said.

Amirra nodded and pulled out the earmuffs and Riddick slipped the cloth band over his hears. Amirra secured the packs and rolled the ropes and tightened them into the grooves. Riddick eased on the sail collapsing the ketch slightly to lessen the wind into the sail and rounded it into the breeze and the ship slowed.

"Keep an eye on the water, there might be sharp points from the reef that could rip open the hull," Riddick said.

Amirra moved to the side of the boat and peered into the darkness. They moved closer to the island and Riddick could make out some of the details of the shore and decided it would be too rocky to make port just yet. He opened the sail and the wind caught hold and jerked the ship sideways. Riddick rounded the ketch pole and yanked the rope and the sail leveled out and the boat turned a sharp corner, and he continued around the south-east side of the island. Amirra tried not to let the sudden movements make her sick but Riddick found the tint of 'sea-sick-green' ease over her face.

"Watch the horizon," Riddick said.

Amirra looked up and found where the starry sky met the blackness of the ocean and the wobble in her head eased. Riddick wasn't going to admit that he suffered from the same condition from time to time and Shaz always found pleasure in teasing him. Riddick carefully scanned the water's surface for protruding landmasses the closer they came to the growing black dot.

A faint tint of light blue emerged under the surface several lengths and Riddick paid attention as the color began to intensify. The color moved toward the island in a wavy pattern, and then he noticed another one and another one. They gave him the impression that they were veins connecting the island to the earth below the water, and he collapsed the sail and secured it to the mast. Amirra was now better and stepped up next to him. The small ship rocked on the waves and continued to drift toward the growing blackness.

"What is this?" Amirra asked.

"Not sure," Riddick said.

He reached out with his echo-location and sent a vibration toward the island. Riddick stumbled back as he received the information. The amount was overwhelming, and he swayed. Amirra tried to steady him and managed to help him to sit down.

"Are you alright? What's wrong?" Amirra asked with panic in her tone.

Riddick breathed in deep and closed his eyes and let the information sink in. He categorized the details and understood how big the island was, that there was indeed a lifeforce he had never encountered before, and the vegetation even seemed to have a kind of knowledge.

"This is definitely the right island, the magic is very old here and quite like Mother Edenochts magic, but stronger," Riddick said.

The ship continued toward the island and Amirra wondered if they were being brought in with the current but on purpose. Riddick struggled to keep his head from swaying. Amirra's panic rose in her chest, and she felt her knees go week. She chided herself for letting her fear get the best of her, after all she was a Necromancer, a Velshari. Amirra dipped into that part of her and pulled her 'get it done' attitude and took the sail. She had been watching Riddick for hours, how hard could it be. Amirra let the sail open enough to let a little pocket form and the ship sped up slightly. She rotated the mast and adjusted the ketch, and the ship rounded the now bright glowing veins.

The sun had lightened the sky enough that she saw the trees

and sand of the oncoming shore, and she maneuvered the boat between the veins. The closer they came the brighter the blue became and soon the colors were glowing. The magnificence of it took her breath away, and she soaked in the beauty. Riddick's head started to ease, and he was able to help her steer the boat. A confidence she hadn't had in a long time eased back into her chest, and she smiled at herself.

"You all right?" Amirra asked.

"Aye, this magic is just so strong, I'm not sure if I'm going to able to handle it all," Riddick said.

"I don't feel anything," Amirra said.

"Let's hope it gets easier once we are shore," Riddick said.

The size of the island wasn't huge, but it would take a few days to cover it. Riddick and Amirra steered the boat the last few lengths through the glowing water.

"This is simply amazing," Amirra said.

"Aye, I have never seen anything like this before," Riddick said.

"You haven't, so this isn't normal?" Amirra asked.

"Nope," Riddick said.

The ship bumped the bottom of the shore and Riddick hopped out and heaved the bow with each wave and got the boat far enough onto the shore, so the tide wouldn't take the vessel back out to sea, and Amirra climbed out.

"Be careful, I have no idea what is here," Riddick said.

"Like what?" Amirra asked.

"Bugs, critters, animals, beings, you know the usual," Riddick said.

Amirra both squirmed and chuckled. Riddick took his satchel from Amirra and slung the canvas bag onto his shoulder, and they made their way up the beach. The glowing water wasn't the only thing to be illuminated, and they found glowing mushrooms and lichen and even bugs, which Amirra didn't find appealing. Riddick stopped every so often and reached out with his mind. Each time he got a picture back, but it made him unsteady, and he learned to crouch each time. Riddick could tell there was a system of partial walls that went around the island in a maze-like pattern and the center of the island was shielded from his view.

He explained what he was seeing to Amirra by drawing the pictures in the sand. But it was hard to understand because it was like it was a new picture each time, possibly like there were multiple levels, but he couldn't figure out where they belonged. He was able to determine where the entrance was, which was on the other side of the island.

"We still have an hour or two left before there is enough light to move forward, let's get some sleep first," Riddick said.

He had been awake now for hours and with the new information, he was becoming very tired. They made a quick camp under the trees and near a cave-like group of rocks. The waves that crashed on the shore was soothing, and they quickly found sleep. Riddick didn't sleep well, however, his mind was busy digesting all the information, and he found himself walking around the island with his essence. It was oddly satisfying though, and he felt a calmness that eased into his body and relieved the soreness of his muscles from the long sailing. He figured it was the energy of the earth healing him and rejuvenating his magic.

13-Too Small, Yeah, We Know

Phanes and the gryphton's carefully scanned the distance as they continued to move into the Kronos territory. Ladtwig spotted several holes in the dirt and pointed them out to Turkill who nodded. They noted the way the holes moved around the earth and found their similarities to be the same as the ground-dogs back home. Phanes sniffed the breeze and lowered to the surface. The others followed and moved to find cover.

"I smell smoke, that means we're not far from the first encampment. Shar, Cluck, you make your way into the camp and blend it, see what you can find out, and meet us back here," Phanes said. They nodded and headed toward the settlement. "We need to head that way a bit more," Phanes said.

Jagwynn veered to the side and Phanes fell in next to her. The daylight was fading quickly, and the mist was beginning to thicken the atmosphere. Phanes readjusted his direction a few times as the landmarks came into view and he slowed as they came closer to the place Azrack had indicated.

"The bugs should be in this general area," Phanes said.

Jagwynn let the Minca off and leaped into a tree and faded into the darkness.

"Where is she going?" Phanes asked.

"To look for the bugs," Turkill said.

"Are they poisonous to her?" Phanes asked.

"No," Turkill said.

"That's lovely, so I'm the only one that can be affected," Phanes grumbled.

"You can go back if you want," Turkill said.

Phanes shook his head.

"What can I do to help?" Phanes asked.

"Stay out of the way," Turkill said.

"Is he always this grumpy?" Phanes asked.

"No, just when his best friends are in trouble," Ladtwig said.

Turkill shot him a glare, but then he quickly turned away and grabbed a stick. He didn't want to admit it, but he was more anxious than usual. Phanes understood and felt a bit of worry for them, not really knowing who the people were, but he could tell that they meant a great deal to the Minca. Turkill unwrapped his satchel and it unfolded to be a heavy leather bag and Ladtwig pulled a rope from his. Ladtwig threaded the rope through the holes at the top and then secured the stick into the ties close to the lip of the bag. Turkill pulled another length of rope and wrapped into a tight circle and slung it over his shoulder. Jagwynn leaped from a tree and landed quietly next to the Minca.

Turkill tossed the rope up over the limb above his head and secured it to a lower one. Ladtwig scurried up the rope like a caterpillar and Turkill tossed him the bag and then climbed up. Turkill yanked the rope and it loosened the knot and then rolled the strap over his shoulder again. They scaled the bulky branches behind Jagwynn and Turkill found the hole that Azrack had described. He moved where he could go in from one side while Ladtwig took the other.

They eased up to the center and Ladtwig held out the lip of the bag, and they carefully covered the hole. Turkill connected the rope he had over his shoulder to the rope around the bag and crisscrossed it underneath the branch securing it to the bag making a tight connection so that there were no holes the bugs could escape from. The Minca moved back toward the trunks of their trees and nodded to Jagwynn who slammed her enormous paw against the trunk.

A low buzzing sound echoed, and a bug shot into the bag followed by several more. The satchel lifted off the branch and started to thrash around as the insects became even angrier. A stinky odor wreaked across the breeze as the Saraswati insects started spraying their venom. Turkill and Ladtwig didn't need all the bugs and it would be easier to carry back, so they waited for the bugs to return to the hole and only a half dozen or so was left and carefully scaled the limb. Ladtwig unlaced the rope on his side as Turkill turned the stick around tightening it around the top of the bag. The brothers worked quickly but quietly so that they wouldn't disturb the hive as they were about to lift the closing bag off the hole.

Turkill moved quickly and tightened the last half-length as Ladtwig let the last crisscross loose. They stood very still as a quiet buzzing echoed from the hole, and they breathed in slowly. There was no movement, so they backed away and quickly returned to where Phanes was. Phanes reached up and took the bag but held it outstretched and the Minca climbed down the tree. Turkill motioned for them to head back to the meeting spot and Phanes took the lead but moved carefully as not to disturb the bugs as much as possible.

They reached the meeting place, and everyone took in a deep breath and sighed.

"That was pretty clever, I have never seen that before," Phanes admitted.

Ladtwig smiled big but Turkill only nodded.

"How long will we have to wait for the others," Turkill asked.

"Hopefully not long, but it could be a bit," Phanes said.

"We have something we need to do, watch that bag, and we'll be back," Turkill said.

Phanes looked at them with a curious scowl but didn't push for an explanation. Turkill and Ladtwig climbed on Jag, and they disappeared into the new darkness. The moon's rays were mostly covered by the thick tree cover, but a few sprigs of light got through leaving a little light to move by. Turkill pulled the map from his satchel and ran his finger over it. He studied the distance and decided they needed to move a bit to the north. Jagwynn caressed the ground effortlessly and soon the ruins came into view. The Minca climbed off Jag and carefully made their way to the door.

There was no handle on the latch, and it was locked shut. Ladtwig pulled his long skinny metal stick out of his pack and stuck it into the hole and searched for the lever inside. He found it and lifted the stick, but the lever wouldn't move.

"Push on the door," Ladtwig said.

Turkill shoved his shoulder into the cool wood door and the lever released with a clank. Everyone froze as the sound echoed through the still night. The door opened a crack letting out a puff of stale air and Jagwynn puckered her nose but stifled a sneeze.

They quickly went inside the building which was nearly the same as the Senate Sanctum in the Shifting Woods in Ebassia, except there was no portal in this one. The old magic tickled their skin and they shivered. Turkill slipped a gold disc out of his pocket and lifted the lid. The compass-like piece of equipment illuminated the few steps around them and the little needle inside bounced and wriggled like a regular compass. Turkill moved the compass around the room until the needle stopped bouncing, and they moved toward the back of the room.

The wall came into view and they could make out the rows of little cubbies with doors on them. Ladtwig pulled out his stick again and stuck it into the tiny notch at the center of the door that was now illuminated by the compass. The latch popped open with a quiet clink and Turkill opened the door. He pulled out the gem in-fused gold choker and shoved it into Ladtwig's satchel. A soft crack outside eased into their senses and Turkill shut the top of the compass turning off the illumination. The room fell pitch black, and they held their breath and scooted against the back wall.

There was another crack and another and Turkill nudged Ladtwig to move along the wall toward the door. Jagwynn moved around the other side, but before they were halfway, the door creaked open and the moon's light illuminated the figure of a human. Turkill wondered what a human was doing here, he was sure there shouldn't be any humans in this realm, and then he remembered Crolos the Desert Warden and wondered if it was an old member of the Dodjen still here in this realm.

The Minca hurried to the front corner and waited for several lengths as the man tried to figure out why the door was open. The figure started to pull the door shut and Jagwynn lurched out of the darkness and knocked him to the ground. The man hollered and the Minca hurried out of the ruins before the man knew what had happened. They raced into the trees and slipped behind a large trunk and Jagwynn leaped into the branches. The man closed the door and hurried into the darkness.

"Who was that?" Ladtwig asked.

"I don't know, maybe an old Dodjen," Turkill half-asked-half-stated.

"I am not sure who it is, anyone who would have been from the old days would be long gone in this realm as time goes so much faster here. It is something we need to figure out, but not now," Jagwynn said.

"We'll tell Azrack when we return and let him figure it out," Turkill said.

They climbed onto her back and hurried back to Phanes.

"Are they back yet?" Turkill asked.

"Not yet," Phanes said.

Turkill harrumphed and Ladtwig pulled out a piece of cheese and stuffed it in his mouth. Jagwynn turned in a circle and curled up in a ball, rested her head on her paws and closed her eyes. Turkill inspected the bag to make sure the ropes were still secure. Phanes perked up and listened as did Jagwynn, and they both rose and searched the distance. Cluck's darkened and beaten figure emerged from the trees and Phanes ran to catch him before he fell.

"What happened?" Phanes asked.

"We were outnumbered, and they have taken Shar," Cluck said.

"How many are there?" Phanes asked.

"I can't be sure, more than we had thought, we need to get her out before they take her to the main camp," Cluck said.

Turkill grabbed the back of Jag's collar and swung himself onto her back and Ladtwig scurried up behind him.

"Where are you going?" Phanes asked.

"To bring her back," Turkill said.

"You can't, there's too many, and your-" Phanes said.

"Too small, yeah, we know," Turkill said.

Jag snickered and Phanes and Cluck shot her a confused

look. Jagwynn leaped into the darkness and Phanes ran his paws through his feathers at the top of his head.

"We need to get farther away from here, in case they come looking for us," Cluck said.

Phanes nodded and helped him stand and grabbed the bag and carefully made their way deeper into the woods. Jagwynn crept close to the ground and the Minca huddled next to her. They pulled their dart guns and loaded them this time with their poisonous darts. Turkill studied the trees and Ladtwig noticed a bright green mushroom that he remembered Helios had said had a toxin in it. He grabbed one as they moved passed it, and he broke it into pieces and dropped them into the little holes the ground-dogs made.

They stopped and listened every few lengths and were able to determine where the Kronos gryphtons were. Ladtwig gave Turkill his signal he was going to jump off and Turkill indicated he was going to go up with Jag. Ladtwig hurried to a hole and opened his water bag and poured some of the liquid into the hole and then another. He took a large leaf and started to fan the air into the hole. Turkill and jag leaped into the trees and scaled the branches until they came close to a sentry. Turkill let go of a quick burst and a dart sank into its chest and then fell from the tree with a thud. The stench of ale and a mix of raw and cooked meat sank into Turkill's nose, and he cringed.

He spotted a group of gryphtons near a fire and a few tents and signaled for Jag to move closer. Phanes landed behind them as he carefully scaled the branches and Turkill let his rapid-fire release a blast of darts as he moved his head, hitting all the gryphton's and before they even knew what had hit them, they were falling over. Phanes had never seen such skill and precision and was incredibly impressed. Ladtwig made a bird call and Turkill and Jag began to make their way to the other side of the next camp where they found Shar tied to a stake in the center.

Ladtwig stood back as a dark-gray ribbard crawled out of the hole with a thick layer of foam on its mouth. Ladtwig climbed a tree nearby and hunkered to the trunk as the rat-bird scurried toward the fire of the gryphton's. It wasn't long before a plethora of ribbards were scurrying toward the camp. Ladtwig crawled along the branches and found Turkill and Jag. They waited as the little rodents bombarded the camp and gryphton's started to panic and fight the rodents.

Turkill and Ladtwig began to shoot as many gryphton's as they could and Phanes made his way toward the center. Jagwynn readied to pounce and watched as the rodents scattered the soldiers. The Minca reloaded a few times and with only a few gryphton's left they ran out of darts. Phanes took out his sling and loaded it and with a quick flick, sent a speeding rock into the skull of a soldier and then another. Phanes landed in front of Shar who looked up through a bloodied eye and face. He quickly united her and helped her out of the camp. The Minca and Jag disappeared into the trees and Phanes and Shar hurried toward Cluck.

"Are you alright?" Phanes asked.

"Yes, how did you get me out of there?" Shar asked.

"It wasn't me, it was all them," Phanes said.

Shar looked around and barely saw the dark-skinned men on the pitch-black jaguar in the middle of the darkness.

"I don't know what to say," Shar said.

"You're welcome, now let's get these bugs to Helios," Turkill said.

Phanes grabbed the bag, and they headed back to the fortress.

14-Move Your Outfit Through Here

Tobis rounded the small ravine and guided his crew toward where they had buried the battle-axes. He was thankful now that they had chosen to bury them separate from the creatures. Tobis slowed as he came to the marsh they had spent their time trapping and found the scoops they used. The late morning was seeping over the sky and it felt as though there was more heat than usual, but Tobis' men started digging while Tobis and a few others inspected the surroundings. The ground under where he thought they had buried the carcasses felt softer than the rest of it and a pit in his stomach raced to his guts and back.

He moved back off the large patch of earth and reached down and picked up a handful of the dirt. Rotten flesh stink stung his nose and he cringed and dropped the dirt as he tried not to gag. A splash from the marsh hit his ears and he froze. His long ears twitched as he dissected the sounds and relaxed when he realized the grunting of the turtlepotomous and stood and turned around. He was relieved to find the squat animal splashing near the tall reeds, but a set of black eyes in the long leaves of the water weeds hit his mind and fear encased his whole frame.

He struggled to make his limbs respond and the bile in his stomach burned his esophagus as it tried to escape his being. His mouth dried instantly, and he couldn't decide if his tongue was going to choke him or not. Heavy breathing mixed with small snort-like growls penetrated his mind and he finally took a step away from the marsh. The black eyes followed his movements and Tobis was certain it was one of the beasts. He carefully reached for the battle-ax with one hand and a spear with the other.

He searched the distance for his herd and determined the rest were still digging. Tobis didn't want to lead the beast to his crew but he knew he would need their help. Tobis noted the beasts soft footsteps through the mushy edges of the marsh and an idea hit his brain. Tobis gripped the ax and sidestepped around to the other side of the marsh. He quickly scanned for the best spot and found it only a few steps from the creature. Tobis' hand wrapped around the staff of the spear and his skin was moist against the dried wood.

He steadied his breathing but found his heart was in overload and sweat dripped down his back. He took another step and the beast continued to crawl nearly motionless toward him. Tobis examined the ground beneath were the beast was about to step and he gripped the spear again. He took another step and the beast followed. The ground under the animal, however, wasn't solid and the water underneath quickly sucked his clawed hoof under the long grassy water weeds trapping him nearly instantly. Tobis watched the panic race across it's long snouted face and a tinge of excited aggression raced through his brain.

Tobis stepped forward with his hoof opposite his spear arm and launched the long shaft at the beast. The razor-sharp bone sank into its neck just above its shoulder and it recoiled with the pain. Anger flashed across it's glassy black eyes and Tobis knew he better make another move before it alerted any others, if it hadn't already. Tobis leaped with two long strides and heaved the battle-ax down through its neck.

The crack of bones and slosh of tissue pummeled Tobis nerves and his stomach lurched with disgust but he kept his nerve long enough to yank the blade out, but as the putrid odor of its blood hit his nose, he lurched forward and expelled his stomach contents, which wasn't much, but he did feel better, for the moment anyway. Tobis shoved the carcass into the marsh as it was having a hard time deciding which way to fall without a head to guide it. Tobis didn't want it in the water, but he guessed it wasn't good to have it in the earth either. The four other stags returned from their rounds and stopped next to Tobis.

"What in the world is that?" one stag asked.

"That is one of the beasts," Tobis said.

The men's faces contorted through a mixture of thoughts and Tobis herded them back to the weapons. He was certain there were going to be more, but he didn't yet understand how many or where they would be and didn't want to find out. They quickly finished gathering the weapons and started back to Antorn and the others. Tobis couldn't get those eyes out of his head. For some reason they were different than the ones they had encountered before. It was if it was thinking, examining, running through scenarios, and trying to outthink him. The last ones just attacked with wild interests, not with a calculated plan. He would be certain to inform Antorn as soon as they returned, and he found himself moving at a faster rate than his usual fast run.

The others weren't sure what to do, but they tried to keep up with him while finagling the new weapons which were much heavier than they were used to. They quickly came upon Antorn and Tobis slowed his pace.

"Antorn, I think we might have some big trouble," Tobis said trying to catch his breath.

"What is it?" Antorn asked.

"While at the marsh I encountered a beast. It was alone and it watched me, studied me, as though it was thinking, calculating, determining it's best attack strategy," Tobis said.

Antorn studied Tobis and noted the energy vibe that radiated from his being and finding the panic and fear he couldn't stop his own from surging.

"Is that different than before?" Soren asked.

"It is," Antorn said.

Pillip and Tobis nodded. Antorn realized there were only half a dozen of his stags that had ever seen one or fought them and his doubt surged.

"So, if this one was thinking, then maybe there are different kinds of them, did it look or smell the same?" Antorn asked.

"It did have a different kind of snout, shorter, with bigger eyes, more like ours instead of the canines, but it smelled the exact same," Tobis said trying to keep his sudden urge to gag from making him look like a fool.

"Did the others have a mark on their shoulders?" Soren asked.

"What mark?" Tobis asked.

Soren drew a resemblance of the mark he saw in the shoulder in the dirt and Antorn, Tobis, and Pillip shook their heads.

"Then maybe that is part of the marking that tells the difference," Soren said.

"It would seem so," Antorn said.

"Have you found anything yet?" Tobis asked.

"No beasts, but we have mapped out the area and have found several patches of the scorched earth. There are no signs of the smaller wildlife that is usually trapped in this area and we suppose they have been eaten or driven out. We have also been figuring out how this weapon works," Antorn said.

Tobis motioned for the weapons to be handed out and his group joined the others in new battle techniques.

"Now that you mention it, we didn't see any of the plains herds we usually would and there were no birds either," Tobis said.

"Alright, so we train on these weapons for a few days and keep moving slowly toward the first sighting," Antorn said.

Tobis nodded and returned to the others. The next few days were filled with new training and Antorn quickly learned the skills of his little army were growing in a unique way. He only hoped it would be enough, but a thought at the back of his mind kept telling him that he needed to gather a much bigger force.

He was certain however, the Herd-Lord would never go for it unless they had enough proof to warrant such a huge change of life. Mazen too sat at the back of his mind. He couldn't stop the feeling that there was going to be trouble, especially on the outskirts, which is where he told her to go. If it were him, that's where he would strike first. On the forth morning Antorn gave instructions to move quickly into the black zone, as they had decided to call it.

"Soren, you move your outfit through here," Antorn indicated on his map, "Tobis, you go here, and Pillip you go here. I'll take my group this way and we will meet up here, if you run into trouble use your echolocation to send a signal," Antorn said.

The new little military nodded and saluted before breaking up into the respective groups. Antorn gave the signal to move out and they did so with eager quietness. The stags were quiet for their size but the number of them made it harder to stay completely hidden. The four groups made their way through the terrain and followed the dark veins of earth until they found a small ridge where Pillip said they had encountered the beasts.

Antorn was trying to figure out how they could sneak up on the creatures, but with how tall they were, it would be nearly impossible. A sticker bush stung his skin as he walked through it. He chided himself for being careless in not paying attention and covered his arm only to find it bleeding from the thorns. He pulled out a cloth an wrapped his arm and then a thought came to mind.

He thumped on his antler and the other leaders replied with their own. They regrouped near several shorter acacia trees.

"We need to make ourselves appear to be bushes," Antorn said.

The men stared at him and he thought a moment. He took the ax and lowered to the ground close enough to be able to chop through the thick trunk and held it out in front of himself. The men understood and spread out and found their own bushes to make their coverings.

"We wait until the sun is just behind us so that if they look this way the sun will hopefully distract them from seeing us," Antorn said.

The army waited until the sun was in the best position in the sky and then started toward the top of the ridge. They spread out into chunks and groups as if it were the natural design of the landscape until the unit was able to see over the ridge. Antorn peeked through the bushy leaves and his heart sank. The beasts were now covering the distance further than his own eyes could see. Pillip gasped as he peeked through his as did the rest of the Forrne. The two mappers began frantically to make the marks they could see as well as describe the sounds and smells. Antorn gave a couple hits on his antlers and gave new instructions to return to the base and the moving shrubs sank back down the ridge.

"What are we going to do, there is no way we are going to fight all of those," Pillip said.

"We need to tell the Herd-Lord immediately," Soren said.

"I agree, but we need to get some kind of proof before Tage will listen and let us form a larger military," Antorn said.

"How many do you think it is going to take?" Tobis asked.

"Everyone, and some clever thinking," Antorn said.

"I don't think we have anyone that can do that," Pillip said.

Antorn smiled, but he was sure, if given the chance the Forrne could be quite creative.

"What kind of proof are you thinking?" Pillip asked.

"I think the head of one them might do it," Antorn said.

"Or a few and put them on a pole in the center of town so the townsfolk can see that they are real too," Tobis said.

Antorn nodded. He hadn't thought about it before, but it did make sense, after all they had elected Tage and they did seem to be very good followers.

"Alright, so how do we get just a few away from the rest?" Pillip asked.

"I'll get close enough for them to see me, and hopefully seeing only one, they will send out a small group. I'll lead them here, Pillip you take your outfit and move around to the left and Tobis yours to the right. Soren and the rest will meet them in the middle while you round behind them," Antorn said.

He indicated on the map that the mappers were busily still adding details too. They agreed and started to make their way to the edges. When they were in position they each gave a tap of their antlers and Antorn stepped over the ridge. His nose flared with the nasty stink, but he kept his nerve and trotted carefully over the side of the ridge. He examined what he could as he moved closer to the beasts' settlements.

The majority of the encampment was rugged with no structures or tents, but they did have heaps of bone piles which Antorn figured were where the smaller savanna animals that had met their demise. He purposely stepped on a twig and nearly jumped in his own skin as the crack broke the dreary atmosphere. Three beasts near the edge pricked their ears and Antorn stepped on another.

The beasts looked up and caught sight of Antorn who froze with a new kind of fear. His heart raced faster than he had ever heard it and his lips went dry. He made eye contact with the larger one and then shot back toward the ridge. The large beast lunged into a dead run and his pack followed behind him.

15-It's So Beautiful And Terrifying

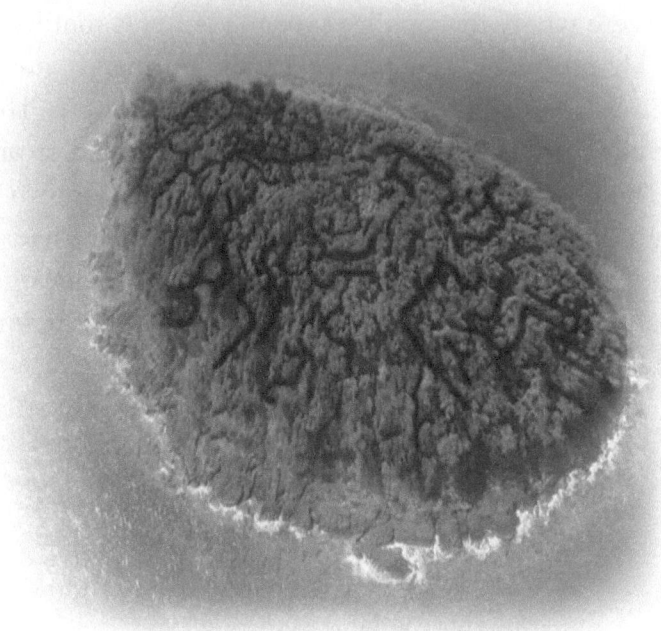

The sun eased over the top of the trees and the birds began to chirp their morning tune. Riddick stirred and listened to the sounds around him for a minute and then sat up and rubbed his eyes. His heart skipped a beat when he didn't find Amirra, and he rose quickly. He searched the shore and found her staring out to sea. He made his way toward her, making some noise so that he wouldn't startle her.

"Everything alright?" Riddick asked.

"Yes, this place is just so beautiful. I'm not sure if it's the magic, but there is a peace here that I have never felt anywhere else I've ever been, which isn't very many places, so I guess it could be like this other places," Amirra said.

Riddick smiled, he like how she rambled when she was

nervous, or happy, or calm, or, well just about all the time.

"Aye, it is," Riddick agreed.

"You slept a while, I was starting to worry," Amirra said.

"I'm sorry, I do feel lots better and a good thing because we have a bit of a trek ahead of us," Riddick said.

"Alright," Amirra said.

They returned to their packs and gathered their bedrolls and ate as they walked down the beach. The tree cover was so thick that without knowing where the beginning of the maze of half-walled passageways where no one would find them, but after his inspection of the island last night he knew where they were. The foliage thickened the further they climbed toward the peak at the center.

"Ah here," Riddick said.

Riddick pulled a bushy leafy plant out of the way and a narrow walkway emerged. The half-walls were made of stones that were smooth and polished and came to their waists. The ground was solid dirt and easy to maneuver. They had to move slowly and move the overgrown vegetation out the way as they went.

"Are we even going anywhere, it seems like we are walking in circles, going up and down and up and down and around and, and have we even heard the hissing thingy's," Amirra said.

Riddick chuckled.

"Aye, it does because we are, but we are getting there, and not yet," Riddick said.

"As long as I'm not the only crazy one," Amirra said.

The sun was now overhead, and the heat brought a surge of humidity that made for difficult breathing, and they began to slow down. Riddick was surprised at how thick the vegetation was, but found the new tickle of magic the ancient island gave him soothing. He had noted several kinds of lizards and birds and plenty of bugs that Amirra had no interest in examining.

"I don't think we are too far off now," Riddick said.

He pulled a large fern out of the way. The bright blue sky opened, and he let Amirra move to the outer edge of the wall. Amirra looked out over the vast landscape and her heart leaped and stomach churned. They were several lengths high, and she gripped the stone wall.

"Oh my, it's so beautiful and terrifying," Amirra said.

"It is," Riddick said.

Riddick wasn't looking at the landscape. Amirra was so beautiful, and he found his attraction to her increasing every day, which he found interesting because just a moon ago he would have said the same thing. A pulsing eased into Riddick's guts, and he stopped. Riddick moved Amirra against the inside of the walkway and put his finger on his lips. Amirra tried not to hold her breath, but she found it harder than she thought. Riddick pulled the ear muffs off and Amirra grabbed his arm with a look of panic. Riddick noted his suspicions were correct, and he looked around where he thought he could hear the sounds.

"What are you doing?" Amirra asked.

The tone in her voice was full of worry and Riddick gave her hand a squeeze.

"I need to listen to the hissing, so I know where the noise is coming from," Riddick said.

"But won't it eat you?" Amirra said.

"Maybe, but I would rather know I'm about to be eaten before it happens," Riddick said.

Amirra heard the jest in his tone, and she scowled, but it made sense too. Riddick snickered and pulled a long skinny vine that was draped across the walkway. The vine wriggled and started to move on its own and twisted around revealing a long skinny bright-green plant that had a peculiar shape on the top that Riddick thought looked like it might open like a blowfish. He watched carefully as the plant breathed gently. Each time the budding tube pulled in air, the thin fibrous gills made a hissing vibration. Riddick understood this to be the first part of the legend and his heart sank.

A tightening in his guts twisted around his core, and he wanted to leave. Riddick found another vine and gently lifted it from the passageway, but there were several tubular plants now hissing around them. Amirra put her hands over her earmuffs and held her head tightly. She couldn't hear them, but she could tell what they were doing. Riddick caressed the plants with his energy and tried to appeal to them, but they didn't seem to respond to his gesture of friendship. The balloon-like top opened and the hissing grew louder, and Riddick scooted away.

He readied himself and searched the vines. He found the tentacles were attached to a massive interlocking joint of vines several lengths up and realized they were part of a tree and instead of branches it had vines that draped all around. Riddick pointed it out to Amirra and she searched the trunk. The tree had long sliver-thin shards of bark organized in jagged and angular patterns that moved up and down the circular structure. Amirra's heart jumped as the shards shivered and rippled showing the sharpness of the blade-like edges. Riddick carefully let go of the pod and eased his way further up the path, but the vines wriggled more. The pit in his stomach lurched, and he shivered as a chill ran down his spine.

Amirra tightened her hands over her ears as the hissing intensified. More of the vines began to wriggle and Riddick was certain they were moments from waking the tree. Riddick knew when that happens, the pods will release a toxin that confuses the mind and makes the persons have the need to go toward it. Then the vines wrap around tightly squeezing the person until they are dead and then the slivers on the trunk prepare the bodies to be consumed. Riddick pulled his energy and wrapped his energy around Amirra and himself and took her hand and took another step. A tinge of magenta emerged and wafted through the air. Riddick squeezed Amirra's hand tight, and he tried to relax but his uneasiness sat heavily in the bottom of his stomach.

Riddick put his finger on his lips and Amirra nodded. Her heart was racing, and her hands were getting clammy. The vines wriggled and started toward them and Riddick pushed his energy away from them. The vines moved and shuddered as his vibrant rust-orange magic sank into them. The bark slivers rippled along the trunk at intervals that gave the impression the tree was breathing, and Riddick took another step. The vines hovered just outside his shield and Amirra tried not to look at them. Riddick pulled another vine and scooted around it holding carefully for Amirra to slide underneath. Riddick stopped and sucked in a deep breath seeing how many more vines there was covering the path they needed to go through.

Riddick ran through several scenarios but nothing he came up with ended up with him not getting eaten. It was a matter of time before it happened, so he decided he might as well get it over with. Riddick pushed Amirra behind him and pulled an armful of vines out of the way. The hissing pods opened, and the misty pink hue emerged.

"Run that way fast," Riddick said.

Amirra gave him a 'are you crazy' look but found urgency covered his face, and she ran through the vines. Riddick gripped his energy and ripped a tunnel for her to run through. The magic was intense, and he wasn't sure if he was going to be able to withstand the effects. He started up the trail himself, but the vines were pushing against his magic, and he began to sweat. Amirra shot out of the pod infested pink mist and turned to see the vines wrap around Riddick's frame. Amirra's heart raged, and she couldn't stop the tears from flooding out. She wanted to race back in there, but she had no idea what she would be able to do.

Riddick gripped the vine that was wrapping itself around his neck and yanked tightly. He focused his energy into the vine but struggled to get a tight enough grip to keep from making it hard to breathe. Riddick struggled with the vines that were now wrapped around his body and the tighter they squeezed the harder his lungs had to work. Riddick tried to think of what he needed to do but it was hard not to start panicking as his lungs were at half capacity. He ran through the story again and a thought came to mind. Riddick pulled in a long steady breath and exhaled. He pictured his energy moving from his body and toward the center of the tree.

The orange earth's energy was strong but not strong enough, and he tried again. The energy again left his body and was a little brighter than before, but the tree didn't respond. Riddick's patience was getting thin and anger formed in his chest. The rust-orange color deepened to hot burnt-brown and the vibration coursed through the air with a thudding. The pulsing grew the angrier Riddick became and the vines began to wriggle with the uncomfortableness he gave but still didn't release him. Riddick became so angry his orange heart fire turned red and a new red-orange heat radiated from his core. The heat withered the vines, and they pulled away, but they tried again. Riddick was getting tired of this tree not listening to him and his new heat surged even more.

"Listen to me you blasted tree, I'm the earth sage and I command you release me," Riddick called.

Riddick's magic shot out from his core and the vines fell from his body. The trunk shivered and the slivers of bark wriggled and ripped from the surface and shot toward Riddick with immense speed. Riddick threw his hands out and thrust the razors to the side and slammed his hands together. The ricochet surged through the barren trunk and it shuddered.

"Now, are you finished?" Riddick demanded. The vines stilled and the pods folded up and the mist dissipated. "Now let me pass," Riddick said.

The vines opened and Riddick could see Amirra's frightened tear streaked face and quickly made his way to her and pulled her into a hug.

"Are you alright?" Riddick asked.

"Yes, are you?" Amirra asked.

"Aye, I just had to be a little more stern than usual, and I thought soggy earth was bad," Riddick said.

Amirra blurted a laugh through a tight throat and then slugged him in the arm. Riddick pulled away and laughed knowing she was mad but not mad at the same time.

"You scared the tar out of me," Amirra said.

"I'm sorry," Riddick said.

"I had no idea what was happening, you said it was going to eat you, I stayed out here trying to figure out how I was going to get back out and then how I was going to get anywhere without you, that really wasn't alright, what would I have done," Amirra said.

"I'm sorry. I'll try to let you know what is going on from now on," Riddick said. He pulled her into a tight squeeze and waited a few minutes for her to process what had happened. "You ready, come on, let's keep going," Riddick said.

He took her hand and squeezed tight and they continued up the path. The path was fairly easy, and Riddick dreaded what he was going to have to do next. If he was going to have to do what Grandfather said the earth sages of old did, then he knew it was going to be painful. He ran the story through his head over and over so that he wouldn't miss anything and wasn't sure what he wanted to tell Amirra. The path ended and Riddick searched for the instructions that would let him into the sacred void. Riddick pulled several large vines out of the way and held them away from the wall.

"Alright, here it goes, I don't know what will happen inside here, so you can't be mad at me this time," Riddick said with a glint in his eye, but Amirra could see the hint of worry under it and smiled.

Amirra stepped back and waited as Riddick called his energy from his core and into his arms. His skin started to radiate the rust-orange color, and he pressed his hands onto the marks at the center of the wall. The pulsing energy rippled over the stone and glyphs lit up and illuminated for a moment and then faded back into the stone. Amirra wasn't sure what happened because nothing happened.

"I am Riddick," Riddick hesitated, he didn't actually know who his actual parents were, he had never been told their names and was suddenly angry as to why, "the Earth Sage," Riddick finished.

The wall began to fade into blackness and Riddick took Amirra's hand and stepped through the doorway. They blinked to adjust to the darkness and Riddick sent a soothing burst of his earth magic into the room. The light increased but not by the sun or fire or even the glow-stones like at the castle and Riddick wondered how it did it. As the light brightened the surroundings, they found there were no walls, ocean, mountains, trees, or anything that would indicate where they were. A faint dusting of glittering particles began to thicken around them, and the swirling mist became an array of colors. The tingle on their skin sent shivers down their spines.

"What is this place?" Amirra asked.

"This is a place where the ancient magic still exists in the world," Riddick said. "At least that is what Grandfather said."

Riddick stepped toward the center of the misty atmosphere and Amirra followed. He waved his hands in and out of the dancing mist and started to search for the tree, or whatever was going to be there, but nothing emerged.

"What happens next?" Amirra asked.

"I'm not entirely sure," Riddick said.

Amirra scrunched her face with curious confusion.

"Maybe you need to ask it what you're supposed to do," Amirra said.

"Aye, I need to find the Sable Cy'ad tree," Riddick said into the mist.

A shimmering movement caught his eye, and he turned to find the image of Mother Edenocht emerge.

"Riddick, how nice to see you again," Mother Edenocht said.

"Oh my," Amirra whispered.

Amirra wasn't prepared for the essence of the planets' form to be so beautiful and her voice was delicate but powerful. The woman's features were combined with the delicate but strong branches of a brilliantly colored tree. She was *so* brilliant, Amirra had a hard time seeing without squinting. The slender figure echoed the strength and sleekness of a trunk and the leaves around her face were elegant and narrow, and gave a hair-like appearance to her frame.

"Who is this?"

"This is Amirra, the Runecaster," Riddick said.

"Greetings Amirra, what can I do for you, Riddick?" Mother Edenocht asked.

"I am in need of the nectar from the Sable Cy'ad tree," Riddick said.

"That is an ancient tree that no longer grows in this world, why are you in need of it?" Mother Edenocht said.

Riddick's heart sank and dread encompassed his frame.

"To make an antidote for Serin's grandfather and uncle," Riddick said.

"I see, there is still a way, but it will take a piece of the Time Tablet of Alisdair," Mother Edenocht said.

Riddick sighed, he was glad he had one and pulled the tablet piece from under his tunic and Mother Edenocht nodded. "This nectar is of the ancient magic of the Teorran Belt and you must first go through a transformation in order to be strong enough to harness its power," Mother Edenocht said.

"Alright, what must I do?" Riddick asked.

Riddick thought back to the story Mathieu had told, and he had an idea of what was going to happen and sucked in a deep breath.

"Put out your hands," Mother Edenocht said.

Riddick held out his hands. Two arm-like tentacles stretched across and Riddick jumped with the prickling heat. Riddick gritted his teeth and hissed as the tentacles crawled into his skin and up into his arms. Amirra's heart raged with the creepy vein-like tendrils that crawled under his skin. She struggled as she watched the heat rip across his being and his body began to shake. He lifted off the ground and Amirra started to panic.

"What are you doing to him?" Amirra shouted.

"His body is advancing, and he is receiving more information on his elemental powers," Mother Edenocht said.

"You're hurting him," Amirra said with tears now flooding from her eyes.

"It is a great strain on him yes, but it is necessary," Mother Edenocht said.

"Please, stop," Amirra said.

"You have the power to help, with your words," Mother Edenocht said.

Amirra struggled to think but wiped her eyes and started the chants that Nitida had taught her and the glyphs flowed to the surface. She changed her chanting to the words that came into her mind, and she stepped under and around the veins, so she could face Riddick. She put her hands on his chest and focused her thoughts into him. Her hands began to glow a sunrise-yellow and the soft hue sank into his core. His body stopped shaking and the tightness in his jaw eased. The soft scent of morning dew that comes with the sunrise eased into her senses, and she smiled as she spoke the words that came to her mind and danced around the new color.

The magic of the Teorran Belt swelled around them and caressed their skin leaving a soothing cool to the heat the information was causing. Riddick's eyes were moving rapidly under his closed eyelids and Amirra kept her chanting calm but strong and steady. The yellow became a strong force and twisted in and around them and merged with his rusty orange with a new synergy her magic made with his. Amirra gasped as the colors blended and surrounded them both, and her mind opened to a whole new level of understanding of the runes and his magic and how they were more connected than she realized. The veins faded from his being and pulled away and his body sank to the floor. He gasped for air and breathed heavily. Amirra sank to the ground with him and wrapped her arms around him. The mist eased and wafted back to the outer edges of the void.

Riddick opened his eyes and looked into hers. She understood him deeper than she ever had, and he saw deeper into her than ever before, and she kissed him. The energy was strong and powerful but soft and soothing, and they embraced one another for several lengths as they regained their strength.

"Are you alright?" Amirra asked.

"Aye, you were there with me," Riddick half-asked-half-stated.

"I was, but I'm not sure what happened," Amirra said.

"Me either," Riddick said.

Riddick struggled to his feet and Amirra helped him.

"You have been transformed into a being of higher understanding and strength and you have Synergized your magics,"

Mother Edenocht said.

"How, I don't have magic," Amirra said.

"Yes, you do. You are the element of Soul, the seventh element. You possess the internal soul traits of kindness, bravery, justice, integrity, perseverance, patience, and determination. Fear is your greatest weakness. Take heed child, let these traits become you and you too will be able to grow and become the power you are meant to be," Mother Edenocht said.

"See, I told you, maybe even a million," Riddick said.

Amirra wasn't sure what to say, but she couldn't deny the fact that she saw the yellow come from her hands and merge with his. She saw his magic, and hers was her favorite color. She remembered what Jagwynn had said, that knowing her favorite color said a lot about her, but she wasn't ready to learn about it then. Amirra smiled at Riddick's bright expression.

"Until next time Earth Sage," Mother Edenocht said.

The essences faded away and a beautiful white and gold tree emerged. Brilliant misty gold pods hung on the strong but fine limbs. The tree was so white Riddick wondered if it was made of a glass-like mineral. He internalized the intelligence of the tree and bowed with reverence and Amirra followed. His mind raced around the many new types of earth elements unlike anything he had ever experienced and understood them to be of the pure and raw magic of the planet that was still deep within the center.

He gained a full picture of what the earth desired and his heart swelled. Heat surged, and he felt the pain the evil had done to the world and how much the planet desired to be free once again. The tree lowered a gold pod and Riddick held out his hands. The cold fruit was soft but firm, and he immediately comprehended its nature.

"Thank you," Riddick said and bowed again.

The limb moved to his chest, and he braced for the pain, but a soft and soothing sensation tickled him, and he soaked in the energy. His muscles relaxed from the pain caused by the transformation and a strong rejuvenation coursed through his body. He smiled with its gesture of healing his body and the tree faded away. Amirra put her hand on his shoulder, and he looked at her. She gazed into his eyes, and they connected on a deeper level than before. Amirra had heard what the tree told him, and she nodded with her approval. Riddick tucked the pod into his satchel and looked around.

There was nothing but mist, and they started back toward the door. Riddick put his hand on what he thought would be the wall and noticed his magic had a bit of sunrise yellow mixed into it, and he smiled. The mist vanished into darkness, and they stepped through the portal. Riddick now understood how important it was to keep people from trying to find this island and wished he could protect it better. He thought about the disguise of Shaz's castle and wondered what it would take to do the same thing for the island.

They made their way back through the maze until they came to the vines and Riddick waved his hand. The vines obeyed this time and parted letting them pass in the now silent darkness as they were both in deep thoughts about what had happened. Riddick could now feel Amirra's heartbeat next to his and wondered if she could feel his. They made their way to the beach and Riddick covered the path with a large fern and instructed it to not move for anyone but himself or Shaz. The stars were out, and two of the three moons were high in the sky with the third being faint in the distance, and they wondered how much time had passed.

"Are we going to start sailing now?" Amirra asked.

"Soon, but I want to try something," Riddick said.

"What?" Amirra asked.

"I wonder how I could give the island a disguise, like the

castle," Riddick said.

"Oh, I know how, but I don't know if I could do it on my own," Amirra said.

"Then, we'll do it together. What do we do?" Riddick asked.

"Well, let me think, I wish you could just see into my head," Amirra said.

"Let's try," Riddick said.

Amirra hesitated, she had never let anyone this close before, but she was certain Riddick was the one for her, was the one who wouldn't, who *hadn't* judged her. He had already seen her call servitors, and perform a crypt ceremony. He already knew what she was, mostly. She sucked in a deep breath and nodded. Riddick held out his hands, and she took them in hers. He interlocked his fingers with hers and closed his eyes. Amirra closed hers and relaxed.

"I don't know what to do," Amirra said.

"Then don't do anything," Riddick said.

Riddick sent a gentle surge of energy toward Amirra, and she wriggled with its warmth. She almost wanted to laugh as the tingle tickled her being. Riddick showed up in her mind, and she tried to keep her feet on the ground with excitement. Riddick smiled, and she started to pull the rune symbols from her mind, and they began circling around them. She picked out the ones that stuck out and Riddick was amazed as she organized the text and ideas into groupings of full thoughts and concepts. He started to understand them the more they circled and realized just how intelligent Amirra was. He added his earth's magic to them, and they started to glow the rusty orange and Riddick allowed his connection with the earth take the message of the runes through his core and into the island. The island absorbed their energy, and they soaked in what was given back to them. The glyphs softened and faded, and Riddick pulled away.

They opened their eyes and looked around. The island now looked like a barren piece of floating rock and Riddick smiled.

"Will that work?" Amirra asked.

"It most certainly will, you're so smart," Riddick said.

Amirra blushed, but she loved it when he said that.

"I guess we need to hurry, we still have a long way back, right?" Amirra asked.

"Aye, but I think I might be able to get some help," Riddick said.

"Really, how?" Amirra asked.

"I'll show you," Riddick said.

16-We Will Be Back

The sun was now behind the horizon again, but the sky didn't darken like before and Shaz was sure it never fully went away from this part of the world and now understood the day and night cycle here. The stars began to shine over the vast sky and the colors of purples, greens, oranges, and yellows painted a magnificent picture.

"How much farther?" Serin asked.

"We're not far but I don't know how easy it will be to find it," Shaz said.

"Why is that?" Serin asked.

"It's in the middle of nowhere... and invisible," Shaz said.

"That's nice to know, do you have a plan Mr. Smarty," Serin said.

"Not yet, I'm hoping that when we get closer, I might be able to sense it with my magic," Shaz said.

Serin tried to stifle a yawn but since they hadn't had much sleep in the last few days, or weeks, or whatever the times been and running all over the planet, the sleep was getting harder to push away.

"Let's make camp, and we'll look for it tomorrow," Shaz said.

Serin nodded, and they veered toward a small group of trees and set up camp. The glowing peddle-like leaves of the underbelly of the tree gave a gentle light to the half-darkened sky and a soothing atmosphere to the new world, and they quickly found sleep. The sounds of the night insects crept across the horizon, but something ate at the back of Shaz's mind, and he stirred. He knew it wasn't the shadow, he hadn't had an interaction since Serin gave him the dream ring, but it was like he was arguing with himself to wake up. A pulse hit his brain, and he woke with a start. He opened his eyes to find the night was on its way into day, but he didn't find anything. Serin was still sleeping on his chest, and he pulled in a slow but deep breath.

Shaz sent his energy into the world and everything came back normal, or at least the same as had been the last day or, so. The familiar pit in his stomach and the hairs at the back of his neck tickled his spine.

"Serin, wake up," Shaz said. Serin stirred and sat up and rubbed her eyes. "Shhhhh, something isn't right, and there's shadow magic," Shaz said.

Serin sat up quickly and Shaz gripped the hilt of the blade. He rose slowly as he surveyed the distance and Serin stood up and searched for their packs.

"Put your shield up," Shaz said.

Serin waved her arms quickly and wrapped her air magic around her body and Shaz lit his fire element around his. Shaz tiptoed out from under the tree and Serin followed. The ground was hot, and they felt the heat radiate from the surface. The tall grasses shriveled and withered into dust the farther they moved from the tree and Serin's nerves began to eat at her. She didn't do well when there was little to no water, and she could sense the dryness in the air. They looked down and watched the earth turn black and recognized it as the same as the pots they had seen the day before.

"This isn't good," Serin whispered.

"Aye, come on, let's get to that portal," Shaz said.

Shaz grabbed her hand, and they headed toward where he believed the portal would be, which was away from the scorched earth. The landscape was as far as the eye can see and only tall beige grasses with the occasional short stalky tree, but there was an odd beauty in it.

"Blast," Shaz said.

"What is it?" Serin asked.

"Jaduuk," Shaz said.

"Where?" Serin asked.

"Just over that bend, but that's where we need to go," Shaz said.

"How many?" Serin asked.

"A couple of hoards," Shaz said.

"Shouldn't be too hard," Serin said.

"Alright," Shaz said.

They made their way over the ridge and found the pack hovering over a carcass.

"Ready?" Shaz asked.

"Let's do it," Serin said.

They both pulled their bows and loaded an arrow. Shaz moved toward one side and Serin the other. Shaz let his arrow loose and Serin hers. Serin commanded the wind to take the arrows directly to their necks and the wind obeyed as they pulled another arrow and another. The beasts fell to the ground without even a sound as the arrows pierced their voice box's. Several fell before the rest of the horde realized what was going on, but the next arrow took its mark and sank deep into their necks. Serin loaded her last arrow and Shaz let his last one go.

Shaz slipped his bow back on and pulled the sword from the sheath. Serin let her arrow go and the whiz through the air left a tickle in her ear. There were only a few left, but they needed to be quick so that they didn't have time to sound an alert. Shaz shot across the distance and Serin pulled the air from around the remaining Jaduuk's mouths. Their eyes flashed with a sense of panic as they struggled to find the air.

The large Jaduuk in the front grabbed for its battle-ax but Shaz reached it first and sliced his blade through the tough bluish neck skin. He rounded quickly with the momentum and leaped over the falling body and stabbed the blade into the next creature's bare chest. The stink of the rancid blood hit Shaz's senses, but he didn't even seem to notice. A Jaduuk fell as the air failed to fill its lungs and Shaz shoved the blade through its spine. The bone and sinew of the massive beasts' spine snapped, and he yanked the blade out. Shaz parried through another strike and finished off the last beast.

Serin grabbed their packs and caught up to Shaz on the other side of the carnage. Shaz put his finger to his lips to signal to keep quiet, and they ran at a quick pace toward the horizon. After several lengths, they stopped to catch their breath and Serin buffed them.

"We aren't too far now, and I don't sense anymore Jaduuk," Shaz said.

"Can you sense the portal yet?" Serin asked.

Shaz shook his head but sent a surge of energy into the atmosphere. The energy came back with a dim image of the portal and Shaz turned directions.

"This way," Shaz said.

They traveled for a little longer and Shaz determined it was now in the middle of the day. They came over another small hill and Shaz found a heard of the large gray animals milling about the portal.

"Do you see the portal?" Shaz asked.

"No," Serin said.

"Try and send your magic out and see if it gives you a picture back," Shaz said.

"Not sure I know what you mean, I mean I get the idea, but how to do you send it out?" Serin asked.

Shaz thought a minute.

"Like, ask the wind to give you a picture of the portal," Shaz said.

"Ah, alright," Serin said.

Serin waved her hand in front of her and with her mind, asked the wind to give her an image of the portal. She studied the wind swirl around the structure and return to her mind. The image was faint, but she could now tell where it was.

"There it is, that's very clever," Serin said.

"Which means it's in the center of all those animals," Shaz said.

"Oh blast, well maybe you could just ask them to move," Serin said.

"Alright let's give it a try," Shaz said.

They moved toward the animals and Shaz took a count and inventoried how big or small they were. Serin made note of where she could hide if she needed to and made her own tally of the animals. A large dark-gray mammal turned its enormous head and started toward them. The size of its three-toed flat soled foot was bigger than Shaz's head and his guts twisted. The animal stared at him with a look that said, 'don't come any closer' and Shaz stopped. Shaz pulled Drafang's fang from his tunic and the animal's eyes widened.

"Are you the Chosen One," the husky voice pounded.

"I am," Shaz said.

Shaz bowed to the animal and a few of the other animals turned to see what was going on.

"You have come to free this land," the animal half-asked.

"Yes, after we have completed another task," Shaz said.

"You are going to leave this land?" the animal asked.

"For a short time, but we will be back," Shaz said.

The animal wasn't sure what to do and Shaz could tell it was having a hard time with the information. The animal started to shake its head and Shaz understood the massive creature wasn't going to let them through.

"No, you must stay here and free this land," the mammal said.

"Tell me what is going on," Shaz asked.

"The land is dying because of the beasts that are killing all the animals and creatures," the animal said.

"We saw that, and you have my word that we will be back as quickly as we can, but we have to return this spider spit to make an antidote for her family," Shaz said motioning to Serin.

Serin bowed to the majestic animal and it searched her eyes. It nodded slowly and stepped aside. The other animals also stepped aside.

"What is your name and what are you?" Serin asked.

"I am Wandi and we are the elephantine," Wandi said.

"Thank you Wandi, I promise we will return as quickly as we can," Serin said.

"We will be right here," Wandi said.

"You stay safe, so if you have to leave, you leave, and we will find you," Shaz said.

The animal nodded and Serin got the impression that Wandi's fear was lessened and had a smile in its heart, and she stroked its long nose as she passed. Shaz put his hand into the center of the portal and the dancing mist sprung into existence. The warm beige-colored mist reflected the grasses and Shaz parted the mist for Serin who stepped through.

"We will be back," Shaz said and stepped through the portal.

17-It's Called Geo-Kinetics

Riddick grabbed Amirra's hand, and they hurried back to the beach. Riddick was excited to try the things he had just learned and helped Amirra into the boat and called the geo-kinetic energy. He understood the idea before, but now, he had a name for it and how it applied to all things of the earth. The boat lifted off the sand and hovered just above the surface. He boosted himself into the boat and gripped the line to the ketch. The sail popped open and the wind was caught and lurched the boat forward. Amirra gripped tightly as the sudden shift threw her backward.

Riddick held the line and searched the stars to determine his directions. The image of the ocean floor came into view, and he moved the boat around the jagged peaks that would rip the boat's hull. The boat picked up speed, and he sent a boost of his new magic into the ship. He imagined the force being similar to Serin's wind-walk but using the physics of matter and its inertia and force. The boat increased in speed and soon Amirra was shielding her face from the onslaught of wind. Riddick looked back to make sure she was alright and found her huddled against the back.

He organized his thoughts to create a windbreak around the boat and the matter obeyed. The boat moved at a fast clip, but Riddick wondered what would happen if he made the salt in the water smooth out the waves he was now fighting. A light-blue eased toward the ship and lightened to a crystal white the closer it came. The waves became smooth and soft and the boat increased in speed.

"Amirra come look," Riddick said.

Amirra lifted her head and found there was little wind and made her way to where Riddick was at the back of the mast. He was barely holding the rope this time as his magic was commanding the forces around them instead. Riddick pointed to the salty waves and Amirra admired the way the tiny particles reflected the moon's light.

"What are you doing?" Amirra asked.

"It's called Geo-kinetics. The use and manipulation of mass and matter and its motion and behavior through space and time. Which is what happens with energy and force, including momentum, friction, vectors, and inertia," Riddick said proudly.

Amirra frowned at not understanding a thing he just said, and Riddick laughed.

"Well, whatever that means, it's wonderful," Amirra said.

"Think of it like Serin's wind-walk but way better," Riddick said.

"Now, don't get cocky," Amirra said with a huge grin.

Riddick smiled, he loved it when she thought he was being cocky. Amirra gazed out over the expansive ocean and noted the little black dots, which she guessed were islands along the reef, pass by at a fast rate.

"How fast are we going?" Amirra asked.

"We'll reach Turob by sunrise at this rate," Riddick said.

Amirra smiled at the sparkling sandy-like salt fade back into the water as they passed over, or did it stay the same and was more like a buffer between the ship and the water. Well, she wasn't sure, but it was beautiful. The moons steadily climbed over the sky and the sun soon etched at the horizon. Amirra stood next to Riddick, and he wrapped his arm around her. She would never have guessed her life would turn out like this. Seeing the world, being with an amazing man who she loved being with. Having magic, that was the real doozy, and she found herself trying to come up with everything possible to convince herself that it wasn't true. But she couldn't deny what she saw and felt and even the essence of the planet said it. How would it not be true? A chant that Nitida had taught her came to mind, and she added the new words Mother Edenocht had told her.

She repeated them in her mind and was surprised to sense the heat of her yellow heartfire lite inside her chest. She focused on the new sensations and allowed them to radiate all over her body. Riddick sensed the energy and gripped her tighter. He liked her warmth, and she rested her head on his chest as they watched the earth move passed them.

The smaller islands closest to Turob came into view, and Riddick decided he would round the backside of the reef to avoid the main sailing route and the other vessels and get closer before having to slow down. He figured they would be near the cave anyway and this way they would avoid running into anyone. He really wanted to see everyone, but they had no time. The sun lifted quickly and Amirra soaked in the soothing light. She realized she was connected to the sun in a way that now made sense, and had been that way her whole life. Riddick slowed the boat and let go of his wind-shield. The brisk breeze was filled with the clean salty air and Riddick sucked in a chest full.

He allowed the salt particles to enter his lungs and fill his body with a new tingle and maneuvered the ship into a small inlet. The waves returned to normal and the boat rocked and swayed back and forth as he moved it through the outward pull. He used enough magic to put the boat onto the sandy shore, and they grabbed their packs. Riddick hopped out and helped Amirra, and they started toward the thick trees.

"This is beautiful," Amirra said.

"Aye," Riddick said.

Amirra was sure he missed his home more than he had expected, and a surge of homesickness hit his heart. Riddick guided her through the island and then stopped.

"What is it?" Amirra asked.

"This is the path that would take us to my house," Riddick said.

Amirra's heart sank, and she rested her hand on his arm.

"I think we have a few minutes, let's go visit your mother," Amirra said. Riddick struggled with his emotions. He didn't think he would feel such a need to see her, but he was having a hard time shoving the lump from his throat. "Come on, I think we need to go," Amirra said.

She took his hand and started up the trail. Riddick's treehouse came into view, and he pulled some of the large ferns out of the way. The treehouse was multiple layers of rooms and walkways in and around the tall, large trunks of the waslick trees. The heavy canopy overhead kept the structure shaded and cool but the sprigs of daylight that now shined through, cast a delicate spiders web of sunlight on the wooden structure. Amirra was amazed at its beauty and how tall the trees were. She was more confident that the trees would hold up the sky and could see herself living here. Riddick pulled the latch the released the plank rope.

"Stand in the middle," Riddick said.

Amirra stepped onto the platform and then Riddick stepped around her and gripped her as he let the rope release. The platform lifted smoothly and Amirra mused at how it worked. She stepped off the platform and he secured the fastener. He led her into the tree-house and soaked in the scents of his childhood. He made his way around the kitchen table and into the main living area of the house. He came back a minute later and shook his head.

"She's not here," Riddick said.

"I'm sorry," Amirra said. Riddick found a pile of papers on the counter and picked one up. He skimmed the words and a perplexed expression sat on his features and Amirra wrung her hands together. "What's wrong?" Amirra asked.

Riddick looked up and around Amirra and found his mother standing in the doorway. Her slightly gray hair was pulled away from her warmed skin and her big brown eyes stared at him as though she wasn't sure what she was seeing.

"Ma," Riddick said.

Riddick hurried around Amirra and pulled his mother into a tight grip. Her soft wrinkles creased her round face and her eyes glassed over as they do just before they start to tear. She was about as tall as Amirra and her curvy figure accentuated the floral sundress she was wearing.

"I have missed you so much, son. Mathieu explained to me what happened but I," she started.

"Shhh, Ma, I'm sorry," Riddick said.

Riddick's mother shook from the emotion that escaped, and he held her. His mind raced around what he had read on the paper and his own feelings.

"Oh my, I'm such a mess, who is this dear," Riddick's mother asked.

Riddick let her go and turned to Amirra.

"This is Amirra, the Runecaster," Riddick said.

"I'm sure that means something to you, but I'm afraid I don't know what that means," Riddick's mother said.

"She's the descendant of Akraven, Ada Yansforth's daughter," Riddick said.

Riddick's mother nodded. She did understand what *that* meant and moved to greet Amirra and took her hand in hers.

"I'm pleased to meet you, I'm Deirdri," Deirdri said.

"My pleasure to meet you," Amirra said.

Deirdri noted the sparkle in Amirra's eye when she glanced at Riddick to make sure she was saying the right thing and understood their relationship and her heart swelled.

"Are you hungry?" Deirdri asked.

"Starved, I'll help," Riddick said.

Amirra took his satchel from him, and he went to the kitchen and washed up. Amirra let them chat and get caught up, and she wandered around the living area that was connected to the kitchen. The house was wonderful, with carvings and statues and fine furniture. Amirra could tell his mother had an elegant taste for things, and she liked how comfortable it made her feel. She tried not to seem nosey, so she sat on the small sofa at the side where she gazed at Riddick and out the windows. A large pink and yellow bird landed on the railing outside and squawked loudly which made Amirra chuckle at its interestingly annoying sound.

A door at the end of the room, that led to the walkway, caught her attention and she stepped into the open tops of the trees. Several of the same birds fluttered around the tops, and she looked over the rail. She didn't realize how high they were and felt her stomach lurch. She decided she was not ever going to fly on one of the flying creatures because if this made her uneasy to be this high, what would it be like to be in the open sky. Riddick came up behind her and slipped his arms around her waist and she smiled.

"You have a wonderful home, this is so beautiful, I would live here," Amirra said.

"Not as beautiful as you," Riddick said and smiled at her implication.

Amirra blushed, she loved the compliments and was getting more used to hearing them, but she still found herself question them. Living with hate for so long left her with a strong sense of fear and it was a daily chore for her to like who she was becoming.

"I still think you're delusional," Amirra said.

Riddick chuckled.

"This is ready, are you hungry?" Riddick asked.

Amirra nodded and they returned to the house. Deirdri tried to look busy but Riddick was sure she had been watching them and smiled. They sat around the table and Deirdri did exactly what every mother does and started telling the most embarrassing stories about Riddick, who blushed while Amirra soaked it all in. Amirra was so happy to hear about his childhood and found herself living a little of her own fantasy within the stories. Deirdri insisted on asking what had happened, where Shaz was, and the Dodjen.

Riddick did his best to tell her what happened while leaving out the scary parts that a mother shouldn't have to find about. Deirdri found amusement that Shaz had a girl and recounted the story of when Mathieu made the boys dance together, which Amirra took great pleasure in, but then told her how wonderful of a dancer he was and told her all about the grand ball at the Ebassia Castle. The morning quickly slipped into afternoon and a sense of time sank into Riddick's mind.

The uneasiness sank into Amirra's chest, and she understood his concern. Riddick cleared the plates and noticed the papers again. He picked it up and Deirdri's heart sank. She swallowed hard and braced herself for the question.

"What is this?" Riddick asked.

"Your lineage and the place from where you come from," Deirdri said.

Riddick's brows scrunched from confused, to interest, and back to confused and Deirdri's heart raced. Riddick knew she wasn't his biological mother, but he never asked, because to him she *was* all he needed. But now it seemed like there was something he needed to know.

"It says my father was Walter Kenon Brouderic, but it doesn't list a mother," Riddick said.

"Aye, it was the way of the Rangers. They didn't list the mothers as a way to keep them from the Velshari. That is also why Shaz doesn't know who his mother is, but I knew them both," Deirdri said.

Riddick looked over the paper and picked up the one underneath it. The paper had a map on it, but he didn't know where it went. Riddick got the impression she didn't want to tell him who his mother was, but also that he needed to ask. He looked up with soft brows. He put the paper down and went to his mother.

"I have always known, but it didn't matter to me, that is why I never asked, and you *will* forever be *my* mother, no matter what," Riddick said.

"I have dreaded this question since I escaped the Velshari with you as a tiny baby. I have had this conversation in my head so many times but now I don't even know where to start," Deirdri said.

Deirdri composed herself and went to the papers on the table and pulled the bottom one out of the pile and handed it to Riddick. He took the paper and started to read and learned it was a letter from his mother.

"This says her name was Maili MacBaron," Riddick said.

Deirdri nodded.

"It says my name is Kenon Riddick Brouderic, and that I was

born in Tirion Alari, the Realm of the Bair Tiornecht," Riddick said.

"Yes, your father was the last heir of the Bair's rightful king-ship, but he bore the mark of the Rangers and was invited to live and train at Hammerstead, when his training was complete, he returned and met your mother, and you were born. Your father Kenon, as he went by, Reinholt, and Merrick were all in the brotherhood of the Rangers. They had determined Shaz was a war wizard and you an Earth Sage. It was no secret that your magic would be sought after especially if you were found out. Mathieu was the Grand Cleric and Denasian, which meant he was the only one with enough magic to harness the Synergy of both of you. We were at the castle to complete the bonding and shortly after the ceremony, the Velshari attacked.

"Reinholt was severely injured, and they had already killed Tallise, Shaz's mother. Reinholt and Kenon begged Merrick to take you boys and Mathieu and escape while they held them off. Merrick and Mathieu took me and Elin, who were your nursery attendants and you boys out through the secret portal in the basement, and we never saw them again. Yerild brought us here where I raised you and Merrick and Elin raised Shaz," Deirdri said.

Deirdri's heart pounded in her chest and strands of her soft gray hair hung at the sides of her face. Riddick stared into her eyes and found them to be full of pain and sorrow. A pit in his guts formed and the urgency for them to leave intensified. Riddick opened his palm and let a tiny bud emerge from his skin. Deirdri's eyes popped open and got bigger and bigger as the bud grew into a stem. The flower opened and blossomed into a brightly colored or-ange and yellow lily. Deirdri looked at him with shock and amazement, and he smiled.

"Take it," Riddick said softly. Deirdri picked it with a trem-bling hand, and he handed a mug with water to Amirra, "give the water some soul magic," Riddick said with a gentle smile. Amirra wasn't sure what to do exactly, but she stuck her finger inside the mug and her soft-yellow magic eased into the clear water. Riddick handed the mug to Deirdri who put the flower in it. "This flower will stay in bloom as long as I live, and from now on, you will always know that I am with you and you are with me," Riddick said.

Deirdri embraced him and he hugged her tightly.

"You have to go, don't you?" Deirdri asked.

"Aye, but I am so glad I got to see you again, and that you got to meet Amirra," Riddick said.

Deirdri's eyes widen and smile with the implication, and then he hugged her again.

"Take these, they belong to you know," Deirdri said.

She handed Riddick the stack of papers and hugged Amirra and tried with all her might not to cry. Riddick knew it would be better to make the goodbye quick and he hurried to his room for a few things he had left behind, and he and Amirra left the treehouse. Amirra could tell he was both happy and sad to have been able to see his mother and understood he would need some time to process it all. They quickly made their way to the cave and Riddick pulled back the long hanging vines that covered the entrance. He pulled a torch from the wall and struck the flick stone and a few sparks hit the torch and popped into flames. Riddick guided Amirra through the winding pathway until they came to the wall that Shaz had always said he had found the room behind.

Riddick waved his hand and instructed the wall to move so that they could pass into the room. The wall obeyed and it rolled into itself and an opening emerged. Riddick stepped into the room and the torch lit up the glyphs. He ran his hand along the wall and read the marks, but not because he could read the symbols but because he could read the memories stored in the mountain's energy. He found the portal sitting at the back of the cavern and put his hand into the blackness. The mist they had grown accustomed to emerged and turned a shade of sky blue.

"Are you ready?" Riddick asked.

"Yes," Amirra said.

Amirra took his outstretched hand and stepped into the portal.

18- Life Gets In The Way, Doesn't It?

Antorn leaped over a small bush and glided over the terrain with a new sense of survival. His long lean legs had a sense of purpose and his chest burned a hot heat, but it wasn't the dreaded kind, it was an awakening kind. The heavy gurgling breathing of the beasts neared his hind legs and at the last second he kicked his hoof into the snout of the beasts.

It hollered and slowed its pace as it shook of the sting and gained speed again. Antorn eased into his new awareness and thumped on his antler to signal Pillip and Tobis' groups that he was passing them. Tobis internalized the echo and gave his commands. The stags moved quickly to the edge where they spotted the last of the creatures and Pillip on the other side. Tobis nodded to Pillip who signaled his attack. The two groups launched into full runs and closed the gap quickly. Tobis gripped the battle-ax and pulled it from the strap on his back and then pulled a spear. He was still unsure how to use the ax, but he was about to find out. He pulled in a deep breath and launched his spear into the air.

The raging pole wriggled just enough with the force that it left a hum in its wake as it sunk into the back of the rear beast. The beast howled and Pillip released his spear. The rest of the men sent their weapons through the air each hitting their marks. The beasts turned and rose onto their hind legs. The stags' hearts raced blood to their limbs, and they maneuvered quickly through the beasts. Tobis ducked the blade of a beasts ax and slammed his ax into its chest. The hit was powerful, and the blade ripped through its ribcage with an unsettling grinding. Tobis yanked the blade and pulled the spear through its thick bluish skin.

Tobis was surprised at how thick the skin was and found he had to add a bit more pressure to get the blade to sink deep enough. The thick oily blood spurted in a pulsing fashion covering Tobis from head to hoof. Antorn shot into the gap that they had made, and Soren and his men launched from the bushes they were hiding behind.

Soren slashed with one hand and stabbed with the other as he encountered the first beasts. It stood on its hind legs and Soren through his body into the beasts center knocking it off balance. The creature stumbled but regained is footing and snarled. It pulled its blade and swung at Soren who ducked in time to feel the wind rush across his sweaty skin. A stag slammed his new battle-ax into the beasts back and its bones snapped as the blade sank deep. Antorn pulled his weapons and descended upon another beast. The stink soon pelted their beings as the oily blood dripped off their weapons and their own bodies.

It was hard not to wretch every time a beast was opened up but the need to live somehow gave them the strength they needed. They were able to quickly take out the pack as there were only about twelve of them to their fifty, but it took more out of them then they had thought. The last beast fell and Antorn instructed them to cut off all the heads, gather all the ax's and return to camp. They cleaned up their camp quickly and hurried back to the Herd-Lord, but Antorn decided to take the long way and make an arch around their lands to identify if there were any other settlements, and to make a quick check on Mazen and her Nama.

The oily blood dried slowly, and the group tried to find ways to get it off their bodies as they returned but there was little that made a difference. Antorn slowed the group to a stop and addressed Tobis, Soren, and Pillip.

"From now on, we stay together. We are now the Forrne Guard, and we must take an oath to protect our people from these beasts, at all costs. We are not loyal to Tage or the Herd-Lord, I fear he or any of the council are going to be capable of understanding what we are dealing with," Antorn said.

Pillip studied Antorn's eyes and found the honesty of his words in his own chest. He gripped Antorn's forearm and gave him the salute.

"We also need a new salute, one that is for the military forces only, I don't want to be mistaken for political nonsense," Antorn said.

"What do you propose?" Pillip asked.

Antorn gave him a new salute. He formed his hand into a long half oval shape and held it at the center of his chest with his elbow bent tight until the others followed. He released his hand quickly to his side and others did the same.

"Now do it again and repeat after me," the stags repeated the salute, "I solemnly swear my allegiance to the Forrne Guard," they repeated the phrase, "and give my life to the cause, to fight and defend the Forrne people," they again repeated, "until the time our oppression is over, or until death," Antorn finished.

"If we don't report to the Herd-Lord who do we report to?" Soren asked.

"The four of us, will be the leaders as of now, and at some point in the future when things are right, we will figure that out, but as for now, we report to our own conscience and to truth. We will be the council to make the decisions, but I will be ultimate leader, if that is agreeable to you," the new Forrne Guard leaders nodded. "Tobis will be second, then Pillip and then Soren, agreed?" The men saluted and Antorn slapped them on the shoulders. "Now gather the men, and put them under oath as well, and as many as we can gather from here on out, this is just beginning," Antorn said.

The leaders formed their ranks and put everyone under the oath and taught them the new salute and then they continued toward the outskirts. The Forrne Guard made their way through the countryside and the four leaders began enlisting stags. Tobis and Soren took the heads of the beasts and put them on the end of poles and began moving through the villages rallying support and fighters. Numbers grew rapidly and Antorn soon realized they needed more leaders to organize their support as well as when and where it would be kept. Soren suggested to include the mappers and send a troop to gather the other trappers. Antorn agreed and Soren organized his men into the new provisions division.

Antorn was impressed at how well the Forrne began to rise to the needs of this soon to be war, and how much they had also been held under a thumb. The thumb of being only great at one thing, sturdiness. Tobis and Pillip made their way through the towns as they moved and organized their men into outfits to start training the stags on how to fight instead of trap. They decided on the grounds near the last settlement as their new Guard encampment and started to organize training and battle strategies.

The days passed quickly but Antorn had yet to make it to

Mazen's nama's and his nerves began to etch at the back of his mind. He found Tobis and studied his movements as he attempted to take down another stag. It proved harder than he had expected and ended up with a black eye instead. Antorn watched another set of stags and wondered if putting their leg's, a certain way and shifting their wight, which was quite a bit for their size, it would get the other off balance.

Antorn walked into the training area and motioned for Tobis.

"I need to make a trip out to the fringes to check on someone, I'll be gone a few days," Antorn said.

"Yes, Sir," Tobis said.

"Oh, and try putting your front leg behind the other guys knee and shift your weight to the side with your front hip and let your rump shift backward," Antorn said.

Tobis' brows squished his face as he pictured what the movements would look like and nodded. He returned to the ring and did just as Antorn said and the other stag hit the ground with a thud. He smiled and Antorn left. Antorn started out a quick pace and made it to the fringes before the evening meal hour. He wasn't sure he remembered where Mazen's nama lived and he wondered for a time until he came across the stream he remembered being a lot bigger. Maybe it was because they were children then, but maybe because there wasn't as much water as there used to be.

"Antorn," Mazen called.

Antorn turned to find her waving happily and he hurried over the stream.

"Are you alright? How is your nama?" Antorn asked.

"We are good, she was pleasantly surprised I came to see her and is still confused that I'm still here," Mazen said with a chuckle.

Mazen wrapped her arms around his neck and gave him a big squeeze. Antorn returned the hug but wasn't sure what do about it. It wasn't like he didn't want to hug her, to be close, he very much did, but what would happen if he allowed his feelings for her change things, would he be able to leave her, would he even want to? Mazen felt the confusion and pulled back and looked deeply into his eyes. They were the same eyes he had had her whole life. The eyes she decided she loved from when she was just a small calf. She tried to tell him once, but he was deep into the study of some random history book or something that he barely heard her, at least that is what she thought. He gave her a reassuring smile and she smiled back.

"Come, you have to say hello to Nama, she would be very unhappy if you didn't," Mazen said.

"Of course," Antorn said.

Mazen led him into the small cottage-like dwelling. Nama came out from the sleeping quarters and Antorn greeted her, but she wrapped him into a hug, and he tried not to get swallowed up in her embrace. Mazen chuckled and Antorn grimaced. The old woman's long white hair was pulled up at the back of her head and she was wearing a brightly colored hand knitted shall that Antorn had never seen on anyone that wasn't old. Her skin was soft and smooth, and the wrinkles looked like they belonged on her delightful expression. Her eyes sparkled though and Antorn could see there was still as much life in her than there ever had been. His heart swelled with the hope and for some reason the knot that had made its place perma-nent in his guts eased.

"Antorn-deer, how have you been, it's been such a long time since the last time I saw you, you're all grown up, but so is my Ma-zen-deer," Nama said.

"It's good to see you Nama, I am sorry it has been so long. Life gets in the way doesn't it," Antorn said.

"It certainly does," Nama said.

"I'll start some supper. I assume you have a little time to stay?" Mazen asked.

"I do, a few days if you don't mind," Antorn said.

Mazen smiled big and a glint in the corner of her eye ignited his heart. She nodded and turned to the kitchen area. He casually answered all of Nama's questions while trying to keep his answers vague but kind. He didn't want to upset her with the details of what was going on, at least not until he could talk to Mazen about things first. Mazen finished some vegetables and meats and they sat outside while they ate. The sun was warm but not too hot and Antorn was glad that they were as far away from the beasts as they could be.

He enjoyed the ladies conversation and interjected here and there, but mostly just listened. Nama decided it was time for her bedtime and Mazen helped her inside and then returned to Antorn who was gazing into the distance.

"Now you can tell me what is really going on," Mazen said softly but sternly.

He was sure she was going to get her explanation and fully expected it which made the corner of his lip tickle into a small grin.

"I have formed a Forrne Guard, and we are gathering forces to go to battle against the beasts. There are thousands of them, maybe even more, I can't say for sure, but if we don't do something they will overtake our kind in a matter of moons," Antorn said.

Mazen looked at him with her gentle eyes but he knew there was a brewing of questions just waiting to pour out.

"You started a Guard? Does Tage know about it?" Mazen asked.

"No, but it won't take long before he does, we have been gathering troops and setting up training and organizing rations and provisions for the last several days," Antorn said.

"Who is 'we'?" Mazen asked.

"Tobis is my second in command and then Pillip and Soren," Antorn said.

Mazen's brain shot into overdrive and Antorn watched with eagerness the gears turning in her head. He wasn't sure what question was going to be next. She had this habit that her thoughts jumped around in her mind.

"Tobis, is he the skinny lanky boy that lived near the marshes?" Mazen asked.

Antorn chuckled and nodded.

"He's not so skinny anymore and he's quite the leader. In fact, they all are. It's been truly remarkable watching these stags evolve from the self-absorbed individuals I hated growing up into diverse and eager individuals with much more to offer than just how strong and fast they are," Antorn said.

Mazen laughed and Antorn's cheeks suddenly went pink.

"You say the craziest things," Mazen said.

"No, it's true, take Gabe for instance, did you know that he draws maps like nothing I have ever seen, and Kade too, they are amazing. Oh, and the Smitting brothers, did you know that they are quite adept at organizing rations," Mazen puckered at the word 'adept' and Antorn decided no one knew that word, "very good," Antorn said.

"I'm not sure what to think," Mazen admitted.

She was right, it was a lot to take in, and would only become more so. Antorn did his best to explain everything and in the proper timeline and Mazen took in the details as if he were telling a story, interjecting, and asking questions as he went. The night quickly overcame the sky, but the excitement was still at full as Antorn finished with arriving at Nama's place.

"So, what are you going to do next, Tage is not going to let you get away with this. In fact, I wouldn't be surprised if he tries to take over the command, and or form his own Guard," Mazen said.

"I was thinking the same thing," Antorn agreed.

"What are you going to do?" Mazen asked.

"Well, the four of us have sworn an oath to each other as the leaders of the Forrne Guard with me as the head and the rest of the stags have sworn an oath to the Guard, so in truth there is nothing he can do. But I don't want this to become a political mess and have to deal with his stupid ego either," Antorn said.

"Oaths can be broken," Mazen said.

"It's true, but most people don't know that, and I want to keep it that way. I do need to figure out what to do about Tage. I guess I could just arrest him," Antorn said.

"Arrest? What does that mean?" Mazen asked.

"I could put him in shackles in the stockyard," Antorn said.

"Oh-deer, I suppose you could, but don't you think that would be worse, I mean all the people that voted for him would surely make a mess," Mazen said.

"Tobis wanted to take the heads of the beasts and put them on poles and place them in the main square so that everyone would understand that we aren't making this up and that we will force them to take arms if we have to," Antorn said.

"Do you think it will work?" Mazen asked.

Antorn shrugged.

"I hope so," Antorn said.

19- How Did Things Go?

The return to the fortress was a bit slower and Turkill tried not to scowl too hard and Ladtwig fidgeted more than usual which earned him a few hisses from Jagwynn. Phanes and Shar had to help Cluck most of the way as one of his wings was badly injured and one of his legs. Even though Cluck continued to tell the Minca they didn't have to wait, that wasn't how they operated. They were aware they needed to hurry, but they also understood the time moved faster here, so they figured they would be alright to take the time.

They traveled through the night and the day became two. Several times they had to stop to rest and let the bugs settle back down. The buzzing made the gryphton's nerves itch, and they tried to keep their focus and the fortress finally came into view.

"Go, I'll get Cluck the care he needs," Shar said.

Phanes nodded, and he and Jagwynn hurried back up the side passage to the fortress. The guard opened the door at the side gate, and Phanes lead them to the war room and knocked on the door.

"Enter," Ralti said.

Phanes opened the door and the room stood up and Jag and the Minca came into the room behind Phanes.

"Sir, we have secured the Saraswati. Cluck and Shar tried to gain information, but they were found out and attacked. Shar was taken captive, Cluck barely made it out and is badly injured, Shar has taken him to the medics," Phanes said.

"How did you get her out?" Ralti asked.

"I didn't, Sir, the Minca did, Sir," Phanes said.

Azrack tilted his head with curiosity but was certain they were capable of it.

"There is also a human in the forest, we saw him while on our errand. He was at the location, but I don't think he saw us," Turkill said.

"Human?" Azrack asked.

"We think he is a member of the Dodjen from rotations ago, but the timing doesn't equate, so we are not sure who it is," Jagwynn said.

The gryphton's dropped their beaks not realizing she could speak and Turkill and Ladtwig snickered.

"Jagwynn, I'm sorry it never occurred to me who you were," Azrack said.

"It's alright Gryphton King, our world is far from what it used to be," Jagwynn said.

"My father spoke of the Sakura when I was a cub," Azrack said.

"We had a long and loyal relationship with your kind, it doesn't surprise me, I hope to continue that legacy," Jagwynn said.

"Of course, you have our allegiance," Azrack said.

"We must go, but please send us word on what you find out, the human may be the answer to your problems with the Kronos," Jagwynn said.

"How so, if I may ask, before you go," Azrack said.

"The Dodjen had a gryphton named Branko and I believe he may have been lost to the realms, he was a Kronos," Jagwynn said.

Azrack rubbed his chin and nodded and Jagwynn and the Minca hurried from the room. They made their way back to the portal and leaped into the misty surface. Helios jumped as the chimes in the portal room sounded, and he rubbed his eyes and hurried down the stairs. The castle portal room was dim and warm and the scent of the Whispmother's cooking hit their brains.

"You're back, excellent," Helios said.

"Anyone else?" Turkill asked.

"No, not yet," Helios said.

Helios took the bag from Turkill, and he hurried up the stairs while the Minca and Jag went to the kitchen. Ladtwig jumped off Jag and through his pack into the corner and snagged a plate from the long counter and dished himself everything that was set out. Turkill too climbed of Jagwynn and rubbed her warmed fur and gave her a quick side-smile. She purred and rubbed up against him and nearly knocked him over. Jagwynn preferred catching her own meals so Turkill opened the back door and let her out.

Turkill slumped onto a chair and sucked in a deep breath. Inelius studied him quietly and noted his tiredness overcome his frame. Inelius was familiar with how hard it was to time shift so quickly and stood to fetch him a plate of food. He set it in front of him and then took his own dishes to the sink. He knew the Whispmother didn't need them to wash the dishes, her magic somehow did all that, but it was something he could do to help.

Helios had moved his laboratory things into another room, so he wouldn't bother the sleeping men, even though the medicine kept them asleep, he figured it would be the polite thing to do. Helios pulled a long glass tube out of his bag and popped the stopper off. He took another container out and pulled the dingy green leaf and tucked it into the tiny opening of the bag. One of the Saraswati bugs twitched and stirred the rest and Helios held the bag away from him. The bugs settled, and he shoved another leaf into the bag. He took another long tubular object and sucked up a few drops of a clear liquid and stuck it into the tiny hole.

The liquid hit the leaves with a sizzle and the fumes emanated into the bag. Helios could feel the bugs fall to the bottom, and he checked his time ticker that was sitting on the table. He waited the several lengths and then slowly opened the bag. The toe-sized bugs were laying on the bottom, and he took a set of tongs and gently lifted the white and green striped flat squat body of one of the bugs and set the insect on the table. He took the glass tube and squished the body at the back end with the triangular stinger, and the bluish liquid seeped into the glass tube. Helios took another bug and repeated the process. He tightened the bag and secured the rope and tucked it out of the way.

Helios began his process to mix the elements of the venom with the effects of the mushroom he had secured. Jagwynn came into the room and sat on the floor and rested her head on her paw and licked her lips. Helios turned and jumped when her yellow eyes were staring at him.

"Oh goodness, Jagwynn, I didn't hear you," Helios said.

"We found a human in your realm who knew about the depository," Jagwynn said.

Helios scrunched his brows tightly over his dark eyes and rubbed his feathered chin.

"Do you know who it was?" Helios asked.

"No, I had thought maybe it would be a Dodjen from the old

days, but your realm wouldn't support the life span for a human that long," Jagwynn said.

"True, did you tell Azrack?" Helios asked.

"I did, but I don't know if he will have the means or knowledge to determine proper measures," Jagwynn said.

"Do you think I should go back?" Helios asked.

"No, but perhaps you should instruct Leeta to secure the information from the academy and become the advisor on the matter," Jagwynn said.

"Yes, Leeta would be a fitting choice," Helios said.

"Then I will return to speak to Azrack, the Minca have retired for the time being," Jagwynn said.

Helios nodded and Jagwynn started toward the door.

"Make sure she gets the transfer records," Helios said.

Jagwynn nodded and left the room. Helios barely noticed the sun fade over the horizon but when he finally couldn't see his notes he started for the lantern on his desk. The lights in the glow-stone in the ceiling turned on, and he inspected the structure. He jumped again as the chimes again sounded, and he hurried to the portal room. He rounded the corner in time to see Shaz and Serin come through the portal. Shaz made his assessment of the room and found Helios coming in the doorway.

"Did you have any trouble?" Helios asked.

"How are they?" Serin asked.

"Still sleeping," Helios said.

"It wasn't too bad, but there is trouble brewing there, so we won't be able to stay long, any word from anyone else?" Shaz asked.

"The Minca are here, but Riddick and Amirra haven't shown up yet, and Jag has returned to my realm to take care of some business," Helios said.

Shaz understood not to ask about Jagwynn's business, she often wouldn't tell him everything anyway but an ache in his stomach lurched. He pulled out the iron cask and handed it to Helios. They followed the gryphton back to the room and Serin checked on Motavo and Asher and an interesting peace came over her. Shaz waited at the door and smiled gently as she pulled the covers up a little bit more. The smell of the food bit at their empty stomachs, and they made their way to the kitchen where they found the hot food comforting, but the time shift hit their being and tiredness ached all over.

They retired to their rooms and Helios started the next steps for the antidote. He took out a clean cauldron and set it on the fire in the fireplace and poured the spider spit from the iron cask and shut the lid tight. Helios added a bit of wood to the fire and poked the existing coals and the fire took hold of the new fuel. He looked at his own version of the map that helped him determine the time passing in the different realms, and figured it would be a few more days, if everything went well, for Riddick and Amirra to return. Helios pulled out some cloth and stuck it in his nostrils and then dipped a glass stir stick into the bubbling spider spit and watched the pearlescent particles dance around the stick. He took his dropper and sucked a few drops from the cauldron and placed them into a small dish and moved it around so that the sticky part of the poison would stick to the edges leaving the clear elements at the bottom of the dish.

Helios sucked up the clear liquid and repeated the process until his dropper was half full. Helios had smooshed the mushroom into a creamy goo and smeared it onto a platter to dry. The flakes of the mucky brown had begun to pop off the plate, and he picked several flakes and dropped them into another dish and drizzled the clear liquid over them. The flakes absorbed the liquid and began to soften. He then took the Saraswati venom and dripped it over the mushroom. A faint but rancid odor filled the room and he moved to the window and slid the pane open a little.

The new night breeze bristled the odor away quickly and Helios continued to mix the two liquids until the mushroom was fully saturated. He took a grinding stick and began to smoosh the mushroom more mixing it until became smooth and glassy. He took the cauldron off the fire and set the dish on. It would take some time for the potion to heat the components, and he sat in the chair at the corner of the room.

The chimes again sounded, and Helios jumped awake as did Shaz and Serin. Shaz was the first to get to the portal room and the lights came on as Riddick and Amirra came through. Serin came around the corner followed by Helios.

"How did things go?" Shaz asked.

Shaz sensed a newness to their magics but wasn't sure what it was.

"Mate, do I have a lot to talk about," Riddick said.

Serin and Amirra hugged and Riddick pulled out the bulbous fruit. The shimmering glow of the golden fruit was intensified by the glow-stone and Shaz got the impression that the magic was familiar to the other. Riddick handed it to Helios who quickly returned to the room.

"You were right, the portal is in the cave, but we came out of the portal in the lower half of the archipelago," Riddick said.

"How did you get back so soon then? That's days travel in Turob time," Shaz said.

"Geo-kinetics," Riddick said with a big grin while nodding his head.

"You're gonna wanna ask him about that after you've had some sleep," Amirra said with a grin that said, 'that's a loaded question'.

"And Amirra here," Riddick started.

"I'm starving, can we talk after we find something to eat," Amirra said.

The three gave her a curious glance but dropped it.

"Come on, let's get you some food," Serin said.

They made their way into the kitchen and Serin went up to check on Helios, but he reassured her he was fine, and he would let her know as soon as things were ready. Serin hesitantly returned to the kitchen where they talked quietly while Riddick and Amirra ate. Riddick gave a brief explanation of his experience with the Teorran Belt and Shaz explained he had an experience too, but Amirra kept her thoughts tight and Riddick wondered why she didn't want to share her new magic. He figured it was her right to tell so he would give her space. They all returned to their rooms for some much-needed rest.

20-Now We Wait

Serin had a hard time letting her mind rest and a knock on the door brought her from her thoughts.

"Come in," Serin said. Shaz opened the door and slipped inside and came to the bed. "What's wrong?" Serin asked.

"Nothing, I just thought maybe you didn't want to be alone," Shaz said.

Serin smiled and scooted over.

"Maybe you're the one who doesn't want to be alone," Serin teased.

"Maybe," Shaz admitted.

Shaz climbed in and pulled the covers up. Serin rested on his warm body and listened to his heartbeat.

"What are your plans for the Timeless Plains?" Serin asked.

"I'm not sure yet. I'm certain there are going to be a lot of Jaduuk, and I have a feeling something, or rather *someone*, else is creating the army," Shaz said.

"What makes you say that?" Serin asked.

"A few things. According to Amirra, Semias *grew* his pack. How, I don't know and neither does Amirra, she was never a part of that, so there must be some process that makes that happen, and just before we found the first scorched earth I felt shadow magic, which I have never felt from the Jaduuk before, so it has to be *someone*. They either have shadow magic or is using something that does. Either way, we need to figure that out. We also need to find out about the Timeless Plains, what is the time difference exactly, do we have some time to make a calculated attack plan or are we winging it. What would be the reason for a Jaduuk army, being the portals are all ski-wampy, it's not like they can easily get somewhere. But if they weren't, where *would* they be going and why. Can we fix the portal first, so we have easy access while we are dealing with the Timeless Plains? We know the Jaduuk are underworld creatures, but what is the point to them, if they, so far, only hunt me, unless there is some-thing we haven't learned about them, except that they are not intelligent and really stink. And it was quite hot there, which I don't think is normal for that realm, and I don't know how to keep you healthy without water to rejuvenate your magic," Shaz said.

"Wow, you've been busy."

"It keeps my mind off other things," Shaz admitted.

Serin ran her hand over his chest and sent a calming boost of her healing and love magic, and he relaxed with the euphoria her magic gave his senses. It didn't take away the grief of losing grand-father, but the cooling effect helped the pain it caused in his body. Shaz reached out and tried to determine how much pain Serin was in, but wasn't sure how to help her, so he just opened his multi-col-ored magic to her. Serin sank onto his frame a little deeper, and he could tell she was relaxing more.

"Go on,"

She was sure he had more he had been thinking about and it was soothing to her to hear him working through the details.

"What about the underground, what kind of situation is there, and why were the spiders there in the first place, I mean, they were obviously driven into the shift by something, presumably the Jaduuk army. Have they broken through other barriers and infiltrated other realms and are we going to find complete realms of paralyzed beings somewhere?" Shaz said.

"That's a scary thought," Serin said.

"I wonder if the Minca know how to make those explosives their kinsman used, that could really come in handy if we are going to have to take on another army of Jaduuk," Shaz said as he ran his fingers through her hair.

"What about the gryphton's, do you think Azrack would send some forces too, and Bowen maybe?" Serin said.

"Aye, I bet they would, that would be quite helpful. I wonder if Helios has some kind of ancient information on the Jaduuk that could help too, or if there is an earth portal somewhere that does, and we need to figure out what the Forrne are like, what will they be willing to do to help or have they all been killed."

"And the other animals that we encountered. They were quite large maybe they could help, except they appeared nervous about something," Serin said.

"Aye, I wonder if Riddick will be able to heal the earth from the scorch marks, and what would be causing them? Is there another volcano or lava, and is it normal that the sun doesn't come up all the way, or is that a problem affected by the Jaduuk," Shaz asked.

"Something seemed a bit different with Riddick and Amirra," Serin said sleepily.

"Aye, I noticed too, I'm sure they'll fill us in tomorrow, and we haven't seen the Minca yet," Shaz said.

Serin's breathing deepened and Shaz was sure she was falling asleep. He tried to still his mind, but it was times like this that his brain slipped into 'constant mode' and he maneuvered through the scenarios and strategies he knew of. This was one of those things of being a War Wizard, and grandfather and his father spent a great deal of time on. Partly because he enjoyed the mind games so much, but partly because it was part of his training, he wasn't aware he was getting at the time. He did somehow find a level of comfort he didn't expect, and he relaxed into the thoughts.

He must have fallen asleep at some point because he didn't know when Serin had woke, but she wasn't there when he returned to consciousness. He slipped out of the covers and went to the window and pulled the curtain enough to see what part of the day cycle it was. Shaz was relieved to see the sun had barely made its way to the morning horizon and he left the room. He started down the hall and heard voices from the room across from Motavo's. He came around the corner to find Helios and Serin working on the antidote. Shaz crossed the room and Serin turned with a smile.

"How are things going?" Shaz asked.

"Nearly finished," Helios said.

"That's great news," Shaz said.

Shaz sensed Serin's excitement, and he was happy for her. He watched with curiosity as they mixed the liquids together. The tincture simmered with a sizzle as they combined, and Helios gently swirled the mixture in the glass tube. The iridescent opal colors mixed into the blue and gold colors. Serin examined the tincture with curiosity and Helios checked his notes.

"I believe this is ready, but it may take some time to reverse the effects of the paralysis, so we should leave them sleeping for at least the first does. We will need to give them two maybe three doses for a complete recovery which will take a few days," Helios said.

Serin nodded, and she followed him to Motavo and Asher's room. The light illuminated the room and Serin gasped at their near blue bodies.

"It's alright, that's part of the toxin, but also the sleeping medicine," Helios assured her.

Serin nodded, but she couldn't help the flutters in her stomach, and she thought she might puke. Shaz gripped her hand and she squeezed back. Helios lifted Motavo's head while Serin opened his mouth and dripped the mixture slowly. They waited for the medicine to ease down his throat since he couldn't swallow on his own and repeated the process. They then moved to Asher and gave him the medicine.

"Now, we wait," Helios said.

"About how long?" Serin asked.

"We should start seeing improvement within the hour," Helios said.

"I'll get you some breakfast," Shaz said.

Shaz pulled a sizeable, tall-back chair with ivory velvet, between the beds for Serin to sit it. He knew she wasn't going to leave at this point.

"Thank you," Serin said.

Serin kissed him and he left the room.

"I see you two have become close," Helios said.

Serin studied him with a 'what are you up to' look, and he chuckled.

"Are you one of the ones that is in favor...or no?" Serin asked.

Helios raised his brows and settled into another sizeable chair at the foot of Motavo's bed.

"In favor, my dear," Helios said.

Helios shouldn't be surprised someone would have clued them in to the dispute, but he hadn't wanted to get too involved in the politics of it all.

"Yes, when this whole mess is over, we are going to be married and have some cute little war wizard babies," Serin said.

"I would very much like to see that," Helios said.

Serin smiled. She would to, but the nagging at the back of her heart suggested that would only be just that, a hope. Shaz came in with a tray of food for them and set it on the side-table.

"Any changes?" Shaz asked.

"Not yet," Serin said.

Shaz read her energy and knew they had been talking about them and her wanting a family someday. He already understood her desire, and it was one of the things that kept him going, wanting to give it to her.

"Riddick is up, so I'm going to go get caught up," Shaz said.

"Thank you," Serin said.

Shaz kissed her and left the room.

"Tell me what has happened back home," Serin said.

Helios popped a bite of the bacon-wrapped ribbard into his mouth and Serin picked up a cup of fresh fruit.

Helios filled her in on the events of the last several rotations in his realm and the dilemma that Ralti was facing with his daughter and Phanes, and Serin found amusement Ralti was a father in the first place. Helios chuckled too, it had surprised them all, but when you find love, life changes, and gryphton's mate for life, so it's nothing to dismiss easily. Serin shared the events since they left them so long ago. The room warmed with the mid-morning sun and Serin observed Motavo's skin start to change, and she hurried to him.

Helios lifted his arm to determine how stiff his limb was and to his surprise, it moved easily. He checked Asher, but his was still a bit stiff, but Helios wasn't surprised based on his size.

"I think we can give them another dose," Helios said.

Serin helped Helios administer another does and put her hands on Motavo's chest and sent her magic to do an inspection. She closed her eyes and tried to understand what was happening. The message was jumbled, but then she remembered something she had learned from the Lavari, and used her light magic to enlighten her own mind. The message became clear and she understood how the antidote was reversing the effects of the toxin.

Serin was amazed to witness the magic of the elements in which she understood them to be from the ancient world. The process reminded her of when she was studying with Mrs. Bailey and now understood what she was trying to teach her about the power the plants and herbs have and how to interpret their nature into her ability to heal. The Saraswati insects that only showed up after the barrier was changed, the mushroom too only returned to this world, but the nectar was the most amazing, then she realized that it was similar to what she sensed in Riddick's new vibes.

The tingle her armlet gave when it added new information tickled her skin, and she breathed out the breath she was holding in. Helios studied Serin as she interpreted the magic of the elements of medicine and was making his own mental notes. She opened her eyes and found Motavo's skin was also beginning to warm and the pink formed under his tanned cheeks.

"Won't be long now, even though they have been sleeping, it will still take several days for them to recover completely. They may also have to relearn things such as walking and moving their bodies, maybe even some speech," Helios said.

"I understand," Serin said.

She understood the idea, but a pain hit her heart as she thought about what that might be like. Serin checked Asher's vitals and was eager to find his skin had started to relax and began to heat up. Serin pulled the drapes open and the sun was now high overhead. She slid the glass pane and the warm breeze blew through the room. Serin sucked in a heavy chest full and held it in letting the wind give her its energy. The room was instantly filled with a freshness and warmth that soothed them. Helios went to his bag and pulled out another jar of medicine.

"This is the medicine that will bring them from the sleep, are you ready?" Helios asked.

Serin nodded, but puckered at its powerful odor as he pulled the stopper. She dripped the thick goo into Motavo's mouth, his reflexes to swallow were functioning and his body took it in. They gave Asher the medicine, but his body was a little slower to respond, but he did show a lot of improvement. Motavo's fingers began to twitch and Serin held them snug. His skin was now warm, and she found her excitement hard to contain.

Motavo blinked and his body jerked. Serin wasn't sure what was happening, but Helios didn't seem concerned, so she assumed it was part of the process. Serin checked on Asher and his skin too was warm. He blinked a few times but didn't stir. Motavo opened his eyes and Serin pulled the drapes closed so that the light wouldn't be too much for his eyes.

"Yappa, can you hear me?" Serin asked.

"Serin?"

His voice was dry and raspy, and she could tell it was uncomfortable for him to speak. She pulled a few drops of water from the air and let the clear liquid seep into his lips.

"Drink," Serin said.

She let a few more drops into his mouth and he swallowed. Motavo took in the water and closed his eyes again. Serin went to Asher and repeated the process for him who took in the water.

"Serin is that you?" Motavo managed, he blinked and opened his eyes.

Serin returned to Motavo's bed and sat on the edge and took

his hand in hers. Motavo tried to focus on her, but she could tell his eyes couldn't make the connections just yet.

"Yes, Yappa your safe and the spiders' toxin is no longer in your system, but you still have the groggy medicine of the sleep, it will take some time."

"Asher?"

"He's recovering too."

"Shaz?"

"We're all safe Yappa."

Motavo nodded and closed his eyes.

"Just rest, you've been asleep for a while, your body needs time to restart."

"How long?"

"We can talk about that later."

Asher tried to lift his head again and Helios lifted his body and propped another few pillows under him to lift him up a bit. Asher's head wobbled back and forth, and Helios stood ready to help keep him down if needed.

"What's happening?" Serin asked.

"Sometimes when people are coming out of the medicine, they can experience the last few minutes of their experience before the trauma. He thinks he is still fighting the spiders. It won't take too long, but we might need Shaz's help to keep him from hurting himself," Helios said.

"Shaz!" Serin yelled in her mind.

Shaz heard and his heartfire spiked.

"Come on mate, now," Shaz said.

Riddick stopped mid-sentence and found Shaz darting out of the room. Riddick's heartfire surged to high alert, and he shot out of the room and up the stairs behind Shaz. Amirra came out of her room at the end of the long hall and saw them running into the room and hurried after them.

"What's wrong?" Shaz asked.

"The medicine can make him remember the last few moments before his paralysis, he thinks he is fighting the spiders," Helios managed.

Shaz and Riddick hurried across the sizeable room and tried to keep Asher from hurting anyone or himself.

"This is one tough guy," Riddick said through gritted teeth as he held onto his left arm. Shaz had the other arm and Helios was holding his body down. Sweat began to form as the three wrangled Asher's extreme size. Motavo struggled to make his eyes focus as he listened to the ruckus.

Motavo spoke to Asher in their native tongue and Asher's expression relaxed and his body eased onto the bed. The three slowly eased off of him but stayed alert in case of a flare-up.

"Let's give him another dose of the antidote," Helios said.

Serin grabbed the tube and started toward Asher. Serin softly touched Asher's arm and made contact with his energy before she opened his lips. Asher responded and let her drip more of the tincture into his mouth, and he swallowed. He rested into the pillows and Serin set the tube back into the holder on the side-table. Serin did a quick check of his body's responses and understood there was still a little paralysis left. She understood her magic wouldn't take the paralysis away, but she sent a boost of her hydro-light magic into his body to help give his mind some clarification as to where he was, and he stilled and rested. Asher blinked and tried to lift his head again, but it was so heavy that it wobbled, and he sank back into the pillow.

"Uncle don't try to sit up yet, you have a long journey back, this will take some time," Serin said.

Serin put her hand on his head to comfort him and a small half-smile crested the corner of his lips. Serin turned to find everyone with worried expressions.

"He's alright, just confused, it's going to take some time," Serin said.

Serin found Amirra peek around Riddick, and she went to her and hugged her. Serin was glad they were all safe again and her heart swelled with gratitude for the sacrifices they had made for family.

"I'm so glad to see everyone," Serin said.

"Me too?" Ladtwig interjected.

Serin chuckled.

"Yes, of course, you too," Serin said.

21-In Theory Yes,

The chimes of the portal room sounded and Shaz and Riddick hurried out of the room. They rounded the corner in time to find Jagwynn, Phanes and Leeta come through the portal.

"What's going on?" Shaz asked.

"Leeta has an urgent matter to speak to Helios about," Phanes said.

Shaz nodded, and they followed him into one of the larger meeting rooms. He figured it might be nicer to address their issues with a large table being that Leeta was struggling to hold onto the stacks of papers and folders as she followed. Shaz fetched Helios who made his way to the meeting room. Amirra took over his place and helped Serin help the men work through the medicines and Shaz and Riddick went to the military room. Inelius brought a few books in and set them on the table and Shaz could see how old his frame was. As hard as it was to lose grandfather, having Inelius around gave him an extra comfort being that he was grandfather's twin brother and looked so much like him. They had the same mannerisms and quirks, and it eased his sadness some, until he thought about when he goes too. Shaz was certain it wouldn't be too much longer, after doing the calculations, he had determined they were over a thousand Ebassian rotations old. Shaz wondered where Inelius had been while Mathieu was in Turob. He had asked him once, but he didn't answer, and it never got brought up again.

Shaz put the thoughts aside and pulled out a large map of the realms and laid it on the table. He had found this map hanging on the wall behind a tapestry and wondered if it had been hidden on purpose. Riddick pulled out the little wooden figures he had made and set them around the map to indicate who and where things were.

"Alright, what do we know about the Timeless Plains?" Shaz asked.

"The Timeless Plains is a realm of a Savanna-like biome which is inhabited by the Forrne, who are an intelligent race. Most of the animal life is docile with the alligators being the predatory creatures," Inelius said.

"When Serin and I were there, the sun didn't cross the sky, it only went halfway around half of the total surface," Shaz said.

"Yes, the Timeless Plains is in the farthest reaches of the planet, where the sun is far from it most of the rotation and so the sun only crosses half the sky," Inelius said.

"So, I'm not crazy," Shaz said.

"Well, no one said that," Riddick said.

Shaz gave him a sideways glare and Phanes came into the room and Riddick snickered.

"Phanes, what's the trouble?" Shaz asked.

"What makes you think there is trouble?" Phanes asked. Shaz

gave him a 'are you serious' look and Riddick put his hands in his pockets. "Alright, I'm not sure if it's trouble yet, but the Minca and Jagwynn ran into another human in our realm. Helios and Leeta are currently going over all the transfer records for the artifacts that were in motion leading up to the End of the Realms," Phanes said.

"Have they found anything yet?" Shaz asked.

"No, there doesn't seem to be any record of humans or the Dodjen being in our realm," Phanes said.

"Riddick why don't you catch Phanes up on the details of the Timeless Plains and I'll go see if I can help," Shaz said.

"Aye," Riddick said.

Shaz left the room and started down the hallway and ran into the Minca.

"Meet Riddick in the war room, we have a lot to cover," Shaz said.

The Minca nodded and Shaz rounded the corner and found Helios and Leeta scanning through the scribbles on piles of papers.

"Is there anything I can help with?" Shaz asked.

"There are so many records, this will take us days to sort through," Leeta said.

"What are you looking for?" Shaz asked.

"The records of the transfers of artifacts," Helios said.

"Find me all the documents with the transfers in the gryphton's realms for the five rotations before the End of the Realms," Shaz said.

Shaz's magic sparkles popped into existence and shot toward the papers. The dancing specs wriggled in and under the papers and pushed them apart as it searched. The tip of the finger-like pointer stopped on a paper and Leeta pulled it out of the stack and then it wriggled some more. It found more sheets of papers and Helios and Leeta admired its diligence. The magic made one more sweep around and fizzled into thin air.

"Does that help?" Shaz asked.

"Why yes, it most certainly does," Helios said.

"Good, because we could use your council in the war room," Shaz said.

"Yes of course give me a few minutes," Helios said.

Shaz nodded and left the room. He took the stairs two at a time up to the bedchambers and found Serin and Amirra helping Motavo sit up in bed.

"Motavo, you're awake. How do you feel?" Shaz asked as he crossed the room.

"Much better, I can't begin to tell you how thankful I am for your help Nipotino," Motavo said.

Shaz liked the sound of that. Motavo didn't replace grandfather, but now he had another grandfather, and to Shaz, that meant a great deal. Shaz gave him a hug and tried to be careful as he had no idea what state his body was in.

"I'm sorry to bother you, but I need Serin's help in the war room," Shaz said.

"War room?" Motavo asked.

"Aye, the Ruin Spiders were fleeing from a Jaduuk army in the Timeless Plains. That's why they were in the underground. We have a big task at hand, and I need all hands-on deck," Shaz said.

"Nipotina, help me to the war room," Motavo said.

"Yappa, you are still too-"

Motavo gave her a stern look and she nodded.

"Me too," Asher said.

Asher propped himself up a little more and Serin studied the large man and wondered how they were going to manage it.

"You buff him, and I'll help Asher downstairs," Shaz said.

Serin agreed and cast her air spell on him and Shaz helped him out of the room. Asher did quite well on his own and Shaz didn't have to help too much, which he was thankful for. Serin helped Motavo, and they made their way down the stairs. Serin was surprised to see how the room was decorated. Well, it wasn't exactly decorations, not like she would do, but with all the maps and stacks of papers Inelius had gathered, it was definitely ready to discuss a war.

Motavo and Asher were impressed too, but Shaz made them sit in the chairs but pushed them up close, so they could see the largest map on the table. Phanes returned to the room with Helios and Motavo and Asher's eyes popped. The size of the gryphton's was astonishing and they had a majesty about them that was inspiring. Shaz was thankful the Whispmother had increased the size of the doorways when they first arrived, otherwise they wouldn't be able to fit through them.

"Motavo, Asher, this is Helios and Phanes, they are gryphton's. Leeta is here too somewhere," Shaz said.

"She has just returned actually, but she may be back," Helios said.

"Are things alright?" Shaz asked.

"Yes, your magic search thing was quite helpful. I have great hope we will finally be able to solve our issues with the Kronos," Helios said.

"Excellent, because we are about to ask some difficult questions," Shaz looked around and everyone was accounted for. "We have a situation in the Timeless Plains. Someone or something is building a Jaduuk army and it has caused significant damage to the land. The Ruin Spiders have fled which would indicate many others will have as well and the earth is being scorched. The problem is we don't know who, or where or how many we're talking about. We need to do some recon and figure out what we're up against, that will decide a few things for us, but I'm thinking this army is going to be even larger than the one we fought in the Minca's realm by a long shot. A bird notified me of the trouble while we were in the Minca realm and after doing the calculations that would be over a rotation for the Timeless Plains," Shaz said.

"What are Jaduuk?" Phanes asked.

"Oh yes, sorry, Inelius," Shaz said.

Inelius opened a book and handed it to Phanes who examined the images and scowled.

"Those are nearly as big as us," Phanes said.

"Aye, and they are excellent hunters," Riddick said.

"Helios do you happen to have any information about them by chance?" Shaz asked.

"Well, they are susceptible to the Ruin Spider spit, which my guess is why they drove them out first," Helios said.

"That's good news, then we can use that as a weapon," Shaz said.

"The only problem is, most beings are," Helios said.

"I can help with that, I can enchant some items to reduce the effects for those who handle the spider spit," Amirra said.

"We are also going to need you to do much more than that," Shaz said.

Amirra's heart jumped and a pit formed in her guts.

"Alright, what?" Amirra said.

"How many items can you enchant at once?" Shaz asked.

"It depends on what kind of items," Amirra said.

"Armor and weapons," Shaz said.

"Not very many I'm afraid, what kind of enchantment would you want?" Amirra asked.

"Lightweight, resistance, and attack," Shaz said.

"*Attack* isn't too hard, but the others would take some time," Amirra said.

"I think I have an idea. With my new geo-kinetics, I can change the mineral components to be lightweight and sturdier, leaving the attack enchantments for Amirra," Riddick said.

"Great," Shaz said.

"How many are we talking?" Riddick asked.

"As many as we can, that leads me to the next point. Helios, how many soldiers do you think Azrack can spare?" Shaz asked.

"I am not sure, we will have to ask, but if this idea works for the Kronos, then quite a bit, if not I still think we can manage a sizable armada," Helios said.

"Excellent, we'll need your men to be in charge of the air support," Shaz said.

Phanes saluted and Helios nodded.

"Turkill, do you know how to make the explosives your kinsman used?" Shaz asked.

"In theory, yes but it is highly volatile, and the Northman are the most skilled at using it, plus the minerals we need are found in the mountains they live in," Turkill said.

"Alright, you and Ladtwig make a trip home and ask the Chief if we can get a crew of your pyrotechnics to join us," Shaz said.

"They will need their mammals to carry it all, but I don't think they will survive in the heat," Turkill said.

"I think I have a solution for that, just get them to the portal, and we'll take care of the rest," Shaz said.

Turkill nodded.

"Riddick can you and Amirra do recon in the Timeless Plains, we need to find out what we are up against," Shaz asked.

"Aye," Riddick said.

"Serin and I are going to go to Ebassia, we'll talk to the Queen and Bowen. Phanes you gather your armada, give us," Shaz calculated the time difference, "six of your day cycles and then have your troops ready to leave. I'll need the coordinates of the best location in your realm to launch as many forces at a time so I can make portals,"

Shaz said.

"How are we going to get all these soldiers to the Timeless Plains?" Motavo asked.

"I'm going to open new portals, here and here," Shaz pointed on the map to the flatlands at the base of the castle. "These will go from Ebassia to here, and then to the Timeless Plains. These here," he pointed to another set not too far from the others, "will come from the gryphton's realm. Until we know what the circumstances are in the Plains, we will set up base camp here," Shaz pointed to the area around the portals.

"What can we do?" Asher asked.

"Nothing!" Serin said.

"Little one," Asher started.

Serin, they could be useful, if I promise to keep them from harm? Shaz asked in his mind. Serin stared into his eyes and found them to be sincere, and she was certain he would, but hesitantly nodded. Motavo recognized their interaction and smiled a grandfather's grin.

"Yappa, you have to *promise* me you won't do anything that can hurt you. You too Uncle!" Serin said sternly.

They both looked at her with raised brows.

"Boy, does she look like her mother," Asher said.

"I could really use you here at headquarters, at least until we have a better idea where we will be stationing the armies, I could use your wisdom and organization skills," Shaz said.

"You have our word," Motavo said.

Asher nodded but Serin could tell he didn't intend on following the rules *exactly* and gave him a stern-er look, in which he chuckled.

"Serin, speaking of, what are your thoughts on healers, there is no way you will be able to heal everyone," Shaz said.

"I think Babbesh and Fionte would be good assets and perhaps other Minca women if there are any, and Mrs. Bailey, and

Yappa, do you think some of the traveler women would help?" Serin said.

"Certainly," Motavo said.

"I would assume there will be healers in Ebassia too. Riddick, can you start another Mrs. Bailey's pain ointment garden?" Serin asked.

"Aye, where?" Riddick said.

Shaz put a marker on the ground outside the castle several lengths.

"Turkill we might need some of your clansman to help rig special pulleys and systems to carry water and supplies to each of the tents," Serin said.

"Ladtwig will take care of that," Turkill said.

Ladtwig nodded with a big grin.

"Asher, you can help us get those tents ready, and the Whispmother can help," Serin said. A tiny soldier floated from the chandelier in the center of the room and saluted to Serin. Serin nodded, and Motavo, Asher, and Phanes' eyes popped out. "Yes, they are tiny soldiers, but they don't like being called tiny," Serin said.

Asher cleared his throat, Motavo rubbed his nose and Phanes stood up straighter.

"What about the portal to the Timeless Plains, where will that take us and where do we need to be to find it coming back?" Riddick asked.

"Good point, I'll fix it before you leave," Shaz said.

"How are you going to do that?" Serin asked.

"I just needed to find it on the other side, then I can make the connection and realign it," Shaz said.

"Aye," Riddick said.

"Alright, anything else?" No one said anything. "Let's go then," Shaz said.

22-Can You Make More

The couple days passed quickly and Antorn wanted to stay forever, which was what he was afraid of so he decided he would leave early the next morning before Nama got up so that he wouldn't have to see her heart break. She had made it very well stated that he and Mazen were to settle down, even with Mazen's constant reassurance that they were just friends, Nama was absolutely certain. Antorn really liked the sound of it and had finally allowed himself to see Mazen as the wonderful woman-stag she was, instead of the annoying play-yard brat she used to be.

Mazen's favorite was thinking of ways to make Tage's life miserable and he wondered what their feud was about. He didn't want to ask in case it brought up stuff she didn't want to talk about. They had spent a considerable time trying to guess what Tage was willing to do to keep his command and what 'they' might have to do about it. Antorn could tell that she desperately wanted to go with him and be a part of it all, but her heart was dedicated to Nama and he found her incredibly attractive for it. Antorn closed his pack and laid down into the soft green grasses at the edge of the cottage and Mazen found him and sat next to him.

"You're leaving tomorrow aren't you?" Mazen asked softly.

"I have to, the list of things I have to do is just getting longer and the longer I stay the harder it is for me to leave," Antorn said.

"I made Nama a promise," Mazen said.

"Oh, what's that?" Antorn asked.

"That when all this is over, I will wrangle you into being mine," Mazen said.

Antorn heard the tiny crack in her voice and he gazed into her eyes.

"I am already yours," Antorn said.

Mazen studied his face and found the look she had been hoping for so many rotations and her heart swelled and then the realization hit, that she might not ever get to see him again, if these creatures are as awful as he says and she struggled to keep her smile intact. Antorn reached up and slid his hand under her long honey hair at the back of her head and pulled her to him and kissed her. His lips were amazingly strong and gentle, and she sank with the energy. Antorn had never been so bold in his life and wasn't sure if he had just crossed the line of no return, but her touch lifted his being to an incredible level that he decided he didn't care. Antorn pulled away and gazed into her eyes.

"I hope I didn't just mess things up," Antorn said.

Mazen shook her head and smiled but what she wanted was for him to do it again. He ran his thumb along her long narrow cheek and took in the softness of her skin. Mazen leaned into his touch and savored the moments creating a memory she never wanted to forget.

"I will come to you when I can," Antorn said.

"What am I supposed to do until then?" Mazen asked.

"Take care of Nama, she needs you. Keep an eye on the area too and send me word if you find any scorched earth or see anything that isn't right. If you do, take Nama to the-"

"She'll never leave this place," Mazen said.

"Then do what you must to stay safe. I will check up on you as often as I can," Antorn said.

Mazen nodded and Antorn pulled her into an embrace. The night was the longest night of his life and Antorn found little sleep. He quietly kissed the sleeping Mazen on the forehead and started back to the camp. He found his new feelings left a struggle in his chest and he chided himself at the same time as relished in the new hope. He was now a mess and that wasn't good, so he tried his best to put her in the best place in his heart to keep it safe but, so that it wouldn't distract him from what he needed to do.

Antorn returned to the camp near the middle of the afternoon and found the stags deep in training and a new set of structures near the back side. He found Tobis and Soren deep in conversation and stopped to listen. Tobis turned to see him and saluted which then Soren saluted.

"Good, you're back, we have a situation," Tobis said.

"Fill me in," Antorn said.

"We have so many recruits that are filing in in droves, we don't know what to do with them all. The Fawn have increased their food production like nothing before and they too have joined the ranks, but they are so much smaller we don't know what to do about it," Tobis blurted.

Antorn rubbed his chin and thought a moment.

"Alright, we form a new division just for the Fawn, what are their specific skill sets?" Antorn asked. Tobis and Soren gave perplexed expressions, they desperately wanted to understand all the words Antorn kept using but it wasn't their way until now. "What are they good at that we could use their help with," Antorn asked.

"I saw one Fawn the other day with a weapon that he launched small spears from, and he hit his mark every time," Soren said.

Antorn was incredibly interested in this.

"Take me to him, now, I want to see this," Antorn said.

Soren turned abruptly and Antorn and Tobis followed quickly behind. The mass amount of stags was overwhelming and every single one of them saluted Antorn as he passed. Their faces were filled with determination and allegiance and it almost scared him.

"Finlo, the Guard General wants to see your launcher thing," Soren said.

The small, even for a Fawn, jumped to attention and stared at the large, muscled stags in front of him. His slender build was sleek, even for the Fawn, and Antorn guessed his age was that he should still be working on the farm with his parents, but he didn't judge, he was just glad that he wasn't in this alone.

"Finlo? We would like to see you launch your small spears," Soren said.

"Oh, yes, Sir," Finlo said as officially as he could.

Antorn smiled. It was energetic to see how much his kind actually had to offer the world. They followed him to the area he had been practicing outside the others, but Antorn noted the Fawn's slight hobble in his gate. Finlo picked up his spear launcher. Antorn dissected the long thin wooden shaft that had an arch to it and watched as Finlo placed a small spear like projectile into the string that was tied to both ends of the shaft. Finlo held it in the center and gripped the string and spear and steadied his arm. He pulled the string back as tight as it would go and raised the tip of the stem and let the spear and string go. The projectile shot out with immense speed and hit dead center of the grain-bail he had that was several lengths away.

Antorn studied the distance between them and was impressed at how well the aim and spear responded.

"I am very intrigued, what do you call this?" Antorn asked.

Finlo's big eyes got bigger and a bead of sweat eased onto his brow.

"I don't have a name Sir," Finlo said.

"How do you make this, can you make more?" Antorn asked.

"Yes, Sir, it's not hard," Finlo said.

"Tobis, let's get on this, this could prove to be very useful," Antorn turned to Finlo, "Do you think you could make it go farther?" Antorn asked.

"I have been trying Sir, but I am at a loss," Finlo admitted.

Antorn reached for the device and Finlo handed it to him. Antorn ran it though his hands and examined the details.

"Explain how this works and how you came up with this," Antorn said.

"Well, you see, I don't exactly run real well," Finlo held out his crippled leg, "and we don't have access to trapping, that's for the stags, so in order to hunt for my family, I came up with this as a way to catch our food," Finlo said with as much pride as he could muster under the shroud of defeat. Antorn understood him exactly and his heart went out to the little guy.

"You might just be the reason to our success," Antorn said. Tobis and Soren looked at him with curiosity but when they saw the gears churning in their leader's head they understood this was going to become a big thing. "And how does it work?" Antorn asked.

"Oh yes, when you pull the string against the wood it creates tension and then when released it propels the spear, but you have to have a spear small enough or the shaft big enough. I'm a little guy so this size seems to work best for me," Finlo said.

"What happens if you make the shaft longer and keep the spear the same size?" Antorn asked.

"I would think the spear would travel farther, but I don't know how accurate it would be," Finlo said.

"Let's give it a try. Do you think you could instruct some of the stags and other fawns to help you?" Antorn asked.

"Sir, yes Sir," Finlo said.

"Very well, you are now the new Fawn Guard whatever this is Expert, do you agree?" Antorn asked turning to Tobis and Soren.

"Yes Sir," Tobis said.

"I do Sir," Soren said.

"Good, make it happen, assign some of the stags to this new division and let's get this device a name," Antorn said.

They all saluted and Finlo jumped a small hop-jump and tried not to throw his hand into the air too high. Antorn smiled as he and the others returned to the main arena. Pillip joined them and began giving his report.

"Antorn, we need to figure out what we are going to do with Tage, I have reports that he has learned of our endeavors and where-abouts and is forming his own forces to come to shut us down," Pillip said.

"Then it's time we make our move. Tobis get the heads on the poles ready. Pillip and Soren gather four," Antorn thought a moment, he didn't want to call them herds or outfits as those were terms for their regular lives, "four troops, which is fifty stags each, and be ready in an hour," Antorn said.

"How do you want to label them?" Pillip asked.

"What do you think?" Antorn asked.

"I think we should have each troop have leaders by degrees as well as by specialties," Pillip said.

"I like it, Tobis, Soren?" Antorn asked.

"I agree," they said.

Antorn liked that they were so willing to work together, he was constantly surprised at how different they were than just a moon ago. Pillip left the group to start his new ranking system and organize the first troops of the Forrne Guard. They assembled quickly and Antorn signaled for Pillip to take the lead. Tobis and Soren filled in after and Antorn took up the end. They marched through the plains with a majesty that every settlement they came to stood with shocked and awed faces.

The young fawn and stags gleefully chased the new regiments until their parents called them back. Antorn ran all the scenarios he and Mazen had come up with, even the funny ones, through his mind as he tried to figure out what he should do. It really all depended on Tage and what he was going to do. They made good time and were about to enter the main village of Kambu when several stags stepped into the pathway and blocked them.

"Move out of our way, we are here on official business," Pillip said.

"Official business? Yeah right, you are here to overtake Tage's command," the stag said.

"You're joking, do you honestly think we care about that?" The stag blinked with confusion. "Look around, do you think that these stags would come here to take over Tage's wonderous rule. These stags could care less about that because they are here to protect you and your silly council from death and destruction," Pillip said.

"Death and destruction, from what?" the stag asked.

Pillip turned and asked for one of the sacks. A Guardsman handed him the sack and Pillip pulled out the head of a beast. The stags recoiled and quickly covered their noses from the stink. Pillip handed it back to the soldier and motioned for he and the rest to hoist the heads on the poles.

"What are those?" the stag managed.

"These are the beasts that have invaded our lands and we are here to make our stand, you either fight with us or against us, but we as the Forrne Guard will not tolerate disloyalty to the life and liberty of our kind and we will take it by force if we have to. There is far more at stake than this ridiculous political movement you have going on here. Now you go tell your fabulous Herd-Lord and his council they have one hour to comply," Pillip said.

The stags were shocked, they had never seen another stag assert this kind of power over others. It was both frightening and exhilarating. The stag signaled for another to give the message and he galloped at a fast pace to the council building. Antorn rounded the back of the troops and started to make his way toward Pillip. Each of the stags saluted as he passed but his guts were in knots. He wasn't the kind to take charge in public, that's one of the reasons he sent Pillip to do it. Antorn stopped just short of the front few lines and waited as he made note of the locals reactions to the new forces.

Antorn studied the end building knowing that was where Tage was. He could imagine what kind of conversation was happening and hoped that Tage was nearly squatting but he didn't think he was going to give in that easily. Mazen and he had decided that he was the kind that was going to fight dirty if he had to. The door of the building opened, and the same stag closed it behind him. He hurried back to the stag at the entrance and whispered in his ear. The stags face contorted through the instructions and Antorn got the feeling the stags didn't want to do what they were being told to do.

"The Herd-Lord and the council will not be fooled by these tactics and refuse to give you entrance to the village, unless Antorn gives himself up and Tage becomes the leader," the stag said.

Pillip scoffed a hearty ga-fa and the stags behind him snickered. The stags skittered uneasily. They were convinced this was not going to go well and they were trying to decide what side they were going to go with.

"Tell Tage that is never going to happen and out of my generosity I will still give him one hour," Pillip said.

The first stag nodded and the second again returned to the building.

"Tell me something," Pillip said to the stag, "what do you think Tage has accomplished in his tenure, other than dividing out people into classes and creating trapping and trading standards that force the populars to be more popular and those that are not be forgotten? Tage hasn't done a thing he claims to have and promised. Do you agree?" Pillip asked.

The stag looked around and found that the stags faces were bright and eager with a pride that he hasn't seen in forever, if ever and he wondered why.

"Tell me something, why do you think that you are suited for this cause?" the stag asked.

"Do you know what these beasts are? Do you know how many there are? Do you know what they are after, what they are going to do, what they have already done? Can you explain why we have little water for this time of season? Can you see that our own kind are starving in the plains and many aren't even allowed to trade their grains anymore because they are of the 'lesser stalk'? What say you? No, you can't answer a single question I ask because one, Tage is unwilling to even look outside his pretty hair-do to see what he is doing to his own kind. Join us, come with us and be part of the solution, not the problem," Pillip said.

Antorn was impressed, he didn't really know Pillip that well before all of this, but he certainly has the means to do what needs to be done. The stag struggled with the new information and didn't answer before the other stag returned.

"The answer is No, and you have been declared an enemy to

the Forrne people. Our orders are to seize them and take Antorn to the stock yard," the stag said.

The first stag stared at him and then looked at the forces of stags all standing in perfect execution and diligence to this leader.

"Are you Antorn?" the stag asked.

"No, and you will never have *my* leader. I will offer you one more time, join us or we will take this village and everyone in it by force. Tage is the true enemy to the Forrne people, and after this is over with the beasts, we will return his Herd-Lordness to the people, but we are doing things our way from now on," Pillip said holding out his hand in a gesture of welcoming.

The stag found his intentions were secured in the wellbeing of his kind and decided he was going to join them and took Pillip's hand. Pillip greeted him and motioned for him to take a place in the ranks and then turned to the rest of the stags.

"The offer is extended to all of you," Pillip said.

The second stag didn't hesitate and hurried into the ranks as did the rest of them. Antorn noticed a dust cloud settling near the back of the building and made his way quickly to Pillip.

"Pillip, I think we have some dissenters, lets round them up," Antorn said.

Antorn pointed to the dust and Pillip nodded. He gave the command for a party of guardsmen to round up the stags and ordered the beasts heads to be secured into the ground leading to the main building.

"Let's go make sure Tage has made his exit and start this. Tobis, secure the buildings, and make the declaration known to the people," Antorn said.

Tobis saluted and took his troops and started toward the buildings. Antorn was glad it didn't come to shedding the blood of his own kind, there was going to be enough of that to come, but he wasn't sure Tage wasn't going to find a way to cause trouble. It did make him wonder why he was so intent on getting him into the stocks. What was it exactly that Tage was upset about? He barely even knew him prior to their run-in when Antorn became the leader of the about to be formed Forrne Guard. Antorn pushed the thoughts out of his mind and went to help secure the buildings.

23- Who Had This Castle Before Your Parents?

Phanes left the castle at a quick pace and the Minca weren't too far behind. Riddick and Amirra took a few hours to gather supplies and rummage through the supply closet for items that might help, while Shaz fixed the portal. Amirra found a long skinny tube that elongated as she twisted it. She put her eye at the skinny end and jumped as she found Riddick's eyeball staring at her. She pulled away and found Riddick on the other side of the large closet.

"Oh fantastic, a seeing eyeglass, that will come in handy," Riddick said.

Amirra handed the seeing eyeglass to him, and he slipped it into the side pocket of his satchel. Riddick bumped a box and caught it before it toppled to the ground. Several jars clinked inside, and he snagged one as it fell out. Amirra took the jar, and he rested the box back on the shelf. Amirra studied the script and tapped her chin as she thought about the words.

"What is it?" Riddick asked.

"A potion that makes a person undetectable," Amirra said. Riddick's face lit up, and he took the jar from her. "Do you think that will help?"

"Aye, does it say what the components are?"

Amirra shook her head. Riddick pulled the stopper and inhaled the aroma. The image that came to his mind was curious, but not complete.

"Can you tell what's in it?"

"Partially, but this is quite complex,"

"I wonder if Helios would have any information, or maybe Inelius,"

"If we can find out, I think it could come in handy, the Jaduuk 'see' with their noses better than their eyes, so if we can disguise ourselves we would have quite an advantage,"

"I'll go ask,"

She left the supply room and searched the rooms until she found Helios in the library with Inelius.

"May I interrupt?" Amirra asked.

Helios turned in his chair.

"Of course, what can we help with?" Helios asked.

Amirra handed him the bottle.

"This is a potion that disguises the scent of something, but there's no list of ingredients, would you by chance know?" Amirra asked.

Helios examined the bottle and handed the blue glass jar to Inelius who studied the marks and handed it back.

"I am not sure, let's see if there is some information somewhere," Inelius said. Inelius snapped his fingers and his magic search spell popped into existence. The diligent finder scurried around the library but didn't find anything, then started toward the door. "You better follow it," Inelius said.

Amirra hurried after the magic to a door at the end of a hall-way on the back side of the castle behind the meeting rooms, but when she went to open it, the latch was locked.

"Hang on, I'll go get Shaz," Amirra said.

The magic bounced and Amirra thought the magic arrow actually agreed and then hurried to find Shaz. She found him in the portal room and waited until he finished the last of his instructions to realign the Timeless Plains portal.

"Do you have a minute?" Shaz turned and Amirra could tell the magic had taken a substantial amount of his energy. "Are you alright?" Amirra asked.

Shaz pulled in a deep breath and nodded but grabbed the edge of the chair next to the small table.

"What's up?" Shaz asked.

"Are you sure you're alright?" Amirra asked.

"Serin will be here in a second or two," Shaz said.

Serin rounded the entrance and moved passed Amirra. Serin sent a boost of her hydro-light magic and did a quick scan of his vitals, especially his heartfire. He wiped the sweat from his brows and sighed as her magic ran through his frame.

"You didn't tell me you were doing this right now," Serin said.

"Aye, sorry, I'm never sure what is going to take so much magic and what isn't," Shaz said.

Serin pulled a bubble of water from the air and handed the wobbly sphere to Shaz who slurped the liquid.

"That took a lot of magic," Serin said.

"Why, I wonder," Shaz said.

"We'll have to research that when we can," Serin said.

"What do you need Amirra?" Shaz asked.

"I was looking for a list of ingredients to a potion I found and Inelius' magic lead me to a locked door," Amirra said.

Shaz stood a bit taller and peered at Amirra who squirmed.

"Take me," Shaz said.

Serin walked with Shaz who followed Amirra out of the room and through the castle to a part she hadn't been before.

"Have you been in this part of the castle?" Serin asked.

"No, but this castle seems to have many secrets," Shaz said.

Serin did a quick scan and found everything to be normal, but she interpreted his uneasiness and her guts twisted. They came down the long hall and found the magic sparkles dancing in the air. Shaz reached for the handle but pulled back.

"What is it?" Serin asked.

"I'm not sure, but there is shadow magic in there," Shaz said.

"What? How? Wouldn't you have sensed it before now?" Serin asked.

"Aye, but I don't think this part of the castle was accessible before, just like the portal room," Shaz said.

"Can you get in?" Serin asked.

"We don't have to, it's just a potion that makes a person undetectable, I don't want to make any trouble," Amirra said.

Shaz gave her a reassuring smile and Serin touched her arm. Shaz held his hand over the latch and allowed the energy to sink into his awareness and then did the same at the door itself. Riddick came down the hall and stopped next to Amirra.

"What's going on?" Riddick asked.

"This is where the magic brought me to find the potion, but it has shadow magic and the door is locked," Amirra said quietly.

"Riddick, can you do a scan of the other side?" Shaz asked.

Riddick reached out his magic and interpreted the image he got in return.

"I'm not sure what to think," Riddick said.

"Aye, girls, I want you two to back up," Shaz said.

"No way," Serin said and Amirra shook her head sternly.

"Didn't think so," Shaz said.

Shaz squeezed the latch and commanded the lever to unlock, but it didn't. Shaz stood back and called his magic from his core and rounded it into a spere and sent it into the door. The wood-looking door faded away and a heavy odor of stale air and nothing good hit their senses and the magic zoomed through the opening. Amirra put up her mind shield on everyone and Shaz stepped over the threshold. The blackness lifted as Shaz commanded the fire element to his hand and looked around. The long stone hallway was covered in a heavy film of dust that stuck to the moist grit of the rotations gone by. Riddick stepped in behind and shuddered at the energy of the entrance. Serin and Amirra too shuddered as they stepped through.

Rows and rows of heavy steel-barred doors sat encased in thick stone cells and chains draped across from one side to the other.

"Is this a dungeon?" Serin asked.

"Aye," Shaz said.

"Why does the castle have a dungeon?" Serin asked.

"All proper castles do, it's a safety measure," Riddick said.

"But why?" Serin asked.

Shaz turned to her and found her face full of shock and disgust.

"Serin, what do you think castles are for?" Shaz asked.

Serin's stomach churned as she understood what he was asking.

"War," Serin said softly.

"I'm sorry love, but yes, war. Castles are strongholds, and places designed to build forces, which also means there is a need for dungeons," Shaz said.

Amirra took Serin's hand and gave it a squeeze.

"Where did the magic go?" Amirra asked.

Shaz turned back toward the aisle and caused the fire element to light the torches on the walls.

"I'll search for it if you like," Shaz said.

The girls agreed and Shaz and Riddick made a quick sweep around the corridors. They found the magic at the back of the square structure pointing to a cell door that was still shut. Shaz stopped next to the gate and carefully peeked around the corner. He pulled the cold steel open and went into the cell. A skeleton of very old bones wrapped in disintegrating cloth laid at the back.

"I wonder how long this has been here," Shaz asked.

He didn't want to think about the fact that his father would have imprisoned anyone, but there was clearly the remains to prove it.

"These are way older than your parents, probably more than a few millennia," Riddick said.

"How can you tell?" Shaz asked.

"The bones have a different composition than anything I have ever seen before," Riddick said.

"How many skeletons have you seen?" Shaz asked with one brow raised.

"Well, not many, but bone matter isn't too much different than earth matter, and I can tell this has components similar to the island indicating it's just as old," Riddick said.

The magic held its position like a trained hunting dog until Shaz knelt next to the bones and reached under the side and pulled out another notebook. The text on the outside was indeed from millennia ago. Shaz flipped through the pages and understood the pages to be a combination of secret records, but most of it he couldn't read right off and was sure he was going to have to decode it. He put the book in the inside pocket of his jerkin and started to leave when another item caught his eye. He gently lifted the fading cloth from the rib cage of the body and found an item of such curious workmanship he had no words to describe it. Shaz reached under the bones and lifted it up.

"What is that?" Riddick asked.

"I have no idea, this the oddest thing I've ever seen," Shaz said.

"Did that man eat it before he died?" Riddick asked.

"Appears so, but why, that's what I want to know," Shaz said.

"Shaz," Serin called.

"Let's go," Shaz said.

They returned to the girls who had worried eyes, and they left the dungeon and Shaz locked the latch again.

"Did you find it?" Serin asked.

Shaz held out the book and motioned for them to leave the passageway. They returned to the library where they met Helios and Inelius and Shaz helped Amirra de crypt the ingredients for the potion. Riddick was confident he could grow all the plants if he had their information, so they went on a book hunt to find them. Shaz wanted to ask Inelius about the 'thing' he found but a nagging at the back of his mind told him not to and Serin studied him intently. He could tell she was focused on what he was feelings and tried to hide them from her, and she scowled.

"Shaz can I talk to you," Serin said.

"I know, come on," Shaz said.

He took her hand and lead her out to the courtyard.

"Something is wrong isn't it?" Serin asked.

"Not wrong, but odd for sure, maybe a bit of unknown, well, a lot of unknown," Shaz said.

Serin's brows scrunched, and she stopped in front of him and crossed her arms over her chest. Shaz chuckled, she was quite cute when she tried to be stern with him.

"I'm not kidding Shaz," Serin said.

"I'm certain of that, I just don't have an answer for you," Shaz said.

Serin scowled harder and puckered her lips tightly. Shaz pulled the item from his jerkin and handed the strange piece to Serin.

"What is it?" Serin asked taking the 'thing'.

"I haven't a clue. We found a skeleton, and this was inside its chest as if the person swallowed it before they died. Riddick is certain this happened long before my parent's time, and I got the same impression," Shaz said.

"Who had this castle before your parents?" Serin asked.

"I have no idea actually. I guess that's a question for Inelius, or the Whispmother," Shaz said.

"That notebook was very old too," Serin said.

"Aye, it's only still intact because of magic, otherwise the paper would have faded millennia ago," Shaz said.

"And that was shadow magic that secured the entrance?" Serin asked.

"Aye," Shaz said.

"So, that was before your parents too," Shaz nodded. "Are you going to ask Inelius what this is?" Serin asked.

"No, not yet, I don't feel right about it, but maybe the earth portal," Shaz said.

Serin handed it back to Shaz who put it into his jerkin pocket.

"I wonder who the person was?" Serin said as they started back inside.

"Aye, and why were they here," Shaz said.

"Looks like we have something else to add to our to-do list," Serin said.

"I guess so," Shaz said as he ran his hands through his hair.

Serin smiled at him, but she understood he was

overwhelmed. Serin stopped just before they reached the door.

"Are you doing alright?" Serin asked.

"As good as can be expected I guess," Shaz said.

"What can I do?" Serin asked.

"I just need to keep busy," Shaz said.

Serin was certain that was not what he needed to do, but she understood the cycle of grief and let him be.

"I'm here for you," Serin said.

"Aye, I'm certain of that," Shaz said.

Shaz pulled her into a hug and kissed her then they made their way to the portal room. Riddick and Amirra came into the room.

"You two ready?" Shaz asked.

"Aye," Riddick said.

Shaz pulled out the map of the Timeless Plains and showed it to Riddick.

"This is where the new portal is supposed to be," Shaz said.

"Supposed to be, what kind of war wizard are you?" Riddick said.

Shaz looked up with a mixed expression and Riddick blurted a hearty ga-fa and slapped him on the shoulder. Shaz shook his head.

"You better be going before I lock you in there," Shaz said.

Riddick looked at Shaz with a mixed expression and Shaz blurted the hearty ga-fa.

"We're going," Amirra said and took Riddick's hand and started through the portal. Riddick gave Shaz a 'you just wait' expression just before he faded into the mist.

24-Things Are Not Looking Good

Riddick stuck his head out of the portal and found the savanna was quite warm and the air was heavy. The mid-day light was barely more than early dusk, and he understood what Shaz meant about the sun not shining, and he agreed that the weather was way too warm for the place. He made a quick scan of the surroundings, both with his eyes and his magic and then stepped out. Amirra followed, and she coughed as the air sank into her senses. The soft oranges of the sun's rays gave them the impression of the sunset back home and gave a soothing but odd sensation.

"This is quite beautiful, but kind of odd," Amirra said.

Riddick pulled out the map and started to examine the surroundings. He noted the few landmarks Shaz and Serin had noted and made a few of his own marks with a writer's tool.

"Aye, Shaz said we would find the scorched earth this way. I think I want to start there to determine if we can find the Jaduuk,"

Riddick said.

"How long is the time here?" Amirra asked.

"About the same as Ebassia, slightly slower is all," Riddick said.

"So, does that make the day's longer or shorter?" Amirra asked while rolling her eyes around her head to figure out the calculations.

"Longer, come on this way," Riddick said.

Amirra followed Riddick through the tall grasses and tried not to be distracted by the newness of the surroundings. She was glad that there was a distant mountain range, which meant she wouldn't think the sky wasn't going to fall on her, but she wasn't sure what would trigger another panic attack. Amirra couldn't help being bothered that it even happened and even though Riddick kept assuring her she was doing alright, she didn't think so.

Patches of short stalky trees speckled the landscape and the gently rolling hills blended into the hilltop they were about to come to. The tall beige grasses that mixed with the rag-weeds gave a familiar scent to the air, but a hint of pitch tickled his senses, and Riddick understood it to be from the scorched earth. His magic indicated they needed to head toward the sun for several lengths, but he also received an image that there were large animals milling about the vast flatlands.

Riddick's initial inspection noted the area would be large enough to house several armies, and he made a few more notes on his map. He took out the looking glass and twisted the device until the distance came into view. The beige grasses merged into dusty greens, and he made out several more patches of trees.

"This place is so big. How long would it take to get to that mountain range?" Amirra asked.

"Without magic, several days," Riddick said.

"That's what I thought," Amirra said.

"I want to check out the scorched land, let's go this way, but we'll travel by magic," Riddick said with a grin.

"How?" Amirra asked.

Riddick wrapped his arm around her and tucked her close to his body, and he called his geo-kinetic magic. A slender oval piece of the ground they were standing on ripped from the rest of it and Amirra threw her arms out to steady herself. Riddick moved his feet so that they were spaced apart and facing partially sideways.

"Stand like this, with your feet between mine," Riddick said.

Amirra moved her feet like his, and he sat back a little to give his body the ability to maneuver the new movements, and Amirra followed. He put his hand facing the ground and his rusty orange light illuminated the land-disc and it started moving forward. Amirra tried not to make too many movements but she found it hard to keep her balance. Riddick brought her closer to his body, and she settled in close and found it easier to just let him lead. It didn't take long, and they were gliding over the landscape with ease. The warm wind rushed over their bodies and through their hair.

Amirra was soon comfortable on the land-board and started pointing out the animals they were approaching. Riddick steered the hovering earth around a large herd of short, stalky, and bulbous-like creatures that were wallowing around a watering-hole that was more than half-way dried up. The savanna beasts casually gazed at them as they raced by but a few skittered. Riddick made note of the different kinds of animal life there was from the field beasts to the birds and the creeping lizards. The sun was shifting toward the horizon, and they had yet to come across any Jaduuk and Riddick was starting to wonder where they were. They hadn't come across the Forrne either and his mind raced around several scenarios and a knot formed in his guts.

Riddick slowed as they came to the place Shaz had indicated

they had seen the scorched earth and searched. The grasses they were racing over began to shrivel and the rich brown dirt was soon replaced with pitch black. Riddick sat backward bringing Amirra with him to slow the hovering earth to a stop and let the earth settle to the ground. They stepped off and took a half-second to regain their bearings on solid ground.

"That was amazing," Amirra said.

"Aye, but look," Riddick said.

"I take it this is the scorched earth," Amirra said.

"Looks like it," Riddick said.

Riddick bent down and scooped the blackened dirt into his hand and found there was more than that. The dirt was burnt to a crisp as if earth could burn, which puzzled him. He absorbed the energy particles and let the identifiers group together in his mind.

"This is a very old magic, similar to the Cy'ad tree but on the evil side," Riddick said.

"That doesn't sound good," Amirra said.

Riddick nodded, and dropped the dirt and brushed off his hands.

"There's also the mix of something else, I can't figure out, but there's a familiarity to the Jaduuk, it's almost as if there's a life force to it," Riddick said.

"A creature that is similar in nature as the Jaduuk, maybe?" Amirra asked.

"Aye, but also from millennia's ago," Riddick said.

"That's really not good," Amirra said.

"Tell me what you see," Riddick said.

"Me? Why me?" Amirra asked.

"Because you're soul magic, if there is a life force maybe you will see something I don't," Riddick said.

Amirra's eyes were wide, but she thought about the idea and

it did make sense.

"Alright," Amirra said.

She bent down and scooped up some of the dirt and a sudden rush of shadow magic shot to her brain, and she jerked away and dropped the dirt and rubbed her hand.

"What is it?" Riddick asked.

"Shadow magic," Amirra said.

"That's what Shaz said too," Riddick said.

"Why can I sense shadow magic?" Amirra asked.

"Because shadow magic has the essence of the Shadow's soul and you have experienced it?" Riddick offered.

"I guess," Amirra said.

"What else did you see?" Riddick asked.

"Nothing, I dropped it too soon," Amirra admitted.

"Try again," Riddick said.

"I really don't want to," Amirra said.

"I know, but we need to know what we are up against," Riddick said.

Amirra nodded, and sucked in. She closed her mind to the Shadow, but let the images of what the soul of the shadow was telling her about. A misty and blurry image surfaced of an incredibly large creature that looked like the remnants of a Jaduuk, but she couldn't tell for sure as the formation was simply the image of the soul and not its actual frame. She could tell it was very angry and had a score to settle with someone or something. She was reminded of the way Semias started to behave the more depraved he became, and she tried to focus through the unpleasant memories. Amirra was getting stronger and learning to overcome her past and was pleased with her efforts.

Riddick watched as her sun-yellow magic emerged from her skin and radiated around the minerals she was moving around in her hands. The shimmering magic danced around and then faded back into her hands, and she dropped the substance.

"We are up against something I can't even describe, but it's extremely large and angry with a score to settle with someone or something," Amirra said.

"Sound's lovely," Riddick said.

"No, I don't think so," Amirra teased.

Riddick chuckled.

"Let's keep going, I have a notion we will find the Jaduuk this way," Riddick said pointing in the direction the scorched earth was coming from and Amirra agreed.

Riddick waved for Amirra to return to him, she scooted in next to him and he called the earth board again. They lifted off the ground and this time Amirra steadied herself well and was pleased she didn't feel wobbly. Riddick maneuvered at a quick pace but not as fast as before and sent out his search and detect energy as he went. Each time the vibrations returned, his mind added more details to the map he was making in his head.

They crossed the scorched earth several times and made note that the marks were forming in vein-like patterns similar to the ones they saw in the ocean and wondered if whatever the thing was, was a similar entity as the island. Riddick hoped not because that meant they were going to be going up against ancient magic that was more powerful than they were. Riddick caught a whiff of Jaduuk and slowed even more. They hunched on the earth-craft to reduce their appearance and spotted a small patch of stalky trees that were still alive in between two veins and veered toward them.

The sun was cresting the horizon, but the atmosphere was still as light as dark-dusk, and Riddick shook his head with amazement.

"I smell Jaduuk," Riddick said.

"I do too, they are quite odiferous," Amirra said.

Riddick snorted and let the earth set down on the ground. He pulled out his looking glass and arranged the lenses as he peered through them. His stomach lurched to his throat and he gasped.

"What's wrong?" Amirra asked.

Riddick handed her the looking glass, and she searched the distance. Her stomach lurched and she wanted to hurl.

"Are those all Jaduuk?" Amirra asked.

"Aye," Riddick said.

"There must be hundreds of thousands, an entire civilization, like ants in an anthill, or worse," Amirra said.

"Aye," Riddick said.

"Things are not looking good," Amirra said.

"No, let's swing around this way and then head back," Riddick said.

Amirra agreed and stepped close to Riddick's warm body. The evening wasn't cold but the drop in temperature was enough to make her feel more comfortable next to him. They started out toward the darkening part of the sky and Riddick was certain they needed to be quick as they were heading into night and it was going to get harder to see, unless the sky stayed like this, which Shaz said it did. He still didn't want to be there more than he had to.

Riddick sent out another surge of vibrations and the return image stifled his breathing. He gripped Amirra tightly and shoved his feet into the earth. He sat backward and threw his feet in an arc to turn around. The hovering earth rounded in a tight arc and Riddick shoved his forces against the ground, so they wouldn't fall off as he rounded the wave-like air pattern and rolled back to standing after they were facing the other direction. Amirra's stomach churned but the thrill raced endorphins through her body. Sweat formed under her cloak and her heart surged with excitement. Riddick shot back the other way and rounded toward the side and found a small ravine and ducked under the short trees that were lining the bottom.

Amirra squatted hard with Riddick's movements, and they shot under the branches at a quick pace. Amirra was having more fun than she thought she should be, and Riddick sensed her enthusiasm and smiled.

He was having a fantastic time riding the earth this way and that and found a bit of his own excitement surge. Shaz was going to have the time of his life with this, and he couldn't wait to show him, and just think how fast they could move with Serin's air buff on top of it. Adrenaline raced through his body, and he rolled over the branch before they would have slammed into it. He regained his bearings and weaved in and out of the branches and smaller bushes until the ravine came to an end.

Riddick decided they needed to stay on task and shoved his feet into the air buffer, and they came to an abrupt stop. Amirra's heart was racing with the thrill, and she was breathing heavily.

"Are you alright?" Riddick asked.

"Alright? I'm better than alright!" Amirra said excitedly. Riddick chuckled. "That was something else, I have no words for that," Amirra said.

"Aye, that was a rush, but we need to be quiet, and find out what is on the other side of this ridge on foot, I'm getting a bad feeling, but we need to check it out," Riddick said.

The glee in Amirra's face quickly turned sour, and she stepped off the hovering earth. They scaled the first few lengths of the ravine and then it started to level out. Riddick lowered to the ground and Amirra followed. Her heart raced, and she suddenly felt the need to wretch.

"What is that stink?" Amirra asked.

"I have no idea," Riddick said.

His face puckered as the odor confused his senses and he stopped. Riddick tucked his head under the tall grass and nearly crawled to the top of the ridge. Riddick slipped his hand through the grass and parted the blades a tiny length and reached out with his energy. An image surfaced and he moved a little closer. He covered his nose and examined the valley below. His stomach nearly lost its contents, and he gagged.

"What is it?" Amirra asked.

She wanted to know but if it was making Riddick sick it had to be bad.

"Jaduuk as far as the eye can see," Riddick said.

Amirra scooted around him and peeked through the beige grass. Her heart surged through her throat and then plummeted into her guts.

"Are those the Forrne?" Amirra asked.

"Aye," Riddick said.

"What happened?" Amirra asked her voice shaky.

"Over there," Riddick said.

Riddick motioned to the side where a sizable pack of Jaduuk were feeding on the remains.

"I think I'm going to be sick," Amirra said.

"Let's go," Riddick said.

Riddick and Amirra scooted backward the way they came.

"This isn't good, now what?" Amirra asked.

"We need to get back to the castle," Riddick said.

Amirra stepped next to Riddick, and he summoned his earth-craft and started back slowly and quietly but the bristling of the grasses sounded louder than before, and his nerves ached.

25-More Jaduuk I'm Afraid

The day quickly slipped into night and the season was start-ing to cool down leaving a crispness in the air. Serin packed a few heavily weaved long-sleeved tunics the Whispmother had made for her, which of course meant they were embellished with a feminine flare which Serin liked. She wasn't concerned and was content to wear a simpler style, but she did like the way the dressier clothes made her feel. The style of her clothes wasn't something she thought about before, but now that she had nice things, she liked it.

Serin had helped the Whispmother with the design of her leggings, and they were also heavier and the Whispmother was able to replicate Amirra's enchantment that held in the heat better, and she had also learned how to make Shaz's clothes more fireproof, since he commonly found himself without a shirt and singed pants every time he lit himself on fire. Riddick even chimed in on how to alter the molecular structure of the cloth to make them stronger to withstand the heat and wear and tear, which the Whispmother was thankful for because that meant their things lasted longer. Serin finished tying her knee-high boots and slung her bag over her head and situated the strap on her side.

"I hope this won't take long, look after everyone," Serin said.

The Whispmother floated down from the eaves of the room and hovered in front of Serin.

"I don't like having to say goodbye," the Whispmother sang.

"Me either, but I'm afraid things aren't going to be any better for quite some time," Serin said.

"I agree," the Whispmother said.

"I have a question, do you know who owned this castle before the O'Connon's?" Serin asked.

"No, one, this has been the O'Connon's for millennia's, but they weren't always called by the name of O'Connon," the Whispmother sang.

"Interesting," Serin said.

"You are wondering who was in the dungeons, aren't you?" the Whispmother asked.

"I am very curious, yes, but that is for Shaz to ask," Serin said.

"For me to ask what?" Shaz asked.

Serin turned to find Shaz standing at the door.

"Who the person in the dungeon was. The Whispmother said your family has always owned the castle," Serin said.

Shaz crossed the room and the Whispmother hovered near him.

"Do you remember when I told you about the Sev-Rin-Ac-Lavah, when you first arrived at the castle?" the Whispmother asked.

"Aye," Shaz said.

"I didn't tell you many things because I wasn't sure what you knew or didn't," the Whispmother said.

"Alright," Shaz half-asked-half-stated.

"This castle isn't only yours because it belonged to your father, this is the last of its kind. This castle has a magic that belongs to the eons before. This is your castle because you belong to the house of Alisdair. That was no accident you were chosen by the elements to return in time to help Alisdair. You have inherited all that he possessed, it was willed by him," the Whispmother said.

The Whispmother materialized a parchment and floated the scroll toward Shaz who let it drift into his hands. Shaz unrolled the scroll and read the text. The writing was the same style as the time tablet and his heart pounded as the words hit his mind. An intense understanding secured the many nights he and Alisdair stood staring at each other through some kind of time portal. Not like the portals from realm to realm where the time turns at different rates, or the earth portals, that share information of the events of history, but actually through time. Serin read his energy but decided it wasn't her right to ask him what it said.

"The remains you found belong to Enric, the last war wizard. He was your kinsman many generations ago. He was tasked to protect the item you found until the next war wizard found it," the Whispmother said.

"Is that why the dungeon is protected by shadow magic?" Shaz asked.

"Yes, he placed the barrier there and then isolated himself in his last days so that no one would find him or the item. He secured the dungeon the way a wizards keep is fortified," the Whispmother said.

"Do you know what this is?" Shaz asked.

"No, that is for you to figure out," the Whispmother said.

"How long have you been here at the castle?" Serin asked.

"Since its creation," the Whispmother said.

"Did you know Alisdair?" Shaz asked.

"Yes," the Whispmother said.

"Did Enric?" Shaz asked.

"No, but you will want to study the notebook he carried. There are many ancient secrets you need to be aware of, that only a war wizard can access," the Whispmother said.

Shaz pulled out the notebook and thumbed through the pages.

"I'm assuming you can read the invisible language," Serin said.

Shaz looked at her with a curious eye.

"You can't see any writing?" Shaz asked.

"Nope, oh wait, turn back," Serin said.

Shaz handed her the book, and she flipped back a few pages and pointed to the text.

"I can read that," Serin said.

"Makes sense, this is talking about the war wizards bonding," Shaz said.

"I like being bonded to you, by the way," Serin said with a playful glint in her eye.

Shaz smiled and tucked the book back into his pocket.

"Even though I'm stubborn?" Shaz asked.

"Yes, because you are stubborn, and I'm just stubborn enough to put up with you," Serin said.

"Aye, you sure are," Shaz said.

"Let's go get this started," Serin said.

They quickly made their way to the portal room and Shaz made the needed instruction to the portals and Serin secured her pack.

"You ready," Shaz asked.

"Yes, let's go," Serin said.

Serin stepped into the portal and the energy tickled her skin. She was more use to the sensation now and there was an interesting comfort she didn't expect. Serin felt the tug on her body as the magic pulled her toward the other side, but she studied the stars as they whizzed by. She was amazed every time how the universe was all around her, and she was safe in a tunnel of powerful energy that transported her to another time and place. Even though they were staying in the same realm this time, she couldn't comprehend the magnitude of the cosmos and the powers they held. She turned to find Shaz right behind her and then the mist on the other side emerged. She put her hand out and the film parted.

The soft glow of the moon's rays that came into the Senate Sanctum eased into her senses, and she took a quick inventory as she stepped out. Shaz too ran through his checklist as he entered the room and found everything to be in order.

"Glad to find everything is still alright," Serin said.

Serin buffed them with wind-walk and they hurried to Ebassia. At the rate, they traveled with the magic they should reach the city gates by early dawn. The coolness of the night left their breath to puff into the night and the moons were sitting further from the earth. The constant mist was cold and the ground underneath their feet crackled from the impending frost. Serin tightened her cloak and was thankful for the warmth it gave. The edge of the forest came into view and the magic started to wear off. They had learned to recognize when the buff was wearing off and slowed their paces, so they wouldn't run off the magic and feel like they were slamming into an invisible wall. The pitch of the working district eased into their senses as they came onto the main road on the forest side of the city.

"Do you have papers?" the guard asked.

"No, but we are here to see Bowen," Shaz said.

"No, papers, no entrance," the guard said.

"Can you at least send a message to Bowen please," Serin said.

"No, now get out of here," the guard barked.

"I'm not sure you want to do that," Serin said.

"Oh, I think I am," the guard growled.

The guard jumped toward them in an effort to scare them, but they didn't budge. Shaz stared at him considering the different options and Serin smirked when he ran through his mind one of her techniques to inflict pain without leaving any marks.

"Fine, we will just go to the main gate and let them know you refused Shaz entrance into the city," Serin said.

The guard blinked and stared, but they could tell a spike of confusion hit his brain. Bowen had told them that they would always be able to get into the city, and Shaz wondered what might be the issue. They started back down the road and toward the city's main gates. It would take several lengths to reach, and they weren't exactly pleased, but they didn't want to make a fuss either.

"Shaz, wait, come back," a guard called.

Shaz and Serin turned around and found a different guard waving them to come back.

"I'm so sorry, we have been in the process of training new recruits and it would seem we need to make sure they are all aware of who you are, please accept our apology," the guard said.

"No trouble, thank you," Shaz said.

Shaz held out his hand for the man to greet and the guard took it eagerly.

"It's a great honor, where may we escort you?" the man said.

Serin admired his round rosy cheeks and jolly eyes tucked under thick brown eyebrows. The traditional soldiers' gear had a slight change to them and Serin decided she liked them. She also wondered if Deagan had had a say in the design change and smiled. The man heaved open the gate and let them in.

"We actually need to see Bowen and the Queen right away," Shaz said.

The man's delightful expression turned solid.

"Is there anything wrong?" the guard asked.

"I'm afraid so," Shaz said.

The man gulped.

"May I ask what it might be? I was one of the soldiers that went with Riddick and Bowen to finish off the Jaduuk," the man said with a proud but cracked voice. The man waved down a wagon, and they made their way toward the side street.

"More Jaduuk I'm afraid," Shaz said.

"But not here in Ebassia," Serin said.

The man sighed with relief.

"But that means we're going to go somewhere else," the man said.

Shaz nodded, and the guard sucked in a deep breath but turned his worried grimace into stern commitment and Shaz decided he liked him.

26-We Have A Situation

The guard operated the wagon through the early morning people which was nice because there weren't too many yet. The clack of the wheels against the cobblestone road echoed off the stone buildings and the clop of the horse's feet had a sharper click and Serin guessed it was the colder weather. The sun cast long shadows over the tops of the aqueducts that were suspended high over the roads and smaller buildings as they made their way toward the castle.

"Open the gates," the guard barked.

The second gate to the castle opened and the horse whinnied as it waited. They passed through the stronghold and noticed several people take second glances and then wave with bright expressions.

"Looks like your still a hero around here," Serin said.

"So, it would seem," Shaz said.

Shaz didn't want all the attention but figured it would be

rude if he didn't at least acknowledge their efforts. He waved casually and nodded a few times and was glad when they entered the last set of gates into the main grounds of the castle. The guard stopped the wagon, and they hopped out and followed him into the grand lobby. The man turned and gave instructions to inform the Queen and Bowen and then returned.

"Is there anything else I can assist you with," the guard asked.

"No, thank you, but I hope to meet you again," Shaz said.

The man nodded with a slight bow and left the castle.

"Wow, it looks great in here, Deagan sure has done a great job," Serin said.

Shaz looked around and noted the details and nodded but Serin could tell he didn't really notice the differences, and she smiled.

"Shaz, what is the matter," Bowen boomed.

Serin jumped and Shaz turned with a slight start to a red-faced Bowen barreling down the hallway.

"Bowen, so good to see you," Serin said.

Shaz shook his hand but could sense the knot in his stomach. Bowen pulled Serin into an embrace and gave her a wink.

"I'm afraid we have a situation, and we have come to ask for your help," Shaz said.

"Serin," squealed Oladesni from the adjacent hallway. Serin turned and hurried to her and gave her a tight squeeze. Oladesni pulled back and peered into her eyes.

"Is everything alright, the message said it was extremely urgent, didn't even put my day clothes on," Oladesni said with a little chuckle.

"I'm so happy to be here, but yes we have an urgent matter we need to discuss," Serin said.

"Bowen let's go to one of the meeting rooms," Oladesni said.

Oladesni escorted them to one of the meeting rooms and gave instructions to bring some breakfast and closed the door. Shaz pulled the map of the Timeless Plains and unfolded and set it on the table.

"This is the Timeless Plains, a realm at the edge of the planet. Riddick and Amirra have gone to do recon but Gavin Rhill is growing a Jaduuk army there. The land is being scorched and animals and critters are on the move. The intelligent species are the Forrne, a dear-like creature, but we have no information yet on their circumstances. A bird notified me of this while we were in the Minca's realm, but we had to deal with Isot first, with that being said, I have a feeling we're going to be up against an overwhelming number of Jaduuk. This is not going to be an easy task and will take time to whittle them all down. So, before you agree, I need you to understand this," Shaz said.

"How many are you talking?" Bowen asked.

"How many can you spare," Shaz asked.

Bowen was positive that was going to be his answer, but he hoped it wouldn't be.

"I figured," Bowen turned to Oladesni who had a concerned expression under light-pink cheeks. Her hair was down in her usual wavy locks and her dark-pink lips puckered into a thoughtful grimace. "Your Highness?" Bowen asked.

"I think there might be someone you might want to meet," Oladesni said.

Shaz stood up with a bit of anticipation but shoved his hands in his pockets. Oladesni rose from her chair and gave instructions to the soldier outside.

"We also have an armada of gryphton's that will be coming and the Minca and their explosions specialists," Shaz said.

"Explosions specialists?" Bowen asked.

"That sounds hazardous," Oladesni said.

Shaz and Serin turned to find a gleeful snicker behind her small hands, and they smiled. A knock on the door startled Oladesni who was still standing right next to it, and she opened it. A young but muscular man with light-brown hair about Shaz's height stood outside the door and Shaz instantly recognized him as a Ranger. It wasn't his physical features that clued him in, but his energy. He held the same aura signature as Merrick, and he was certain he was a born Ranger, not just a trained Ranger. Shaz's heart skipped and Oladesni invited the man into the room and closed the door.

"This is Declan, a Ranger from Hammerstead," Oladesni said.

"How do you do?" Declan said.

"Declan this is Shaz, Reinholt and Merrick's son, and his companion Serin," Oladesni said.

Declan's hazel-green eyes popped out of his strong brows which nearly left his forehead. Declan knelt on one knee and bowed his head low and Shaz wasn't sure what to say.

"Please, stand," Shaz said.

"Zis is honorrr," Declan said.

Declan rose to his feet and Shaz took his hand in the Rangers salute. Declan's heart skipped as he understood how much that meant to them for him to know the handshake of the brotherhood.

"I thought they were all gone," Serin said.

Declan turned to Serin and bowed deeply. Shaz knew it wasn't their custom to make such a fuss and to bow like that wasn't their way either, which made him wonder what was going on.

"May I ask where are you from?" Shaz asked.

"I vas borrrn in Hammerrrstead, but I vas small child when ve verrre locked avay frrrom rrrest of vorrrld. Some time ago shield just disappeared, but zings verrre so different zat it took time forrr us to figurrre out wherrre Ebassia even vas," Declan said.

"Aye, about the time I came through the barrier the first time. It must have removed the shield," Shaz said.

"You said RRReinholt and Merrrick's son," Declan half-asked.

"Reinholt was my father but died when I was a baby, Merrick raised me," Shaz said.

What is your intuition telling you? Shaz asked Serin in his mind.

He is genuine, but something's not right, I can't figure it out though, Serin returned.

Aye, Shaz agreed.

"Exkuse my behaviorrr, I know it's not vay of RRRangerrrs, but ve have been locked avay in ourrr village forrr so long zat zis is just overrrwhelming," Declan said.

"I wasn't aware Hammerstead was in a different realm," Serin said.

"It didn't use to be, just high in mountains but after last battle everrrything vas kut off," Declan said.

"That's when the islands of Srinna Vossa were sunk and the Queen cut off the realms," Serin said.

Serin didn't want to say it was her mother that ruined so much. She understood why, but she also understood that most people wouldn't understand.

"How many of you are left?" Shaz asked.

"Ve have substantial grrroup, while not being able to find rrrest of vorrrld, ve decided to crrreate ourrr own. I vas sent to find out what happened after barrrier changed and made my vay herrre. I vas quite surrrprrrised zat Queen and Boven herrre vas even avarrre of us, but I guess zis explains why," Declan said.

"My father will be most happy to find out about this," Shaz said.

"Wherrre is yourrr father? Zat vould make him rrrightful leader," Declan said.

"He is on an errand," Shaz said.

Declan nodded, he understood what that meant, but Shaz sensed a dread hit his heart.

"I have to ask you where your loyalties are," Shaz asked.

"To United Forrrces, unless zat is gone now too, zen I guess ourrr loyalties lie vith you, as son of RRReinholt and Merrrick," Declan said.

"Why?" Shaz asked.

"RRReinholt vas next in line to bekome leader of RRRangerrrs, and Merrrick after him, which vould default to you, since Merrrick is on errrand," Declan said.

"The Rangers don't do leaders based on birth," Shaz said.

"Trrrue, but I," Declan started.

"Who is your current leader?" Shaz asked.

"I am," Declan said.

Declan tried to hide the hesitation and insecurities and Shaz understood exactly how the young man felt.

"Well, then Declan, leader of the Rangers of Hammerstead, I am honored to accept your friendship and loyalties, but you are the leader and I honor you as such," Declan took Shaz's hand in the Rangers handshake and agreed, but Shaz could tell he didn't want to be the leader. "Excellent, then we have a lot to cover," Shaz said.

Shaz looked at Serin who gave him a smile, and he understood her inspection agreed. A servant dished plates of food onto a smaller table at the back of the room and set out dishes for them to help themselves. Serin dished Shaz a plate while he explained the situation in the Timeless Plains to Declan and Bowen and recapped the time in the Minca's realm. He tried to stay on topic, but it became evident that Declan was in great need to figure out what all had happened and was astonished at the events with Isot and the Biding of the Crypt.

Shaz did his best to fill him in on what he could, but a gnawing at the bottom of his guts, that he and Serin needed to go to Hammerstead, settled in. Bowen offered the details of the efforts he and the queen had made to increase the skills in the army to include fighting the Jaduuk and Declan explained his troops and the needs his people had, which was what he was there for.

They needed more land and medicines. Oladesni began arrangements to send them what they needed plus gave them more land to expand now that the boundaries were open.

"Ve have sizable forrrce, but ourrr veapons von't be up to parrr, ve don't have rrrunekaster to enchant ourrr gearrr vith needed skill points," Declan said.

"Amirra can do that, she is the Runecaster," Shaz said.

"I don't think she can do all that, plus Bowen's forces," Serin said.

"Maybe we can get Nitida to help," Shaz said.

"Nitida?" Declan asked.

"The Runecaster at the Mountain Temple," Declan nodded but Shaz could tell he wasn't sure exactly what that meant. "Are you familiar with elemental magic?" Shaz asked.

"I vas schooled in old days' knowledge, so in zeorrry, da," Declan admitted.

"Good," Shaz said.

"Vhy?" Declan asked.

"We'll be traveling by wind," Shaz said.

The twinkle in Shaz's eye gave Declan and unsettled sensation and he studied his face.

"You arrre elemental of airrr?" Declan asked.

"No, well yes, I'm a war wizard, but Serin is the wind and water mage," Declan looked around the room and no one was laughing or snickering, and he found no indication they were playing a joke on him. Shaz was curious about Declan, he seemed to understand what was going on, mostly, but there was definitely a gap somewhere and Shaz wasn't sure what all he understood. "Bowen, how long until you can get your troops ready?" Shaz asked.

"I'll need a few days," Bowen said.

"What kind of medics do you have?" Serin asked.

"We have medics in the ranks, they'll be sufficient," Bowen said reassuringly.

"Alright, make ready to leave, here," Shaz pointed to a mark near the rear of the castle next to the large barracks.

"How?" Bowen asked.

"By portals of course. When Riddick gets back, and we have a better idea what we are up against we will solidify our strategies, but Riddick needs time to strengthen all the armor and make it lighter," Shaz said.

"I'm excited to see that," He stood from the table and scooted his chair back in and started toward the door. "I'll see you in a few days," Bowen said.

"Aye," Shaz said.

"Serin do you have just a minute?" Oladesni asked.

Serin nodded, and excused herself, and she followed Oladesni into the hall.

"Is everything alright?" Serin asked.

"Yes, well no, well yes, I don't know," Oladesni said. Serin sensed her mixed feelings and gave her a little burst of calming energy and Oladesni smiled. "This is going to sound dumb, and it's certainly not important, so never mind," Oladesni said.

"I think he likes you too, you should just ask him to join you for a walk around the courtyard every day at noon and things will work out the way they should," Serin said.

"Oh, my goodness, how can you tell?" Oladesni blushed.

Serin was amazed at how red her cheeks turned, and she chuckled.

"I'm a girl, and I can sense it in you," Oladesni sighed but blushed again. "You'll have to point him out to me," Serin said.

"I'm so embarrassed," Oladesni said.

"You have every right to be happy," Serin said.

Shaz opened the door, and he and Declan left the room and started down the hall.

"You coming?" Shaz asked.

"Yes, of course, I'll be right there," Serin said. "If you need an excuse at first, tell him you need the escort as part of your daily routine."

"Alright, I'll do it," Oladesni said.

"Good, and I'm going to check on you when we come back," Serin said.

Oladesni blushed again and gave Serin a hug who then hurried after Shaz.

27-Repeat This To Antorn

Tobis returned with only a few of the council members and locked them in a smaller building until Antorn returned to talk to them. The day was now evening and Antorn made his way from the last of the grain storage containers after making assessments on how to organize the food and rations.

"Antorn we are ready for your questioning of the prisoners," Tobis said.

"They are not prisoners, yet, they haven't been given all the information," Antorn said.

"Yes, Sir," Tobis said his cheeks turning a blush of pink.

Antorn pulled the door open and went inside the once open market building. He scanned the room and found the half dozen stags and fawn leaders along the back wall.

"What are you doing Antorn, this is anarchy," one of the

leaders said.

"I can appreciate that is how you see it, but let me show you what I see," Antorn motioned for them to follow him from the building. The leaders looked at one another not knowing what to do. "I'm not the one to be afraid of, but I will show you what we should be afraid of," Antorn said. He motioned again and left the building leaving the door open. A moment later the leaders hesitantly came out of the building. "Follow me," Antorn said.

Antorn led them to the poles in the ground and pointed to the beast's heads. He pulled a good-sized bag off a pull-cart and opened the flap. He handed the bag to the first stag and pulled out a hand full of dirt.

"Smell that, what does it smell like to you?" Antorn asked.

The stags sniffed the rancid dirt and crinkled their noses as they passed it around.

"What is this?" the first stag asked.

"That is burnt dirt. Have you ever seen dirt burn before?" Antorn asked. The Forrne shook their heads, "and those heads, do you think we made them up and went through this huge plot of scheming just, so we could take over the position of Herd-Lord, when all it would really take is to call for a new vote based on the laws of our land?" Antorn asked.

The stags looked around at the newly formed Guard and noted how stately the stags were as they executed their duties with diligence. There was a strange sense of pride and duty that seemed very natural to them but had been many rotations that anyone had ever felt that way or seen it.

"What is happening then?" another stag asked.

"I don't know, but what I do know, is that these creatures are real, they attack and kill us and are growing in numbers. This dirt is burned, and have you noticed there is less water this time of the rotation than usual? Did we have less rain? No, we didn't so where is the water? Why didn't Tage investigate this moons ago? Why didn't he send for word from the outskirts to find out their conditions? Why has he encouraged those of popular status to treat those of unpopular status with unkindness and scrutiny. That has never been our way, we are a herd who takes care of our own, not hurts them in ways that don't leave marks," Antorn said.

The first stag sagged with a kind of relief.

"We have been busy being popular," the stag said.

"It's time that we stop that nonsense and get back to our roots, our real selves, will you join us?" Antorn asked.

"We are not militant, we know nothing of these practices," the second stag said.

"Then do what you do best and help lead, we need men in positions to make decisions to keep the village progressing and to support the guardsmen," Antorn said.

"Guardsmen? Is that what you are calling all this?" the stag asked.

"Yes, we are the Forrne Guard, I am the leader, and you will report to me, Tobis, Soren, or Pillip," Antorn said.

The stags didn't exactly like the idea of having to report to anyone, but there was too much proof to argue they weren't right.

"What about Tage?" the stag asked.

"He has decided not engage in a civil conversation and therefore is an enemy to the Forrne, unless he agrees to keep out of trouble, when all this is over, I will relinquish his duties back to him, until then you as a collaborative group will begin to oversee his duties, that's if you know what those duties are," Antorn said.

The stags nodded.

"I have some books that will teach you what you *should* be doing to govern our people, I expect you to read them and follow its directions," Antorn said.

"And if we don't accept your offer?" another asked.

"I shall lock you up and treat you as an enemy of the Forrne until the time come that you should deserve a hearing, then it will be up to the people as to your fate," The stags were impressed that he had such an understanding of the rules of their kind, and he glanced over the excitement. "Who do you elect among yourselves to stand as leader of the council?" Antorn asked.

The stags talked amongst themselves for a brief moment and the first stag rose his hand.

"I will," the stag said.

"What are you called?" Antorn asked.

"I am Slat the Herd-Council-stag," Slat said.

"We are no longer going to use those terms, how about Slat the Head Official of the Forrne Guard," Antorn said.

Slat thought a moment.

"Would you consider Head Official of the Order of the Forrne Guard?" Slat asked.

"Why Oder?" Antorn asked.

"It sounds better," Slat said with a hint of embarrassed tone.

Antorn chuckled.

"Very well, Head Official of the Order of the Forrne Guard. That is kind of long, how about Slat of the HOOF?" Antorn asked with a tiny flick at the corner of his mouth.

The stags chuckled, but they all agreed and kind of liked it. Antorn welcomed them into the new Order and put them under the same oath that the rest of the Guardsmen took and started to give them their instructions and formulate the needed items of business. The day turned to night and then day and the village was a busy place. The news spread rapidly, and forces continued to come in droves. Slat and the rest of the Order was impressed at how well everyone tended to their new duties and decided they had long awaited this kind of people. They removed their jewelry and adopted the more militant look that the guardsmen had and found their new purpose to be fulfilling.

A startling cry came from the near distance and Antorn lunged from his discussion with Slat and made his way to where the cry came from. A young stag was barely able to stand and Antorn caught him in his arms.

"What happened?" Antorn asked.

"Beasts," the boy managed.

"Where?" Antorn asked.

"In the west Valleys, everyone is gone," the boy staggered.

A few women-stags came for the boy and took him to tend to his wounds. Antorn quickly rounded the throng of stags and fawns until he found Tobis and Pillip.

"Make a unit ready, the West Valleys have been attacked, as soon as you're ready, leave immediately," Antorn said.

"Sir," Pillip and Tobis said.

They rushed off shouting orders and the guard immediately quieted and began to prepare to leave. The Forrne Order members noted the command Antorn had and appreciated his gesture of unity. It was clear to them that he did indeed have the power to change things. Antorn pulled Soren aside and neared him closely, so he could talk quietly.

"I am not convinced the Order is totally committed, who do you trust to set as an informant?" Antorn asked.

Soren wasn't sure what the word 'informant' meant exactly, but he got the idea and thought a moment.

"I'll put the Smitting brothers on them, they are a bit odd and bicker a lot which will give them a good cover, but are totally loyal to the Guard," Soren said.

"Perfect," Antorn said.

"Do you have certain information you desire?" Soren asked.

"Not particularly, anything to do with Tage and or loyalty to the Guard, I want to know, or if they start acting different, perhaps speaking in code or…well I have no idea, I just don't trust them yet," Antorn said.

"Yes, Sir," Soren said.

"Are your men ready? How's that contraption thingy Finlo was working on?" Antorn asked.

"He's calling it a 'speared ballista', and yes we have fashioned several and my troops have been training with them. It's an impressive device and they have all gotten quite good, the stags' launch further but I must admit those little fawn are by far the better aim," Soren said.

"Interesting, let's make sure we use that," Antorn said.

"Of course," Soren said.

The hooves of the four troops that made up the new units pounded the ground as the stags and fawn Guardsman raced toward the Western Valleys. The fawn were surprisingly fast for their smaller frames, and they had no problems keeping up with the larger stags which was a nice addition to their forces. Tobis and Pillip pushed the troops hard as the Western Valleys were over a days' journey at a fast pace. The men however found the charge invigorating. The sound of their hooves hitting the ground in such numbers gave the locals a shuddering in their frames and the little ones stared with complete awe.

It was an interesting feeling, to be revered, but also to know that you might not come home and Tobis found the mixture of emotions sink into his chest. The time passed quickly as Tobis managed his thoughts, and they came to the ridge just before the valleys. Tobis slowed the troops and Pillip came up to him.

"What do you see?" Pillip asked.

"Nothing, no stags, fawn, structures, streams, nothing," Tobis said.

Pillip internalized the words as he too searched the distance. Several stags came up next to them and peered out over the horizon.

"Where did everyone go?" the stag asked.

"I have no idea, Adwen, take your troop and search the west banks, Ranton, you take yours around the east, I'll go down the middle, and Pillip you make your sweep behind and around this ridge," Tobis said.

"Yes, Sir," they confirmed.

The teams split up and started to search the valley. The crews met up on the other side with complete confusion.

"The only thing we found were tracks as though something had been dragged," Adwen said.

"Us too," Ranton said.

"Do you think the beasts carried them off?" Pillip asked.

"I do, and that secures my thoughts that the beasts are more intelligent than we thought. Deri, report this to Antorn, tell him we are going to follow the tracks, and we need reinforcements, immediately, go as fast as you can," Tobis said.

Deri saluted and launched into a dead run.

"This is where we turn back into trappers, we need to follow these and find out what happened and quickly," Tobis said.

Pillip nodded and the herd of soldiers became trappers again and started to follow the tracks in their quiet stalking mode. The valley was vast and sat at the bottom of a low mountain ridge. The troop didn't have to go too far before all the tracks merged into one path and it became obvious that the Forrne had been drug through the mountain pass. Tobis stopped and ordered two troops to fan out along the bottom of the mountain and search for anything that was out of place and one troop to stand guard while he took his troop up the pass.

The path was wide at first but began to narrow the higher

they went but then it leveled off, and they found another valley they didn't know about. They usually didn't trap the mountains since there was nothing that lived there. Tobis flicked his long ears and listened as he motioned for the stags to stay low and out of sight. The sounds of the beasts crept from around the bend and Tobis carefully crept close to the side of the rockface. He peeked around and found the beasts covered in the blood of his people and their bodies were mangled and half-eaten. His stomach lurched, and he quickly scooted back behind the mountain. Tobis struggled with his stomachs' need to hurl, but he made himself return to the others.

"They are just around this bend, and there are a lot, but I think if we can get them into the valley we can spread them out and take them out," Tobis said.

"What's your plan for that?" Pillip asked.

"Let's do what we did last time. You go back down and divide at the clearing, I'll lead them out and then you attack from the back," Tobis pointed to two stags, "hurry back and inform the others to attack from the sides as soon as we have them into the valleys and stay hidden," Tobis said.

The two soldiers started down the path quickly and then Pillip moved his forces. Tobis kept a handful of men with him and waited until he heard Pillip's echolocation. Tobis stepped out from behind the rock and gripped a spear. He wriggled his fingers until he found the grip he wanted and hurled the long staff into the air. The whipping sound it made ended as it sank deep into a creatures neck. The beast reared back and howled but it was cut short as another spear landed in its neck.

The beast fell with a thud, but the others were now on high alert. Tobis launched again and it hit the shoulder of another. The beasts' black eyes flashed red and the pit in Tobis' stomach hit his brain.

"Go!" Tobis commanded.

The stags raced down the path and could feel the thudding of the beasts coming. The path was narrow in places, and they had to be careful but made it though and into the downward slope and picked up speed. Tobis looked over his shoulder and found the beasts coming at full charge. Their size was frightening, and they were fast. Tobis was glad that they had spent time running lately and felt he was actually faster than he used to be. The group raced into the valley and headed straight down the center in a close formation. The beasts spread out and tried to circle the troop, but they weren't quite fast enough to get completely in front of Tobis.

Tobis continued his heading until he sensed Pillip's echolocation and signaled to split up and turn on the beasts. The stags pulled their battle-ax's and spears and the beasts howled. Drool dripped from their upright fangs and their breath left a stiff stink in the air as they moved into their upright standing position. The beasts' pulled their battle-ax's and Tobis signaled the attack. Tobis rounded the ax in his hand and ducked the oncoming swing. He swung the blade in an upward strike, and it sliced the beast's chest. The beast roared with pain and its eyes shifted to red. Tobis' heart raced, but he slammed his fist into the creatures jaw. It didn't work like he had hoped and instead of sending the creature flailing, he heard several of his own bones break.

Tobis recoiled and winced with the pain but whipped the ax around in a side strike and the blade raced across the beast's throat. Its oily blood splurted and Tobis leaped over its falling body. He shook off the pain in his hand, but he was certain it was going to be difficult for some time. A torrent of small spears penetrated the atmosphere and landed their marks into the beasts. Tobis found the line of Fawn with their new ballista's, and he smiled. The Fawn loaded another round and the stags in Soren's troop engaged.

Pillip took up the rear and the last group fell in on the last side. The beasts were tough, and were more agile and calculated than the first time they engaged and Tobis tried to figure out why. Pillip flipped around and launched his hind legs into the chest of a beast sending it flying. Several stags mimicked the movements and kicked them and then another wave of stags stabbed or sliced as they were down which proved to be a quick assassination, until another wave of beasts funneled out of the mountain pass.

Pillip turned to see a fresh wave and signaled to Tobis, who organized his men to divide and separate from the group. The first troop rounded to the left and the other to the right and Pillip moved up the center. Soren's troop spread out to ease the new creatures into the kill zone, and they began another attack. The Fawn continued to launch the spears and the stags were impressed with how accurate they were.

A beast noted the spears-man and snorted giving a signal to another and a small group escaped and started toward the Fawn. Tobis and Soren saw their actions and immediately ordered an interception. Niclas, the fawn leader, signaled another launch, but they found they were more skilled from a distance and the targets moving directly at them proved harder to hit. One of the stags snared a creature and another tapped one more leaving one very large beast headed straight for the Fawn. Niclas's heart raced and the pit in his stomach shot to his brain causing a flurry of panic to encompass his being.

He took a step back and his hoof slipped off a small stone, and he cursed. He sucked in a deep breath and gripped a spear, loaded it into the ballista and instead of raising it upward to launch it into the air he pulled the string straight back and squared his shoulders. The breath steaming out of the creature's snout temporarily shielded its face which gave Niclas the needed wake up call. He steadied his breathing and waited until the animal's heaving blueish chest came into view.

Niclas released the string and the spear sizzled straight through the air and sank deep into the beast's neck. It's eyes flashed red with a glossy panic and it gripped at its throat as it began to lose consciousness. Niclas and the others watched with their big eyes as the beast staggered and fell into the dirt. It's momentum propelled it into a heap of earth and came to a stop only a few small lengths from Niclas's hooves who was too stuck to the ground to move.

The Fawn broke into cheers and slapped Niclas on the back and the stags peeled away and saluted and Niclas saluted in return. The Fawn eagerly started talking about how he did it and began to adjust their angles and where the best point on the string would be to make the spears shoot like that. They could tell the spear had more power and was more direct, and they were excited to try the new approach, which came sooner than they wanted.

Another three beasts escaped the throng and headed toward them. Niclas loaded the ballista and squared his shoulders, adjusted the ballista like he did the last time and pulled extra hard on the string. He released the spear and it shot out with great speed and reacted the exact same way. The spear sank deeper into the creature and it recoiled. Several spears from the others too shot out with more exactness and sank into the beasts stopping their movements almost instantly.

They turned their attention to the rest of the group and reloaded. The spears reached their targets, but they realized they were not as impactful the further away they were, so they returned to the higher launch.

28-As Many As Possible

Riddick and Amirra heard the snarl of a Jaduuk and knew it was time to pick it up. Amirra settled into him and braced herself along his frame and let him do all the steering and movements. Their new synergy was getting stronger, and she was sensing more and more of his movements and thoughts and allowed her body to lift her knees when he did and bend and roll when he did. Bright pinks and oranges faded into the moon's purple rays of the impending night sky and it was almost as if the night and day were competing as to which one was going to win.

The wind rushed passed them so quickly it filled their ears with its whooshing that talking wouldn't be possible. Heavy pounding echoed from behind them and Riddick took a quick inventory of how many beasts were chasing them. The terrain became harder to navigate as the flatlands became rocky. Riddick quickly learned he had to avoid the sharpened peaks protruding from the ground when the earth they were on was sliced down the center.

Riddick shoved his foot into the one side and kicked out the other sending it flying into the face of one of the larger beasts. He reached out with his hand and ripped a new piece of earth from the bottom and merged it into the one they were on and again picked up speed.

The Jaduuk seemed to have a different vibe about them than before and Riddick tried to determine what it was but found it was too hard to focus on flying over the land and that, so he figured he would run it by Shaz later. The further they went the bigger the rocks became, and Riddick was banking off the side-walls and rolling in complete circles in a tubular fashion as the rocks tightened at the top.

The tube was starting to narrow, and Riddick didn't want to get caught in a dead-end but the Jaduuk were keeping a quick pace along one side. Riddick found a small opening in the rock up ahead and readied himself to take a hard turn upward. He rolled again and was nearly upside down when they reached the opening, and he shot through the hole. Riddick and Amirra lifted off the earth-craft for several lengths before descending back toward the ground.

Riddick spotted the earth-craft and swung his legs catching it again with his energy in time to land a few lengths over the earth. He steered and snagged Amirra who re-situated herself next to him. The force was still in motion, and they reset their footing, but now they were on the other side of the tunnel and the Jaduuk. Riddick wasn't sure where exactly where they were, and they were moving so quickly that it was hard to get a beat on the images the vibrations were giving him. He scanned the distance and found they had lost the pack, and he slowed down.

He retraced their steps and examined the surroundings and realized they were on the complete opposite side of the realm they needed to be on. Riddick started a smooth curve, and they rounded the peaks and boulders of the lower half of the mountain range they had seen when they first arrived.

The energy was different under the slickness of the rockface, and he didn't have to expend as much energy to make the magnetic propulsion of the minerals move as much, but it didn't last long as they needed to swing back around and head back to the portal. The excitement started to wear off and the endorphin release was now being replaced with the cool-down and a weariness overcame them. Amirra tried not to lean too much against him but her eyes were getting heavy and Riddick was wearing out too.

Riddick decided they had made enough distance that they could stop, and he carefully slowed down and found a place with tall grasses. He let the earth ease back into the surface, and they wobbled as the motion of moving no longer propelled their frames.

"How are you doing?" Amirra asked.

"I'm exhausted, you?" Riddick asked.

"Yes, do you think we will be safe here?" Amirra asked.

"Aye, after I do this," Riddick said.

Riddick pulled up a ground bubble, and they settled into the soft dirt and quickly found sleep.

****

Turkill and Ladtwig stepped through the misty tingles and hurried into Shaz's new mountain temple. Shaz had given them the instructions on how to pass through the barrier he had created when he sealed it, and they hurried back into their realm. They shielded their eyes from the high sun until they adjusted and started down the trail. Jagwynn padded behind them as they maneuvered back down the jagged rock-face until they reached the bottom and then leaped onto Jagwynn's back and raced to the village.

The humid air instantly made Ladtwig's now longer hair puff out like a dandelion plant. It was why he kept it short, but he hadn't had the time to shave it, and he kept shoving Turkill's face away each time he teased him about it. The heat bore down on them, and they started to sweat but it was a mixture of sweat and humidity that made their clothes stick to their bodies. Jagwynn shoved her beefy hind legs into the ground and flung her claws out as she leaped over the small ravine that they had used a rope bridge to cross before. The Minca squeezed their legs tightly and gripped her fur as they soared over the distance. Her front claws gripped the earth on the other side and propelled them the last length until her hind legs gripped the next leap.

The village came into view, and she slowed as they rounded the last few huts. Turkill and Ladtwig leaped off her before she came to a complete stop and scurried toward the Chief's hut in the center of the village.

"Father, father!" Turkill called.

They threw the flap of his hut open and searched but the chief wasn't inside. They turned around to find a few of the elder Minca staring at them startled.

"Where is the Chief?" Turkill barked.

One of the men pointed and Turkill and Ladtwig hurried into the jungle. They ran quickly through the heavier underbrush and found the Chief near the river.

"Father," Turkill said.

The Chief spun around with a surprised and shocked expression.

"What is the matter?" the Chief asked.

"We need your help, there is a Jaduuk army taking over the Timeless Plains, and we need a pyro-crew and healers right away," Turkill said.

"Oh, this is very bad," the Chief said.

They started their way back to the Chiefs hut and Turkill caught a glimpse of his lady friend. His heart skipped a beat, and she smiled with an excited wave. He grinned at her and tried to give her the 'I'm sorry things are dire, but I hope to see you soon' look, but realized that was probably too much to say with just a look. She nodded as though she understood, and he caught up to his father.

"Tell me everything," the Chief said as he hurried them into his hut.

They rehearsed the whole matter quickly and the Chief scratched out a note to the clan leaders and rolled up the several papers and tied them onto the legs of several birds.

"We should hear back soon, but for now let's get Babbesh and Fionte involved and see what we can organize," the Chief said.

They made their way to the tents that were still set up and the Chief peeked inside. He spotted the Chieftess and Fionte at the back of the tent, and he cleared his throat. The ladies made their way to the door, and he motioned for them to come out. The Chieftess jumped with a little squeal when she saw her son's and threw her arms around them. Turkill squirmed, but she didn't care and Ladtwig hugged her tightly.

"What is the matter?" the Chieftess asked.

The Chief rehearsed the matter and Turkill filled in the spots he left out in which she gasped and ooh and ahhed as they told the story.

"Do you think Babbesh and you can form a medic team?" the Chief asked.

"Of course, how many?" Fionte asked.

"As many as possible, but we need to leave someone here to take care of our own people," the Chief said.

"Yes, I have just the person," Fionte said.

"Wonderful, but we have to hurry our time moves slower

than theirs," Turkill said.

"We need a crew of men to help with the tents and rigging," Ladtwig said.

"You know who you want?" the Chief asked.

"I do," Ladtwig said.

"Alright, go do it," the Chief said.

Ladtwig hurried away.

"How are the Northman going to carry all the explosives without their mammoths?" the Chief asked.

"Shaz says he has a plan for that, we just need to get them to the portal, and then he will take it from there," Turkill said.

"Alright, let's go," the Chief said.

Turkill spun around and nearly knocked his lady friend over.

"Oh, I am so sorry Shati, I didn't see you there, I mean, I saw you, I just didn't," Turkill stammered.

Shati reached up and planted a kiss right on his lips. Her touch was riveting and Turkill blushed under his deep rust-brown skin. She pulled away and found his expression that of complete shock and her eagerness shifted to fear. He quickly pulled her into him and kissed her back. Turkill pulled away and looked deeply into her eyes.

"I have missed you so much," Turkill said.

"I have missed you too," Shati said.

Turkill spotted Feungrid standing next to a hut with a scowl that rivaled his own, and he snickered. Turkill took Shati's hand and lead her with him as he headed toward the prayer hut.

"Where are we going?" Shati asked.

"In here," Turkill said.

"I can't go in there, that is only for the leaders," Shati said.

"That's right," Turkill said.

He held the flap open and motioned for her to enter, and she hesitantly crossed the threshold. Turkill closed the flap and pulled her into another embrace.

"I shouldn't have left you, but I had to, and I have to again, but this time I'm going to take you with me," Turkill said.

Shati studied his face and found he wasn't kidding, and a rush of emotions surged through her. Her warm-brown skin enhanced the deepness of her eyes and Turkill studied them as she processed what he had just said.

"I don't think my father will agree to that," Shati said.

"What do *you* say?" Turkill asked.

"Yes, I will go with you," Shati said.

"This won't be easy and there is still a lot of things that we have to do, we will be fighting the Jaduuk again, but we need healers, and people to stay and help with the food and such, you will be safe at the base of operations," Turkill said.

"What about you?" Shati asked.

"I will be there too, but I am a warrior and Shaz needs me," Turkill said.

"I'll do it," Shati said.

Turkill hugged her tight and kissed her again.

"We got to hurry, you go to Fionte and tell her you volunteer to go, I need to head to the Northman's village and organized things there, and I will see you again in a few days," Turkill said.

"Alright," Shati said.

They made their way out of the prayer hut and passed Feungrid, and he glowered at Turkill who didn't even look at him. Turkill gave her hand a tight squeeze, and she hurried to Fionte.

****

Phanes rounded the corridor and knocked on the door. Ralti opened the door and Phanes saluted. Ralti saluted and let Phanes in the room. Phanes rehearsed the details and the plan indicating on the map the details for the new portals and what they would need to do and Ralti studied him with a sense of surprise and honor. He was certain Phanes had the potential but listening to him organize the details as well as showing the command and leadership now assured him he had chosen well.

"We only have six of our day cycles to make this happen, where are we on the issue of the Kronos?" Phanes asked.

"Peace talks are going well, Azrack believes we are not far from a peace treaty," Ralti said.

"Good, we will need as many forces as we can spare," Phanes said.

"How many Jaduuk are we up against," Pontos asked.

"Riddick went to do recon, but Shaz believes it will be a formidable force, and he is wanting to strike hard and fast," Phanes said.

"Do you know what would be good, if we had those fireball launchers we battled at the Battle of Small Creek," Pontos said.

Phanes looked at the gryphton with a 'someone fill me in' look.

"It's a human's weapon, I bet Shaz will already be aware of those, but if not ask Helios, he studied the designs," Ralti said.

"Helios is working on creating a toxin using the Ruin Spider Spit that we will be in charge of dropping from the air, the toxin is a paralytic, and he's hoping to add the poison from the Minca's dart guns to make it deadly," Phanes said.

"Sounds like Helios," Pontos said.

Brigdon grunted with a quirky side grin and Phanes studied the older gryphton's. It was evident that they had rotations of history together, and he found a peculiar excitement surge for his ability to learn from them in battle.

"I'll notify Azrack of the developments while you gather the forces and begin making the arrangements," Ralti said.

"Sir," Phanes said.

"Dismissed," Ralti said.

Phanes saluted and hurried from the room.

"He's nearly a spitting image of you," Jaxton said.

"I know," Ralti said.

"He's already got her heart," Jaxton said.

"I know, what?" Ralti said.

"Leeta, he's already won her heart," Jaxton said.

Ralti sighed.

"I know," Ralti said.

"You'll be alright," Jaxton said.

Ralti looked at him with a cross glare and Jaxton laughed. Jaxton slapped him on the shoulder and the team dismissed.

29- Suit Yourself

The sun was now sitting in the second half of the sky as Shaz and Serin followed Declan to the stables. The scent of fresh-cut grass wafted over the strong essence of the lilac bushes and ivy that covered the outer wall the castle. The young stable boy ran to help them and when he recognized Shaz and Serin he bowed deeply. Shaz didn't like the attention and tried to be nice, but it made him feel as though he were under a looking glass and everyone was watching his every move. An eerie thought came to his mind, and he searched the distance and found that everyone *was* looking at him.

Serin pulled out a coin and handed it to the boy who smiled big and hurried to the first stable. He pulled a saddle off the wall and heaved it over a chestnut mare and Serin gazed around the large stable. A horse near the other side caught her attention, and she made her way to the stable door. The horse looked up with sad eyes, and she wondered why. She reached for the latch, but the boy grabbed her hand and pulled it away. Serin startled and stared at the lad.

"No one is allowed to go in there, that horse is possessed," the boy said.

Serin searched the boy's face and found real concern, even fear but there was something about the animal that intrigued her. She didn't usually sense animal's intentions, but she did with this horse, and she wanted to know why.

"I'll be alright," Serin reassured.

"I'm sorry Miss, but I have to insist," the boy said squaring his shoulders. Serin appreciated his commitment, but she pulled her hand from his grip, and Shaz stepped next to him followed by Declan.

"I'll be here if the lady needs a hand," Shaz said.

The boy wasn't sure what to do and studied them. He agreed but hurried out of the barn and Shaz figured he was fetching the stable master.

"What's wrong?" Shaz asked.

"I'm not sure, but something about this horse is pulling at me. I understand his intentions, and I've never sensed that in an animal before," Serin said.

"Interesting," Shaz said.

Shaz lifted the latch and opened the gate slowly. They walked into the stable and the white horse nickered uneasily. Serin moved closer to the animal, but the horse backed up until it hit the back wall. It pawed at the ground and snorted as it moved its ears back and forth. Shaz understood this was a warning signal and his heartfire jumped.

"You're alright boy, I want to introduce myself, my name is Serin Svirtari," Serin said.

The stable master rounded the corner at a fast gate and began to holler at them. Serin ignored him and Shaz left the stable and blocked the way.

"What in tarnation are you doing in there, that animal will take your head off, get out of there," the stable master billowed.

"She understands horses," Shaz said.

"I don't give a horsecurd," the man snarled.

Shaz had never heard that term before and struck him with a humorous but curious intrigue. He found himself both wanting to laugh and investigate where the term came from. Serin pulled something out of her pocket and rolled it in her fingers a few times and held it out to the horse's nose and the horse jockeyed several times and pawed at the ground.

"I'm a traveler and I understand you," Serin said.

The horse stared into her eyes and Serin closed the little figurine into her palm and moved her clenched hand toward his nose.

"She's going to get herself killed," the man said.

The horse nickered but his energy relaxed and a chill ran across its back and the tail swished back and forth. Serin touched the horse's nose with her closed fist and gently ran her hand along the long nose. The animal moved his head into her touch and the stable master started to move past Shaz.

"Let her try," Shaz said holding his arm out to stop the man.

The man glared at him and searched his face and Shaz found fear and anger both for her safety and their disrespect to him as the stable master. Serin moved to the horse's neck and ran her hands along its warm body. She picked up a brush from the adjacent wall and began to smooth out the mangy hair. The animal leaned into the caress and Serin began talking to it in her father's native traveler's tongue, which was different than her mother's. The horse understood the language instantly and Serin now understood why she was drawn to it.

"This is a Branagan, the breed my father's people bred, they are incredibly rare," Serin said.

"A what?" the stable master asked.

"Where did you get this horse?" Serin asked.

Serin tried to keep her tone calm but Shaz could tell she was feeling anxious.

"We corral wild horse a couple times a rotation and this horse was in the mob, but this is the wildest I've ever seen, we were going to have to put it down,"

"Well, you won't need to do that, I'll take him," Serin said.

"I'm sorry Miss I can't let you do that," the master said.

"Shaz open the gate, I think I'll saddle him out there where he can stretch his legs a bit," Serin said.

Serin put the trinket in her pocket and returned the brush and Shaz opened the latch. The stable master grabbed his hand and Shaz heated it up and the man pulled away with shock in his eyes. Shaz opened the gate and Serin led the horse from the stable. The horse calmly walked next to her with his head high and the stable master and the boy scurried into a stable and closed the door. Shaz gave Serin a saddle, and she moved to the animal.

"Do you want to get out of here?" Serin asked.

The horse jockeyed but with a level of excitement instead of anger. Serin threw the saddle over the horse's back and reached under and pulled the billet strap under its belly. The horse shifted with the unfamiliar sensation of the saddle and Serin reassured it. Declan stood watching with amazement as did the rest of the stable hands. Serin ran her hand along the horse's neck and then tightened the strap and wrapped the extra leather strap in a knot and secured the rest of the fittings.

"Where's your horse?" Serin asked.

Shaz turned and found a second horse saddled next to Declan's, and he pointed. Serin put her foot in the stirrup and slowly lifted herself onto the animal. The horse shifted and pranced with the newness of the saddle and her weight but settled quickly.

"This is the most amazing thing I have ever seen," the stable master said.

A hushed commotion sounded over the other horse's noise and Shaz and Declan mounted their rides.

"Thank you," Serin said.

The stable master nodded, but he was more thankful than she was and came out of the protection of the stable next door. Shaz kicked his horse and the steed lurched forward and Declan too urged his horse, but Serin waited an extra minute.

What are you waiting for? Shaz asked in his mind.

This horse is going to blow past you so fast your mind will spin, Serin returned.

Serin held the reins back and kept the animal from launching itself forward.

"You ready to catch them?" Serin asked.

The horse pulled against the reins and Serin leaned close to the animal's neck. She relaxed the reins and spoke her father's language. The horse lunged from the stable and gripped the soft dirt with its majestic hooves. The horse was gone so fast the people darted out of the building as fast as they could and watched Serin nearly laying on the animal. The animal's gate was so long it almost disturbed their senses. The crowd broke into hoots and hollers and Serin and the white horse disappeared over the landscape. Serin gripped the reins gently to give the horse direction and scanned for Shaz's energy and found them up ahead and adjusted her course.

Shaz looked back and saw her coming at a quick pace and was surprised at how fast the animal was.

You better pick it up, this horse wants to run, Serin said.

Shaz nudged his animal and Declan looked back and found her right behind them and nudged his. Serin could tell the other two horses were going to need help, so she quickly boosted them with her wind-walk. Shaz eased his horse into the magic, but Declan didn't have a clue what was going on and his horse jostled about until Serin blasted passed him. The horse took the challenge and found a new gate behind Shaz. They crossed the countryside with such speed that Shaz was starting to wonder how long the Branagan was going to last, but it showed no signs of slowing down and Serin could tell it needed the run.

Her father had taught her that the Branagan was the off-spring of the wyvern, but she never believed it. But maybe now it might just be true, at any rate, it was bred for running, hard, fast, and for a long distance. Declan indicated the direction to Shaz and Shaz told Serin who shifted the horse's direction as the sun was making its way under the horizon.

"How much further?" Shaz asked over the rushing of the wind.

"Not long, just over zat rrridge," Declan said.

Shaz whistled and motioned to Serin toward the ridge, and she pulled back the reins for the first time. The horse slowed its pace, and she let Declan and Shaz catch up to her.

"I'm totally shocked zat ve arrre herrre alrrready, what vas zat you did zat made horrrses go so fast," Declan asked.

"I call it wind-walk, or in this case wind-run," Shaz said with a few eyebrow raises and a grin.

Declan searched his face to decide what to say back.

"This is air magic, which makes you as light as air so can move faster," Serin said.

Declan nodded but his mind raced around the idea and Serin chuckled.

"It's about to wear off so let's give the horses a few minutes to cool down before we head into town," Shaz said.

"Oh, I figured out how to remove it too, hang on," Serin said.

Serin gripped her fist and rolled her other hand over the top and the air buff dissipated from their beings and the horses settled to the hardened surface. Shaz's eyes gleamed with amazement and Declan wriggled with the weirdness the energy made on his body.

"You're always amazing me," Shaz said.

Serin blushed and Shaz smiled.

"Let's go," Serin said.

The township of Hammerstead emerged as they eased over the ridge. Hammerstead was as unique as Ebassia and had many intricately carved buildings but were nowhere near as tall and was surrounded with smaller older style buildings. Shaz's need for details and military evaluation kicked in, and he began making note of the exits, buildings, structures, people, and anything that seemed odd, out of place, or different. Serin read his energy and soaked in the interpretations she received from it. It was part of their synergized magic, even though she didn't have all the skills he did, she was able to tap into them as needed and had learned how to understand his motives for doing things based on the things he learned such as the city's layout.

She was certain that he, if needed, was aware of the exits, the place they keep prisoners and how he would make an escape, fight back, and so on. It was a different kind of mentality than her own, and it initially took her by surprise that he was so methodical and capable of doing the hard things that come with war. But then she decided that was what made him capable of so much will to also protect people. The faded sun left little light in the sky and the lanterns and fire pits illuminated the surroundings. The main gate of the city opened as they approached and Shaz took another inventory of the armed guards and positions. What weapons they had and how they held them. He was convinced the people of Hammerstead were highly capable of hand-to-hand combat as well as weapons. Declan led them through the gathering people to a building in the center and hopped off the horse.

Shaz and Serin climbed off their horse and a couple young men took the reins.

"Be gentle, he's an excitable one," Serin said.

The boy nodded with deep concentration. Shaz and Serin followed Declan into the building and found it was warm and had modest furnishings. A gently aged woman came from a room at the back with a smile that quickly shifted to confusion. Her medium-length dark hair framed her sun-kissed skin and her dark-brown eyes sat on a trimmed but soft face.

"Mother, zis is Shaz and Serrrin. Shaz is RRReinholt's son. Zis is my mother Crrristen," Declan said.

Cristen's confused eyes shifted back and forth for a minute and settled on disbelief. She crossed her arms over her chest and gave a similar look as Turkill's and Shaz shoved the chuckle down. He put his hand over his heart and nodded with a slight bow in the Rangers greeting and the woman uncrossed her arms. Her tight expression relaxed, and she struggled to allow his greeting to convince her.

"How kan you be surrre?" she asked.

"Just look at him, he looks just like him, and he gave old grr-reeting," Declan said.

Shaz wasn't sure how Declan would know what his father looked like and figured he would ask later.

"You kould have taught him zat," Cristen said.

"Why would I do that?" Declan asked annoyed.

"Pleasure to meet you," Shaz said.

"I don't believe you arrre son of RRReinholt," Cristen said.

"I guess I could ask you the same question, how do you know about Reinholt since he died when I was a baby," Shaz said.

Shaz tried to keep his tone gentle, but he found a bit of annoyance in her lack of trust.

"He vas ourrr leader," Cristen said.

"That died before, by the looks of it, you were born too," Shaz said.

Cristen's brows crinkled and her expression turned sharp. Shaz wasn't sure what to do, but he was getting the impression they weren't welcome, and he was going to leave.

"I don't blame you, it has been a very long time," Serin said.

Shaz understood Serin was telling him he needed to give the women a little more time and perhaps something she would be able to believe.

"I never knew him, I was raised by Merrick and Elin. Elin died when I was a boy, so it's been just Merrick, Grandfather, or Mathieu and myself, oh and Riddick, son of Kenon Brouderic," Shaz said.

Cristen's eyes bulged and her knees went weak. Declan steadied her and helped her to a chair.

"I don't believe it, how, wherrre?" Cristen asked.

Cristen's tone was shaky and her hand trembled. Serin wondered why the news would be so overwhelming to her, but they did look young and wondered how they understood the information.

"I met zem at kastle in Ebassia," Declan said.

"So, Ebassia still exists?" Cristen asked.

"Da, it's all zerrre," Declan said.

"Can I ask, how many rotations has it been here in Hammerstead?" Shaz asked.

"About hundrrred, until barrrier shifted, now day cycles arrre going at much faster pace, and ve have niet idea why, and niet one is aging vay ve used to," Declan said.

"How long has it been forrr you?" Cristen asked.

"About twenty-five in Turob, but over three-hundred for Ebassia," Shaz said.

"Zat kould explain why days have been going faster, ve arrre now parrrt of rrrealm of Ebassia again," Declan said.

"What do you understand about the realms?" Shaz asked.

Declan went to the kitchen and organized some dishes onto the counter.

Serin was sure Cristen was still trying to process the information, and wasn't finding some answers in her mind.

"Ve know about zem in generrral, but most of zose zat trrraveled zem arrre gone now, zerrre arrre only handful of older folk zat still speak of 'old days', rrrest of everrryone, if zey rrremember don't say much," Declan said.

Declan made them up a plate of roasted meat and vegetables and Cristen tried to help, but she found her emotions near the surface more than she had expected. Serin wanted to give her a boost of calming energy, but she figured that might be too much for her to process. The food was tasteful, and they were happy for the nourishment.

"Can I ask, how you know what my father looks like?" Shaz asked.

Declan set his plate down and retrieved a book from another room. He flipped through the worn edges of the pages and set the book on the table when he found the one he was looking for.

"Zis is book of instrrruction forrr leader of Hammerrrstead," Declan pointed to the images in the book and Shaz found his father and Merrick in the center with seven other men and small child. "Zis is RRReinholt, and Merrrick," Declan said.

Serin took a peak.

"Wow, you do look just like him, even more so than in the mural," Serin said.

"He vas about yourrr age zerrre, and yourrr mother," Cristen said.

She pointed to the young woman standing at the corner of the image like she wasn't supposed to be in it but was. There were only a few images at the castle of his parents and for some reason this image gave him an interesting emotion he couldn't explain. Serin listened to his feelings and tried to get an image of what he was experiencing but it was confusing at best. Cristen too observed as he processed the information, and he set the book on the table.

"Tell me what happened at kastle? What did you tell King?" Cristen asked.

"She's Queen," Declan said.

"Zat kan't be, zerrre's not been Queen ever," Cristen said.

"I know, but she daughter of late king, Oladesni is name of her. Anyvay, I made my vay into city and sought audience vith queen I vas surrre it vasn't going to happen, but when she vas made avarrre I vas zerrre frrrom Hammerrrstead she rrrushed out to meet me in kourrrtyarrrd. Apparrrently, she had met RRRanger and had been told zey had all been destrrroyed. She vanted to make surrre I vas who I said I vas, so she starrrted grrrilling interrrogation. She vas one deterrrmined young voman, but I passed her questions, and she invited me to stay at kastle. I hadn't even had time to make my kase when zese tvo kame, and I vas voken frrrom sleep to kome to queens meeting," Declan said.

"Vait, young voman?" Cristen asked.

"Quite, I didn't darrre ask her age, but she kouldn't be morrre zan tventy," Declan said.

"She's too young to be queened, she'll never surrrvive," Cristen said.

"Oh niet, she vas quite imprrressive, and she knew what she vas doing," Declan said.

"Did you get chance to plead ourrr kase?" Cristen asked her pitch high.

Cristen took the dishes from the table and Serin helped.

"Da, she has grrranted us land ve need, and I have svorrrn ourrr loyalties to her," Declan said.

"Why did you do zat? Ve don't even know if she's going to keep her vorrrd, she's just girrrl," Cristen said.

"Bekause she has svorrrn allegiance to Shaz herrre, and she knows Merrrick, and Cerrros frrrom Kouncil is one of her Vizierrrs," Declan said.

Declan pulled out the declaration of land and alliance agreement and handed it to Cristen who read the text.

"It's real zen?" Cristen asked.

Serin wondered why the woman was so skeptical and guessed that she had trust issues just as she used to, and her heart swelled with compassion for her.

"Da, quite rrreal," Declan said.

Cristen threw her arms around his neck, and he wrapped her in a tight hug.

Shaz perked up and his instincts kicked in, as he sensed a large group of men coming toward the house. Serin felt it too and they started toward the door.

"We won't stay here if it will cause trouble," Shaz said.

"Vhat do you mean?" Declan asked.

"You have some unpleasant company outside," Shaz said.

Shaz gripped the hilt of his blade and Declan's heart raced.

"Stay herrre," Declan said.

Cristen nodded but Shaz and Serin were right behind him. Declan flung the door open and stepped out in time to catch the man coming up the stairs off guard.

"What in blasted horrrsekurrrds!" Declan shouted.

The tall bulky man at the door wreaked of anger and Serin instantly understood his main goal in life was to seize the leadership from Declan. Serin gave Shaz her rundown and he nodded. Shaz and Serin came out of the house and closed the door behind them keeping Cristen out of view.

"What do you zink you arrre doing brrringing strrrangerrrs herrre," the man barked.

Shaz was impressed with the strength of his voice and it reminded him of Merrick.

"Zis doesn't koncerrrn you, Trrristan," Declan said.

"Zis koncerrrns all of us, zat's why you shouldn't be leader, you'rrre young spoiled rrrat and you kan't underrrstand basic rrrules of Hammerrrstead," Tristan barked.

The crowd outside laughed and jeered and Declan sucked in a deep breath. Serin could sense Cristen's energy and understood it was him who she was afraid of.

"Da, it koncerrrns zem, but not you," Declan said.

"The basic rules of Hammerstead or your rules?" Shaz said. The man shot him a glare and his eyes rippled with anger. Shaz didn't even as much as flinch, and he glared right back. Tristan searched his face and clenched his jaw tightly. Tristan was a good ten rotations older or more and at least half a man's weight bigger.

"Who arrre you?" Tristan barked.

"Shaz son of Reinholt, actually," Shaz said.

Tristan burst into a rolling fit of laughter and Shaz shoved his hands into his pockets and waited for the man to stop. Serin crossed her arms over her chest and stared at him. Tristan contained another bought of laughter, but the crowd was still amused. Shaz was still trying to piece together the mystery of their time laps and what they knew or remembered.

"Zis is funniest zing I've ever hearrrd," Tristan said.

"Suit yourself," Shaz said.

He motioned for Serin to return to the house, but Tristan slammed his exceptionally large hand against the door. Serin shot him a glare and was about to unleash a flurry of something but Shaz grabbed her arm.

"Zis little lady zinks she kan hurrrt me," Tristan said.

Serin's blood boiled under the surface and Shaz tried to keep his urge to laugh at the man hidden.

"She could, but that's something I will do," Shaz said.

"You'rrre fooling me, you arrre going to challenge me to fight?" Tristan asked.

"Shaz," Serin said.

"Yes, I am. Isn't that the Rangers way, if you were actually a Ranger that is," Shaz said.

"You better vatch it, boy," Tristan snarled.

"Or what you'll beat me up," Shaz said.

The crowd started to murmur and Serin could tell they were starting to question Tristan's motives.

"I'm ten times man you'll ever be," Tristan growled.

"I guess we'll see about that, tomorrow then?" Shaz said.

"Da, tomorrrow. You'rrre bigger fool zan I kould have ever guessed," Tristan said shaking his head.

Tristan turned and started through the crowd and the crowd moved away from the house. Shaz waited a few minutes and studied the man's movements as he walked.

30-I Have Been Told I'm Stubborn

Cristen came out from the backroom and wrung her hands.

"Vhat happened?" Cristen asked.

"Shaz, you don't have to do zis," Declan said.

"Yes, I do, and you know it, plus I'm not afraid of him, he's left side dominant, which is my best side," Shaz said.

"Best side for what?" Serin asked.

"Dodging," Shaz said.

Serin gave him a sideways glare and he chuckled.

"You'rrre not going to fight Trrristan, he'll kill you," Cristen said.

"Niet, zey arrre going to leave tonight, rrright now in fact," Declan said.

"I understand how you feel about this, but I have my reasons, and I need you to trust me," Shaz said.

"I don't zink I kan let you do zis," Declan said.

"If you would prefer, we will stay in the countryside for the night," Serin said.

"Oh goodness niet, please you'rrre ourrr guests, kome I vill show you to rrroom," Cristen said.

Shaz nodded, and they followed her to the back of the house where the bedchambers were.

"I'm sorrry I only have one bed," Cristen said.

"I'll take the floor," Shaz said.

She nodded and closed the door behind them.

"What is your plan Mr.," Serin asked.

"Get my can kicked a bit and then kick his," Shaz said as he set his pack in the corner of the room.

"That sounds like fun," Serin said.

Serin pulled off her cloak and hung the heavy wool on the peg on the wall. Shaz unlatched the buckles on his jerkin and hung it next to her cloak.

"As long as you don't lay any bets as to how many of my bones he'll break, I guess we're alright," Shaz said.

Serin started to unlace her boots and Shaz took off the sword and stuck it under the mattress near the top where he was going to lay on the floor.

"I'm going to wager-"

"I don't really want to know. Just don't let me break too many," Shaz said.

Serin unlatched her thigh knife belt and removed the little dagger she kept next to her breast. Shaz pulled off his boots and tucked them under the bed.

"Seriously Shaz, are you really going to fight?" Serin asked.

Serin pulled down the covers of the bed and sat on the soft padding. Shaz looked around for a blanket but didn't find one and Serin patted the cushion.

"Aye," Shaz said.

"Is it so you can win their allegiances?" Serin asked.

Serin scooted to the far side of the mattress and Shaz climbed in, and she cuddled next to him.

"Aye, so if there's a way for you to *not* let me feel the pain that would be nice, but you can't heal me, that is considered cheating for this kind of thing," Shaz said.

"I'll do my best," Serin said.

"Aye," Shaz said.

He kissed the top of her head as she was now laying on his chest.

"I wonder why Declan seems so uneasy," Serin said.

"Aye," Shaz said.

"And Cristen too," Serin said.

"Aye," Shaz said.

"Do you think Tristan has something to do with it?" Serin asked.

"Aye," Shaz said.

"Is that all you're going to say?" Serin asked.

"Aye," Shaz said.

"I figured," Serin said.

"Whatever the story is, there is something wrong for sure. The Rangers don't act like this, at least not according to my father," Shaz said.

"Aye," Serin said.

Shaz blurted a quick snort of laughter and Serin chuckled.

"Alright Miss Sass," Shaz said.

"Quit talking, you're making it hard to sleep," Serin teased.

"Well, aren't you on a roll," Shaz said.

Serin chuckled and Shaz ran his fingers through her hair. The lantern on the other side of the door went out and the light that had come from under the door now left the room dark.

Morning came quickly and Shaz stirred as a spec of morning light danced through the mostly closed curtains. Shaz lifted the covers and sat up carefully but Serin stirred too. They could hear gentle clinks coming from the other room, and they quickly dressed. Serin took a few minutes in the washroom across the hall and washed the dirt from her face and freshened the gentle waves in her long hair. She wrapped part of it up and away from her face and secured it with a fastener and made her way to the kitchen.

"Good morrrning, how did you sleep?" Cristen asked.

"Well, thank you," Serin said.

Serin took the pitcher of cold milk from her and set it on the table and then set out the stack of plates and utensils that were on the table.

"Wherrre arrre you frrrom? Declan told me about yourrr horrrse and how you verrre able to make it herrre so fast, but neither of us knows wherrre you arrre frrrom?" Cristen said.

"My parents were travelers," Serin said.

"I'm afrrraid I'm not surrre what zat means," Cristen said.

Serin wasn't sure how to explain the complexity of her identity. How does she tell people that her mother was the lost heir of a supernatural race of people who was raised by a group of people who traveled around to avoid the supernatural people, who then became the Queen of the most powerful city in Edenocht, therefore making *her* the next queen, *and* who was raised with wyverns in another realm also making her the Wyvern Priestess, and synergized to *the* war wizard making her one of the most powerful being on the planet?

"Well, let's just say I moved around a lot and I have a few places I call home," Serin said.

Cristen nodded, but she could tell that there was more to it than that. Shaz came into the kitchen and took a plate from Serin and set it on the far side of the table.

"Can I ask you a question?" Shaz asked.

Cristen looked up from the griddle and examined him.

"I suppose," Cristen said.

"Who was the last leader?" Shaz asked.

"RRReinholt, but some arrrgue Ean MacKullif vas last alive, why?" Cristen asked.

"Does he have any descendants here," Shaz asked.

"Tristan," Cristen said.

"I wondered," Shaz said.

"He's trrrying to take leaderrrship," Declan said as he came into the room.

"Why haven't you stood up to him?" Shaz asked.

"I have many times, but his tactics arrre strrraying frrrom ourrr trrraditional values and arrre bekoming morrre aggrrressive. He's rrriling up people and kausing zem to side vith him," Declan said.

"When is the time set for the match," Serin asked.

Shaz looked at her surprised. He hadn't figured she would be familiar with hand-to-hand combat, and was instantly intrigued.

"Mid-morning," Declan said.

Cristen motioned for them to sit, and she set a plate of griddle cakes on the table. The room fell silent except for the clinking of dishes and sounds of the morning rush of people outside.

"Sounds like people have kome to find out who you arrre," Declan said.

"What am I supposed to tell them?" Shaz asked.

"Tell zem who you arrre," Cristen said.

"How do I prove it, I have no paper record of my lineage, at least not here. I don't usually need to prove myself that way," Shaz said.

"How do you prrrove yourrrself elsewherrre," Declan asked.

"Shaz, no magic, we don't need the sqwalls on our trail," Serin said.

Shaz's enlightened face frowned.

"Plus, *you* don't even believe me entirely," Shaz said.

Cristen looked up and her cheeks turned a shade of pink.

"It's not zat I don't believe you, it's just harrrd to believe. Zerrre vas such chaos after barrrier vas forrrmed and it vas harrrd enough to rrraise Declan in vay to be leader when he vas old enough. But when he rrreached age of man, Trrristan rrrefused to hand it over," Cristen said.

"I see," Shaz said.

"So, how will you fighting Tristan give Declan the leadership, shouldn't it be Declan who fights him?" Serin asked.

"Things aren't that simple. There are exceptions to the exceptions. As a child of an appointed leader, if I want to challenge I can, which is what Tristan has done. When a challenge is made, all those who have an interest in the leadership, be it relation, appointed or simply wanting power, must participate in the challenge. The challenge is over when the last man is standing, or the last challenger has fallen. Declan won't challenge me, which is his right as actual leader. That way he doesn't lose the appointment by a fight and I won't challenge his right, and then will retain the leadership and the people will be forced to comply," Shaz said.

"Assuming zey still vant to follow old vays," Declan said.

"What number were you?" Shaz asked.

"That's an odd question," Serin said.

"Leaderrrs pick next ten in line to take over, in kase somezing happened, and if ve lost all ten zen it vas to go to heirrr of last known leader. I vas tenth chosen, but I vas just small child when leaderrrs verrre all killed, I bekame leader. Bekause I vas boy, and kouldn't asserrrt my rrright effectively it has been divide forrr some time," Declan said.

"Does anyone have the birthmark?" Shaz asked.

Declan showed him the mark under his shirt on his side.

"Just me, zat I'm avarrre of, which is why I vas tenth selected bekause I vas next child to have marrrk, but I vas told you had it, and you verrre borrrn beforrre me," Declan said.

"Vhich is why Trrristan hates him so much bekause he konsiderrrs himself trrrue blood, but he doesn't have marrrk and is angrrry about it," Cristen said sharply.

Shaz lifted his tunic and showed them the birthmark on his lower back. Serin now understood that it was more than a birthmark. She found it a little odd that she was still learning about him, even though she knew him so well and had been together for a few rotations now, well who really can tell how much time had passed with all the realm traveling they've done. Shaz tried to add it up once, but they gave up and decided it didn't matter anyway.

"It's getting time, arrre you rrready," Declan asked.

Shaz nodded and Declan opened the door, and the crowd began to cheer, but Declan knew it was not for him. Shaz came out followed by Serin and the crowd half gasped, and the other half cheered more. Serin guessed it was his blonde hair and wondered how many saw his likeness of his father. It was quite a sight and it made Shaz a bit irritated that they would put so much emphasis on the whole thing. He was certain Merrick would be very angry and according to Merrick, so would Reinholt. They held the honor of the brotherhood as a sacred calling and this was a meaningless sideshow.

"Let's get this over with," Shaz said.

Declan led them through the crowd and around several buildings to the back part of the city and the crowd followed. The noise only intensified when they made their way to the box. Shaz took a quick inventory of the people, structures, and the box itself. Log poles were nailed together in a crisscross-like pattern and about waist high. It was nearly identical to the one Merrick had fashioned as he and Riddick grew and started training. It brought a sense of comfort, but he wasn't looking forward to getting hit.

Another group of people came from the adjacent side of the box and Shaz found Tristan in the center. He gauged his movements paying particular attention to his hip movements. He wanted to determine if he was going to use his core force or if he was going to favor the arm strength. Tristan stopped at the other side of the box and removed his shirt. His large frame rippled as he flexed his muscles and Shaz rolled his eyes.

"Arrre you surrre you have to do zis?" Declan asked.

"Aye," Shaz said.

"How much can-kicking should I allow?" Serin asked.

"I'll let you know," Shaz said.

Shaz gripped the back of his collar and pulled his tunic over his head. The crowd on his side of the box roared with cheers and a pit in Shaz's stomach settled in. Serin touched his arm and Shaz looked at her. She reached up on her tiptoes and kissed him. Her kiss was tingly as she sent the boost of her pain magic into his body. He took in the magic and then smiled at her.

"Don't die," Serin said.

"I'll try," Shaz said.

Shaz ducked under the top rail and entered the box. Merrick had taught him, to always be first in the box and take the corner you want. Tristan climbed into the box and rolled his shoulders. Shaz hopped a little bounce-jump and swung his arms to ease his mind into gear. It wasn't necessary, but he found it gave the opponent the idea that he needed time to warm up, which gave them the false understanding that if they came at him hard and fast they could take him out easily.

Tristan gripped his fists together and Shaz determined he wasn't quite as big as Merrick, which was a nice advantage. He had fought Merrick so many times, he had a pretty good idea what his strategy was going to be, but what he didn't know was if Tristan was a dirty fighter or an honorable one. His first impression was that he was going to take as many cheap shots as he could, and he counted on that. Declan entered the box and held out his arms to address the crowd and waited until they quieted down.

"Let it be said zat Shaz son of RRReinholt challenges Trrristan son of Ean in hand-to-hand kombat of skill, what arrre yourrr konditions?" Declan said loudly.

He motioned to Tristan.

"When I vin, Declan vill rrrelinquish kommand to me, and leave Hammerrrstead forrrever," Tristan growled.

Declan motioned to Shaz.

"When I win," the crowd laughed, "when I win, you relinquish command to Declan, and leave Hammerstead and never return, and shave that ugly scruff on your face," Shaz said.

The corner of Tristan's lip curled and the glint in his eye told Shaz that he had no indication of leaving.

"Niet hitting below belt, fight ends when I say," Declan said.

Shaz and Tristan nodded, and Declan left the box. Shaz squared his shoulders and lowered his center of gravity onto his heels as he sat in a slight crouch, assumed a high guard, and took in a deep breath. Tristan lowered his body and brought his hands up. Shaz stared into Tristan's eyes and waited for Tristan to take the first shot. Tristan moved his feet in a sidestep and Shaz countered moving in the other direction. They circled each other for a few lengths and Shaz was certain Tristan was trying to find a beat on him.

Shaz slowed his heart rate and focused on his training. Tristan lunged forward with a direct jab and Shaz felt the wind rush by as he rolled his head out of the way. Tristan followed with a backhand strike. Shaz instinctively threw his hands up and blocked, ducked out of the way, and sidestepped. Tristan cut from the other side, and Shaz again parried away. Tristan spun quickly and threw his closed fist around and Shaz ducked the back-handed slap. Tristan steadied himself and squared his shoulders. Shaz moved around the box and Tristan closed the gap and shot his fist outward in a large swinging side-strike over-extending his reach to maximize impact and aimed at Shaz's head. Shaz ducked, stepped on Tristan's foot, and slammed his fist into Tristan's ribs. Shaz heard the crack of Tristan's bones as he recoiled and hunched over with the sudden force. Shaz stood up and delivered an alarming elbow to the back of Tristan's head. Shaz jumped out of the way as Tristan's body ricocheted with the hit, and he stumbled forward.

Tristan spun around and a deep animal growl escaped his throat. That's what Shaz was looking for, how long it was going to take to get him riled up. Tristan took two fast steps toward Shaz and swung with a barrage of fast upper side-cuts. Shaz dodged and weaved the hits and his heart-rate flashed adrenaline to his limbs. The warmth it gave his muscles eased the stiffness, and he moved easily. Shaz rounded Tristan and stepped into a hit to Tristan's kidney. Tristan roared as his body absorbed the impact. Pain raced through his brain and Tristan pulled his elbow backward.

Shaz saw it coming and bent backward but not in time to avoid part of the hit. The pain didn't sear his brain like usual, but his head jerked with the sudden force, and he stumbled backward. The increasing heat bore down on them and sweat splashed the crowd as he hit the wooden poles of the box. Shaz shook his head to clear the fog but the pressure of Tristan's large fist sank through his guts and to his spine. Shaz's body collapsed, and he struggled to get air in his lungs. The ringing in his ears overpowered his thoughts but Shaz rolled away from Tristan's large boot nearly landing on his face. Tristan chased Shaz as he rolled and Serin's blood boiled. She found it extremely difficult to not buff him with her magic.

Shaz wrapped his arm around Tristan's next stomp and threw his body, leading with hips upward and Shaz kicked toward his face. Shaz's foot planted a solid strike into Tristan's throat and Tristan's body jerked away. Shaz analyzed Tristan's gasps and sputters as he rolled through the motion and came to his feet. The discomfort of the puffiness from the welt on the side of his face irritated his mind, and he skittered toward Tristan. Shaz threw a shuto hand strike into the side of Tristan's head. Shaz followed his foot's movement and shifted his weight striking with a buffeting of fist-strikes. Tristan hollered with shock and pain and Shaz rolled around to his front. Shaz struck with a double-hand-slice and hit the corners of Tristan's neck. Tristan's knees went weak and his stomach lurched with the overload of chemical releasing from his body. Shaz slammed his closed fist into Tristan's face shattering his nose. Blood sprayed Shaz in the face and he flinched. Tristan fell backward and hit the ground hard. Dust puffed around his frame and the crowd gaped in total disbelief.

Shaz's guts were now on fire as the pain block Serin had given him was wearing off. A hush over the crowd made Shaz's nerves ache as if they knew something he didn't. Tristan stirred and moaned as his limbs regained their ability to move. Tristan struggled to his feet and touched his face and found the blood dripping. He licked the blood as a frenzy surged from his guts. Tristan dug his toe into the dirt and Shaz saw the shift in his hips as he darted toward him. Shaz shifted his weight onto his back foot and threw his forward leg into a snap-kick that caught Tristan in the chin. His head jerked upward, and blood flew in a spray as his bottom jaw slammed his teeth into his upper teeth. Tristan shuffled backward and struggled to shake off the fog and spit the rest of the blood into the dirt.

Shaz rounded Tristan and ducked the side lunge and swept his foot and hooked it around Tristan's ankle. Tristan yanked his leg out of the grapple and shoved his foot toward Shaz's thigh. Shaz rolled out of the thrust and came to his feet. Tristan quickly rolled his shoulders and caught Shaz in the ribs with a double-fist-punch. Shaz heard and felt the crack of his ribs, and he stumbled backward. Tristan wrapped his beefy arms around Shaz's body and picked him up and body-slammed his full-frame onto Shaz. They landed on the wooden fence and it shattered under their weight.

The impact expelled all the air from his lungs and Shaz's brain shot into overdrive with pain. Shaz's limbs instantly went numb from the crack in his spine and his eyes teared. Tristan rolled off him and Shaz tried to roll out of the way, but his body didn't respond. Tristan stood and the crowd was silent. Tristan looked around and could see the terrified expressions of the people. He had expected cheers and applause, but the people were completely shocked.

Shaz closed his eyes and reached out to Serin. Shaz could tell Serin's energy was raw and angry. She gave him a mental picture of his heartfire wrap around his frame and ease the pain and force the bones in his spine to realign. The crack and pop of the tissues obeying irritated his senses, but the sensations returned to his limbs. Pain receptors called for more adrenaline and a boost of energy filled his frame. He called the air to his lungs and it filled them to capacity.

Shaz started to move and struggled to his feet. The crowd broke into cheers and Tristan smiled, until he realized it was Shaz they were cheering for. Shaz allowed his heartfire to fill his body with heat and Tristan turned to see Shaz steady himself on the half-crushed fence.

"You have to be insane," Tristan sneered.

"I have been told I'm stubborn," Shaz said.

Tristan lunged and Shaz sidestepped and stepped in with his front foot, pivoting towards the incoming punch, snapped out a right-hand shuto just below Tristan's elbow blocking with one hand and the other made contact at his voice box. Shaz whipped his body around to follow his forward foot and rammed his fist into Tristan's inner leg. Tristan's leg faltered and released his heavy frame. Shaz spun around with a reverse roundhouse sending the heel of his boot into the center of Tristan's face. Blood poured from his mouth as Shaz released a fast upper-side-cut to his temple. Shaz closed and interlocked his fists. He swung his arms over his head like he was swinging an ax and slammed them into Tristan's spine at the base of his neck. Shaz cringed as he felt the bones snap under his strike.

Tristan's body fell limp with a thud and Shaz breathed heavily. The crowd cheered and Shaz stepped backward as blood pooled from Tristan's open mouth. His eyes stared blankly and Shaz was positive he had just killed the man. An odd sense of relief overcame him, but it was accompanied by a new sense of shame. He wasn't even bothered at all, which then made him wonder if he was slipping closer to his shadow magic. Merrick *had* taught him, that you either kill or be killed, but the manifestation of that made Shaz's guts lurched, and he wanted to hurl. Declan hurried into the arena and checked Tristan's pulse. He stood and took Shaz's hand and held it up.

"Arrre zerrre any other challengerrrs?" Declan asked. The crowd was silent, "I declarrre Shaz is vinner," Declan said.

Serin ran to Shaz and wrapped her arm around him to help him. She sent an instant boost of pain magic into him as she touched his heated skin. He sighed with the relief, but his broken body struggled to regain its proper form. Declan dismissed the crowd and a group of men helped make way for them to return to Declan's house.

31-We'll Leave You To Your Planning

Declan opened the door and Serin helped Shaz inside. Cristen came from the backroom and gasped as she internalized Shaz's battered frame.

"Oh, my goodness," Cristen cried.

"He'll be alright, I just need to get him to our room," Serin said.

"I'll fetch medicine maker," Cristen said.

"No, I'll take care of everything," Serin said.

Cristen wasn't sure what to think but Declan gave her a nod, and she moved out of the way. Serin helped Shaz to the bed and closed the door.

"You certainly got your can kicked," Serin said.

"Aye," Shaz said.

"Can you lay down, or would you rather sit?" Serin asked.

Shaz eased slowly into the mattress and winced and hissed as his body adjusted. Serin put her hands on his chest and searched for all of his injuries. There were more than when the Shadow Selket slammed him into the floor, and she frowned.

"Shaz, you're in awful shape, why did you last so long," Serin asked.

Serin wrapped her hands around the invisible energy of the water and air element and her soft blue aura illuminated in front of her.

"I had to beat him in an honest fight," Shaz said.

"You call that an honest fight?" Serin asked.

"As honest as beating each other up can be," Shaz said.

"I suppose," Serin said.

Serin let the tingling energy ball sink into his skin, and she wriggled her fingers instructing the magic to go to the different areas of his injuries. Shaz focused on the warmth the magic gave his mind and allowed the euphoria to tickle his senses. He hated the scraping his bones made as they returned to their proper places, it made his teeth hurt, if that was possible. Serin breathed in careful and deliberate breaths as she moved the magic around his body.

"How bad is it?" Shaz asked.

"Well, you're not dead, but if a wager had been made, I would be paying up," Serin said.

Shaz smiled, but his body, even though was under her magic, didn't feel happy. Shaz mused as her face scrunched the way it does when she focused, and his heart swelled. He was even more thankful for her than before, and she stopped her work and leaned over and kissed him to reassure him and then returned to her mending.

Declan paced the hall outside and struggled with what he had witnessed. It was their custom to be highly skilled fighters, and they taught to kill or be killed, but there was something almost rabid about the way Tristan acted during the fight. His guts knotted up as he replayed the fight in his mind and Cristen tried not to ask, but she was worried about the way Declan was acting. He had explained in general, and she too was filled with an emotion she didn't expect. She was tired of Tristan's threats and bullying, but to have him dead hadn't quite sank into her being. Cristen busied herself with cleaning the house and checking on the smoked meat in the back smoker, but the worry in the house was so thick it could be cut with a knife.

Serin moved to the last bit of mending on Shaz's face and hoped the cut in his cheek wouldn't leave a scar. He already had enough, and she wanted so badly to make them disappear. Her armlet tickled her skin and she examined it. The symbols rearranged into new instructions, and she read them carefully. Her mind filled with a unique procedure, and she thought about it for a minute.

"Is everything alright?" Shaz asked.

"Yes, I'm just thinking about how I want to heal your cheek," Serin said.

"So, it doesn't hurt," Shaz said.

"No, I think I'm going to leave a big orange boil on your face," Serin said.

Shaz snorted and was pleased his insides weren't on fire anymore. Serin smiled but closed her eyes and let the symbols in her mind organize with the symbols she was seeing in Shaz's scroll markings on his back. The glyphs settled into a specific place on the old language and formed new ones. Shaz felt his magic being called from his core and mix into hers, and she fused the skin together in a new manner. The slow and calculated formula erased even the slightest mark on his gently tanned skin and Serin's excitement surfaced.

Shaz remembered the first time she used magic to 'sew' him up in the shifting woods so long ago and found she had the same glint in her eyes as she did then.

"There, finally, no scar," Serin said.

She reached over him and kissed it anyway, and Shaz pulled her onto him and wrapped her into a tight hug.

"You're not going to get sappy are you," Serin asked.

"No, happy, remember," Shaz said.

Serin was certain that was what he was going to say, and she sank into his embrace. They laid together for a little bit but knew they needed to wrap things up and get back to the castle.

"I think Declan is going to need a bit of calming energy," Serin said.

"Yes, I think he's passed the room now for the fiftieth time," Shaz said.

They climbed out of the bed and Shaz opened the door. Declan spun around at the end of the hall and hurried to greet him.

"Arrre you alrrright, I've been vorrried sick," Declan said.

Declan investigated Shaz's face and torso, which Shaz realized he had left his tunic at the box and sighed. He always seemed to be half-dressed lately.

"Aye, good as new," Shaz said.

Serin came out of the room and rested her hand on Declan's shoulder. She sent a soft dose of calming energy into his body, and he shivered with the caress.

"How?" Declan asked.

"Magic," Shaz said.

"I don't underrrstand, I mean I underrrstand idea of elemental magic, I've just never seen it," Declan said. Shaz sensed several people in the outer room of the house and started toward the opening. "Oh, da, memberrrs of old rrregime have kome to addrrress you," Declan said.

"Regime?" Serin asked.

"Another name for Council," Shaz said.

Declan looked at Shaz with a curious glance but nodded in agreement.

"Would you like a new shirt first," Serin asked holding up another tunic from his pack.

"Thanks, I keep losing these," Shaz said.

I don't mind Serin said in her mind.

Shaz blushed and hurried and pulled the ivory silk shirt on over his head and Serin smirked. Shaz cleared his throat and made his way into the next room. The group of men ranged from old to older with a few more like Merrick's age. The men arranged themselves into an order Serin guessed was a rank of some kind and Shaz took each of them by the Ranger's handshake. The men were surprised, both with his understanding of the culture and the fact that there wasn't a single scratch on him. These men, however, were familiar with the powers of the elements, but it had been such a long time since they had seen it.

"Pleasure to meet you," an elderly man said as Shaz reached him in the back of the room.

"The honor is mine. My father has told me so many things about the Rangers," Shaz said.

"I understand you were raised by Merrick and his wife," the man said.

"Aye," Shaz said.

"But he looks just like his father Reinholt," another man said.

"That's what I have been told," Shaz said.

"I'm sorry for your loss," a third man said.

"Thank you," Shaz said.

"Declan filled us in on what happened," the older gentleman said.

"We hear you are recruiting an army to fight Jaduuk," the second man said.

"Aye, you have seen Jaduuk before?" Shaz asked.

"Some of us, yes," a man said.

"Then I must ask," Shaz started.

"You don't need to ask, ve arrre at yourrr serrrvice," Declan said.

"Now that things have been put back in order, you have our allegiance," the second man said.

"Thank you, Declan, you remember the plan then?" Shaz asked.

"I do, ve vill be zerrre," Declan said.

Declan took Shaz's hand in his and Shaz recognized a new vibe from the man. Shaz was confident things would return to the ways of the Rangers now that Tristan was out of the way.

"That was some fight, I can't believe how much you reminded me of both Reinholt and Merrick," one of the men said.

Shaz didn't know what Reinholt's fighting style was, and always figured he had learned from Merrick, so he must have his, but maybe it was more of the physical mannerisms he inherited from his father.

"I am sorry, but we need to go," Serin said.

"Of course," the elderly gentleman said.

"It's getting nightfall, arrre you surrre," Cristen said.

"Aye, we'll be fine, we'll leave you to your planning," Shaz said.

Shaz excused himself and returned to the room, and he and Serin gathered their things quickly. Serin could tell Shaz was in a hurry but wasn't quite sure why. Serin stopped in the kitchen and gave Cristen a hug and thanked her for her generosity and Serin could tell she too had a new vibe about her. They tried to leave quietly but Declan followed them out of the house.

"If you vant to leave vithout being seen you should go zis vay," Declan said.

Declan motioned to the stables at the side of the town.

"Thank you," Serin said.

"I've sent forrr yourrr horrrses to be rrready forrr you," Declan said.

Shaz slapped his shoulder and Serin gave him a hug. At the stable they found a young lad finishing tightening the harness on the chestnut.

"We'll take the Branagan together," Shaz said to the lad.

Serin gave him a questioning side-glance but nodded as Shaz removed the saddle the boy had strapped on. Shaz pulled a few coins out of his pocket and gave them to the boy who smiled big.

"And, please don't say anything to anyone," Serin said.

The boy nodded and they made their quiet escape and Shaz started out toward the mountain range in the opposite direction of the castle.

"Where are we going?" Serin asked.

"I realized last night as we were heading toward the mountains that I never closed the Mountain Temple in this realm and with the Jaduuk becoming a bigger issue, I need to get that done," Shaz said.

"I see, how far is it?" Serin said.

"Not far, but it will set us back a day or so," Shaz said.

"Alright," Serin said.

Serin buffed the horse and Shaz guided the magnificent animal over the landscape. His night vision took over and Serin wrapped her arms around him, rested her head on his back and closed her eyes. The air magic, the natural ease of the animal, and Shaz's warmth made for a smooth ride and Serin found the motion hypnotic. She drifted in and out of drowsiness as she tried to stay awake through the night. The sun began to push out the night, but it didn't help much as the mountain was now shielding them from the light. Shaz slowed the Branagan and Serin stirred. Shaz eased the horse over a small stream and Serin sat up and looked around.

The coolness was bitter, and her breath steamed as she exhaled. Her nose was on the verge of getting cold and if that happened she would be cold for hours.

"How much farther?" Serin asked.

"The entrance is just over that ridge, but there is a bit of trek once we reach the inside," Shaz said.

"Will we be on foot?" Serin asked.

"I have no clue," Shaz said.

They continued up the path and luckily it wasn't too steep for the horse, which seemed to enjoy the challenge and would have done it anyway. The path widened and the natural dirt was replaced with hand honed stones placed tightly in rows. They rounded a bend, and a grand doorway came into view. A large stone header topped pillars that sat next to a set of stone doors. Shaz let Serin off the horse and then climbed off. He patted the horse and stroked its nose as he took in the details of the surroundings.

"This one won't be like the last one will it?" Serin asked.

"I don't think so, but I don't actually know what or who was the last to access this one," Shaz said.

He ran his hand along the engraved marks on a rail that led to the doors. The magical signature eased into his senses and understood this was the access to get in, but there was another place that the Jaduuk most likely used when they came after him last time. Shaz studied the images in the stones for a quick minute and understood how to open the door. He pushed the marks needed and the latch unlocked. He swung the door open and the entrance was large enough for the horse. Serin called the animal and it nickered and followed them. Shaz found a torch on the wall and ignited the cloth. A large lobby opened and the murals in the walls were very similar to the mountain temple of the Minca. Shaz took in the details and understood what this was.

"This is Cornelia's temple, the Temple of the Enlightened. This is where the Dodjen was organized," Shaz said.

"It's quite lovely, not at all like the Velshari temple," Serin said.

"Aye, but it has a violent past and is as old as the realms," Shaz said.

"Are they all that old?" Serin asked.

"I believe so," Shaz said.

Shaz instructed the horse to wait, and they quickly made their way through the corridors until they found the main intersection. Shaz examined the notes in the carvings and they found the portal room near the back side of the temple.

"I'm not sure how much energy this is going to take," Shaz said.

"Alright, I'm ready," Serin said.

Shaz called the multi-colors of his magic into a sphere and rolled it into a tight ball. He let the energy hover in the air and began the ancient language and thankfully he found all but two of the portals already secured, plus the portal to the other temples, which he left open but secured it with his new instructions. The light of the magic grew as he spoke the secured language and the room began to lighten. He closed the two that were open but committed the names so that he could look into them when they got back to the castle. Shaz also instructed them to notify him at his castle if anyone or anything tries to access them. He found the portal from the underground and secured it. Sweat formed at his hairline as the heat of his magic swirled around the vast room. Serin dug her toes into the ground and gripped her hydro-light magic. She rounded her head with her little dance and focused on sending the energy into Shaz.

The force left her being and traveled into Shaz, but on the way Serin caught a glimpse of something move through the light. Her heart pounded and she took a step back and checked again. Panic raced around her heart and Shaz turned to see her with a surprised but unsteady expression. His heart jumped and he looked around.

Serin tried to find the object she thought she saw but nothing was there. Shaz's nerves itched with a need to hurry, so he gripped the energy and imagined the three underworld accesses close shut. He secured it with his shadow magic and instructed that he was the only one that could open it. The mountain rumbled deep and Shaz was confident the doors had been shut and locked. He let his magic fade and the brightness it gave eased back to only the firelight at the entrance of the room. Shaz sucked in a deep breath and turned to Serin who was nervously waiting near the exit.

"Are you alright?" Shaz asked.

"Yes, but let's get out of here," Serin said.

Shaz took the torch and left the room. On the other side he disguised the entrance to appear as the mountain with instructions never to reveal itself unless they give it his passkey. They hurried back through the temple and found the Branagan. Shaz wanted to ask Serin about what had her spooked, but he figured she would tell him when she was ready, she usually did. They returned down the path and where the stone pathway started Shaz instructed the mountain to disguise the entrance to appear as the rugged mountain and a dead end.

32-This Is Treason!

Deri peeled around the corner and skidded in the gravel as he barreled into the camp. The stags jumped with the sudden intrusion but felt his eagerness as the sweat was dripping down his bare chest and his tanned skin was pink with the warmth of running hard and fast. Deri slowed quickly and tried to catch his breath before rounding the edge of the pavilion which was being used as the headquarters. Deri didn't wait too long and hurried around the corner. He was still out of breath but at least he was able to make at least one sentence at a time.

"Antorn, we arrived at the valley, and we found nothing, not a single soul, no structures, stags, fawn, grain stacks, nothing. Tobis believes they were carried off, we found tracks leading into a mountain pass. They need reinforcements immediately," Deri said.

Antorn's eyes searched his reddened face then gave orders to make ready the next troop. The troop raced across the distance and Antorn struggled to know whether he should go or stay and keep an eye on the Order. It wasn't that they were still thinking the old way, but he understood it wasn't easy to change your mindset overnight. He was still waiting to find out if Tage had been found and so far there was no word. He wondered where he would have gone being there were no hoof prints. A thought came to mind, and he tried to remember if they had actually searched his chambers. Antorn took a couple stags and returned to the council building.

The guardsmen split up and searched the lower levels and Antorn went to the room he had encountered him the first time. The building was empty, but an interesting feeling lingered in the air. Antorn didn't like being inside either and figured maybe that was the reason. The room was empty, but he made a sweep anyway and noticed a tiny gap in what looked like an old wood trim along the side of the door as he was about to leave. He stopped and heard a faint gasp. Antorn pulled the board open and found Tage hiding in the dark of a secret room.

Antorn flicked his antler and the stags hurried toward him.

"Well, how about that? You are as crooked as you look. What a coward," Antorn said.

"You'll never get away with this," Tage said.

"Away with what exactly? What do you think is going on?" Antorn asked.

The stags entered the room and yanked Tage out of the cubby. Tage wriggled and squirmed under their heavy grips.

"This is treason!" Tage shouted.

"Let me ask you, do you suppose to sit upon your high and mighty seat and do nothing while we face a clear and eminent danger and have not committed treason? Do you suppose when the initial indications of the beasts appeared, and you did nothing you didn't commit treason? Do you suppose you are protected as long as you stay inside these walls while the rest of your kind are slaughtered and taken is not treason? No Tage, I have not committed treason, you are who has committed treason and you are lucky I am only going to lock you up and I won't even mess up that hair," Antorn said.

Antorn indicated to the guards to take Tage, and they wrestled him out of the room. Antorn wondered if the council was aware of the secret room and if they were hiding other things as well. Antorn returned to the camp and instructed a group of Fawn to inspect every inch of the building and secure everything. Antorn's mind quickly returned to the battle at hand and made his way to the guardsmen. He organized another troop to head to the area they first met the beasts and sent another to the midlands. He sent a recon group of Fawn to scour the edges and report back but to stay out of conflict.

Even though he had plenty to do his mind returned to Mazen often, and he struggled to keep his fears from overtaking him. The night was quiet as much of the new Guard was now on duty. Antorn gazed into the sky and observed a bright flash across the darkened night. He had seen them before and wondered if it was one of the glowing spheres falling from the atmosphere. A flicker caught his attention, and he squinted to inspect the light. A hint of green specked the atmosphere, not like fire or any other light in the sky. He held out his hand to judge the distance and found it was coming from the tip of the farthest mountain peak. He made a note and decided he would send a recon unit in the morning.

"Antorn, Sir, a recon unit has returned, but they have been injured," a guard said.

Antorn hurried to the Fawn and found one of them had been injured quite badly and the others were hurt but would be alright.

"What happened?" Antorn asked.

"We were scouting the outskirts examining the blackened earth and didn't see the beasts until they were upon us. We barely made it out alive," a fawn said.

"What about the inhabitants?" Antorn asked.

"We didn't have time to find out, but I don't think there are many, if any left. We found a lot of the black earth though," a fawn said.

Antorn thought about the statement. The amount of blackened earth related to how many beasts there was intrigued his mind. It made sense though, and he wondered what the correlation was. He thoughts quickly jumped between Mazen and Nama and the beasts and his heart raged with anger. His intuition told him they were dead, and his hope said they were still alive, but he knew from his history that hope rarely won the argument and his anger grew.

"Take them to the healers and you follow me," Antorn said.

The Fawns nodded and the others helped their kin as the first followed Antorn. He took him into the tent where the new maps were laying out on a table.

"Explain to me where you were and what you saw," Antorn said.

The fawn began to explain where they were and outlined the dark earth with a marking tool. Antorn was right, it was in the exact place that Nama was, and his blood boiled. The fawn shrunk back a little as he watched Antorn's expressions rage from angry to angrier. Antorn realized his guards fear and tried to soften his tight jaw.

"This is where some of my kin are," Antorn said.

The fawn nodded with understanding, but he kept a safe distance.

"We did see hoof tracks lead to the falls, but were unable to follow them," the fawn offered.

Antorn nodded, but he was convinced they had no hope to their survival. He dismissed the fawn and paced the tent for several lengths. His body ached from the rawness of the new emotions, and he was both exhausted and invigorated. He poured over the maps and struggled to keep his anger from overtaking him, but he picked up a tankard of brewed grains and chucked it. The tin clapped and clanged through the still night, and he covered his face with his hands.

"I won't presume to understand what you are experiencing, but I can tell you I too have had moments like these," Slat said. Antorn looked at the older stag and found a kind compassion in his eyes he didn't expect. "I know you don't trust us yet. Even as old as I am, I can still learn things and what I have learned in the last half moon, is you have more to offer our kind than anyone I have ever met. I have learned there are things out there we have never encountered before, and you are the right one to figure things out. I have learned even when you think you have it all together, no one really does, and we're all just trying to do our best," Slat said.

Antorn looked at him. He had no idea what to say or what to think for that matter. Slat gave him a gentle smile and patted his shoulder.

"I am sorry I don't completely trust you yet," Antorn said.

"You have every right to doubt our loyalties, as we had been caught up in the wrong set of thinking. I can tell you we all feel we have been liberated and are now free to follow our own conscience," Slat said.

"Those are big words, no one really knows those," Antorn said.

Slat laughed.

"But you and I do, which is refreshing to me. To have a leader who is as intelligent as he is brave," Slat said.

"I'm just a weirdo no one understands," Antorn said.

"That is may be what you used to be, but not anymore," Slat said.

"What am I supposed to with that?" Antorn asked.

"I have learned you are a doer not a sayer, and people follow that. I will hold things here while you check on your kin," Antorn gave him a curious look and inspected his face. "The Smitting brothers won't let me get away with anything, they are quite good at their job," Slat said with a smile.

Slat held out his hand and Antorn took it into a grip of friendship and nodded.

"I won't be long," Antorn said.

"What are your orders?" Slat asked.

"Keep building the forces and provisions, let's get this under control and fast," Antorn said.

Slat saluted and Antorn hurried out to find a small troop to take with him. The night quickly turned into morning as the stags closed in on the area the fawn had indicated seeing the black earth. They slowed their paces and Antorn signaled for them to spread out. They quickly but carefully moved through the fields which were now burned and heavy with pitch. Antorn waved his men toward a group of trees but to move with caution. He understood the beasts hid in the grassed and were able to slink low to the ground.

Antorn halted the group and searched. He found a set of black glassy eyes just as Tobis had described and signaled his findings. The troop scrutinized deeper and tapped their antlers to signal their findings. Eighteen beasts were counted and Antorn initialized the group to divide into two sides and circle the creatures. It was their turn to surround them and Antorn had learned they hunted as a pack but didn't do as well when they themselves were surrounded. He also learned there was a leader and when taken out the group struggled more.

He wasn't sure how to find the leader until they were up close when he could search for the marking on the shoulder, but he guessed it was the first set of eyes he found. That's how he would do it anyway. The guardsmen fanned out and readied their position to strike but Antorn knew this group of stags had never fought the beasts before and worried if their lack of skill would become an issue.

The grasses underneath the acacia trees started to move slightly and Antorn was certain the pack was on the move. He stepped closer and waited a length then stepped closer. His heart hit overload as the glassy eyes emerged only a length in front of him, and he turned and lunged back the other way. He pulled his battle-ax and winced as the sharp clawed hooves of the beast ripped through the skin of his back leg. He stopped and lifted his hind legs and slammed them into the chest of the beasts sending the sizable animal flailing backward.

Antorn lunged again and shot out of the grip of another beast. His troop descended on the beasts with great vigor and Antorn rounded his speed and ripped the ax upward and into the side of the head of a beast. The beasts evaded more of the strikes as though they were learning from their attack styles and Antorn gripped a spear. He hurled the shaft at a beast which was hot on the tail of a stag and the tip sank deep into its back. The beast slammed into the ground and howled. Antorn released another spear as did several of the stags.

Each took turns using the ax if they had one, and the spears. Antorn decided every unit needed the fawn ballista-ers and slammed his fist into the side of a beast he rounded before it could lash out with its clawed grip. The beast recoiled but spun on its hoof and snarled. Antorn swung the blade at the beast but it jumped out of the way and sidestepped. The awkward fineness of the beast alarmed his senses, and he skittered out of its reach, but turned in a backward strike and caught the beast in the back of the neck with the ax blade.

The beast fell with a thud and Antorn turned to another. A stag launched his spear into the air, and it landed in the leg of a beast immobilizing it, and then he ran straight at it. He stayed just out of reach and ran the blade of his bone spear across its neck and the rancid oily blood squirted him. The fumes made the stag gag, and he tried to keep his nerve but didn't succeed and hurled. Another beast turned to him and with long powerful strides it covered a great distance quickly.

Antorn reached for another spear but his quiver was empty. He frantically searched for something he could use and found the spear he had first launched. He lunged toward it and yanked the staff from the lifeless body. He spun and quickly made his mark and launched the staff. The humming it made as it sizzled through the air eased his nerves, but his anticipation ate at his heart. The spear raced across the beasts side causing it to recoil but it didn't detract it from his target.

The stag regained his composure and turned to find the beasts about to overwhelm him. He ducked low to the ground and rolled under the beasts leap and hurried back to his feet. He spun around as did the beast, but he was prepared to kick with his powerful hind legs. The stags' hooves planted square in the beast's chest with so much strength that he felt the creature's skin break before the force pummeled it backward. The beast launched into the air and plowed into the dirt. The other stags also used their hinds legs to their advantage and Antorn gathered another spear from a dead beast. He turned his attention to the last few beasts and aided the fight until they had overpowered the pack.

33-No Time To Visit

Turkill and Jagwynn made good time getting to the Northman's settlement high in the mountains. Turkill was glad it was a bit cooler than in the jungle biome of his realm as he had become accustomed to wearing more clothes. The watchman sent a signal overhead and Turkill and Jag slowed down as they closed in on the little squat building. An older man with a long white beard and lighter skin came out of one of the buildings in the center and Turkill slid off Jagwynn.

"Turkill, we just received the news, tell me what is going on?" the man said.

"Tomos, how are you?" Turkill asked.

"We are good, come," Tomos said.

Tomos pulled the latch and opened the wood door to the building. The brightness of the mid-day's sun left his eyes the need to adjust, and he blinked. Several men were sitting around a long table each with a mix of hurmpf looks and Turkill chuckled to himself. He was the best scowler according to Serin, and he mused at what she would think about these men.

"Please sit," Tomos said.

Tomos indicated a chair and Turkill dismissed it.

"I'll stand thank you," Turkill said.

"Tell, us what can we do to help?" a man asked from the center of the table.

"We are in need of a mass-scale pyro-crew and enough explosives to detonate a city," Turkill said. The men looked at him with blank stares, and he realized they had no idea what a city was. "Enough to blow this mountain," Turkill said.

Gasps and instant murmurings sounded the room.

"Are you serious?" another man asked.

"I am afraid so, you know how many Jaduuk we fought last time? Well, there are ten times that or more, and our explosives were the most powerful tool we had in winning against them, the creatures of the Timeless Plains are in great need of our help, and if the Jaduuk take over that realm, they will take over the rest of them. I wish I could say this is all a big gag, but its serious, and we only have a few days to make ready," Turkill said.

The men could see the seriousness in his features as well as his tone and dread settled over the hut. The oldest Minca stood and held out his hands to quiet the crowd.

"You have our support," the Eldest said.

Each man stood and gave Turkill a salute and Turkill returned with his own.

"Frebin, Drager, take your men into the caverns and start loading up the explosives, Harmus you and Orn gather the animals,

Abban you gather your experts and organize several crews," the Eldest said.

"How are we going to get our animals there?" Orn asked.

"We're not, Shaz has a plan for that, all we need them to do is take the material to the portals and Shaz will take care of the rest," Turkill said.

"It will take us a few days to travel to the jungle and impossible to bring all this up the mountain," Tomos said.

Turkill pulled out a map and unrolled the paper onto the table.

"Shaz is going to make us portals, here and here," Turkill said pointing to the marks. "That way we can have access to more if we need," Turkill said.

"More, but this will be more than half our supply," Orn said.

"Then we will need to start mining," Turkill said.

"How much to think we will need?" another man asked his voice and brows raised.

"I can't say for sure, but I don't think this will be the last time Shaz will need our explosives, so I think we need to plan on having ten times our normal supplies," Turkill said.

"That is going to make us a target," Tomos said.

"I know, so we will have to make some improvements to our safety measures, I have an idea for that," Turkill said.

"Alright, how quick can we make this happen?" the Eldest asked.

"My crew can start transporting as soon as we have the mammoths," Frebin said.

"They are grazing in the peaks, it will take a day to bring them down," Harmus said.

"Alright, let's go," Tomos said.

The Eldest dismissed the clansman and Turkill waited until the men began to disperse.

"Eldest, Shaz has a special request," Turkill said.

"What is it?" the Eldest asked.

Turkill handed him a piece of parchment and the Eldest read the script and nodded. Turkill saluted and left the hut.

****

Shaz and Serin rounded through the valleys of the highlands until they came to the travelers' encampment that they had spent time in not too long ago. Shaz didn't have to steer the horse as the Branagan seemed to already know where it was going and Serin believed it did. They slowed as they rounded the last bend toward the tents. A round stout man came out of the first tent and Serin smiled at his red cheeks and excitedly waving arms.

"Shaz, Serin what a surprise," the man boomed.

They dismounted and the man pulled Serin into a tight squeeze.

"Lashi, how are you?" Shaz said.

Shaz held out his hand to shake Lashi's but Lashi pulled him into a hug anyway.

"We are good, what is the matter?" Lashi asked.

"Why is it that everywhere we go everyone always asks us that?" Shaz asked.

Serin gave him a 'serious' look and Shaz gave her the 'yeah your right' look.

"We need your help," Serin said.

"Of course, of course, come," Lashi said.

Lashi led them toward another tent where he summoned Barsoli, Kaven, and Ruslo who followed them into the place where the leaders met which was a good distance from the tents. Shaz filled them in on the details and explained the need for healers and warriors. The men engaged in a discussion and made the arrangements.

"I'm sorry, but we are in a hurry, we have no time to visit, I wish we could, but we can catch up when we see you at the castle," Serin said.

"We are honored you have come," Lashi said.

"Where is Rat?" Shaz asked.

"Why?" Barsoli asked.

"We need him to come with us and bring the horse back here," Shaz said.

"I couldn't help but notice, is that a Branagan?" Kaven asked.

"It is, and he belongs with you," Serin said.

"I thought they were all gone," Barsoli said.

"It's said, they are the offspring of the wyvern you know," Kaven said.

"They only appear when there is one noble enough to need them," the Choovino said as he winked at Serin.

"For such an old man you sure have a way of sneaking up on people," Lashi said, and he gripped his beating heart.

"I'll fetch Rat," Ruslo said.

"Thank you," Shaz said.

"You must be hungry, please eat before you leave," Barsoli said without a question.

Shaz agreed but Serin could tell he was still feeling anxious. Shaz tried to enjoy the quick reprieve but with the extra time at the temple, his guts were in a constant tightness. Rat hurried around the tent and gave a little hop-skip and Serin excused them.

"We really do appreciate your help, we will see you in a few days," Serin said.

Serin buffed them which made the stallion Rat was on run as quick as the Branagan, and they were able to reach the Senate Sanctum by nightfall. Serin buffed again and Rat returned with the horses while Shaz and Serin slipped through the portal.

The castle was quiet and dark when they returned and Shaz did his quick assessments and found that they were the first ones back. Shaz changed the chimes in the portal room to sound but by sending a vibrating pulse instead of loud bell-like noises when the crew traveled through, that way those who weren't magic wouldn't be woken up if it were at night as he didn't know how Motavo and Asher were doing.

By Shaz's inspection of the landscape as they passed the large windows in the front lobby, half the night was gone. They quietly stopped at the kitchen and got a quick bite of the Whispmother's mixed vegetable and meat hash and Serin decided on a bath. She loved the new improvements that the Whispmother had made when she added a private bath in her quarters and new windows. The Whispmother also took the liberty to soften the harsh cold stone floor with some plush rugs that accented the soft blues, ivory's, and golds in the room.

Shaz sat at the desk in his room and unfolded the few maps he had been collecting and marked one with the new locations of Hammerstead. He spent some time calculating the distances and placements of the portals and what it was going to take for him to make them big enough. He ran several ideas through his head as he tried to figure out how to secure them with so many people and equipment they had to move and from each of the places. Things made sense in his head and even on paper but a tinge in his guts made him question how practical it would really be, and he couldn't help the nervous vibes which sat in his guts.

"We'll get it figured out," Serin said. Shaz looked up with a bit of bloodshot in his eyes and Serin frowned, but she now understood what she had perceived. "I came to check on you because you have an odd sensation I haven't felt before," Serin said.

"Oh," Shaz ask-stated.

"I saw your dream last night, and there was a lot of dead Forrne," Serin said.

"Aye," Shaz said.

"Is that foretelling, or already happened?" Serin asked.

"I'm not sure, maybe both," Shaz said.

"That's not good," Serin said.

Serin took the writers instrument from him and moved the maps out of the way. She sat on the desk in front of him and ran her hands through his hair. Her touch was soothing, and he sensed a sudden sleepiness overcome his mind.

"What are you doing?" Shaz asked.

"Helping you relax," Serin said.

"With magic?" Shaz asked.

"Mmhm," Serin said.

"It's working," Shaz said.

"Good, you're not good to anyone if your grumpy," Serin said.

"Are you saying I am grumpy when I'm tired?" Shaz said slowly.

"Mmhm," Serin said.

She motioned for him to move to the bed where she tucked him in, and she pictured in her mind what it would be like to call the fire element and a burst of Shaz's magic ignited the fire in the fireplace. She jumped with the start and looked at Shaz who had his eyes closed and was breathing heavy, which made her wonder if he called the fire or if she did. They had learned that the fire crackling was more soothing to him than the water noise, and when his mind was in overdrive he had a hard time relaxing enough to find sleep. She closed the door and retired to her own room.

A crack of thunder ripped over the castle and the room shook with its rumbling. Shaz jumped out of bed and ripped the sword from under his mattress where Serin had tucked it the night before. Shaz scanned the room and found nothing was out of place but his heart was thudding in his chest. The drapes over the tall windows let in a tiny bit of light from the darkened sky but Shaz could tell several hours into the next day had passed and cursed.

Shaz threw his clothes on, hurried from the room, and started down the hall but sensed Serin still in her room and crossed the hall instead. He lifted the latch quietly and started to open the door. He peeked in and found her soft curves tucked under the covers, and he was about to close the door when she stirred.

"I'm not asleep," Serin said.

"I wasn't sure if you would be able to sleep with the rain," Shaz said.

"It's been obnoxious for hours now," Serin said.

Shaz tucked the sword under her mattress and pulled the covers back and slipped in next to her.

"You're freezing cold!" He propped himself on his elbow and rolled her over, so he could look at her face. Her eyes were red and puffy, and her teeth were chattering, "What is wrong? Do I need to fetch Helios?" Shaz heated up his body and pulled her tight. The magic coursed all around them and wrapped around her. He searched with his magic all over her body for anything that might be causing this but didn't find anything. "Are you sick? What's wrong, you're totally wigging me out," Shaz said.

The pit in his stomach surged, the hairs on the back of his neck stood out, and he searched Serin's face. Her deep green eyes were now black, and her skin started to crack. He frantically tried to put her skin back on her bones, but she continued to fall apart, and panic raced around his body. Tightness gripped around his shoulders, and he struggled from the grip of whatever was trying to pull him away.

A blast of magic pricked his senses, and he grappled at the chaos in his mind. Another surge ripped over his body, and he searched for Serin again but found she was no longer in sight, and he was in his own room.

He opened his eyes and turned to find a fully intact Serin with panic in her eyes. He jumped up and gripped her tightly, and she wrapped her arms around him. Shaz looked out the widow and it was barely early morning, and the sun was cresting the clear sky. He was certain now it was a nightmare, and his mind raced around what he saw.

"Are you alright?" Serin asked.

"It was a nightmare," Shaz said with a heavy sigh.

"I figured, but I thought you didn't have those anymore," Serin said.

"It was shadow magic, but not *the* shadow, it was my own shadow magic," Shaz said.

"How lovely, now what do we do?" Serin asked.

"I wish I knew," Shaz said.

"What was it about?" Serin asked.

"You couldn't see it?" Shaz asked.

"No, not like others, I only could tell you were in great panic," Serin said.

"You were dead and crumbling to dust," Shaz said.

Serin looked at him and found an unusual angst inside, and she hugged him tight.

"I'm sorry you had to see that. Do you think it has to do with that notebook you found?" Serin asked.

Shaz pulled away and looked at her.

"You are so smart," Shaz said.

"Well thank you, but you're being kinda weird right now," Serin said.

"What's new?" Shaz teased.

"That's true, you better go study that book before you explode," Serin said.

Shaz's face crinkled and Serin laughed. Shaz hurried out of the room and back to the book box where he pulled out the notebook he found in Isot's lair and then headed to the dungeon. He wasn't sure he would find anything there, but maybe he needed to inspect the rest of the cells and or the walls. If every other wall in the castle had hidden glyphs then maybe something else will show. The hallway was dark and Shaz called his magic and rolled it around and sent it into the door. The wood façade vanished, and the dungeon came into view. He stepped over the threshold and the prick of shadow magic bit at his skin. He waved his hand across the air and the sconces lit up.

The warm fire light throughout the hall was somehow comforting, but an awkward sensation sat in his chest, and he opened the first cell. He scanned the room and sent a wave of magic to inspect it and it came up empty. He repeated the process through all the cells and found that there had been many prisoners over the millennia's. His magic gave him faint impressions of who they were and why they had been incarcerated, and he found an odd interest in their stories.

He closed the cell door and came to the one that had the skeleton in it. He pulled the iron grate open and the bones were gone. Small piles of a powdery substance he assumed were the bones sat in the same shape and he found it interesting that they would become dust and so quickly since he was last in there.

Shaz put his hand on the wall and asked it to reveal any runes or glyphs which it did. One whole wall was covered with the marks and Shaz pulled out booth notebooks and sat on the floor. He opened each one and started to compare the markings. There was quite a bit that were the same as the notebook left by Enric which indicated they were a dialect of the ancient language, but Gavin's book wasn't the same, and he figured they were a type of shorthand note system.

He discovered that Enric was a scholar, he wasn't a full war wizard, and was only able to use shadow magic under limited circumstances. Shaz also learned that that was the way Gavin Rhill was. Shaz started to understand how it was that Gavin became the leader of the Velshari and was able decode the night Gavin banished Art-Te-Bus to the underworld. Time passed quickly but Shaz found his mind was infused in the stories that he couldn't disengage, even when Serin came to check on him. She set a plate of food next to him and left the dungeon quickly. She had a strong distaste for them after her time in the dungeon at Ebassia.

There was really nothing that Motavo and Asher couldn't take care of, so she figured he needed to finish his intrigue. Shaz found a marking on the stone wall that reminded of him of the thing he found, and he pulled it out of his pocket. He twisted it in his fingers while searching for the mark he remembered and when he found it he put it next to the glyph to compare the details. The rest of the marks began to glow and illuminate more marks that weren't there before. His mind shot into overdrive as a sudden influx of information raced across his eyes. His heart thumped and he struggled to breathe. Serin felt the distress and raced down the corridor. Her heart pounded with a fear she couldn't explain. She rolled her hands around each other and readied for a large dose of her hydro-light magic. She rounded the corner quickly and her assessment was correct. She launched the magic into Shaz's stiff frame and gripped another surge of magic. Shaz's body eased but she could tell he was in a state of interacting with another being or some kind of entity.

Serin sucked in a deep breath and tried to read his energy. The information she experienced sucked the breath she was about to inhale from her being and she gasped. Sweat ran down their faces as the magic of the eons of time wrapped around them. Shaz and Serin spent the next several lengths being elevated to yet another higher plane. The magic eased as the information dimmed and they sagged onto the cool stone floor. Serin's chest burned and she coughed and sputtered through her reflexes need to gain air and Shaz coughed through his responses returning to normal.

"Are you alright," Shaz managed.

Serin let out a cry as her body regained the ability to move. Shaz scooted over to her and wrapped her into his arms and held her tightly.

"What happened? Serin managed.

"It would seem we have been lifted to another level of magical understanding," Shaz said.

The image of the thing sat at the back of his mind and he now understood they had just unlocked the powers of the cosmos.

"That means we are going to have to something hard soon," Serin said.

"Aye," Shaz said.

"I don't think I like this," Serin said.

Shaz smiled but he felt the same way.

"We'll figure it out," Shaz said.

"Are you done causing trouble?" Serin asked.

"No, I'm nowhere close to that," Shaz said with a smile.

Serin smiled back but her body still didn't want to move. They rested for several lengths until they were able to make it out of the dungeon. They're minds were spinning with all the new information and Shaz was certain the thing was an ancient artifact just as the Sev-Rin-Ac-Lavah was and an intense need to secure it from the shadow hit his chest. He had no idea how he was going to do it, but he understood the need to figure it out.

****

Riddick stirred and let a small hole in the earth-bubble open at the top and examined the sky. He had no idea how long they had slept, but he could tell it was mid-morning and woke Amirra. Riddick let down the earth and the hot air hit their lungs.

"Why is it so hot here?" Amirra asked.

"I'm guessing it has to do with the scorched earth but what is causing that I don't know, I receive the readings that there is a great deal of lava closer to the surface than it should be, but why I don't know. Let's get moving, we're not far from the portal now," Riddick said.

Amirra swung her satchel over her shoulder and situated the strap across her chest and snagged a portion of rations for her and Riddick who shoved it into his mouth as he gripped a piece of earth. Amirra ate hers quickly and then stepped up onto the solid dirt turf. She settled in next to Riddick which allowed him to operate the hovercraft, and they started back toward the portal. The tall oval rock structure that framed the portal came into view and Riddick's nerves eased. He maneuvered the last little valley and slowed the craft just in time to jump off, and they ran through the mist.

34-Heat It Up Real Hot

The vibrations radiated through the castle and Shaz stirred and sat up. He quickly made his way to the portal room in time for Riddick and Amirra to come through.

"How did things go?" Shaz asked.

"Oiy mate, we have big problems," Riddick said.

"That's no good," Shaz said.

The pit in Shaz's stomach settled in, and he tried to relax, but he had already been feeling a dread and this just confirmed it.

"How about you, did you get Bowen's help?" Riddick asked.

"Aye, and the Rangers," Shaz said.

Riddick stopped mid-step and turned to Shaz with a confused look.

"Rangers?" Riddick asked.

"Aye, I'll fill you in over some breakfast," Shaz said.

Riddick nodded, and they made their way to the kitchen where they found the Whispmother's magical food sitting on the table, which was the best perk about have a magical castle. No one had to worry about being hungry, especially with the way the Whispmother loved to take care of everyone and Amirra who also loved to cook. She however had to cook the regular way but the Whispmother never minded sharing the kitchen.

The vibration of the portal buzzed and Shaz hurried back to the room. The Minca came through and Turkill gave their report and Ladtwig hurried into the kitchen. Shaz filled Riddick in on the details of Hammerstead and what happened to the people and Riddick gave his findings in the Plains. Motavo came into the room and welcomed them back. Motavo explained that Helios had returned to the academy, but would be back soon and Asher was out making a sweep around the castle boarders.

They finished eating and made their way to the war room where they began to strategize their plans. Asher returned from his inspections and Serin and Amirra busied themselves with new items to enchant.

"If the Timeless Plains are as dry as you say, I'm going to need something to rejuvenate my magic," Serin said.

"Oh goodness, I didn't think of that," Amirra said.

"I have no idea what to do though," Serin said.

"Humm," Amirra said. She rummaged through a box and found a small glass jar about the size of her thumb and examined it.

"What is that?" Serin asked.

"It's just a plain glass jar, but I was wondering if you could make a mini-rain cloud and then I could enchant the jar to keep it inside so when you need water you just pour out some rain from your cloud," Amirra said.

"Oh, my, you're brilliant," Serin said.

Amirra smiled.

"But it might not work, if the cloud has too much power it might break the glass," Amirra said.

"But if it's too small it won't do any good," Serin said.

"Oh wait, I could try to give the glass the enchantment I used on Ladtwig satchel, that way the jar can carry a cloud big enough," Amirra said.

"Oh, perfect, let's give it a try," Serin said.

Amirra ran through her chants quickly to organize her thought and completed the enchantment and then Serin called a mini-rain cloud and with her wind magic wrapped her hands around the energy, making the raincloud become small enough to push into the jar. The jar held the cloud for a few minutes but then shattered and the raincloud popped to full size drenching the girls who snarled with the displeasure of instantly becoming soaked. Amirra found another jar, and they tried again but that too shattered, but this time Serin stopped the cloud from releasing its stored water. Amirra's frustration flicked her nerves and Serin decided that maybe they needed to think of something else, especially if the castle was going to keep getting soaked. She didn't think the Whispmother would appreciate that.

"Wait a minute, I have an idea," Amirra said.

Amirra grabbed another small jar and cast her enchantment and then hurried to the war room. She threw the door open and all the men jumped. Amirra rounded the table quickly and stopped next to Riddick who gave her a glance of intrigue. Serin came into the room and Shaz gave her a perplexed glance. Their intrigue as to why the girls were dripping water all over was somewhat amusing but Serin kept her thoughts focused.

"I need you to change this jar," Amirra said as she pulled a wet lock from covering her eye.

"Alright, how?" Riddick said slowly.

"Make it *really* strong, strong enough to hold a raincloud," Amirra said.

Riddick scrunched his face and searched hers and when he found she wasn't even the slightest bit teasing, he closed his eyes and focused on what he would need to do to make the glass strong enough. The orange dusting of his magic seeped out of his skin and wrapped around the jar and the glass absorbed the new information. The minerals in the glass infused into a tighter space and the jar shrunk a tiny bit. Riddick handed it to Shaz who took the jar with a curious gaze.

"Heat it up real hot, just hot enough that it doesn't turn to ooze," Riddick said.

Shaz nodded and wrapped his hand around the little object and the fire element consumed his flesh. He turned off his heat when he could feel the glass soften and held open his palm.

"Now Serin, you use the wind to cool it down," Riddick said.

Serin twirled her finger around the jar and Riddick sent another dusting of orange particles into the glass. The new glass was ultra-shiny with a delicate twist of shimmering specs throughout. Serin called her raincloud and shrunk the darkened cloud and then pushed it into the jar. The cloud resisted, but she managed to force the stubborn energy inside the jar, and she and Amirra held their breaths. Motavo, Asher, and the Minca watched with curious anticipation. Serin smiled and put the stopper on the top and Amirra took the jar and slammed it onto the stone floor. The group jumped as the sharp clang coursed through the room. The jar didn't break and Amirra picked it up and handed it to Serin.

"Now open it and see if you can pour water out," Amirra said.

Serin opened the jar and poured a little puddle on the table.

"It works," Serin said excitedly.

Amirra took the jar and wrapped a chain around the neck of the jar and handed the temperamental force to Riddick.

"Secure this to it," Amirra said.

Riddick looked at her and took the jar without taking his eyes off hers.

"Please, sorry, I'm just excited," Amirra said.

Riddick smiled and organized the molecules to secure itself to the glass and handed it to Amirra who handed it to Serin who fastened the chain around her neck.

"That was quite creative," Shaz said.

Serin sensed relief overcome him with one less thing to have to worry about and touched his arm before leaving the room. Amirra gave a little hop-jump and hurried after her.

"That was interesting," Asher said.

"Most certainly was," Turkill said.

"Is that what you were thinking for the armor?" Shaz asked.

"Aye," Riddick said.

"If glass was that strong, how strong will you be able to make armor?" Asher asked.

"I hope strong, those beasts were different than the last time," Riddick said.

"How so?" Motavo asked.

"I can't place it exactly, but it was as if they were smarter," Riddick said.

"That's great, just great," Turkill said.

The chimes sounded and Shaz made his way to the portal room and found Phanes coming through.

"Shaz, we are ready when you are," Phanes said.

"Excellent, I'll get to the portals right away," Shaz said.

"Oh, and I am supposed to ask you about the trebuchets," Phanes said.

"The what?" Shaz asked.

"A weapon made by humans that were used in the Battle of Small Creek, Helios can tell you about them," Phanes said.

"I think I can figure it out," Shaz said.

"Sir," Phanes said.

"As soon as the portals open come on over, we'll set you up in the west quadrant," Shaz said.

Phanes saluted and disappeared back into the portal and Shaz returned to the war room.

"Riddick, do me a favor and look up trebuchets," Shaz said.

"Oh, I know what those are," Turkill said.

"You do?" Shaz asked.

"Oh, yes, we have used something similar to launch the explosives," Turkill said.

"How far do they launch?" Riddick asked.

"It depends on how big they are," Turkill said.

"Get all the information you can, let's add those to our strategy," Shaz said.

Turkill nodded and he and Ladtwig hurried to find Inelius. Shaz left Riddick to finish the last of the details with Motavo who was going to be in charge of the castle base and went to find Serin. He found her in the lounge now dry and refreshed.

"Hey there, how are things?" Shaz asked.

Serin looked up from her book she was reading on how to use her healing magic on large groups at a time, or at least aid in their healing and recovery.

"Alright, how about you," Serin asked with a smile.

"The gryphton's are ready, I'm going to go create their portal and could use your help," Shaz said.

"Of course," Serin said.

Serin put her book down and Shaz waited for her to cross the room. He wrapped his arms around her in a hug, and she hugged him back. Serin heard his deep exhale and felt the same way. She looked into his soft gaze and could see a mixture of emotions. She understood one of them was the ache in his heart for Grandfather's loss, which never went away, even with all this planning to fight a war didn't appease the heaviness and Serin was starting to worry. Serin reached up and kissed him gently in which he returned, but his energy was scattered. She pulled away and gazed into his eyes.

"Are you doing alright?" Serin asked with her gentle concern.

"Not really, but what can I do?" Shaz admitted.

"This won't last forever, but I understand, mostly, what you are going through," Serin said.

Shaz nodded and gave her another squeeze, and then they headed through the castle. The sun was bright but there was a chill in the air that meant the cold months wouldn't be far. They took the side road from behind the stables and walked through the tall green grasses and over a small hill. The valley below the hillside the castle was built on was vast and from this vantage one could see most of the surroundings. The water had all disappeared from the flood a few moons ago and the animal life had returned, but now the fields were going to be filled with armies and tents and large-scale weapons.

They didn't have a lot of time either and Shaz's energy was starting to tire. Serin tried to keep her calm demeanor so her own nerves wouldn't add to his, but she couldn't help internalizing the stress of what was about to happen. If they even knew what that was exactly.

"I think this should do," Shaz said.

Shaz took out the piece of the time tablet and ran his hand over the energy.

"Sheltet narata noshari. Sa nate te she'late narata noshari. Sa nate te narato." The unique metal began to hover in front of him and wriggle. "Tarren menin shelt la noshari tere mea'aha. Shatyoha re mevina charera no'ha latenta," Shaz said.

The time tablet started to spin quickly and Shaz gripped his toes into the ground as the magic stung his being. Serin boosted him with her pain relief magic and wrapped him with a blanket of wind to steady his body. A small oval disc formed in front of Shaz, and he held his hands out and *stretched* the magic. The purple mist rippled and swayed as the conduit began to make its way through the time shifts until the magic located the place Shaz indicated.

The mist formed a rounded-oval shape that was several lengths taller than Shaz, and then he moved a few lengths and began another. The energy was impressive as the force was sucked from his being and sweat dripped down his back. Serin gave him her wind power, and he soaked it in. The first portal began to sway with the movement of things entering.

Phanes and his armada of brightly colored feathered men-like eagle-lions, wearing full armor and armed with swords, spears, and slings, emerged and Phanes barked his orders to where to set up their camp. Shaz released the next portal and stepped back as more gryphtons poured out. Riddick whistled from the castle and gave Shaz the signal that Bowen had reported in, and he and Serin moved to where he was going to make their portals. He repeated the process three more times with each one getting harder.

Bowen emerged with the beginning of his massive army. The rest of the day and into the night was a constant flow of new beings into the valleys of the castle and instructions and orders. The noise and sudden odor of smelly men consumed the atmosphere, and the night didn't happen to have sleep in it.

Motavo grouped the leaders and organized the forces with their instructions. Several patrols were put in charge of building the trebuchets. Another was put in charge of large barriers that were used to secure battle lines, and another in charge of catapults. Helios headed the instruction of the units and started to train the men on how to build and use the machines and were instructed that when the Minca arrived they would show them their needed adjustments.

Riddick began making the needed structure he had thought up to enhance the armor and each brigade, company, troop, command, contingent, outfit, squad, detachment, flock, horde, unit, team, and patrol would be given instructions on when and where to turn in their respective equipment. Riddick wasn't sure what it was going to take to alter it all, but he started out with shields, since those would be the hardest and the first line of defense. Amirra helped him by adding her rune skills to make his earth magic encompass as much as possible. Riddick stood in the center of the large room that was fashioned to have several hooks to hang the weapons from.

Riddick closed his eyes and focused on the kinetic energy of the earth and allowed the imprint of the current mineral structures to enter his mind. Amirra buffed him with her Runemagic which helped give him the way to effectively organize his thoughts and a new way to distribute the needed changes. She also added as many alterations of her own, such as, owner adaption, which would teach the shield how to be the most effective based on the owners skills. She also added absorption, which was a Velshari enchantment, and allowed the shield to absorb a level of the opponents' energy giving the owner of the shield more strength which Riddick found quite fascinating.

Riddick's rust-colored magic wafted around the room and mixed with Amirra's sun-yellow magic. The pulsing vibrant colors sank into the shields and a sizzling crackle came as the mineral components rearranged. It didn't take long with both of them making the changes, but with the sheer amount that was needed indicated they would still take days to complete them all. Serin stopped in to buff them with her refreshing magic giving them a boost that they needed.

The Ebassian soldiers were shocked and amazed at how light the new shields were and got busy trying them out. Clanks and thunks sounded through the night as no one was eager to sleep. The shields were so much stronger that even without anything else changed, they would make a big difference.

Shaz and Serin both were wearing out, but they made their way to the area they were going to put the Minca and the Rangers and again made a few more portals. He then made another very large portal next to it that went to the same location as the old one in the Timeless Plains where Wandi and his herd was.

"I'll be right back," Shaz said.

"I'll come too," Serin said.

Shaz nodded and they walked through the fuzz. They reached the other side and found the daylight was near the high-afternoon point and looked around for Wandi.

"Do you see him?" Serin asked.

Shaz shook his head and sent out his energy and waited for the return.

"Ah, they are over there," Shaz said.

Serin buffed them with wind-walk, and they hurried over the small ridge. The large elephantine herd was milling about the nearly dried up watering hole when Shaz and Serin came into view.

"Hello Wandi, how are you?" Serin asked.

Wandi turned his very large head and flapped his sizable ears.

"You did come back," Wandi said.

"We did, and we need your help," Shaz said.

"To do what?" Wandi asked.

"Well, we have a lot of very heavy minerals that we need transported and thought you would be able to help," Shaz said.

"We are not load animals," Wandi said.

"I respect that, but if you want us to stay and help you then you need to do your part too," Shaz said.

Serin cringed, that was most certainly not what she would say to the ginormous animal. Wandi flapped his ears and twisted his long trunk around for a few lengths. He studied Shaz who stood with a quiet confidence and kept his shoulders square and sturdy. Serin guessed it was the way of the elephantine, and she amazed at how instinctively Shaz understood them.

"Alright, what do you need us to do?" Wandi said.

"Follow us," Shaz said.

Wandi began to give instructions to his herd and the large animals started out at a slow but powerful pace. Serin caught a glimpse of three young elephantines who seemed to have an eagerness but their little, for them anyway, legs had a hard time keeping up with the grownups. She waited as the littles caught up to her, and she smiled and rubbed the snout of one of them who was trying to investigate her whole being. Shaz chatted with Wandi at the head of the pack and gave him the rundown while Serin made quick friends with the babies and their mothers. The pachyderms entered the portal and Serin wasn't sure if the tunnel was going to hold them with the way the energy wall shifted and waved around. To her relief they all made it to the other side with no issues.

The enormous beings gave the people quite the spectacle but Turkill went in to fetch his people and the morning encompassed the organization of them and their explosives.

"You're exhausted, you two need to go get some rest, we will take it from here," Motavo said.

Shaz turned to see his warm brown eyes under concerned brows, and he nodded. He was exhausted, and so far everyone was on their way and there was nothing he needed to do for now.

"Go, we'll be fine," Asher said.

Shaz and Serin nodded, and they made their way back to the castle.

35-These Knuckleheads Almost Blew Us Up

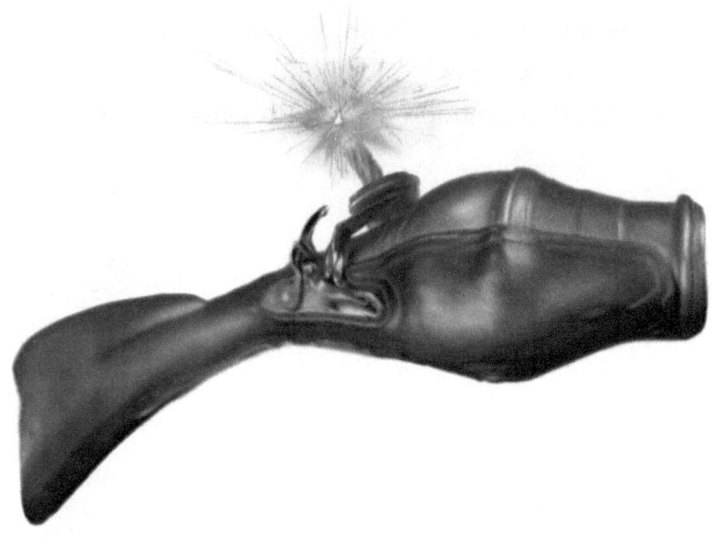

The sun was bright as the rays pelted Shaz in the face, and he rolled over and covered his head. He knew he needed to get up, but he didn't want to. For the first time since they returned to the castle after defeating Isot, his body ached a different kind of pain. A heavy weight sat on his chest and tears sat just under the surface of his closed eyelids. He had no idea what his problem was. At first, he thought maybe he had extended too much magic making the portals, but the idea of his grief over losing Grandfather settled in. He understood he would feel bad, sad, and even angry about losing him, and knowing his father was still alive should make things better, but that wasn't the case. He and Serin had talked a few times about the process of grief and in theory he understood it, but this was nothing like what he thought it would be.

A soft knock sounded and Shaz knew Serin was at the door. He loved having her around, in fact he craved it, but at this moment he didn't want her to see him being such a baby.

You're not a baby, and I don't see you that way, Serin thought from the other side of the door.

Shaz rolled over and kept his face under the covers but faced away from the door, and Serin interpreted his permission for her to enter, and she opened the latch, crossed the room, and sat on the bed. His muscular frame under the sheets trembled and Serin rested her hand on his shoulder. Serin sent a soothing wave of magic into his frame, and he relaxed a little. She pulled the covers away from his face and lifted a blonde lock off of his defined features. She leaned over him and kissed his cheek. The heat radiating off his skin sent alarm bells shattering her quiet conscience. Serin searched his heart-fire and found he was alright, but she made note of it.

The sky darkened and a heavy wind picked up and blew against the window. The minutes passed as Serin gently stroked his cheek and played with his hair and Shaz continued to fight the urge to cry. Sounds of the armies outside rippled over the horizon and Shaz could tell the day needed to get started, but the wind was getting stronger and the sky darker. Serin soaked in the energy of the weather, but she could tell it wasn't the same kind of rainstorm as usual and wondered what was going on. Heavy drops fell from the dark clouds and hit the ground with a pattering of sounds from the dirt to the cobblestone paths and main entrance. Serin wrapped her arm around him and laid her head on his shoulder.

Why do I feel like this? Shaz asked in his head. He was afraid if he used his mouth his voice would crack from the huge knot in his throat.

"Do you remember when we found Helen, and she was unresponsive?" Shaz nodded. "This is what she was experiencing. The overwhelming sensations of loss. I think there is a great deal of fear which drives this emotion. The fear that whatever that person brought to your life will leave you broken, and empty. When I look into a person's aura, their energy, the chaos of all those feelings always makes me experience fear, and as I have learned, it's *their* feelings I sense. Your fear of not ever getting to see him again is overloading your emotions. Unlike Helen though, I can't give you a reason to keep going, other than *I* need you, *I* want you, and the world needs you. But I also understand that that kind of pressure only weighs heavier on you, so only you can decide what you are going to do," Serin said.

Serin sat against the headboard and Shaz rolled over and rested his head in her lap. Serin moved his hair from his face and ran her fingers through his hair. Shaz's chest heaved with the building emotions and Serin rested her head against the soft padded headboard. The rain increased and hit hard against the castle. The tears in her eyes were as real as his, and he broke down and let out the energy stored in his being.

Serin listened to his fears, his loneliness, his sadness, his anger, his disbelief, his frustration with himself, and her heart sank. Serin sucked in a deep breath as she kept an eye on the storm outside. She didn't know what to do, it was much easier to separate herself from others as they suffered grief, but with their shared magic and the fact she loved him so much made the task nearly impossible to separate herself from his. Shaz let out a breath and pulled in another and wiped the tears from his face. Serin got the distinct impression Shaz's grief was causing the storm outside and wasn't sure what to do. She tried to find a read on the rawness of the magic, but the result was just a jumble of messy information.

"I need to get up and do something," Shaz said.

"Riddick and Yappa can handle everything, I think you should take some time to be sad. Pushing the pain away won't make it go away, only postpone the issues," Serin said, but she wondered if that meant there would be rain for the whole time.

"I don't want to be sad," Shaz said.

"I know, but your body does, and you need time to process the information it's receiving, both from your mind and heart, and right now, your heart wants to be sad," Serin said.

Shaz didn't say anything, but she was right, at this moment his heart did want to be sad. He decided he didn't like it, but he figured he couldn't keep fighting it either, plus with the rain there wasn't much he could do anyway. A scrunched scowl overcame his face and Serin smiled at understanding his quandary.

"I don't remember this happening when my mother died on the island," Shaz said.

Serin thought for a minute, why didn't he?

"Maybe that was part of the Synmagic with Grandfather, maybe he harnessed the pain for you," Serin said.

"Great, now I feel worse. Knowing he took this upon himself too," Shaz said.

"But you don't know if he had suffered grief before, and how he might deal with it," Serin said.

"True, does it get easier?" Shaz said.

"I don't think so, but I do think people learn a different way to deal with it. Perhaps taking all the good things about them into your own life is the best way to heal the loss. That way they are always with you because you are always thinking about them," Serin listened to Shaz's feelings include his fear of losing Merrick, and herself, and Riddick, and the Minca, and she wanted to race inside his heart and take away all the pain. "I'll stay here as long as you want me to," Serin said through a stiff throat herself.

"Which means you will become a permanent fixture to my bed," Shaz said.

Serin chuckled.

"I would like that," Serin said. Shaz looked up at her with a curious intrigue, and she smiled. "Whispmother, would you bring us some breakfast and let my Yappa and Riddick know we will be here if they need us," Serin said.

An Inugami soldier floated down from the rafters and nodded and then floated back into the ceiling. Serin wondered how they did it. Was there a secret set of tiny doorways in the ceilings no one but Shaz could see or did they just materialize through the walls. A few minutes later Serin watched a tray of morning foods materialize onto the side table and decided they materialized through the walls.

"Are you up to eating?" Serin asked.

"No, but you can," Shaz said.

Serin took the cup of fruit from the tray and put a grape into her mouth and Shaz closed his eyes. It did comfort him some that she was there, and she didn't think he was a baby even though *he* thought he was. Serin examined his heartfire and tried to think of a way he wouldn't roast her out while she sat with him. She waved her finger and a breeze formed and circled the room and the sensation was refreshing. She wondered if his extra heat was also part of his magic's way of suffering. Which then begged the question, what is he capable of without knowing? Maybe that is part of what Inelius was trying to explain to her about his connection with the shadow magic.

Serin kept running her hands through his hair and rubbing the skin on his neck and chest while she finished her cup of fruit and noted the notebooks on the side table. She picked them up and a prickling sensation bit at her skin. She understood the shadow magic's aspect on them and wondered how Shaz dealt with the shadow magic always inside him. Did he deal with the same irritation or was it different somehow?

"It is different, kind of like having a constant tickle in your throat and you always want to clear it, but when you do there is nothing there to clear. The irritation was worse after Grandfather ended the Synergybond, but now I don't hardly notice anymore," Shaz said.

"Have you made any progress on the notebooks?" Serin asked.

"A little, the language is very different, this is the ancient language, but I can't figure out how its organized," Shaz said.

Serin put the books back on the table and sent another boost of calming energy into Shaz's body. A commotion broke out outside and Shaz lifted his head and listened.

"Uh oh, something is about to happen," Shaz said.

A loud boom ricocheted off the walls and Shaz sat up, leaped out of the bed and over to the window. Serin hurried to the glass and peered outside. Frebin, Drager, Harmus, and Tomos emerged coughing and sputtering and covered in metallic smudges while waving their hands across their little bronzed faces to rid them of the smoke. Shaz chuckled at their amazing windblown hair. Turkill barked his grumpy commands and the Minca started a heated 'conversation' as to what happened.

"I wonder what that's all about," Shaz said.

"You up to finding out," Serin asked gently.

Shaz nodded and pulled her into a hug and then kissed her.

"Thank you, I love you so much," Shaz said.

"I love you," Serin said.

Shaz pulled on a tunic and his boots and secured his sword and ran a brush through his medium-length light blonde hair and pulled the stray locks out of his eyes. His hair wasn't long enough to pull back like Riddick did, but it wasn't short either, just the way he liked it. Serin followed him out of the room, and they made their way into the courtyard where the Minca were still arguing.

"What's going on?" Shaz asked.

"About time you got here, these knuckleheads almost blew us up," Turkill barked.

"What were you trying to do?" Shaz asked.

The fresh scent of wet dirt sank into Shaz's awareness, and he soaked in the comfort he received, and the rain came to a soft drizzle.

"Well, I thought if we could carry smaller cannons with charges in them then we would be able to have a better advantage, but the canon was too small and it blew up," Frebin said.

"And I tried to tell him this wouldn't work, but he didn't listen," Drager said.

"Quite an intriguing idea, what was your design," Shaz asked.

Turkill grunted with a 'are you serious' look.

"Well," Frebin pulled out a sketch and handed the paper to Shaz who studied the marks.

"This is quite clever," Shaz said.

"But it doesn't work because as soon as you light the wick the explosives ignite," Drager said.

"What if you add a mechanism to change how the wick is lit and maybe move the lever around to the bottom, and then you can pull the mechanism here," Shaz pointed to the underneath part of the barrel that was a bit like a bulbous root, "that would give more time for the charge to get to the powder," Shaz said.

"That might work, but how are we going to keep adding charges," Frebin asked.

"We can make them very compact, that way they will shoot out of the barrel instead of blow it up," Drager said.

"Not sure how you're going to do that," Tomos said.

"Maybe Riddick will have a solution," Shaz said.

"Good idea," Drager said.

The Minca men hurried away to find Riddick and Shaz examined the remains of the little hand-cannon.

"They are quite clever," Shaz said.

"Aye," Serin said with a smirk.

Shaz smiled and Serin followed him out into the mass of tents. They made their way through the Ebassian's and every man saluted as they walked by. Serin wasn't sure what to think of it. She didn't know if she was supposed to salute back or wave and smile, so she just kept a gentle smile on her lips and nodded every so often. They reached the edge of the camp and found their way to the gryphton's and found several large trees laying in a stack. The construction of the trebuchets were in full swing and Shaz inspected the progress. Another loud boom sounded but it was followed with cheers and excited shouts.

"It looks like the hand-cannons were a success," Shaz said.

"At least it didn't blow anyone up, that is," Serin said.

"True," Shaz said through a chuckle.

Serin was glad he seemed better, at least for now anyway. An interesting sensation rippled over the ground, and they turned to find Riddick riding a piece of earth while he hovered over the surface. Shaz's eyes popped out of his head and his heart jumped with the excitement. He studied Riddick as he banked off one of the tents at the outer edge and rolled in a complete circle before leveling off. Riddick sat back a bit and stuck his front foot into the earth-craft and is pushed against the inertia and force of the earths energy and came to a stop in front of them.

"What in the world is that?" Shaz blurted.

"Oh, this, I call this a piece of earth hovering over the ground, so I can ride very fast," Riddick said with his snarky side grin.

"How do you do that? You have to teach me," Shaz said excitedly.

"Oh, it's really easy," Riddick said.

He hopped off the craft of grassy turf and it lowered to the ground. Riddick gripped the earth next to Shaz and the new turf rose off the surface and hovered in the air a few lengths. The long narrow oval-like shape was sleek and gave the impression it was designed for speed and maneuverability, "Alright, you stand like this," Riddick showed him how to stand partially forward and partially sideways and how to put his feet for the most maneuverability. Shaz hopped onto the turf and an instant understanding of the new magic entered his mind. His balance was nearly perfect, and he bent his knees and swung the craft back and forth gently as he interpreted the information.

"Now what?" Shaz asked.

"Then you steer it, kind of like a horse, in the direction you want to go, and you go, and if you want to go faster you sit forward a little and to stop you sit back. The faster you sit back the faster you stop. To steer you twist with your hips and bend your knees back and forth," Riddick said.

Shaz leaned forward and the craft started moving over the surface. He twisted his hips back and forth, side to side and the earth-turf responded and within a few lengths he had figured out how to steer it. Riddick hopped onto his craft and Serin smiled. She was glad for the distraction and could tell this would help Shaz enjoy something, even if it were small and for a little while. Riddick gave Shaz a few instructions as they moved at a fair pace and Shaz settled into the movements.

Shaz leaned forward a little more and the craft picked up its pace. Shaz's heartfire ignited with the thrill, and he and Riddick darted in and out of the tents at a quick pace. The gryphton's at the edge of the camp stopped what they were doing and stared with wonder as Shaz and Riddick blasted passed them. Serin chuckled and started back toward the castle and figured it would be awhile before they would return.

36-She Hasn't Stopped Talking About You

Antorn and the troop gathered the battle-ax's and continued toward the outskirts. They made it to Nama's house and Antorn didn't want to go inside so another stag made the inspection. The stag returned and shook his head, but Antorn wasn't sure if that was 'they didn't make it' or 'they're not here' and the fear crept deeper. The stag returned and Antorn questioned if he should ask.

"They're not here," the stag offered when he realized the look of confusion on Antorn's face.

Antorn sighed heavily but without knowing where they were his heart thumped faster.

"We need to follow the tracks," Antorn said.

The stags split up and began searching for survivors. They made their way to the falls and found the water was still drizzling over the top, but the pool was quite a bit lower than it had ever been. The terrain steepened and Antorn wondered if Nama have been able to make the trek. Antorn heard a noise from behind the falls and held out his hand. The guards stopped and readied themselves and Antorn studied the noise.

He decided it was a small one and continued to the waterfall. He slowly peeked around the water and caught the large pole before it hit him in the head but then stepped back as arms were flung around his neck. His eyes adjusted, and he found Mazen gripping him tightly, and he gripped her with eagerness.

"Mazen, you're alright," Antorn said his voice cracking.

She nodded in his embrace, and he understood her adrenaline was still surging through her body, and she was unable to compose herself yet. "Nama?" Antorn asked.

Mazen sniffed and sucked in a deep breath and then pulled back. Antorn pulled a lock of hair from her face and found her eyes red with tears. He searched the cave and found several stags and fawns huddled in the farthest back corner. Nama's fair complexion emerged from the darkness, and he relaxed. "Is everyone alright?" Antorn asked.

"Everyone we could convince to come before the beasts attacked, but we couldn't make everyone," Mazen managed.

"You're safe now, there's a troop ready to take you back to the main village, and we'll search out everyone we can find," Antorn said.

A small stag touched Antorn's leg, and he looked down.

"Did you kill the beasts?" the young one asked.

Antorn bent down and pulled the little girl's hair from her teary face.

"I certainly did, and so did the big stags that are outside waiting to take you to safety," Antorn said.

The little girl wrapped her arms around his neck and gave him a huge squeeze. An interesting sensation overcame him, and he was now even more determined to save his people.

"Come on, let's take you somewhere safer," Antorn said.

Antorn helped the Forrne out of the falls and the guards started to escort them back to the main village.

"We need to start gathering the herds and moving them to Kambu, we can't protect everyone in the outskirts," Antorn said.

"Yes, Sir," the stag guard said.

Antorn turned to find Mazen in a gentle argument with Nama, and he made his way over to them.

"Nama, are you alright?" Antorn asked.

"I'm not going, there is nothing out here. Everyone is overreacting," Nama said.

"Can I show you something?" Antorn asked.

Nama studied his fine long features and found he had a serious but gentle look and nodded. He took her hand and guided her to the dead beasts, and she gasped and covered her mouth as she nearly gagged.

"These are the beasts that are attacking our herds, and they seem to be increasing in numbers, I can't protect you if you are so far out here and I really want you to survive long enough for me to ask Mazen to be mine," Antorn said.

Nama looked him in the face with a surprised but eager expression and nodded with accepted defeat. He patted her hand and escorted her back to the herd and placed her with the main group. Mazen came up behind him and put her hand on his shoulder.

"What did you say to her?" Mazen asked.

"I showed her the beasts and told her I needed her to be closer so that I can protect her better," Antorn said.

Mazen smiled, but she had a skeptical glint in her eye. Antorn smiled.

"Oh, so I was going to tell you that Tage didn't act at all like we had figured," Mazen gave him an 'oh' look, "he acted so much worse," Antorn said.

Mazen laughed, and he then told her the whole story as they made their way back to main camp. Halfway a stag raced toward them with great eagerness. Antorn ran out to meet him figuring the herd didn't need to know the possible details and gave him more instructions, and he raced back the other way. Antorn returned to Mazen, and she looked at him with admiration and dread.

"I have some urgent matters to attend to, but you take Nama to Kambu, and I'll meet you there," Antorn said.

"Is everything alright?" Mazen asked.

"Not really, but don't worry about it, you just get Nama and the others back to Kambu," Antorn said.

Mazen nodded and Antorn turned and started out, but turned around and hurried back to Mazen, pulled her tight and kissed her. The guards snickered quietly but understood their responsibility was to protect their leaders family, and they straightened with solid determination. Antorn returned to Kambu and found Slat and the Order organizing the provisions.

"Slat, I need you now," Antorn said.

Slat startled, jumped, and turned to find Antorn half-turned away heading toward the war pavilion. Slat hurried after him and so did a handful of other guards.

"The outskirts are no longer safe, we need to mobilize everyone and bring them into smaller areas and station guards around about them," Antorn said.

The stags nodded but had scrunched expressions.

"We need to group everyone into smaller areas and guard them," Slat offered.

The stags nodded and Antorn pointed to the map.

"Grier, you round up this area and Brandt you take this area. Where do you want to make new villages?" Antorn asked.

Slat looked over the map.

"What about here and here, this will give us the needed closeness but with some room to stretch if we need to, but Antorn, what about the grain fields, we will still need Forrne to tend to them, so we continue to have provisions," Slat said.

"What if we take this area and fortify this for grains, we can move herds here and here, that way we can do both," Antorn said.

"That would work, but what if the people won't go," Slat asked.

Antorn looked at him out of the corner of a questioning eye.

"Why wouldn't they?" Antorn asked, but then he remembered Nama and understood his own question. "We can't make them. All we can do is hope they will. Take a couple of the poles with to show them what we are up against, and maybe the Order should go with the Guard. They know you and trust you are of the government, maybe they will go if you ask them," Antorn said.

Slat nodded and left with the guards. The noise of mobilizing guards increased and Antorn kept an eye on the path that Mazen and others would be coming in on. There was no sign of them yet, but he understood they were traveling with younglings and the elderly so it would take longer, but it didn't ease his anticipation. He busied himself with the orders and organizations of the new settlements and dividing the Guard into troops to begin the new living arrangements. He was surprised however, at how many Forrne had come to join the Guard and found Soren's men deep in training them all as quickly as possible.

Antorn turned to find a ruckus going on and made his way. He searched the distance and found Tobis and his troops running at a steady pace. Antorn ran to meet them and Tobis filled him in on the details. Soren's troop emerged from the distance and caught up with Antorn and Tobis, and soon Pillip's troop came into the valley. Antorn rejoiced that they all returned and there was no one lost and dismissed the troops to recoup.

Antorn filled them in on the new plans for the settlements, and they filled Antorn in on the details of the battle and the mountain pass.

"Get some sleep, in the morning we need to figure out a way to create a stronghold around the settlements and block off that mountain pass," Antorn said.

"Sir," the three agreed.

They hadn't realized how tired and hungry they were until they filed into the food arena and the hot roasted meats and grains wafted through their senses. Antorn kept watch over the trail and waited for the herd to make it to the camp but the evening turned to night and there was no sign of them. A knot in his stomach bit at his nerves again, and he tried to still his mind, but it didn't work. The camp quickly quieted with the impending nighttime, and he struggled to stay awake even with the irritating sounds of the night insects.

A hushed sound of voices entered his mind, and he jumped alert. It was the herd and he hurried over to them. He directed the stags on where to put the Forrne, and they ushered them into the camp. Antorn waited as the Forrne followed in line and waved back at the little girl who was waving eagerly at him with a big smile and tired eyes. He found Mazen and Nama toward the back of the line.

Antorn sucked in a deep breath and chided himself for being such a derp. He had never felt this way about Mazen before, or anyone for that matter, and he wasn't sure if he was losing his mind. Well, he *was* certain he was losing his mind, come on, who becomes the leader of a new army, runs into the government and takes it by force, arrests the leader and forces the people to go to arms against an impending and possibly undefeatable enemy, and falls in love in the meantime. He was living someone else life for sure, but he couldn't deny what he was experiencing.

"How did things go?" Antorn asked.

Mazen slugged his arm, and he pulled back with shock and a feeling of instant 'what did I do?' overcame him.

"You didn't tell me you promised Nama you were going to ask me to be yours," Mazen said.

Antorn did leave that part out, but he mean it. He studied her intense amber eyes and couldn't decide if he was in trouble or if she was teasing and his heart raced but for a different reason. The corner of Mazen's lip twitched, and he went with the, she was serious but also not at the same time and grabbed her face and kissed her before she could unleash anything else. Mazen sank into his embrace and wrapped her arms around him. He pulled back and inspected her eyes to find out how much trouble he was in, and she gave him a relaxed 'you're still in trouble for not preparing me first' look, and he smiled.

"I take it things went alright?" Antorn asked.

"How are things here?" Mazen asked.

"The beasts are certainly increasing in numbers and there is no way to protect everyone with them being so spread out. We are going to start more condensed settlements that we can fortify so that we can protect them better, but that will mean a lot of families will have to give up their lands, at least for now," Antorn said.

"That's going to be hard for them, that's like asking them to give up their families," Mazen said.

"I know, I only hope they will understand what is at stake and see that we are trying to keep them alive," Antorn said.

"I think they will, rumors have been spreading about several outskirt settlements being attacked and the people being carried off," Mazen said.

"Is that what happened to you?" Mazen nodded. "How many do you think?" Antorn asked.

"Does it matter, one is too many," Mazen said sharply.

Antorn stopped and turned to her.

"I agree, I am only trying to figure out how many of the beasts there are and what they are capable of," Antorn said softly.

"I'm sorry. I'm not sure, maybe half the number we have left," Mazen said.

"Let's get you and Nama settled in, and we can talk more in the morning," Antorn said.

Mazen nodded but she didn't want to leave his side. They helped Nama and the others into the group of non-guards in one of the covered pavilions and gave them some food. Antorn returned to his post and finished the notes he was making before Tobis and the others arrived. He stretched and yawned and turned around to find Mazen standing in the door.

"Mazen, is everything alright?" Antorn asked.

"I couldn't sleep and saw the light on and thought you might still be in here," Mazen said.

Antorn rubbed his face and Mazen could see the wear on his features.

"Come on, you can stay with me, or rather I'll stay with you and Nama," Antorn said.

"I would like that, but you'll have to stay with Tissa too," Mazen said.

"Who?" Antorn asked.

"Tissa, the little girl from the falls," Mazen ask-stated.

"I see," Antorn said.

"She hasn't stopped talking about you since we left the falls. She's going to marry you someday you know," Mazen said.

"She is, is she?" Mazen nodded with a smile in her eye. "What does that mean for you then?" Antorn asked.

"I don't know, we'll have to see about that," Mazen said.

Antorn chuckled, and they made their way back to Nama and settled in together for the night. Antorn woke with both a sleeping Mazen and Tissa on him, and he smiled and wondered at what point Tissa made her way to him. He watched the sun brighten the sky and knew he needed to get an early start on the day but didn't want to wake the lady-stags. He waited a bit longer and then decided he needed to be going. Antorn ran his hand along Mazen's slender cheek, and she stirred.

"I need to be going," Antorn said quietly.

Mazen blushed as she found she was on the upper part of his long torso and sat up. Antorn nodded to Tissa's small frame which was draped across his long back and nearly drooling on him. Mazen snickered and pulled the sleeping little one off, and he got up quickly as to try, and keep the child asleep. He nodded with a smile and Mazen snuggled with the girl. She knew her parents had been killed or taken and was now an orphan, who by the looks of it has adopted Antorn. The girl shuffled but stayed asleep and Antorn made his way back to the guard.

37-Run From What?

"Serin, where is Shaz?" Asher asked.

"He and Riddick are-," Serin thought a moment, "checking on things," Serin said.

"Looks like they are messing around," Asher grumbled.

"I understand, but they need the break. Can I help with something?" Serin asked.

"Helios needs the spider spit," Asher said.

"Oh, dear, what are we going to do about that?" Serin asked.

"I guess we're going to have to go find some spiders," Asher said.

"How do you suppose we do that?" Serin asked.

"Which is why I wanted to ask Shaz," Asher said.

"I see, well let's think of something while Shaz de-stresses for a bit," Serin said.

Asher grumbled, but he understood she was making an executive decision and decided not to make a fuss. They made their way back to the castle where they found Helios in his new laboratory that the Whispmother made for him.

"Serin, where is Shaz?" Helios asked.

"He's out joyriding," Asher grumbled.

"He's checking on things," Serin corrected.

Helios noted the sternness in her voice and nodded.

"I wanted to start working on developing our toxin, but I don't want to use the spider spit we have just in case," Helios said.

"How much do you figure we are going to need?" Serin asked.

"Unfortunately, quite a bit. If we are going to make bombs and gasses *and* poison the arrow tips, we are going to need a substantial amount," Helios said.

Serin thought about it and ran several ideas through her head. She wasn't particularly a fan of spiders either, but she didn't want to hurt any of them.

"They live in the ground, like ants but I have no idea what they eat," Serin said.

"They eat mushrooms," Inelius said.

Inelius' slow frame crossed the floor.

"Do you know which ones?" Helios asked.

"The same ones you secured for the antidote," Inelius said.

"How did you secure the spider spit from them last time," Helios asked.

"I held them with an air bubble and Shaz scared them and then caught the spit when they tried to slime him, but it seems kind of mean to scare them all the time," Serin said.

"They're spiders," Asher said.

Serin gave him a glare and he cleared his throat.

"Yes, but we don't have to be cruel," Serin said.

"How do you supposed then?" Asher asked.

"Haven't a clue," Serin said.

"The book indicated that they use the spit to digest their food as well, maybe if put some mushrooms behind glass and then when they spit on the mushrooms it hits the glass and drips down and into canisters, that way we're not scaring them," Inelius said.

"How brilliant," Serin said.

"So, how are we going to get them here, and where are we going to put them?" Asher asked.

"We can put them in the hillside behind the castle, and we can make them a home of tunnels but block it off with stone walls, so they can't move in permanently, I don't think Shaz would appreciate them as neighbors," Serin said.

"I don't think the Whispmother would like it either," Inelius said.

"I'll go fetch Riddick and Shaz and get that started," Serin said.

Serin returned to the courtyard of the castle and was about to start her long trek through the tents of soldiers but stopped when the wind told her Shaz was coming. Serin stopped and listened and for the first time she could understand what the wind was telling her. An excitement rose from her chest as she interpreted all of its ramblings until a certain set of words crossed her understanding. She looked around and searched the sky, but nothing was there and a pit in her stomach ate at her guts.

Serin closed her eyes and reached out with her magic the way Shaz had taught her when searching for the portal. She wanted to find out if she could find the source of what she heard. A pale blue hue of energy wafted around her and then dissipated into the atmosphere. She stood quietly taking in all the sensations she received back but still nothing what she was looking for. Shaz rounded the edge of the camp on his new toy and a prick at his mind made his heart jump.

Shaz turned quickly to see Serin lifting into the air surrounded by her blue magic. He was amazed at how her form was so still with all the wind's energy around her. She was beautiful but there was something about what was happening that made him uncomfortable, and he maneuvered his hover-craft toward her. He wasn't sure how high the turf would go, but he lifted the turf up and it only reached a half a story high.

He settled it back to the ground and waited for Serin to return to the surface. Serin's toes touched down, and she blinked and found Shaz watching her with concern in his eyes. Shaz hopped off and took the last few steps toward her.

"Is everything alright?" Shaz asked.

"I'm not sure," Serin said.

"What do you mean?" Shaz asked.

"Well, I finally heard what the wind was telling me," Serin said.

"That's great," Shaz said.

"I thought so too, until I heard something I didn't want to hear," Serin said.

The joyful expression on Shaz's face turned serious, and he braced himself.

"What did you hear?" Shaz asked.

He almost didn't want to.

"My father's voice telling me to run," Serin said.

Shaz's face scrunched.

"Run from what?" Shaz asked.

"I don't know," Serin said.

"How recent?" Shaz asked.

"Just a minute ago," Serin said.

"I mean, how long does it take for the wind to carry information? Did this happen a long time ago or only a short time ago," Shaz said.

"Oh, I see. I can't tell. But I reached out with my magic like you taught me to search for my father, but I didn't find anything," Serin said.

"That was good thinking," Shaz said.

Serin smiled but a weird dread entered her mind. Shaz did a quick scan himself and came up empty too.

"Are you going to be alright?" Shaz asked.

Serin shrugged.

"I hope so, but I get the impression something isn't right," Serin said.

"Aye," Shaz said.

"Where is Riddick?" Serin asked.

Shaz could tell she needed some time to think about her new awareness and what she heard, so he tried to only listen to her thoughts, but not, at the same time. He wanted to give her privacy, but he also was sure he would hear bits and pieces anyway. They found Riddick, and Serin rehearsed the idea for the spiders and Riddick headed to the hill to start the spider colony while Shaz and Serin figured out how to best bring the spiders there. They decided on a small portal that would lead into their new nest but figured they would need to be on the other side to encourage them to travel through it.

Shaz and Serin again made their way through the portal and into the Timeless Plains but this time they crawled through the small portal which Shaz was able to place near the entrance of their existing colony. He was getting quite good at creating the portals and it seemed like his magic was getting stronger which was a nice relief. Shaz searched the colony and found the best place to start driving the insects out by dropping fire balls into the holes. The spiders emerged and Serin formed a wind tunnel between the distance and the spiders scurried into the portal.

It didn't take too long and Shaz closed the portal and made a new one, and they returned to the castle. The spider farm worked great and the spiders were happy to have a new home and didn't seem bothered that they couldn't access the mushrooms behind the glass because Riddick had made them grow well for them elsewhere too. The canisters filled quickly, and Helios began working through his process to isolate the components that made the paralysis and used the Minca's poison from their jungle plants to make a new toxin.

The days passed quickly, and the preparations went smoothly, but Shaz couldn't shake the agitation of urgency from his mind and several times found himself being short and grumpy with people. Serin understood what he was sensing, but she had no explanation for everyone and hoped that they would be ready soon. She was also experiencing her own worry as the words repeated in her mind often.

The metal manipulations didn't take a long as Riddick had anticipated, so he moved onto the swords and with Amirra's help they had enchanted everything by the end of the week. The gryphton's and Ebassian's erected the trebuchets also by the end of the week and were now working with the Minca to fine tune the launching mechanisms and sequences. Helios had made good advancements and was certain it would only take another day or so to be ready which was good because Shaz was getting more and more moody. He tried really hard but there was a driving force that kept him going at a steady but urgent pace, which seemed to add to his seeming grumpiness.

Shaz, instead of dealing with people, spent several hours poring over the maps and making his preparations so that the process of opening the portals to the Timeless Plains would be quick. He needed one very large portal to allow for the elephantines and all the heavy timbers of the machines and figured that if he made at least two portals on each side of the large one, then each group could easily be directed to where they were going to be stationed.

"Are you doing alright?" Serin asked.

Shaz looked up from a map and smiled an 'I guess' smile and Serin's soft brows comforted his soul.

"That's a silly question," Shaz said.

"I suppose, but what else am I supposed to say, 'Are you going mad and making everyone nervous on purpose or are you just being a derp'," Serin said.

"I'm sorry, I can't make this stupid pit in my stomach to go away and the image of all the dead Forrne keeps coming to mind. I'm certain we need to be there already and it's making me crazy that we aren't ready yet," Shaz said.

"Well, I think you were a little bit crazy before all this, after all you picked me," Serin teased.

"Aye, well then I'm the craziest being there is," Shaz said.

Serin chuckled.

"We're getting real close, aren't we?" Serin asked.

"Aye, but I'm wondering if I need to take a quick trip over there and make sure things are alright for us to make the move," Shaz said. Serin nodded but her stomach churned, and she wasn't sure why. "I'm going to start the portal on this side and when I'm sure we're good to go, finish it on the other side, but if I don't come back in a few, I'll need you to finish the cast to open the portal," Shaz said.

"You're kind a twigging me out right now," Serin said.

"I'm sorry, but I keep getting the need to just go," Shaz said.

"Then we should go," Serin said.

Shaz ran his hands through his hair, exhaled, and nodded. He held open the flap, and they found Motavo with Riddick and Amirra making a final check through the list.

"We need to move now, get everyone ready to leave in an hour," Shaz said.

Motavo studied Shaz's face. He had started to learn Shaz's mannerisms and found he was serious. Serin too was serious, and he nodded and turned quickly giving orders as he left. A gentle ruckus picked up as the troops began taking down tents and organizing equipment and gear. They found the Minca and gave them the instructions and Turkill and Ladtwig began organizing their powders and material onto the elephantines. Riddick and Amirra hurried to their rooms to dress in their new armor they had made for themselves.

Amirra enchanted them with the same fortifications as the rest, but added a few extras to accommodate their magic skills. Riddick grabbed the set they had made for Shaz and Serin and met Inelius at the bottom of the stairs.

"Be careful," Inelius said.

"Aye, you too," Riddick said.

Amirra gave Inelius a hug and gave him a surge of her soul magic. He blinked with the newness but smiled as the new force gave his body a renewed sense of purpose.

"We'll be back before you know it," Amirra said.

They hurried back to the portals and found Shaz and Serin who began to put on their armor. Serin put her Whisperwood bow on and secured the quiver and checked for all of her hidden blades. Shaz liked the new armor, it was light and flexible, but was very strong and his enchantment allowed for the metal to stay in its shape and strength even when getting hot with his fire.

The sun sat low in the sky and the day began to shift into night as Shaz and Serin made their way to where he was going to make the portals. He began his cast and formed the smaller portals and started the large one. The words flowed off his tongue so naturally that he didn't even have to think about it anymore. The misty wall emerged and rippled in a circular pattern until it found the outside edges and snapped into place with a pop.

Bowen's forces marched up the small hill in full gear and the sight was amazing. The sounds of the new metal clinking on the chainmail under armor left a tingle in the air and Shaz made a quick scan over the forces. He found the gryphton's standing at attention waiting their turn with Phanes looking a bit older than a half a moon ago. A sudden pang of angst hit Shaz's chest as he was asking these people and creatures to sacrifice their lives, if needed, for creatures they had never met, for a cause they didn't fully understand. The Rangers fell into place and the weight sank deeper.

What was he doing? What was going to happen? How many lives would be lost? Shaz wrestled with the thoughts.

Serin took his hand and her cool skin caressed his warm skin. He turned to her and found her 'I love you' smile she always gave him.

"We didn't start this, but we have to do something to end it," Serin said.

"Aye, but that doesn't make me feel better," Shaz said.

"Maybe after killing a few hundred Jaduuk you'll be a little better," Serin said.

Shaz smiled.

"Maybe," Shaz said.

38-I Have A Favor To Ask

Antorn found Tobis, Pillip and Soren in the pavilion, and they began making the arrangements to build the settlements and fortifications. The days were quickly filled with Forrne filling into the new settlements and Guard consistently growing. At first many of the Forrne were hesitant but the majority of them did leave the outskirts and bigger plains for the smaller more compact settlements and the Guard continued to fight the beasts.

They used many tactics as it seemed that the more they used a tactic the smarter the beasts became and started to adopt their tactics. Antorn ended up moving the head base camp toward the outer area so that he was closer and between the beasts and the Forrne. They managed to keep the beasts from attacking the strongholds which were now named Shuhani and Nimbalia. The Guard became excellent at their battle-ax's and the Fawn grew steadily with their ballista's which proved to be a quite important strategy, but they began to suffer more and more loss as the beasts attacks increased in frequency and numbers. As the moons flew by the beasts started to overpower them. Antorn's frustrations sat heavily on him, and he tried to keep his focus and hope, but he was now faced with the need to retreat and unite the two settlements into one.

Antorn slammed his fists into a pole that held up one of the arenas and then pulled them back and shook out the pain that raced to his brain.

"Antorn," Mazen said. Antorn turned to find Mazen's face full of worry, and he tried to soften his jaw. She knew him well enough now to know how frustrated he was and that there was little she was able to do to help. Antorn rubbed his face and squeezed the bridge of his nose with heaviness. "Things will be alright," Mazen said.

"I wish I could believe that, but no matter what we do, no matter how many stags we send we just keep getting wiped out. I've already lost Soren and Pillip is badly wounded. So far Tobis is holding together, but there is no way we can keep the strongholds. We're going to have to retreat and bring everyone together, which means we're going to lose half our fields which also means half our food. We already can't find much to trap anymore, and we are barely getting by on the grains we *are* able to grow," Antorn said.

Mazen didn't know what to say, she hadn't realized how bad things had gotten. Antorn tried not to talk about it when they were together, and he didn't want Tissa to know about it either. Tissa stayed with Mazen and Nama now and every time Antorn was around she wanted all of his attention, which he tried to give her the best he could. He was very fond of the little one, and even felt as though she belonged to him now, which added to his stress. Mazen crossed the arena and wrapped her arms around his waist and leaned into his chest. He draped his arms around her with a heaviness. It wasn't that he didn't want her affection, but it was that he didn't feel he deserved it.

Tobis rounded the corner and found them together and didn't want to disturb them, but he cleared his throat. Antorn looked up and nodded for him to come in. Mazen pulled away and squeezed his hand as she left the pavilion.

"What's going on?" Tobis asked.

"It's time we merge the settlements, we just don't have enough resources to keep both villages, and we need to pull back more. Gather the Fawn and start to gather as much of the grains and seeds as possible. We'll start moving out in two days," Antorn said.

"Yes, Sir," Tobis said.

Tobis' voice was soft, and his once eager desire was tamed with the experience of death and pain. Antorn too, understood the pains of death and loss and his heart was filled with a chaos he had never had before.

"What is the last report from the perimeters?" Antorn asked.

"Our numbers are sufficient, but we have lost over a hundred in the last few days," Tobis said.

"Tobis, I don't know what to do, I am losing hope that we are going to survive this. I promised so many that we were going to defeat these beasts and I have done nothing but get them killed," Antorn said.

"Stop. One, there is absolutely nothing you could have done differently, you didn't bring these beasts here. Two, under your command we have killed far more of them than they us. We simply don't multiply the way they do. Three, you have done more for this people than any other stag I have ever known or heard about, and four, you are the most determined stag I have ever met. It's the highest honor to have associated with you and even more so to die by your side," Tobis said.

Antorn couldn't help the tear at the corner of his eye, and he cleared his throat and gave Tobis a thankful smile.

"I have a favor to ask, if at any point I don't make it through this, you are to take over and make sure you look after Mazen and Tissa," Antorn said.

"I won't have to, because you are going to do it yourself, and you're even going to marry her properly," Tobis said.

Tobis squeezed Antorn's shoulder and left the pavilion. Antorn sighed heavily but managed to pull himself together. The merger went as smoothly as possible and the Forrne had learned to be diligent when the Guard told them to do something. The Guard had earned the total respect of the Forrne nation and the Order which was still governed by Slat and a few of the others. The rest had been captured during a trip through the outskirts to gather the rest of the stragglers. The attacks seemed to ease a bit, and they were able to regain some the territory around Nimbalia which was quickly farmed, but they were running out of enough water to grow the grains. Antorn had come up with a unique way to irrigate the water and to create a recycling of the moisture back into the ground with using system of thin bone slats that covered the fields. As the sun heated the ground and the water evaporated off, the vapors would get caught by the thin sheets of bone and drip back down to the ground.

It worked quite well, and they were able to grow more grains with less water than before, but he worried it still wouldn't be enough. The move took only half the moon cycle and Antorn and Tobis redoubled their efforts on securing the perimeters. Antorn had been watching the same green light in the sky for moons and over the time he noted several more. He wanted to know what they were and felt like that was part of the answer but each time they tried to sneak close enough to find out what it was, they had to retreat, so they didn't lose men.

Antorn and Tobis decided to make another attack at the south borders in an effort to regain territory to build another farm. Pillip recovered but was permanently disabled as his front leg was mangled so badly that there was no way to fix it without amputating, which he decided against. Antorn left him at camp as the leader, and he took to the battlefield with Tobis. They waited until daylight when the sun disguised their luminescent marks which they figured was how the beasts found them since many of the raids happened at night. They had also gone to dressing in as many skins as they found to keep their markings from becoming targets.

Antorn gave them the signal as the sun peeked over the horizon. The troop moved carefully and slowing toward the beasts camp. Antorn stopped at a group of trees and lowered close to the ground, which wasn't as easy as he had wished. Their long legs didn't bend in the way that would be useful to crawl through the grasses, and their taller frames stuck out anyway.

The beasts camp was different this time and Antorn noticed one of the beasts speaking in a rough gurgling fashion that mimicked their growls mixed with grunts and words. He couldn't understand what was being said, but his anger grew. They were evolving at the same rate they were multiplying, and he was out of ideas. He eyed a tall structure that had been constructed with the crude trunks of the acacia trees and secured together creating a platform at the top and Antorn wondered what it was for.

A beast's ear flicked, and it sniffed the air. It turned toward Antorn and Antorn quickly stepped behind the tree but peeked out. The beasts sniffed again and then turned to search in Antorn's direction. Antorn quickly realized their sense of smell was heightened, and he figured that was what gave them the advantage. His breath struggled under the panic in his chest, and he kept perfectly still until the beast returned to what it was doing.

Antorn backed up and quickly made his way back to the others.

"We have a big problem, they 'see' with their noses, and they are building lookout towers," Antorn said.

"Why lookout towers if they can detect us with their noses," Tobis asked.

"Maybe it allows them to pick up our scents better," Antorn said.

"Then there is really no way to do this except fight," Tobis said.

Antorn nodded but his mind raced around every scenario he could think of. He looked at his troops and his heart sank. They were strong and determined, obedient and loyal. They were willing to fight to the death but wished they didn't have to. Antorn flicked his ears as did Tobis, and they readied themselves.

They engaged the beasts and the battle started off with the beasts taking the advantage. Antorn watched three of his men go down right away, and he yelled at the top of his lungs. The beasts turned toward him, and he started to run from the group. Tobis gritted his teeth and shot out after him taking out one of the beasts from behind. Tobis was certain Antorn was trying to lead the pack away from them, and he signaled for the group to attack. Antorn was fast but had learned that the beasts cornered as well as they ran, but he wondered if they could jump.

Antorn shot across the distance and leaped over the small ravine. The beasts didn't see the ravine and fell into the void. The beasts behind them tried to leap over too, but they were still holding their battle-ax's, so they struggled to get a grasp of the other side and fell into the ravine. The ballista's launched their spears at the beasts, and they sank into their flesh, but another wave of beasts came out of the distance. Antorn ran again and leaped back over the ravine lower down, and they resumed their chase. The Guards circled the creatures and fell upon them with vigor and Tobis lead another troop toward the oncoming beasts. They rounded the pack and launched their spears and ballista's, and many of the beasts fell.

A stag skidded around a tree and turned and kicked the beasts square in the chest. The bones in the creature's chest cracked as it flew backward several lengths. He rounded his battle-ax through the arm of another and the beasts recoiled with the sudden shock and pain. Tobis let a spear loose and it sank into the back flank of a beast, which only slowed it down. The creature turned on him and swung his ax. Tobis jumped out of the way but not before the blade raced across his shoulder. The pain hit his stomach and shot panic into his brain, but he leaped over a fallen beast and turned around in time to kick the beast in the head.

The recoil launched the creature backward and it slammed into another beast and then tumbled to the ground. Tobis hurried back to the guardsmen and found Antorn rounding his ax into the skull of another beast. Tobis searched and found there was another pack headed their way and sent a signal to Antorn who yanked his blade back and ran to meet up with them.

Tobis pointed to the next pack of beasts and Antorn closed his eyes. He nodded and readied himself but a weird sizzling like fuzzy sound emerged. Antorn turned to where he thought the sound came from, and he saw a wriggling purple haze wafting in the middle of the air. His heart thumped against his chest and his mind raced with ideas, but nothing settled in. The sound deepened and Antorn thought it was growing. The wafting mist solidified into an oval shape, and he struggled to make sense of what he was seeing. The pounding of the beasts hooves brought him back to his reality and dread encompassed his frame.

Realms of Edenocht

39-I Know What This Casting Is About

Nitida closed her eyes and tried to figure out what the casting meant. She had never seen one so detailed. She had seen an Empyral casting before, but she had never known one to include the Zod-Kal stone resting in the place on the altar that represents the 'Prime Power'. The Zod-Kal stone isn't its own stone but becomes a single stone when the Zod stone touches the Kal stone, and both stones have to have landed in the same section. The rune circle consists of the future, past, presence, as well as mind and memory, the connection to the deities, the appearance of the person, not to be confused with the actual traits, but their 'vibe' they appear to have, their highest self and their animal nature. Each section is divided into colors that when looked at the whole resembles an eye. This is used as a way to peer within ones whole self.

Nitida rolled the Zod stone, which represents 'nectar', in one hand and the other, the Kal stone, which means 'deity'. It wasn't so much that they were touching indicating that they meant there would be a 'godly' influence in the casting, but they were sitting on the lines that intersect appearance, deity, the highest self, and the animal nature. It was truly perplexing, and she was at a loss on how to explain it. Nitida placed the stones back on the rune cloth and heaved a sizable book onto her lap. Her old delicate fingers tickled the edges of the papers as she chanted her own beginning chant. This was the most important part of reading the runes. To put herself in the frame of mind to only be thinking of the person to whom she is casting for and not her own interests. She finished her chant and turned the pages carefully. She understood by rotations of practice that the meanings would come to her when the information was needed but not before.

Nitida couldn't help the urgency as Serin had come moons ago and this casting has been her main focus, but she had yet to resolve the understanding. Her eyes skimmed over the glyphs of the ages, many were of the current language, some were of the older languages and a few were of the ancient language. The interesting thing about this book was it was initially compiled as a series of notes but then re organized as an instructional. The intention was to allow the reader to understand how the notes lent to the understanding of the means and methods but Nitida wasn't finding anything.

She continued to scan the pages and then set it down when the last page offered no insights. Nitida decided to return to the library and managed her aged frame from the soft cushions. She pulled her heavy weaved shall over her shoulders and started toward the door. The long corridor to the library was the one that was filled with the large vaults and arched window like structures. The day had turned again to nightfall, and she examined the moons' beams trickle into the open courtyard. The first star in the sky emerged as she gazed into the atmosphere.

A sudden understanding hit her mind, and she examined the star. Images of the constellations raced through her mind. She wasn't very good at knowing them all, but she loved to star gaze anyway. She preferred to make up her own names of what she found in the sky but at this moment she understood that the casting had something to do with the cosmos in a different way than usual. She searched the sky and waited until the next star emerged, and she was certain now how to find her answers.

She gave a silent nod of thanks to the universe and hurried to the libraries section of the cosmos. She picked out several books and laid them out on a nearby table and began searching. She had no idea what it would be, but the answer usually 'popped out' when she found it, and she knew she might have to be patient. It was also a skill she had been learning since the time of her beginning so may rotations ago. Several books into the pile she found an image of one of the constellations she had never heard of before and on the next page was the scaled-out version indicating where it was in the sky. She turned the book around in different ways and decided she would take it outside to determine if she could identify it for herself.

She managed the book to the courtyard and placed it on the altar under the pavilion and turned to the now dark night. The lights in the atmosphere gave a wonderful, illuminated essence that she missed so many nights as she was usually sleeping. The same star in the sky was now brighter, and she examined the books images to find the star and then located where the new constellation would be. She turned to that point in the sky and found it. The first point was marked by a large star that had a slight red appearance and went into the next star and the following three until it rounded back up into the corners of the markers.

The book indicated it was the unified constellation of the 'Gods' and then the book showed each individually. She admired them and found Alisdair, Malita, Todan and Baltair, except the last star for Baltair was in the book, but not in the sky, and she wondered if maybe it was the wrong time of rotation to see it, or if there was something bigger. She settled on something bigger, and she shivered as the truth of it ran through her body like a cold wind.

Nitida pulled all the stones and casting cloth from her purple velvet pouch and organized them back into the exact placement as the original cast. The way the moon shined on the stones from the spaces in the top of the pergola illuminated the exact constellation. Nitida gasped and covered her mouth but her eyes were wide as the information pummeled her mind. Nitida gripped the edges of the altar and sucked in a deep breath. Images of the deities flashed before her eyes and circled through the events of the times of peace and times of wars since the beginning of time.

The information was astounding and Nitida wasn't sure if she was going to have the strength to perceive it all. The flashes went by so quickly that some of them she only received ideas of what happened, but she was certain the eons of time was divulging information to her. She wasn't aware of a runecaster ever receiving this kind of knowledge but felt that this understanding wasn't 'for her' but 'through her' and the information was for Shaz, Serin, Riddick, and Amirra. The images faded, and she heaved as her chest sucked in the cool night air. She pulled away from the stone carefully and waited until she was steady on her feet and combed her long silver hair from her sweaty skin.

She put the book of notes on the altar and began to scribble as much as she could from the exchange into the back of the book. Her fingers were tired after the constant writing, but her brain refused to let them rest until she had made as complete of an inscription as she could. Her mind was eager and energized, and she found there were enough forces to support her frame. The night faded into the early day and Nitida was still diligently inscribing the details and didn't sense Inelius standing behind her.

He slowly made his way to the altar and examined the rune cloth and the stones as they were placed. He noted the book on the constellations and looked into the early dawn, but the sun was shielding the stars now, and he was unable to see what she had seen. He waited patiently as not to disrupt her efforts and when she was nearing the last of the details he noted a small tear form at the corner of her eye. Inelius examined the script and understood what her emotions meant. Nitida realized his presence and looked up. His soft gaze was gentle and reassuring and his company was too.

They had spent many rotations together in the Mountain Temple while Shaz and Mathieu were in Turob and had found their friendship grew to a deeper and more profound level. He offered his old arms and she embraced him. He wrapped his arms around her shaking frame and watched the soft ice-blue flowers open as the sun's rays hit their sparkling pods.

"We have to find Shaz and Serin right away, I know what this casting is about, and we have little time," Nitida said.

"They have gone to the Timeless Plains, but there is a portal that will take you," Inelius said.

"I wish you could come with me," Nitida said.

"I do as well, but we both know, I am only able to continue living as long as I stay here, or at the castle," Inelius said.

"I know, which I am forever grateful for," Nitida said.

"I have a feeling our time here is nearing its end," Inelius said.

"I do too, I don't know if I am happy or sad for it," Nitida said.

"I feel the same way, but if we leave together we will stay together," Inelius said.

"I hope so," Nitida said.

"Let's get you to the portal," Inelius said.

40-Go, We're Right Behind You

Antorn dug his front hoof into the soft ground and gripped his spear and battle-ax. The shiny sharpened bone at the top glistened in the less than bright sky and reflected the now soft light of the low sun. The knot in his stomach churned and his breath heaved his human-like chest.

"Are you sure you want to do this?" Tobis asked.

"No, but what choice do we have? We can either die by fighting to protect our lives or die because we didn't," Antorn said.

"Alright, then let's do this," Tobis said.

****

Shaz's energy pricked the back of his mind, and he turned to the portals.

"Serin there's trouble right now," Shaz said.

"Go, we're right behind you," Serin said.

"Riddick," Shaz called.

Riddick turned to see Shaz disappear through the mist and darted towards it.

"Go, there's trouble now," Serin said.

Riddick threw up his shield and ripped his battle-ax off his back as he stepped through the portal. He rounded the handle in his palm so that the blade would be ready for an uppercut as he ran through the shift's force pulling him faster through to the other side. Turkill and Ladtwig shot into the energy field behind him. Riddick was only a second behind Shaz and saw Shaz run straight for the first Jaduuk. The Jaduuk's eye flashed a hint of confusion and it snarled as drool dripped from the corner of its tight lips. Shaz launched himself over the beast and pulled the blade across its neck.

The Jaduuk's eyes widened with the realization but was unable to control the blood spurting from its main artery and hit into the ground plowing the soft surface into a heap over its head. Riddick swung his ax into the gut of the first Jaduuk he came to and the blade sank deep into the softer midsection. Turkill and Ladtwig thrust their rapid-fire darts with speed and precision hitting a Jaduuk behind Shaz. The beast staggered as their darts were now laced with the poison of the Ruin Spider Spit. The spider spit paralyzed its body allowing their poison time to stop their heart and the Minca jumped a hop-jump with the success. Turkill found a large boulder and motioned to Ladtwig who veered around a stump toward it. Shaz dodged the swing of a smaller Jaduuk and stabbed his blade into its side and pulled the edge through the thick blueish hide.

The Jaduuk howled and Shaz shoved his feet into the ground and somersaulted over another Jaduuk. The rancid odor of the Jaduuk's blood was starting to be less gross than before and Shaz figured it was because they had fought so many. Riddick launched another side-strike and dodged a flared claw and Ladtwig and Turkill let more darts fly. Shaz rolled through a strike and followed as the blade reached through the neck of another beast.

Riddick pulled up a wall of earth and several Jaduuk slammed into the force and the earth toppled on top of them. Riddick stomped his foot and several more fell into the holes and were buried alive. Shaz called the fire element and sent a blast of fire from his palm that blew his hair all around him. The force ignited the closest beast in an instant inferno and dripped over the others with a slow ooze taking in the glory of its nature. Howls ripped over the atmosphere and Antorn stood in complete shock. He couldn't make his mind explain what his eyes were seeing and Tobis too was stunned.

"What in the world is happening, what are those things?" Tobis asked.

"I have no idea," Antorn said.

The memory of the two-legged stags from moons ago surfaced and Antorn shook his head and dug his front hooves into the ground.

"Are we going to help them?" Tobis asked.

"Of course," Antorn said.

Antorn gave three quick thumps on his antlers and the sound vibrated over the atmosphere. Riddick felt the sounds and turned to find the small army of Forrne. Riddick whistled and Shaz turned and found Riddick nodding to where they were. Shaz leaped out of the reach of a Jaduuk and swung the blade through the creature's neck. Serin came through the portal and saw the oncoming beasts and gave the signal. The largest portal opened, and rows of armored men came running through. The thunderous sounds of feet hitting the ground and the clanking of chainmail armor against the new and improved breastplates sent shivers through the Forrne who turned to see the ruckus.

Ebassian soldiers with their long-shields formed into a wall of protection and ran at a steady pace directly at the oncoming Jaduuk. The first row slammed their shields into the ground and the second row rested on top leaving small openings for the archers who quickly began letting arrows sizzle through the air. The paralyzing poisoned arrowheads landed their marks into the neck and chests of the beasts and Jaduuk began falling in droves.

The shield-wall picked up and advanced and more soldiers poured out of the portal. Antorn's heart raced with a sense of instant devotion but couldn't figure out what was going on. He flicked his antlers again and the small but determined force shot out of the trees. They galloped at a fast pace and gripped their spears and battle-axes. The Forrne Guard engaged the Jaduuk with a new sense of determination and their hearts swelled with hope.

Serin sent a blast of wind shards careening through a pack of Jaduuk and blood spurted from the instant gashes. Amirra came through the portal leading a group of Minca and their cannons. They stayed back and loaded the first set of explosives and aimed the cannons to shoot clear to the back of the hoard and lit the wicks. They blasted across the sky with an undeniable force of awe and the crackling explosives tore the Jaduuk to shreds. Antorn side-sliced a Jaduuk through the guts. Riddick slammed his hand into the chest of a Jaduuk and it went flying backward and plowed over several more.

Declan and several of the Rangers shot out of the portal, gripped their newly enchanted weapons, and hollered the Rangers battle cry. The sound was gripping as it struck fear in the enemy and formed a heightened determination in the allied forces. Their large statures and sturdy determination was the same as the Ebassian soldiers, and they veered to one side and slammed their blades into the creatures with such speed and fierceness they sent a flicker of fear through the beasts a second before they fell lifeless.

Shaz dodged and rolled through an oncoming attack and sliced the backs of their tendons. The beasts roared with the pain and fell immobilized. Antorn slashed a beast and leaped over a fallen one. Shaz made eye contact with him and gave a smile-wave as he back-flipped over another beast and stabbed the blade through its spine. The blade barely even felt the resistance of the bone as it sliced it on its way back out. Serin blasted Shaz with her wind and flung him out of the way of a forward strike, and he eased into her magic.

Shaz took the advantage and sliced the head off another as the wind brought him back to the ground. Another blast of explosives careened overhead, and Tobis barely saw the ax of a Jaduuk coming straight for his heart but an instant before it made contact Serin's wind gripped the blade and yanked it from its grip. The Jaduuk's stunned face, as the weapon was no longer in its claw, allowed Tobis the time to slash his spear through the creature.

The soldiers again advanced and the Jaduuk forces dwindled quickly as the explosives continued to barrel out of the sky. Bowen halted the next set of soldiers from attacking and redirected them to their original plan. Shaz doused the last pack of Jaduuk with flames and Antorn and Tobis and the rest of the Guard gazed around at all the strangers and dead Jaduuk. Shaz, Riddick, and Serin made their way to Antorn and the others.

"Are we dreaming the same dream?" Tobis asked from the corner of his mouth.

"If we are, that's pretty creepy," Antorn said.

"I think they are looking at us," Tobis said.

Shaz chuckled, Serin smiled and Riddick put his hands in his pockets.

"Are you alright?" Shaz asked.

"Is it speaking our language?" Tobis asked.

"Yes, we speak your language, I'm Shaz the war wizard and these are my friends, Serin and Riddick. I'm sorry we didn't make it here sooner,..." Shaz's tone ended in a question as to ask their names.

"Antorn and this is Tobis, what is a war wizard?" Antorn asked.

Shaz thought about it and remembered a different term.

"Battle Mage," Shaz ask-stated.

Antorn's eyes widened, and he stared at Shaz and then looked around. The soldiers continued to march out of the portal and organize into their ranks.

"Battle Mage? You mean from the legends no one ever talks about anymore?" Tobis asked.

Shaz bowed and gave them their greeting and Antorn bent one knee, but his head was spinning with the details. The rest of the Forrne followed.

"I am unsure of what to say," Antorn said.

"Where are your people, are they safe?" Shaz asked.

"We are few in numbers now, our settlement isn't far from here," Antorn said.

"Well, we are here to take over this battle for you, I have three more armies still to bring, and we will need to occupy some of your lands," Shaz said.

"You can have it all," Antorn said choking back the lump in his throat.

"Well, not all of it," Tobis said.

Shaz chuckled and Serin smiled. Shaz gave Bowen the go-ahead, and he started the next brigade.

"Riddick let's clear these ugly's," Shaz said.

"Aye," Riddick said.

Riddick gripped a piece of turf off the ground and hopped onto it and hovered around the masses. The Forrne stepped back with the oddity and watched with wide eyes as Riddick stopped every so many lengths and stomped twice until he surrounded the carcasses. He hopped off the craft and slapped his hands together and the ground shook. The Forrne shifted uncomfortably as the ground wriggled around all the bodies, and they sank into the dirt. Riddick hopped a few times and the earth compacted tightly over the now buried bodies and he returned to Shaz.

"That was fancy," Shaz said.

"Aye, it's a new trick I learned," Riddick said.

"I like it," Shaz said. Shaz turned to Antorn. "We are going to set up camp here moving that way and over there," Shaz motioned to the locations and Antorn nodded. "Do you have any wounded?" Shaz asked. Tobis nodded and pointed to the trees. "Come with us, we have a lot to discuss. Serin and our healers will take care of your wounded," Shaz said.

Serin waved at Amirra and the Minca women, and they hurried toward the trees with another raincloud following behind them. Antorn gave commands for his troop to return and show them where the wounded were, and then he and Tobis followed Shaz and Riddick to where Bowen and Declan were eyeing the raincloud with huge eyes. Antorn and Tobis were having a hard time taking in the mass amount of new creatures and turned as the ground rumbled. They slowed down and stared as the elephantines came pounding out of the portal with heavy cords over the horns on their backs pulling the gigantic trebuchets unassembled on large wagons. Shaz and Riddick stopped and waited for Antorn to take in the sight and then directed Wandi where to take the wagons.

Bowen and Declan made their way over to Shaz and saluted. Shaz wasn't sure why they saluted this time when they never did before and wondered if maybe it was just instinctual. He fully recognized them as equal in leadership, if not better. Shaz nodded with acknowledgment. It *was* a comfortable feeling, but he had a hint of doubt in it too. In *his* mind, he was only twenty-six now and there were people that had a great deal more experience than he did. Grandfather had always taught him that he was never to let his powers make him entitled and that he was to treat every creature of every kind with respect.

Shaz used to resent the fact that Grandfather was so diligent to teach him to serve every being there is, instead of letting him appreciate his full potential at being the best at everything, but he was now starting to see why. It was Grandfather's way of earning instant respect, and if not, at least consideration. Shaz didn't even feel like he had done that much, but just being kind to people was Grandfather's way and, more now than ever Shaz wanted to live up to that.

"We're about halfway, and then we'll bring over the Minca, the rest of the Rangers, and then the Gryphton's," Bowen said.

"Great. Bowen, Declan, this is Antorn and Tobis, the leaders of the Forrne," Shaz said. The two men saluted and Antorn and Tobis returned with their own salute. Turkill and Ladtwig jumped off one of the baby pachyderms and made their way over to them. "This is Turkill and Ladtwig, the leaders of the Minca," Shaz said.

Antorn and Tobis nodded and returned the Minca's salute but tried to keep their intrigue for the tiny humans from overloading their faces. Turkill snickered under his harrumph scowl. He secretly liked being the 'tiny human that ended up doing huge things leaving everyone speechless', but he wasn't ever going to admit it.

"We'll have the war tent set up in a few minutes, and then we will be able to get to work," Bowen said.

"Excellent," Shaz said.

"I really have no idea what to say, I have so many questions, I think I'm in shock," Antorn said.

"I understand, there is a lot to cover and details to exchange. Bowen where is Motavo?" Shaz asked.

"He's helping Helios with the poisons," Bowen said.

Shaz tilted his head with a concerned expression.

"Don't tell Serin," Shaz said.

"She's already aware, come to find out, Motavo and Asher are now immune to the toxin. We didn't have time or enough Saraswati venom, or Helios would have made the antidote for everyone, but he's confident that he was able to adjust the Ruin Spider Spit to be less harmful to humans. Should now only cause mild stiffness and a stomachache," Bowen said.

"Ruin Spiders? They are not toxic to our kind," Antorn said.

"That's very good to know, but the Jaduuk are affected so it's going to be one of our best tools, especially when mixed with the Minca's poison," Riddick said.

"Is that what those beasts are called?" Antorn asked.

"Aye, Gavin Rhill has been growing the Jaduuk, but we aren't sure how he's doing it. Our top three priorities are, find out how the Jaduuk are being bred, build the fortifications for the camp and find out about the water shortage," Shaz said.

"We have noticed new lights in the night sky that comes from the mountain, but we haven't a clue what they are. There are so many beasts that we can't get through them enough to find out what it is," Tobis said.

"The land is nearly half covered now with darkened earth and the heat that comes from it has evaporated almost all the water we have," Antorn said.

"We don't have many trees here, so I'm not sure what kind of fortifications we can offer," Tobis said.

"We're not going to use trees, we're going to use the dirt," Riddick said.

Antorn gave Riddick a perplexed glance. A crew of soldiers finished the last stakes of the tent and heaved the heavy canvas into place and secured the ropes that held the poles inside. Shaz pulled open the flap and they went in. Antorn ducked and maneuvered his antlers through sideways with a bit of cautious embarrassment.

"I guess we're going to have to make a few adjustments," Riddick said.

Phanes rounded the corner and Antorn's heart thumped from his chest. Phanes crawled on all fours through the doorway as his upright status wouldn't fit either. Antorn and Tobis took in his sizable frame and features and instantly knew he was a predator type of creature, and they stepped back. Shaz sensed the energy change and stepped between the Forrne and Phanes. He remembered what Azrack had said about elk being his preferred meal and wondered if that was going to cause an issue.

"Phanes, these are the Forrne leaders, Antorn and Tobis," Shaz said.

"Sir," Phanes said without even the slightest indication of there being an issue, and saluted.

Antorn returned the gesture and an odd sense of security settled in. Phanes rose to full height and pulled his satchel off and unlatched the canister at his hip and put it on the table that a soldier had just setup.

"What is this?" Shaz asked.

"These are the only antidotes Helios was able to make, he has put another crew on getting more of the Saraswati bugs, but that might take some time with everything going on. So, these are to be kept for the leaders," Phanes said.

Shaz nodded, and was about to unroll a map when Serin and Amirra came through the tent. Shaz and Riddick turned to them and smiled as they made their way to the table. The sparkle in their eyes for Shaz and Riddick was undeniable and Antorn got the distinct impression they were the force that made up this company.

"How are the Forrne?" Shaz asked.

"They are all on their way to a full recovery. The Minca women are tending to everything they need and Ladtwig's crew has begun setting up the medic tents," Serin said.

"Excellent," Shaz said.

Shaz, Riddick, Declan and Bowen all began to organize the maps and Phanes chimed in the details of his armada and Turkill made his report. They worked extremely well together and Antorn studied the crew. He could tell there was history between them, but more than that, there was a fierce loyalty to Shaz, which for some reason he felt too. It was as if there was a kind of vibe about him that not only asked for it, but commanded it, but in a 'I'll fight for *your* life without you having to ask' kind of admiration.

"Antorn, what can you tell us about the Jaduuk's presence here?" Shaz asked.

Antorn blinked his thoughts away and stepped toward the table.

"We don't really know a lot about what these things are, but we have been fighting them for over a rotation. They just started to appear, at first in small groups but eventually they were so numerous we just couldn't keep any ground and started retreating, the animals of the savanna are nearly all gone, whether they are in hiding or killed I don't know. I now understand where the elephantine went, but everything else...," Antorn shrugged.

"What about the scorched earth?" Riddick asked.

"It showed up just before the beasts did, and spread out as they did," Antorn said.

"Do you know where it began?" Shaz asked.

Antorn pointed to the map in the area they had first met the Jaduuk.

"And the water?" Serin asked.

"The reserves have been dried up for some time," Antorn said.

Antorn indicated where the reservoirs were in relation to the scorched earth.

"I think I might have an idea. Riddick can you make me a pond?" Serin said.

"Aye," Riddick said.

"What are you going to do?" Bowen asked.

"Make a raincloud over the pond," Serin said.

"Won't the heat make the raincloud fizzle out?" Shaz asked.

"I'm thinking if I can wrap it with a breeze, that will keep the warm forces out," Serin said.

"Oh, I can help with that, if we keep the cloud low enough then the heat can't get underneath and dissipate it. It's basic weather pressure," Riddick said.

Shaz nodded with that 'of course, why didn't I think of that' kind of nod and Bowen and Declan chuckled.

"So, we make a few of them around the camp for easy transportation," Serin said.

"What about the lights in the night, where are those?" Shaz asked.

Tobis pointed to the map in the several locations and Shaz took the markers Riddick had made and set them on the marks and stood back. An interesting notion came into his mind, and he ran through all the constellations.

"Antorn, are your people safe where they are?" Shaz asked.

"We have a force around the settlement, but we are tired and wounded," Antorn admitted.

"We need to scout out the surroundings and start setting up the fortifications to the base and move the settlement here. Riddick, can you and the Forrne make a sweep around the perimeter," Riddick and Antorn nodded, "Bowen, we need to get your crew ready to start the digging and rigging the fortifications," Bowen agreed, "Turkill, make ready to start production of the bombs," Turkill grunted, "Declan, you help Helios with the launchers," Shaz said and Declan nodded.

Shaz stepped around Riddick to examine the map and then moved to the other side of the Forrne and twisted his head back and forth with a scrunched face. Riddick eyed him, he had seen that face many times before and was certain he was working through something of importance.

"Phanes, make ready a crew to make a sweep over the encampment, we'll meet you here, I want to get a birds-eye view of where the heaviest concentration of Jaduuk are and find out what these lights are," Shaz said.

Shaz pointed to the map and Phanes saluted.

"Sir," Phanes said.

Riddick studied Shaz as he moved one of the pieces on the map a small degree and started to examine the map more closely.

"Alright, let's get to it," Shaz said.

The leaders saluted and everyone left except Serin, Riddick, and Amirra.

"I'm certain you're working on something, what is it?" Riddick asked.

Shaz waved Riddick to stand where he was standing, and Riddick rounded the table.

"What do you see?" Shaz asked.

"A map with markers on it," Riddick said.

"What do the markers remind you of without the map," Shaz asked.

Riddick rethought the idea and studied them. He picked up another and placed it in the middle of three of the markers, and they both lit up.

"Baltair," they said in unison.

"What is Baltair?" Serin asked.

"It's a constellation," Riddick said.

A sudden thump hit Shaz's being, and he pictured the other three constellations of the 'Gods' series. Alisdair was one of them, which meant *Alisdair* was one of the God of Glory's children, and he chided himself for not seeing it sooner. Which also now meant, that this was something important and not just a coincidence. The heavy heat now in his chest indicated that this was part of the puzzle, and if the lights indicated one of the 'Gods' they could be in for a big fight.

If he inherited everything, including the magic of Alisdair, the *son* of the God of Glory as was written in the will, what did that mean? How would that play into this new information? He didn't feel like he had more magic, and or what did that actually mean. Would that mean that they would have to fight a God? And how powerful is a God, what kinds of things can a God do? What could he do if he now had Alisdair's magic too? Serin listed to his feelings and tried to interpret what he was thinking but his emotions jumped all over the place, and she didn't know what to think.

"Does this mean something?" Riddick asked.

"Aye, but I'm not sure what yet, I have an inkling Baltair, one of the actual Gods, is a key figure in all this," Shaz said.

"What do you mean?" Riddick asked.

"I'm starting to wonder if Gavin Rhill is really the force at play or if he's just another pawn of a bigger and more powerful force," Shaz said.

"Now, you're totally twigging me out," Riddick said.

"You and me both," Shaz said.

41- You're Going

Antorn and Tobis examined the humans and gryphtons with awe and wonder and had a hard time getting their brains to accept the new information. They stopped and let a troop of Ebassian's march to their designated area with tents over their shoulders. Their expressions were tight with focus, but they had a familiar feel to them. The dimmed sky didn't reach full darkness this time of the rotation, so they could see just about everything. Distant howls echoed over the plains, and they turned toward the noise. They weren't sure where they were coming from, but a sense of panic overcame them.

"Go get the troop ready, we need to get our people moved as quickly as we can," Antorn said.

"Yes, Sir," Tobis said.

Tobis galloped toward the trees and Antorn returned to the tent. He pulled the flap open and stepped inside.

"May I bother you for a moment," Antorn asked.

"Of course," Shaz said.

"I heard the beasts in the distance, and I fear they will attack our settlement," Antorn said.

"I'll ask Bowen to send out a force," Riddick said.

"Great, I'll meet up with Phanes," Shaz said.

"Aye," Riddick said.

Riddick followed Antorn out of the tent and pulled a piece of earth and hopped onto the turf. Antorn's eyes widened as he watched him maneuver the thing over the surface but lurched after him when he realized he had fallen behind. They maneuvered through the armies until they found Bowen and explained the matter. Bowen nodded and ordered his red brigade to leave immediately and the forces picked up their gear and was ready in less than ten minutes. Antorn lead them to the others and explained the plan but was again shocked to find every one of his men in complete health and with the largest smiles that could be formed on their faces. Riddick and Bowen smiled as they too knew how it felt to be healed by Serin's magic. There was a euphoria that went with it, which was the best part.

The soldiers set out at a quick pace, but they were nowhere close to being as fast as the Forrne, and Riddick tried to think of a way to make the earth move them faster without wearing himself out. Antorn didn't want to ask his stags to let the soldiers 'ride' them, it was never anything they had ever had to do, but the notion kept returning to his mind.

"Tobis, what do you think about us letting the soldiers ride us, I realize this has never been done before and I don't have any clue what the others will think, but we really need to move faster," Antorn said.

Tobis looked at him and had been thinking the same thing.

"I've been thinking that as well, I already counted, and we are about even in numbers. I think if you command it, the men will do it," Tobis said.

Antorn stopped and turned to his men.

"I understand this is not our way, but-" Antorn started.

The guardsmen didn't even wait until he finished his request and began organizing the soldiers on their backs. Riddick popped an earth board for the few remaining and quickly instructed them on how to operate it. Antorn smiled to himself and once situated, they galloped toward their settlement. It didn't take long to reach the outer perimeter and Antorn couldn't get the dread out of his guts that he might find what he didn't want to find. The Jaduuk howled again and this time they were much louder. Riddick sent out his earth magic and waited for its report on the whereabouts and indicated to the soldiers.

"We'll take it from here, you get your people back to the camp," Riddick said.

The Forrne let the soldiers off, and they organized into their ranks and Riddick started out toward the beasts.

"Tobis, you head that way, Gabe you head there, and I'll head this way," Antorn motioned each direction and the Forrne lurched into fast gallops. Antorn moved at a quick rate but his mind was all over the place. He wasn't sure how he was going to explain everything to the people and feared that if he didn't they would refuse to leave *again*. He slowed his pace as he came up to the camp and tried to be quiet until he found Slat and the others. The pavilion came into view, and he rounded a pile of bailed grains and scanned the sleeping stags. He found Slat on the far side of the pavilion and started toward him when he felt a tap on his leg.

His heart skipped, but he looked down into Tissa's big eyes. He bent down as much as he could and gripped her into the tightest hug he could muster without squishing her. She wrapped her arms around his neck and squeezed tightly.

"I was afraid you weren't coming back," Tissa said with a tight throat.

"So was I, but the most amazing thing happened, and I'm here to take you and everyone to meet my new friends that are going to help us," Antorn said through the knot in his throat.

Tissa pulled back and looked him in the eye with a 'are you teasing' look, and he chuckled.

"Where is Mazen and Nama," Antorn asked. Tissa pointed to where they were sleeping. "I need to talk to Slat for a minute, but I'll be right there," Antorn said. Tissa nodded but didn't leave his side and instead of making her return to them, he gripped her hand tightly and took her with him. "Slat, I'm sorry to wake you but we need to talk," Antorn said.

Slat stirred and looked up and then hurried to his hooves.

"What is the matter?" Slat said.

"I can't explain just yet, but we need to move the herd, now," Antorn said.

"Move the herd?" Slat said loudly until shooshing himself.

"Yes," Antorn searched his brain for a way to explain, "do you believe there is more to this world than just us?" Antorn asked.

Slat searched his face with scrutiny and when he found he was serious he searched his own brain.

"I suppose, I wouldn't have before the beasts, but I guess anything is possible now," Slat admitted.

"Well, the Battle Mage has come to help us with these beasts which are called Jaduuk, and they have set up camp near the ravine. We need to move the herd close to them, so we will be safe," Antorn said.

"Battle Mage, you mean the stories from the old tales that no one ever talks about anymore?" Slat said.

"His name is Shaz, and he has brought three huge Guards," Antorn said.

"Three Guards," Slat said.

"Riddick, his," Antorn had no idea what they were, "other mage and a troop has already gone after the beasts we detected in the distance, but we need to hurry," Antorn said.

"I'm not sure what to think," Slat said.

"My head is still swimming too, but it's true," Antorn said.

Shouts sounded from behind them and Antorn found Riddick standing between four guardsmen casually standing with his hands in his pockets, but the guardsmen had him boxed in with their spears. Riddick nodded and waved with a big grin and Antorn signaled to the men to let him pass. Mazen woke to the noise. She frantically searched for Tissa and found her standing next to Antorn holding his hand. Mazen jumped up and started toward them. Slat's eyes popped out and his mouth fell to the floor.

"That's what I did," Antorn said.

"Antorn, we took out the Jaduuk, turns out it was only a scouting party, but that means we need to start moving. The men are standing guard so you can inform your people and we'll escort you to the main camp," Riddick said.

"Excellent, Riddick this is Slat the head of HOOF," Antorn said. Mazen touched Antorn's shoulder, and he looked to find her confused but excited face. She was beautiful, and he had missed her more than he thought possible. Slat closed his mouth and swallowed and was able to hold out his hand and Riddick took it in a grip. Slat startled with the touch and was convinced Riddick was real and Riddick chuckled.

"And this is Mazen and Tissa. Please, forgive my kind, we have never seen, well I don't know what you are exactly," Antorn said.

"No biggy. We're humans, those of us on two legs that is, but then there's the gryphton's who are another mixed being," Riddick said.

"Is he speaking our language?" Slat asked.

Antorn chuckled again and nodded and wrapped his arm around Mazen and gave her a squeeze. She wasn't sure about the display of affection in public and especially in front of Riddick whom she was still trying to assimilate. Riddick noticed Tissa's eyes gloss over, like they do before you cry, and held out his hand. She stepped back and leaned into Antorn who wrapped his arm over her small shoulders.

Riddick opened his hand, and a small stem grew from the center of his skin. Tissa's eyes widened with the growth and tried not to watch while keeping her eyes fixed on the now budding flower. The bright yellow peddles unfolded and settled into a wonderful array of beauty. Tissa looked up at Antorn with trepidation and wonder, and he nodded for her to take it.

"Go ahead, take it," Riddick said. Tissa slowly picked the flower from Riddick's hand, and she smiled a small grin. Riddick grew another one, this time pink and put it in her hair next to her slender ear. "You'll see, thing will be alright," Riddick said.

Tissa smiled but leaned into Antorn and smelled the blossom.

"It's a good thing we speak the same language, because I'm terrible at learning other languages," Riddick said.

"I don't know what to say?" Slat said.

"Then don't say anything, but we need to move and quickly," Riddick said with a playful grin.

"Of course," Slat said.

Mazen took Tissa and admired her new flower as they returned to Nama and began organizing their things, which wasn't much. Slat began waking the Forrne and getting them organized to move. It helped quite a bit that Riddick and the soldiers were there because the others could see for themselves, the things that Antorn and Slat were telling them. The herd moved quickly, and the first wave headed out with half the troop. Antorn put Mazen, Tissa, and Nama in the first wave to leave but Nama was having a hard time keeping up with the herd so Riddick made an earth board for her to ride and it followed Mazen who was not happy that she had to leave Antorn again, but he had been firm, and she understood his need and agreed, but not before giving him a small piece of her mind. Riddick liked her instantly. There was definitely a woman's flare to her *piece of her mind* lecture, and he was positive she would fit right in with Serin and Amirra.

Riddick gave instructions to send another troop to help transport their goods, but Antorn was certain his stags would be able to take everything. Tobis and Gabe retuned with everyone they could find, and Riddick made sure they took their tools for farming and as many seeds as they had. The stags and fawns moved quickly, and Riddick was impressed at how quiet they were for their size.

"Looks like all we have left are the sick and injured," Antorn said.

"Where are they?" Riddick asked.

Antorn took Riddick to the group that was ill, old, or injured and Riddick pulled out a large bottle Serin had given him. He dished out a dose for as many as could be healed and then made earth boards for the rest.

"Where is Pillip?" Antorn asked.

"I have no idea, I thought you already sent him," Tobis said.

Antorn shook his head.

"I think I do give me bit, Pillip is going to need one of your thingy's," Antorn said motioning to his earth-board.

Riddick nodded and sent the others on their way with the last of the troops. Antorn made his way to one of the building that no one used anymore and Antorn found Pillip in the corner.

"I'm not going Antorn, you can't make me," Pillip said.

"Wanna bet?" Antorn said.

"I'm useless, there is nothing I can offer, just let me be," Pillip said.

"No, do you know why? Because I believe there is much more to this universe than just us, and it's upon us. I can't do this without you, I never have. You're the one that truly leads this Guard," Antorn said.

"That's the furthest from the truth and you know it," Pillip said.

"Well then, let's agree that you are both super studly and get going," Riddick said.

Antorn turned to Riddick standing in the doorway and smiled. It was the first time he didn't know what a word meant, and he liked the sound of it.

"What in the world?" Pillip said.

The urge to jump up and grab his battle-ax hit his brain a second before he squashed it. Riddick walked over to the wall where it was hanging and picked it up.

"Now that is one nice battle-ax, looks like the Jaduuk's, I bet your quite handy with it. I favor this one too," Riddick said as he handed his own battle-ax to Pillip who took the weapon and looked at it.

Pillip was unsure of what to say or do but his heart lunged in his chest with a renewed sense of, something. Riddick sensed the energy shift and gripped the ground below Pillip.

"Now, I understand you don't know me, but I have a mate that I would do anything for, and by the looks of it, you and Antorn here are just like me and Shaz, so I'm going to say this only once, you're going," Riddick said.

He lifted the earth and Pillip threw out his arms to steady himself. Riddick gave the turf instructions to take Pillip to the camp. Antorn smiled as Pillip's face contorted through the range of emotions he had already experienced, and they hurried after the others.

42-How Long Will You Be Gone

Turkill hurried to his camp where he found Frebin and Melog and instructed them on the plans for the bombs. They had been diligently working on the new designs for the hand-cannons and found after working with Riddick they were able to compact the igniting components into small round balls which launched from the barrel and exploded on impact. It was quite the addition to their arsenal.

They found the hand-cannons process needed a great deal of heat and force to make and the Minca were too small to offer the needed force so several Ebassian's began to hammer the smelting ore as the Minca made the ammunition.

Turkill turned to where Drager and Harmus were working with the toxin. He snickered under a harrumph with his fellow comrades donned in an interesting layer of heavy leather apron-like dress and large leather mittens that went to their armpits with a shield of glass covering their faces which made their afro-braids stick out of the top of their heads. Turkill almost chuckled with the sight until he saw Feungrid. His scowl shot to the surface and settled into his chest. Feungrid looked up and smiled his obnoxious grin and Turkill turned to leave, hesitated, then shook his head. He wanted to punch the portly man in the face but that wouldn't solve the problem. It would make him feel a little better, until he got in trouble for it.

Turkill huffed away and made his way to Helios and the gryphton's. He relayed the message for where to begin moving the equipment and then started toward the meal tents. His thoughts ran around the event from rotations ago. It was actually quite a dumb excuse to stay mad at for all these rotations and it really shouldn't have happened. Turkill was the Chief's son, and the best at everything, and the best looking in the clan, so he had nothing to worry about. He even told a few funny jokes and could argue with the best of them, but there was something about Feungrid that just got under his skin.

Every time Turkill advanced in some way or another Feungrid would have some sarcastic remark or excuse as to why he advanced. If he had just said 'good job' and meant it, there wouldn't be an issue now. And then, when they were old enough, he was always getting in the way of every girl Turkill wanted to talk to. He so wanted to punch him in the face, but continued to take the high road. Maybe that was what bugged him more, the fact he was always expected to be the better person and Feungrid understood that. Turkill picked a few red berries, a bread roll which was half the size of his plate, a slab of meat and made his way to a table at the side of the tent.

A soft set of lips touched his cheek, and he jumped and turned to see a smiling Shati holding a plate of her own. His cheek quickly turned pink, and she held in a chuckle.

"Is it alright I sit here, or is this for the leaders only," Shati asked.

Turkill cleared his throat.

"Of course, I would like if you did," Turkill said.

Shati sat next to him a little closer than he would have, but he liked it.

"Is everything alright?" Shati asked.

Turkill gazed into her warm amber eyes and smiled. He wanted to tell her everything, but he didn't want to bother her with the details and how boring it was to be a leader. Don't get him wrong, I mean, he liked bossing people around, well he didn't like it, but he was good at it, and it needed to be done. A few rotations ago he would have loved it, but now, he wished it could be the way it used to be.

Not knowing anything about the rest of the world and only worrying about whether Feungrid was going to try and steal Shati. If only that were his biggest worry. Shati watched the thoughts move across his face and wanted to help, but she also understood men were funny that way and didn't usually share the details unless they had to.

Shati quietly ate a few bites while Turkill struggled with the heaviness of his duties.

"I hear the bomb squad and the throwers are heading out," Shati said.

"Umhum," Turkill said.

"Are you going to be going with them?" Shati asked.

He stabbed his meat and cut a bite sized piece and shoved into his mouth.

"Umhum," Turkill said.

"How long will you be gone?" Shati asked.

"Not sure," Turkill said.

"I know this is war, and things are going to get a lot worse, but I want you to know I am happy to be here with you, even if you don't want to talk to me," Shati said.

Turkill looked up with a bit of painful acceptance.

"It's not that I don't want to talk to you, I very much do, it's just that everything that is on my mind are things I can't talk about," Turkill said.

Shati gave him a reassuring smile, and he relaxed a little.

"Well, then we will need to talk about something else," Shati started.

"Why don't you tell me about what you have been doing?" Turkill said.

Turkill gave her hand a squeeze and she smiled. She began telling him how they had set up the tents and organized the medicines and how much she had already learned about the art of healing. She explained she had barely returned from a lecture on the aspects of the gryphton's anatomy that Helios was teaching and after lunch she was to go to another lecture on the human anatomy. Turkill smiled at her enthusiasm of all the neat things she had learned, but he understood as soon as those things were to be put in actual practice it would change quickly. Fionte and Babbesh had also taken to instructing the others, on the matters of herbs and poultices. How to harvest the herbs and crush the leaves to make the pain medicine that Mrs. Bailey made. Turkill wondered if Mrs. Bailey knew how famous she was with her pain medicine and smiled to himself.

Turkill enjoyed listening to Shati and finished more of the food than he would usually, but he figured if he kept eating she would stay, and the moments would last longer. He stared at the next bite stuck on his fork and debated whether or not his stomach had room and decided he better not chance it. The last thing he needed was a side ache in the case he was called out suddenly. He put his fork down and pushed his plate away but listened to Shati finish her details on the use of the magic water from the raincloud, which was under strict observance.

A commotion broke outside the tent, and he turned to listen to see if it was something he needed to address.

"What is it?" Shati asked.

"I'm not sure, but I better go take a look," Turkill said.

"Alright," Shati said.

"Thank you, for sitting with me," Turkill leaned in and brought her to him and kissed her. Her touch was soft and beautiful, and he took in the details of her lips. He pulled away and looked her in the eye. "I will come find you this evening if I can,"

Shati smiled and nodded and he left the tent.

43-I'm Still Mad At You

Shaz kept busy by moving about each camp and making sure everyone had what they needed. After making sure the military forces and fortifications were in full operation he made his way to the Forrne's new settlement. The settlement was filled with a lot of commotion as they tried to make new shelters and begin their farming. Shaz was impressed with how well they made their grain fields and tried not to be in anyone's way. He wasn't sure how many Forrne he would find and by Antorn's description, they had dwindled to small numbers, but he didn't have a clue what 'small' meant.

Most of the Forrne tried not to stare at Shaz either, but he could tell that they too were checking him out and wondering what all this crazy was about. He watched a few young stags trying to carry a sizable pole and admired their determination.

"Battlemage, is there something wrong?" Antorn asked.

Shaz turned to find Antorn's brows tight with concern and Shaz shook his head.

"No, no, please call me Shaz. I'm just checking in on you to make sure you have what you need," Shaz said.

Slat peered from around a tall bushel of grains and scrutinized Shaz with curious intrigue.

"I think we are all doing well, considering," Antorn said.

"Good to hear, I want to make sure you understand you are not required to join our ranks, but you are certainly welcome to do so. I want you to take care of your people first," Shaz said.

"I thank you, but we will continue to fight until this is over," Antorn said. Shaz figured they would, he would to, and nodded. "Tell me, where do you come from?" Antorn asked.

An interesting vibe sitting several lengths away tickled Shaz's awareness, and he started to move toward it. Antorn wasn't sure if he should follow but Shaz motioned for him to go with him.

"I was born in the realm of Ebassia but raised in the realm of Atamar on an island called Turob. I fear that I am the cause for all your troubles," Shaz said.

"How would you be the reason for all this?" Antorn asked.

Shaz passed a stable-like structure and kept moving toward the vibe. The energy grew in strength and Shaz recognized it as an earth portal. He wasn't sure what 'interesting' formation it would be, but he was curious to find out.

"When I traveled through the first barrier, or portal from my realm, I opened them all. I wasn't aware of that of course, but it started a chain reaction of the events that are to come which will realign our world," Shaz said.

"How many realms are there?" Antorn asked.

"That we are aware of, twelve, but I have a suspicion there are more than that," Shaz said.

"Do you believe in the stars?" Antorn asked.

Shaz stopped and turned to Antorn's large stature. Antorn squirmed with his anticipated reply as Shaz examined him.

"What do you mean?" Shaz asked.

"I mean, do you believe there is more to our world than just us," Antorn asked.

"Aye, I do. How big it is, that I have no clue, but there is a much bigger world out there, and we have only begun this journey," Shaz said. Antorn swallowed hard. His chest heated with the truth of his words, and he nodded. "I want to show you something," Shaz said.

Shaz rounded a small pathway and found the earth portal. Three tall slender stones sat in a slightly off centered triangle and Shaz touched the first stone. The glyphs of the magical informational lit up under his touch and Antorn stepped back with uneasy caution. Shaz illuminated the rest of them and scanned their meanings as they descended down the stone.

"This is an earth portal. It's not like the ones we came through, it's more like a really big book, but with pictures," Shaz said.

Shaz opened his hands and focused his multi-colored magic from his core and into the center of his palms. Antorn was struck with an intense curiosity but also a heavy dose of fear. Shaz rolled the wobbly force around until it formed a sturdy ball, and he sent it into the rock.

"May I?" Shaz asked.

The magic sank into the form and illuminated into a glistening shimmer of the colors of the savanna at night. Antorn's eyes were fixed on the mesmerizing illuminations.

"Shazmpt, the war wizard, how may I help you?" the earth portal asked.

Antorn shifted back several steps with the sudden voice.

"What portal is this?" Shaz asked.

"This is the portal of the constellations," the deep voice said.

Shaz wasn't sure if this would take a lot of his magic and wondered how long it would be before Serin showed up and what kind of lecture he would be in for because of it. Shaz held out his hand to Antorn who hesitated, but put his hand in Shaz's. Shaz put his other hand flat on the stone and the sudden information dumped into his mind. Antorn too shifted with its heaviness and his eyes widened with all the information that was now pummeling his attention.

Shaz's chest heaved as he absorbed the energy so that it wouldn't affect Antorn, since he had no idea if his body would be able to handle it. Shaz was right, Serin felt the tug on her emotions and her nerves raced through her body at lightning speed. She put down the jar of powder she was about to pour into a bowl and darted out of the tent. Fionte, Babbesh, and the other Minca healers jumped with her sudden movements. Serin wrapped herself with a hefty dose of wind-walk and blasted toward the Forrne's settlement.

The wind gave her a clear picture of where Shaz was, along with the frantic words of her father again, and she cringed. She had been so busy that she had forgotten about the stark warning and her heart thumped. She was confused at the sudden race of emotions, both for Shaz and her own heartache and rounded the outer edge of the settlement. Shaz and Antorn tried to assimilate the stars as they painted vivid pictures of the organization of the cosmos and the beginnings of the first peoples.

It raced through the effects the universe had on the people and the beings of highest enlightenment and Serin came around the corner in time to watch them both sink to the ground with exhaustion. Serin whipped her hands around her and sent a surge of healing magic at them both and skidded to a stop next to them.

"What in the tarnation are you doing?" Serin said sternly.

Yep, just like Shaz thought, he wasn't upset though, he actually like that she got so worked up when he did stupid stuff. It meant she really cared about him, and she was passionate about their safety. Serin helped Shaz stand who then helped Antorn, but waited with a tight glare for his explanation.

"I found an earth portal," Shaz said.

"And you just had to access it, because you can't wait until I'm here to help you," Serin's voice was filled with angry fear. Shaz pulled her into a snug squeeze and Serin sucked in a deep breath. It was his way of diffusing her quickly and it worked every time. Antorn smiled at the exchange but was consumed by the influx of information still rolling around in his head.

"We have a lot to talk about," Shaz said. Serin looked up into his eyes and found a heaping dose of fear and frowned. "Are you alright Antorn?" Shaz asked.

"Yes, but I'm not sure what just happened," Antorn said.

"Earth portals are like record keepers, this one keeps the records of the cosmos and the universal powers that regulate our planet and the beings that lived here," Shaz said.

Antorn nodded, he understood that from what he saw and Shaz and Serin understood it would take time for his mind and body to process it all.

"You scared the tar out of me, I hate it when you do stuff like this," Serin said.

Serin studied his compelling and magnetic eyes and tried to decide what she was going to do.

"I'm sorry," Shaz said.

Serin shook her head and gave him her clenched teeth 'I could punch you' scowl.

"Maybe next time I'll let you lay there and suffer," Serin said.

Shaz chuckled, but searched her being to make sure she was kidding. He swallowed when he found that she would in fact let him suffer and cleared his throat.

"I won't do it again, I promise," Shaz said.

"Umhum," Serin said, but her tone was a convinced skeptical.

Slat came out from around the pathway and tried to interrupt quietly. Antorn turned to find the shock and bewilderment on his face and started toward him.

"What's wrong?" Antorn asked.

"Pillip is in a rage again," Slat said.

Antorn turned quickly and hurried after Slat, and Shaz and Serin followed. Antorn came through the cloth covering over the entrance and Pillip threw a large jug at him. Antorn ducked and it slammed into the post and shattered to the ground.

"Pillip, what is the matter with you?" Antorn asked.

"Get out of here, leave me alone," Pillip shouted.

Serin listened from the doorway and read his energy.

"He's dealing with the rage of grief, only he didn't lose a person, he lost his legs," Serin said.

Shaz nodded and understood, to a degree anyway.

"Can you do anything for him?" Shaz asked.

"I'm not sure, but I'll try," Serin said.

Shaz pulled the blanket back and stepped in before Serin to shield her from anything that might come flying at her. Not that she couldn't catch the item in mid-air herself.

"You brought these strangers here?" Pillip growled.

Serin rolled her hands around a soft pale blue ball of mist and sent her calming magic into his frame. His body relaxed but his mind raced with the event. He struggled against the euphoria and his anger ultimately settled on comfortable irritation.

"I'm Serin, I'm a healer, can I take a look at your legs?" Serin asked.

"No, there's nothing that can be done. Just leave me alone," Pillip said.

"Actually, there is, and I understand what to do, if you'll let me," Serin said.

Pillip stared at her. His face ran through everything he understood, but he couldn't figure out how she could do anything.

"It's alright to doubt, I doubt all the time. I doubt that Shaz here will ever stop making my heart thump when he does stupid stuff. Or rather, I doubt that he will ever stop doing stupid stuff," Serin said with a teasing but serious tone.

"It's true, I can't argue that," Shaz said nodding.

Pillip closed his eyes. He wanted so much to be normal again. To be able to fight those blasted beasts that did this to him. To run across the savanna again. He sucked in a deep breath and Antorn gave him and encouraging nod.

"Fine, but when it doesn't work, you'll leave me alone," Pillip said.

"Deal," Antorn said.

He didn't actually intend to leave him alone, and he couldn't argue with the hope he had. He had seen them shoot fire from their hands and hover on pieces of earth. Whip the air around and slice the beast's flesh with it. The other guardsmen were healed, so why not Pillip? Serin knelt in front of Pillip's large frame and put her cool hands on his warmed leg. She closed her eyes and sent her inspection magic into his frame and waited for the report on the damage.

The structure of his bones formed in her mind, and she understood what she needed to do.

"I need to break your bones and reset them, then I'll heal them in the correct placement. It won't hurt but it will feel...," Serin searched her brain for the words.

"Irritating, it's the weirdest irritating and creepy sensation to have your bones grow back together. I have had it done several times," Shaz said.

Pillip looked at him and Shaz gave him the 'that's what she means by doing stupid stuff' look and shrugged.

"Ready?" Serin asked.

"No, but go ahead," Pillip said.

Serin gripped his leg on either side of the twisted bone and sent a sizable boost of her pain magic into his frame. The warmth the magic gave made him shiver and as soon as the area was numb she gripped tightly and began to twist the bones. The loud pop and crack of the bone separating made them all jump and cringe with the sound. Serin stroked the surface while she pictured the nature of his bones realign to their proper shape and then began to smooth them into the correct place. Her blue magic pulsed and shimmered around the disfigurement and Shaz remembered when she did that to him after getting slammed into the ground by the shadow Selket. Antorn and Pillip's eyes bulged as the once twisted and mangled calf-bone realigned and became the straight appendage it once was. Serin then moved to the other leg and repeated the process sending a second dose of the pain-numbing. It took several lengths for Serin to organize the fibers and tissues around the bones and fuse the muscles back into their proper places.

Shaz felt the drain it was causing on her, and he boosted her with his magic. Perspiration crested her hairline as the magic heated up the room, and then she ran her hands along his legs one last time to make a final inspection.

"All done. How do you feel?" Serin asked.

Pillip tried to speak but his throat was stuck shut with a lump of gratitude. Serin patted his arm as he ran his own hand along the sleekness of his legs. Serin stood and held out her hand to him indicating he should get up. Pillip took her hand but hesitated. He pulled in a deep breath and then lifted himself up. To his great astonishment, his body lifted easily and was solid and strong. Antorn embraced him and slapped his back with enthusiasm. Pillip pranced a tiny prance-hop and let the smile encompass his face.

"I still don't have words for all this," Antorn said.

"It will take time, but for now, we have some Jaduuk to kill," Shaz said.

Shaz held out his hand and Pillip took it in a tight grip. He wrapped Serin in a tight embrace.

"Thank you," Pillip whispered, it was all he was able to do.

Shaz noticed how much energy Serin had expended and excused them and returned to their camp.

"I'm still mad at you," Serin said.

"I know," Shaz said.

"You make me nuts," Serin said.

"I know," Shaz said.

"What if,"

"I know," Shaz said.

Shaz pulled her close and she relaxed into his touch and then pushed him away.

"Schmoozing me won't get you out of this," Serin said.

"I know," Shaz said.

They rounded the corner and found Riddick and Amirra with her arms folded across her chest glaring at Riddick who was trying his best to 'explain' what had happened hoping for the least amount of damage as possible.

"Looks like we're both out in the cold," Shaz said.

Serin smiled and nudged him with her 'I guess you're off the hook this time' and Amirra spotted them.

"Serin, maybe you can help us out," Amirra said.

"Oh dear," Serin said.

Shaz chuckled and waved to Riddick to hurry and come with him while the girls were distracted. Riddick took Shaz up on the invite and with a few long strides, they were out of sight.

"Men," Amirra said with a huff.

Serin chuckled and agreed completely, and they began explaining, with emotion, why they were right, and the men were in big trouble.

44-Alright, Here's The Plan

"Thank goodness you showed up, Amirra had her scary Vel-shari face on and I wasn't faring well," Riddick said.

"Serin's none too thrilled with the way I handled something either," Shaz said.

"Women," Riddick said.

"You said it. How are the fortifications coming?" Shaz asked changing the subject.

"Good, mostly done, just the few timbers on the far side, and we've started on the barriers for the Forrne, who are still funneling in. The ponds are ready and Serin is working on getting them filled and the Minca have finished getting the tents set up. Amirra is helping the Minca women get the garden organized and pain medicines made. Motavo and Asher have secured the poisons and are starting to set up the assembly line for the new explosives. Helios has finished two of the six trebuchets and several catapults. Several of the elephantine have left for the savanna to gather the animals that are left. Wandi thinks he might be able to enlist the Rhino-moa, whatever they are," Riddick said counting on his fingers with each addition as not to forget something.

"Excellent, let's get going," Shaz said.

Shaz was filled with excitement, the thrill of the hunt, and dread. He couldn't keep the shadow magic's itchy sensation from sitting at the back of his mind and struggled to figure out why. Shaz and Riddick hurried through the bustle of the Ebassian's and met Phanes, Cluck, Shar, Brigdon, and Jaxton and a flight of their comrades.

"Brigdon, Jaxton, so good to see you," Shaz said.

"Where is the pretty one," Brigdon grunted.

Jaxton snickered and Shaz smiled. The memory of Brigdon carrying Serin to the rift from so long ago surfaced and a comfortable peace sat in his chest.

"She's helping the Minca, but I'll make sure she gets to go with you on the next mission," Shaz said with a half-shoulder grip of the extremely bulky, even for a gryphton, soldier.

"Jump on," Jaxton said.

Jaxton and Brigdon leaned down and Shaz jumped on Brigdon and Riddick climbed onto Jaxton, but wasn't sure if he was doing it the right way and Jaxton snickered. Cluck and Shar starred with wide eyes and shook their heads. They had never seen such a thing. It wasn't their way to let anything *ride* them and to see their superior officers readily offer was nearly too much. Of course, this whole thing was beyond their imaginations so why did this surprise them. Brigdon released the claws from his paws and lunged against the ground, unfurled his mighty copper-colored wings, and launched into the air with Jaxton close behind.

Riddick eased into the motion quickly and Jaxton's royal purple and dark tan frame maneuvered to the soft right of Brigdon who took the lead. Phanes launched into a fast run and shoved his hind legs into the earth, lifted his massive ice-blue wings, and shot into the air. The others followed with the same eagerness and rose in altitude quickly.

The gryphton's pulled up their lion legs and tucked them in tight and from the ground, only looked like a huge bird but with a long tail instead of the normal tailfeathers. Their stunning colors created a glow-like residue as they shot across the sky, and they looked as though they belonged in this realm. The landscape was vast and flat, and it was different than their own world of forests and mountains that even the gryphton's felt a sense of curiosity. They formed into a tight V formation as they flew toward the area the green lights were.

They maneuvered toward the glowing dots and Shaz was impressed at how powerful they were as well as precise and wondered how many hours of training they had been through to be this uniformed. The gryphton's used their tail feathers at the end of their long lion tails as their 'rudder-like' adaption for steering which lent to having more maneuverability for their large size and lion and human-like limbs. The sleek form they pulled into was amazing as their muscular frames pulled in tightly giving them a very aerodynamic shape. They glided through the air with ease, at least to those watching it looked very effortless.

The small flight banked in a wide arc. Their sharp eagle-eyes were highly adept as seeing small things from long distances but instead of hunting ribbards, they were scouring the surface for large, ugly, and stinky beasts.

The Jaduuk weren't hard to spot either, as they were highly stinky, and they could smell them at the same time as they could see them, well they almost couldn't see them through the mist of stink that emanated from the foul creatures. Their large blue hides also seemed to blend into the colors of the savanna as the moons came out and the bio luminescent properties of the grasses and plant life left a myriad of shades on the bottom surface. Phanes' heart sank as he internalized the sheer number of creatures. There wasn't even a number he could come up with in his head. If it weren't for the fact that they were organized into what appeared to be outposts with a large number of Jaduuk in each, his dread might overcome him.

Shaz and Riddick laid close to their necks and Shaz's nerves itched with the numbers, and he began running all the scenarios through his mind. He noted the ravine and decided that would be an excellent place to funnel them through so that the ground patrol could keep the advantage. It would take some effort to get them there, and he thought of a few ideas that he would discuss with Riddick later.

Brigdon indicated to the mountain range and the first yellow-green-ish light came into view. They lifted higher in the sky as the mountain range diminished the distance between them and the ground. The hordes of Jaduuk lessened as the mountain range began to encompass the surface and the greenish light came into consciousness. Brigdon indicated his aerial moves to the flight, and they kept their tight formation lifting higher into the sky.

The coolness of the high altitude was refreshing, and their noses were glad for the reprieve. The first green *thing* came into view and the gryphton's had a hard time figuring out what it was. They circled a holding pattern as Shaz, and the others made notes of everything they could see. Riddick noticed a warmth that came from the large oval-like sphere which confirmed in his mind that the structure was causing the heat to radiate into the atmosphere. He guessed that was part of the problem with the water supply and the scorched earth and made mental notes of the surface area the heat covered.

Shaz tried to keep the bile from surging through his esophagus as he watched several full-sized Jaduuk emerge from the green *thing*. They were covered in a glowing green ooze and began to clean it off by licking their bodies. The wretched sight made them all gag, and they tried not to make any noise. Even though they were quite high, they didn't know for sure how well the Jaduuk 'heard' things. The ooze appeared to be fuel for their newly formed forms and Shaz now understood how they were 'grown'. They flew to the next mark and then the next and made mental notes of each one and headed back to camp.

Shaz and Riddick and the gryphton's hurried toward the war tent and gave instructions for the rest of the leaders to meet them there. Shaz searched for Serin but didn't find her anywhere. He sent out his magic and found her in the healer's tents. He sighed a quick exhale and wondered why he was, so anxious about her whereabouts. An interesting notion crept from the back of his mind that she was in danger and a flash of the nightmare he had of her being dead crossed his mind.

He didn't have time for this nonsense and tried to push it out of his thoughts, but he was smart enough not to completely dismiss those kinds of impulses, and he cursed under his breath. The flap opened and Declan, Bowen, and Motavo entered. Jagwynn slipped through followed by Turkill and Ladtwig and then Helios.

"Alright, here's the plan. As soon as the first bomb hits, we are going to need to hit hard and fast. I got a good layout of how they are camped, and if we separate our attacks we can keep our forces from getting overwhelmed," Shaz moved Antorn's map and put his finger on the ravine. "I want to take a crew around this side and drive as many as we can through the ravine. Declan, we're going to use you and your Rangers as bait, here. Drag them through the ravine this way," Shaz moved his finger along the center of the ravine, "Bowen, your forces will move in here, and here, and attack from both sides and move toward the back to continue pushing them through the ravine.

"Phanes, you'll be air support here, and here. I want you to make sure the Ebassian's can drive them through the ravine. Turkill, Ladtwig, Cluck, I need two crews with cannons, here and here," Shaz indicated they would be on the top ridge behind the line of site from the opening of the ravine. "Station the catapults here, and here," Shaz pointed behind the cannons, "that way they can reach to the back as the cannons direct their fire into the ravine," they nodded. "That will be theater one. In the second theater, I want several troops to be stationed here, and here," Shaz pointed to the flatlands, "there is little coverage, but that is what I am expecting. I want to draw out as large of a horde as possible. Brigdon, the trebuchets will go here and here. These are the marks for impact, but we will use this whole region. Phanes, I want another flight to drop the dust here and here, so the trebuchets can ignite it," Shaz pointed toward the sides of the flat area and tapped his finger on the map as he thought through another scenario.

"What if we take some troops here, and use the marshes as an advantage," Riddick said.

"Aye, good idea, then we can use the trebuchet's here, here, and here. Declan, send another group through this valley and draw them this way," Shaz ran his finger along the map from the narrow ridges of the bottom of the mountain range and toward the marshes.

"Da Sirrr," Declan said.

"How long will it take to move the trebuchets and men into place?" Shaz asked.

"If we leave at first dawn, we can make the marshes by late afternoon, early evening. The ravine won't take as long, but we will have to heave the cannons and catapults up to the top of the ridge," Bowen said.

"We can help with that," Antorn said.

The group turned to find Antorn and Tobis coming into the tent.

"I'm sure the elephantine will help as well," Riddick said.

"They aren't here," Bowen said.

"But they will be by morning, and they have friends with them," Riddick said.

Shaz nodded and was sure he had detected them with his magic.

"In theater three, I need a flight with bombs here," Shaz pointed to where the pathway and the hordes of Jaduuk were. "This one is going to be critical. We need to take out as many beasts as we can, but the main objective it to block the entrance. How are the poisoned arrows coming?" Shaz said.

"We have a major supply now, and we have outfitted a few flights of gryphton's with the Forrne's ballista's. We tried to poison their rocks for their slings, but they would have to touch the poison, and we didn't want to risk it," Helios said.

Shaz nodded, but the pit in his stomach settled in and he struggled with the irritation in his mind.

"Motavo will stay here at base and be point. Everyone report back here to him," everyone nodded or saluted, "Alright, everyone get some sleep, when the elephantine arrive we'll move out," Shaz said.

The leaders dismissed and moved about their crews dishing the needed orders and finalizing their last-minute details. Shaz made his way to the healer's tent where he found Serin giving instructions on the use of the herbs. Serin looked up and found him watching her with a forced smile, and her guts churned. Serin finished her instruction and dismissed the group and Shaz made his way to her.

"Is everything alright?" Serin asked.

"Aye," Shaz said.

"You do know I know better," Serin said with a snarky tone. Shaz chuckled.

"Come on," Shaz took her hand and led her from the tent. They walked a little ways from the last tent, and he pulled her close.

"You're twigging me out," Serin said.

"Shh, just listen," Shaz said.

Serin listened, but she didn't hear anything, and then she *heard* his emotions and her guts tightened. Her nerves tingled with his, and she wanted to itch at the shadow magic.

"What's going on?" Serin asked.

"I'm not sure, but I keep seeing the part in my nightmare of you being dead and it's twigging me out," Shaz said.

"I'm sorry, is there something I can do?" Serin asked.

Shaz shook his head. He had no ideas. He didn't quite understand what was going on. He was certain it was *his* shadow magic but what that meant was a mystery.

"Just be patient with me, I have a feeling I'm going to be a mess," Shaz said.

Serin looked at him with curious scrutiny.

"What do you mean by that?" Serin asked.

"I'm really not sure, maybe it has something to do with Alisdair and his magic mixing with mine, or the fact that we are going up against a lot of shadow magic, or, it could be that there's an entire civilization of evil creatures that hunt just me. I just want you to know that I'm doing what I can, but I might become a bit of daft head," Shaz said.

Serin chuckled, he didn't usually use that term, it was, however, Riddick's favorite word as of late, but she smiled at him and tried to shove the nervousness out of her being.

"A daft head huh? Well then, there is cause for concern," Serin teased. Shaz chuckled. "So how did the flight go today?" Serin asked.

"Good, Brigdon asked about you, I told him you would ride with him on the next mission," Shaz said.

"Brigdon is here?" Serin asked.

"Aye, and Jaxton," Shaz said.

"I'm excited to see them," Serin said.

"We leave as soon as the elephantine get back, Riddick said they are on their way and should be here sometime in the early morning. Tomorrow is going to be a big day," Shaz said.

"Are you going to be able to sleep?" Serin asked.

"I hope so, but I don't think so," Shaz said.

"I figured, maybe I can come up with some kind of concoction for you," Serin said.

"If it tastes nasty I'm not drinking it," Shaz said.

Serin gave him mock indignation and he smiled.

"Come on, I want to say hello to Brigdon before it gets too late," Serin said.

45-Pretty One!

Shaz and Serin made their way into the gryphton's camp and even though they had been around the mighty animals before Serin was suddenly aware of how small she was compared to so many of them. They were truly magnificent, and she was glad she had the chance to know them. Brigdon, Jaxton, Shar, Cluck, and Phanes were discussing the details of their assignments around the campfire as they came out from around one of the tents. Brigdon looked up and found Serin rounding the large fire pit.

"Pretty one!" Brigdon said.

"Brigdon," Serin said.

Serin threw her arms around his thick neck, and he pulled her into a snug squeeze. Shar gazed at Serin and wondered why she was so special. She couldn't help sensing a tinge of jealousy for this human woman, and she chided herself for being such a cub about it all.

"Oh Brigdon, it's so good to see you," Serin said as she regained her footing back on solid ground.

Jaxton cleared his throat and Serin turned to him.

"Jaxton, I'm so happy you're here," Serin said.

Serin wrapped her arms around his neck in a tight squeeze, and he pulled her snug.

"You two sure know how to plan a party," Jaxton said.

"Well you know us," Serin said.

Everyone laughed, well, except Shar and Cluck. Phanes even chuckled. He was beginning to understand what their connection was with the humans, he was feeling it too. Serin turned toward Shar and Cluck, and smiled, but she was certain they weren't yet ready for the friendship.

"This is Shar and Cluck, part of the command," Jaxton said.

"Pleasure to meet you," Serin said.

They nodded but didn't offer an audible greeting which Serin didn't worry about. Brigdon was about to snarl at their lack of courtesy but Serin put her hand on his beefy shoulder.

"How is Azrack? Tell me, what's been going on in your realm," Serin said.

Brigdon gave them the stink eye but began telling her about the last several rotations in their realm and how excited he was to meet the other pretty one, meaning Amirra, and how that lead him to this detail. He basically told Azrack he was coming without giving him the option to say otherwise. Jaxton and the others' jaws dropped to hear so many consecutive words leave Brigdon's mouth and Shaz smiled. Serin listened with eagerness and Shaz engaged with Jaxton and Phanes as to the details of the mornings attacks. Cluck joined in the conversation and found Shaz to have a kind of vibe that he was drawn to. Shar too listened to his voice of command, how well he listened, as well and understood the art of war, but she kept a further distance from the whole thing.

What she didn't understand was, that she had never known Brigdon to have so many words. In all the times they had interacted, he barely spoke much and if he did, Jaxton often 'interpreted' for him. But now, he was speaking with clarity and enthusiasm and interest. A tinge of anger sat at the back of her mind, and she didn't know what to do about Serin. Serin listened to her vibes and could tell that she didn't like her much. Serin searched Shar's energy and found that she meant her no harm or that she was going to cause any trouble. It took a good part of the evening until Serin was able to piece together the complexity of the eagle-human-lion way of thinking, and then she understood that Shar secretly liked Brigdon and was jealous.

The time passed quickly and Serin couldn't stop the huge yawn escape her being.

"My goodness, the time has gotten late, I'll shut up now," Brigdon said.

The whole group was quite impressed, as well as shocked at how much talking Brigdon was capable of and Serin gave him a hug. She whispered what she determined about Shar and Brigdon pulled back and peered into her eyes with scrutiny. Serin nodded and smiled and Brigdon blushed.

"You ready Shaz?" Serin said.

Shaz looked up from the map with his mind still engaged in the current thought. He held up his finger to tell her to give him just a second and returned to finish his thought. They wrapped up their conversation and Shaz and Serin returned to their tent.

"I don't know if I have ever heard Brigdon say so much, ever," Serin said.

"I think he has a secret love for you," Shaz said.

"You think so?" Serin asked.

"What, you can't see it?" Shaz asked.

"No, I can see it, I just don't think it's that kind of love," Serin said.

"What kind of love is it then?" Shaz asked.

Shaz wasn't sure how many *kinds* of love there was, but he did understand what he felt for Serin wasn't what he felt for Riddick or his father.

"I think it's more like, there's a connection that we have that he doesn't have with anyone else, that's all," Serin said.

"Well, whatever it is, it's certainly unsettling to Shar," Shaz said.

"You noticed that too, I got the distinct impression that she likes him, a lot, and for some reason he doesn't notice her," Serin said.

"Oh, the joys of love and romance," Shaz said.

"Yeah, about love and romance," Serin said.

Blood rushed through Shaz's body at lightning speed. The tone in her voice indicated he had forgotten something, or said something he shouldn't have or, well it could be anything. Girls were quite confusing at times and even though he was able to read her thoughts, they changed so often he was still at odds with knowing what he was supposed to do sometimes. Serin was impressed with how many emotions her tone stirred and watched his face contort through them at high-speed.

"I love you," Serin said.

Shaz breathed out the breath he didn't realize he was holding in and Serin snickered at his distress.

"You about gave me heart failure," Shaz said.

Serin kissed him and he sank into her embrace. Serin could sense the struggle inside and decided she better not tease him too much. She sent a boost of calming energy, and he soaked in the euphoria of her magic. She pulled away and he smiled at her.

"Come on let's get some sleep. Maybe I can make my heart rate go back to normal," Shaz said.

Serin laughed and slugged him in the gut which he flinched with mock exasperation, and they retired for the night. Sleep came quickly but Shaz stirred more than usual. Images of Alisdair and the constellations circled his vision of Serin's crumbling face, and his heart pounded. He jerked awake and he sucked in a deep breath. He rolled over and listened to Serin's breathing. They had talked about it and Serin mentioned the idea, that it might be a way his mind was processing a fear, which Shaz agreed with, but he *was* sure there was something more to it. Shaz closed his eyes again but Serin stirred and rolled over to face him. She ran her finger along his arm.

"I'm sorry I woke you, again," Shaz said softly.

Serin felt bad. He either slept a long time when he could, or couldn't sleep at all.

"We'll get it figured out. Maybe we need a fireplace in here so you can keep embers going all night," Serin said.

"That might help," Shaz said.

He didn't think it would, but he would give it a try. Serin let her pink love magic pick up her bright light magic and soothing healing magic as it left her being and let it eased into his mind, and he was able to find sleep again. This time he slept longer than he would have and woke to the commotion of the soldiers forming their ranks.

"Serin, wake up, time to go," Shaz said with a start.

Serin didn't reply and he rolled over. She wasn't there and he hurried out of bed and dressed in his heavy leather jerkin and gaters. Strapped on the Honor Blade, shoved his feet into his boots and ran his fingers through his medium-length hair. He made his way to the food tent and found Serin with Riddick, Amirra, and the

Minca. He hurried to the front and the soldier let him get in line. Shaz gathered the prepared food onto the tray and made his way to their table.

"It's about time you got here," Turkill grunted.

Shaz gave him a sideways glare and Serin the 'you euphoriaized me' look, and she snickered behind her mug of a hot herbal drink. Riddick and Amirra mused at the exchange and tried to hide their own snickers.

"Everyone ready," Shaz said.

Shaz hurried through his breakfast as the others filled him in on their last-minute details, and they hurried from the tent. Bowen was already moving his forces toward their destinations when Antorn, Pillip, Tobis, and their small but ready and determined Guard arrived.

"Pillip, how are you doing?" Serin asked.

Pillip smiled from ear to ear and pranced and Serin smiled at his lack of words. She could tell from the amount of energy he had that he still didn't have words to express his gratitude for her.

"We are here to do whatever you ask," Antorn said.

"We haven't had this much hope in forever," Tobis admitted.

"That's good to hear," Shaz said.

Serin internalized Shaz's hint of doubt of himself, and she sighed. There was nothing she could do to take that away and his extra shadow magic was a concern for both of them.

46-It Begins

The Minca found their way to the elephantines and gave them the instructions, and they headed toward the enormous trebuchets. The humans found it amazing that the ginormous animals were taking orders and talking with the smallest of humans. Wandi curled the end of his trunk and the Minca stepped onto it, and he carried them with him. The Forrne helped haul the catapults and wagons of cannons dividing into the necessary groups to assist in the different theaters. One army headed toward the marshes in the flatlands of the savanna and marched at a quick pace while another force began the hike to the upper ridge of the ravine. Bowen's soldiers made good time across the savanna as did the Rangers.

Phanes and his wingmen were the fastest flyers, so they were assigned the furthest egg and were to drop the combustible dust over the savanna as they flew, so they headed out first. Shar and Cluck headed their flight and flew toward their mark, and the last flight headed by Phanes' first in command, Coby, headed for their mark. The group of sleek, brightly-colored feathered animals rose into the atmosphere at incredible speed.

****

Shaz was thankful it was the perfect time of the rotations, as the sun didn't set completely, and they could attack at any time without having to deal with the darkness of night. They didn't need to leave camp as early as the others which ate at Shaz's nerves. He decided they would head out anyway and make another sweep around the area. Brigdon knelt down and let Serin climb on his back and Shaz jumped on Jaxton. The flight of gryphton's gripped the earth with strength as they ran to get a bit of speed before they launched themselves into the air.

Shaz was filled with endorphins and uneasiness. Serin too experienced the eager anticipation. They made good time across the sky and the green egg-like sphere came into Shaz's view as did the wretched odor. His upper lip peeled at the stench and Shaz indicted to Brigdon who had also spotted the spawner. Shaz waited for the signal from Riddick and the Minca, who sent up small flashes of explosives to signal they were ready and in place. With a few strong strides Jaxton bent in half and dove toward the ground.

The rest of the flight split into two groups and circled around the spawner. Staying in twos, they flanked the mountain side and in a spiral, dove toward the target. Jaxton dropped his bomb with the needed timing, so that the explosion would occur when it hit the egg. Jaxton pulled in his wings and arched his head upward leading his body back into the sky. Shaz gripped tightly and kept close to his frame as he threw open his wings and slammed them against the air and shot back into the atmosphere. Brigdon followed close behind and dropped his bomb and was nearing the end of pulling out of his nosedive when the bombs sank into the rubbery egg. A sucking sound echoed in their heads before the whiplash of the forces encompassed the distance.

The combustion of the explosives ignited the energy of the lava and life forces of the egg and the gryphton's fought against the suction. Jaxton lunged his neck out and flapped his wings as he 'ran' against the forces, but the suction was too strong, and he began to be pulled backward. Shaz turned and gripped the combustion but internalized the force that was about to be unleashed and his heart thumped against his ribs.

"Watch out!" Shaz yelled.

Serin ducked low and gripped tightly around Brigdon and the blast shot them into the sky at such speed that they tumbled in the air for several lengths. Shaz's stomach lurched, and he tried to keep his bearings as the forces threw them like rag dolls. The gryphton's regained their command of the air, pulled in their wings, and let the forces propel them into the distance. They turned to see an enormous green and orange mushroom-cloud billow from the detonation point and sparks and sizzles of the mineral components left a spectacular sight.

Shaz gave a little jump-hoot. He didn't expect the blast to be that intense, but he was pleased with the impact.

****

The first blast erupted into the air and Declan and his Rangers darted from their hiding places and ran full speed into the nearest pack of Jaduuk. They hollered their war-cry and the beasts jumped to alert. Declan whipped his longbow and shot an arrow into the neck of a Jaduuk. The beast gripped it and broke it with its thick clawed hoof before the paralysis left its body motionless and it fell to the ground. The Rangers let loose a torrent of arrows and then turned and ran toward the ravine. A large Jaduuk howled a throaty sound and the ground began to thump under the Rangers feet.

****

The heavy billowing cloud encompassed the distance before Shar, and Cluck heard the blast and dove toward their target. The spawner was tucked into the rock face and it would take a tighter descent to get the bombs to the correct place for maximum detonation. Shar bent at the waist and tightened in her wings, stretched out her neck, and pulled in her legs tightly. Her body descended at an incredible speed and the slick stream of wind-reverb that came from her splitting the atmosphere, left a high-pitched crack in her wake.

Cluck too bent in half and flanked her side tightly. Shar let go of her bomb and then Cluck, and they raced back into the atmosphere, but instead of trying to reach a higher altitude, they shot across the distance in an effort to out-fly the combustion. The bombs hit with near precision and the same explosion ripped across the sky. The pulsing the reverberation made, coursed through their bodies, and they squirmed with the icky sensation. Shar and Cluck turned and saw the green and orange mushroom-cloud shoot into the air.

They braced themselves as the blast shoved the air particles outward at an incredible speed and power. The gryphton's pulled in their wings and let their beaks slice through the force. They didn't make any distance, but they were able to stay in the air until the inertia weakened enough for them to steer toward the next checkpoint.

****

The boom echoed across the sky and Riddick, who was riding his earth-board, and a group of Rangers who were riding the Forrne Guard, all let go of their long-range arrows and ballista's. Riddick shot his geo-kinetic energy outward and gripped the Jaduuk's attention. The horde howled and started out after them. The Forrne had excelled at running from the Jaduuk and raced across the savanna. The Rangers continued to fire their arrows keeping the charge in motion as they darted across the flatlands.

Antorn and Riddick peeled around to one side of the marshes and Pillip and Tobis the other. The Jaduuk pack divided and followed and met up on the other side and continued after the Forrne. Riddick spotted the trebuchets and reached out with his magic to find out how many Jaduuk had mobilized. There was sizable amount but not enough, and he motioned for Antorn to return, so they could gather more.

Pillip and Tobis continued toward the weapons and as soon as the Minca saw them on this side of the attack line, they let go of the long handle of the launching mechanisms. The heavy weight in the center of the upright poles fell to the ground with immense speed and the slings were whipped around the tall poles. The slings released the loads of explosives and shot into the air. The crackling fireballs soared the long distance with a buzzing sound that irritated the nerves and breached the Jaduuk landing their expected target plowing over several beasts and igniting the dust. A soul piercing crackle from the explosives splitting the atmosphere careened across the sky and the crew loaded another ball into the slings.

The dust heated up and burst into flames that consumed the Jaduuk. The landscape lit up with the immense heat and another round of fireballs careened across the sky.

****

Coby's flight dropped in a direct shot to release their bombs. The disarray of Jaduuk intensified their emotions as the Jaduuk were now on alert. The wind was sharp and stung their feathered heads, but they stayed the course and when they had dropped far enough to make an exact hit they let go of their bombs and twisted, leading with their beaks, and pulled out of the nosedive with precise ambition. Their sleek but large bodies slipped through the air easily until the suction of the ground imploding, before it exploded, pulled against them. They tried to lift their wings to shove away from the force, but they found it much harder than they had expected. Their bodies lowered toward the ground but then the orange-green mushroom-cloud billowed from the green soup-like ooze and the force shoved them into the atmosphere. They rolled and tumbled with the velocity for several lengths and then caught the wind stream and banked a hard corner to get out of the impeding impact.

****

Phanes made good time and the force of the next blast aided in their speed. When they reached the spawner, they hovered above the sphere and noticed a hoard of Jaduuk running around in disarray. His heart leaped with both excitement and a tinge of worry. It wasn't like they would have any kind of weapon that could be launched into the atmosphere, but he couldn't deny the weird feeling in his gut. The blast rippled across the sky and Phanes gripped the long cylinder and dipped his head toward his mark. He folded in his ice-blue feathers and shot toward the egg. His wingmen dipped in the same fashion and clung tightly to his side and the wind rushed over their mixed shades of blues and yellow feathers. Phanes neared the target at high-speed and shoved the bomb toward his mark.

The bombs fell to the ground with their heavy noses pointed downward. Phanes rolled his body and continued his dive but changed its course so that he would be lower than the belt of concentrated inertia. The bombs hit a split-second from each other and Phanes and his wingmen lifted their beaks to direct their descent. They blasted over the Jaduuk and allowed the force of the new blast to shove them away.

They rolled tightly to avoid the suction that happens a second before the mushroom-cloud erupts. The high pitch of the air splitting in half wreaked havoc on their ears, and they doubled their focus. Their speed was incredible, and they had a hard time keeping the savanna floor in their sights as they raced away from the blast.

****

The flight flew with fervor and was pleased with how successful the mission was, but Shaz wanted to fly as close to the first blast and inspect the damages. Shaz and Serin pulled their tunics over their mouths as the debris from the blasts began to return to the ground. The ground was a ginormous hole filled with a green ooze that Shaz guessed was the remains of the egg-like structure. The surroundings were covered in a layer of greenish-black film and left a bitter and rancid odor in the air. Brigdon and Jaxton circled a few times until Shaz gave them the go-ahead to head to the ravine.

****

The ravine was steep with a dried-out riverbed that had carved out the bottom from under the more jagged rock bed above. Jagwynn decided she would climb the acacia trees that lined the walls of the ravine and find her perch. Declan directed his men into the ravine, and they rounded the sharp corner of the small canyon walls and skidded on the loose gravel before making it into the shade of the tall rocks. The Rangers dashed through the widest parts of the riverbed until the canyon walls began to offer cut outs and small alcoves. They hid quickly as the beasts barreled around the corner. The warriors tried to steady their breathing as they tucked into their hiding places, but they knew that the beasts detected them through their noses, and it wouldn't take long for them to find them anyway.

The first Jaduuk gripped his battle-ax, sniffed the breeze, and snarled as he caught the scent of the men. His long fang crested his ragged eyebrow and Declan eyed him sort through the amount of scents. Declan held out his hand to steady his men and waited for their next move. They needed to get more of the beasts within range of the catapults that were waiting above. Declan motioned for his men to stay put and came out from a tall bushy fern.

Declan slammed his sword on his smaller round shield and the sound echoed off the two walls. Declan's heart pumped blood throughout his body, and he absorbed the endorphins as though it was a fine meal. The Jaduuk turned and its black eyes narrowed as the large creature analyzed his frame. Declan now understood what Antorn had said about them having a kind of intelligence, he just wasn't sure what that meant. Declan spun on his toe and shot into the ravine. The Jaduuk snarled it's commands and the pack thundered after him. The Rangers kept low and behind their bushes, trees, or lumps of earth as they waited for their prey.

The largest Jaduuk scanned the surroundings as his horde chased after Declan. One of the Rangers scrutinized its expressions and was sure it was calculating its next move. Declan hopped a fallen tree and shoved his foot into the side of the ravine wall and back-jumped to the other side. He gripped the tree limb that was protruding from the dirt wall and lunged upward. He kicked off with eager strength and back-jumped again to the other side. Declan puckered his lips tightly and let out a high-pitched whistle. He looked down in time to witness Jagwynn launched from her perch and snagged the beast with her claws. Jag swung her hefty hide and slammed her massive jaws into the beasts neck before they hit the ground.

A soft hum whistled into the tops of the ravine as a series of arrows plummeted into the flesh of the Jaduuk. The paralytic effects of the spider spit worked amazingly well and the Jaduuk quickly stiffened. The Rangers sprung from their hiding places and took out the Jaduuk with exactness.

The ravine went quiet and the Jaduuk Captain flicked his long-tufted ears. He sniffed the breeze and found the scents of the men still there. He sent another horde into the ravine and the Jaduuk pounded through the gravel of the riverbed. Turkill gripped the large trunk and Wandi swung him onto his back. Ladtwig swung onto Imka's back with his backpack of hand-cannon ammunition.

Frebin, Drager, and Harmus all lifted onto the elephantines and they headed around the top part of the ravines high ground that slowly shifted toward the lowest level of the river. Wandi listened carefully with his large ears for the pounding and thudding of the Jaduuk's and used it to disguise their own heavy feet. The slope was gradual and would take a little bit of time for the massive animals to maneuver, but they hurried as quickly as the terrain would allow.

47-You Sure Did Make A Mess

Riddick and Antorn raced toward the edge of the tree line Antorn had first seen the beasts and their noses let them know they were getting close. Antorn loaded his ballista and Riddick searched the distance. Riddick indicated to Antorn which way would offer the best exposure and Antorn let his spear soar into the sky, and they heard the howl as the blade pierced a Jaduuk's shoulder. Antorn quickly loaded a few more and Riddick gripped the ground with his magic and released a multi-shot of rock-shards into the pack.

More howls ripped across the sky and Riddick repeated his rock-blades as Antorn released another spear. Riddick's sharpened material was laced with thin glass-like blades as it moved through the distance. The farther they went the sharper they became. Intense stink of the Jaduuk's rancid blood sank into their noses and again another howl pierced the horizon. A heavy thud rippled toward them and Riddick was sure they had a sizable mob. He waited another half-second until the creatures emerged from the tree line and turned his hover-board, and he and Antorn darted back toward the trebuchets. The Jaduuk ran on all four hoofed claws and Riddick shuddered with the itchy vibration it left on his nerves.

The gryphton's launched into the air with more of the explosive dust and hovered over the trebuchets until the sizable company of Jaduuk had mobilized and darted toward the back of the pack. They opened their dust bags and let the flammable powder drift to the surface. The wind was calm and the Jaduuk hardly noticed the dust settle on their thick hides. The gryphton's made it to the edge of the oncoming creatures and dropped their bags, pulled out their new ballista's and struck the flick stick against the stone and the tips of the spear-like arrows burst into flames.

Gryphton soldiers aimed and let loose their strike sending a barrage of flames into the mob. The flames ignited the dust as the sharpened tips sank into their flesh. Several Jaduuk howled as the combustible combination consumed them. A massive mammal half the size of the elephantines pounded the ground and snorted. Riddick turned to find a very large herd of the animals he guessed to be the rhino-moa's, and he let out a hoot. The three unbelievably huge horns that protruded from the center of its long and narrow head gave him a tingling excitement. Antorn raced toward the four-legged gray and leathery beasts. Antorn raised his arm high over his head and shouted a thrilled howl of his own and the rhino-moa snorted. The exhaust escaped their flared nostrils that Riddick figured he could put his whole foot in. Antorn shoved his hooves into the dirt and shot back toward the outer edge of the oncoming Jaduuk.

The rhino-moa gripped the earth and thundered after Antorn. Pillip and Tobis joined Antorn in the charge and the ground shook. Several packs of Jaduuk turned in time to find the beasts moving at a fast clip for their size. The Jaduuk Captain in the center of the pack raised its arm and howled a gurgling grunt-like howl. The packs turned and ran toward the rhino-moa. The lead bull lowered his head and lifted his light-colored eyes and gauged his attack. The following bulls lowered their heads, and they plowed into the enemy. A Jaduuk's body was lifted into the air as the powerful animal skewered his horns into its torso. The bull flicked his head and the Jaduuk went flinging into the air as the bull skewered another.

Antorn, Pillip, and Tobis engaged the Jaduuk now wearing the enchanted armor that was outfitted for their size and abilities. Antorn sliced the neck of one and brought his blade up into another. Pillip's elated excitement to take his revenge was filled to the brim, and he hacked and sliced with the eagerness of ten Forrne. Pillip rolled his spear in his hand and hurled it into the mid-section of a beast and with the other hand slammed his battle-ax into another, then yanked his spear out of the first in time to swing it around and catch another across the neck.

The bulls barreled through the hordes and bowled them over with hefty strength. The lead bull turned and circled back out of the pack taking out as many as he could. They regained their attack and began another assault.

****

The Rangers returned to their hiding places and hushed their breathing as the new wave of Jaduuk crossed their path. The Jaduuk raced down the ravines dried waterway snorting and sniffing the breeze. The Rangers held their breath as the Jaduuk began to search for them. Declan whistled again and another flood of arrows whooshed overhead. They sank into their marks and the soldiers again hurried out and killed them. A tall dark-haired Ranger near the wide opening of the ravine, studied the Jaduuk Captain and watched as he struggled to make sense of what was happening. He hesitated and signaled for the next tide of creatures to halt. The Ranger made a clicking sound with his tongue and several more men began to mimic the night insects. Declan repeated the instruction to the crew at the top and the catapults were armed and aimed to the back of the large pack.

Wandi and his herd slowed as they came to the bottom and the Minca loaded their cannons. They pulled the lever back and held the rounded end on their arm as they squinted over the narrower chamber. The Jaduuk came into view and Wandi stopped. Turkill sucked in a deep breath and steadied his aim. He wanted to take out the Captain, or at least get a head start. Turkill surveyed the distance and found the rest of the Minca ready and called his commands.

The balls shot from the barrel and ripped across the distance plowing into the beasts. The Jaduuk turned and started toward them. The Minca quickly loaded more charges and began firing at will. Turkill pulled his dart-gun and shot a rapid-fire burst of the poisoned darts and Ladtwig repeated. Turkill caught a glimpse of one of the Jaduuk almost smile at the sting of the dart but then its expression turned to panic as the paralysis took over its body.

The large fireballs ripped across the sky and blasted the back of the pack sending them flailing in all directions. The gryphton's unfurled their wings and caught the updraft of the wind coming from the ravine. They beat their wings against the force and rounded in a tight V formation to the outer edge of the horde. They dropped the flammable dust over them and pulled their ballista's. Hit their flick sticks and ignited the combustible tips and launched them into the back of the horde.

The beasts bellowed an obnoxious mix between a growl and a howl as the flames ignited their flesh. They ran around and tried to subdue to flames and the chaos unsettled the group which was waiting for their turn to funnel into the ravine. They started to shove each other and soon the havoc reached the front of the line. The lower intelligent Jaduuk shoved their way into the ravine and the soldiers repeated the process.

The gryphton's continued to launch their ballista's and when they were out, they dove into the pack. A gryphton released his talons, flared his claws, and lifted upward in time to sink his talons into the flesh of the beast. He gripped tightly and yanked the beast off balance. The gryphton behind him lifted from his nosedive and brought his sword up in a jab-slice through its neck. The beast recoiled with the instant pain but couldn't keep his focus as his life force faded quickly.

****

The battlefield came into view and Shaz could see the masses of men trying not to be distracted by the mushroom-clouds. The gryphton's landed near the trebuchets. Riddick made his way back from the front lines to regroup.

"Well, you certainly know how to start the show with a bang," Riddick said.

Shaz chuckled.

"It was quite a bit more than I expected," Shaz said.

"I only hope it didn't start a cascading effect that we'll be sorry for," Riddick said.

Shaz stopped and gave him a *stink eye*.

"What do you mean?" Shaz asked.

"With explosions like that we could start a series of earth shakes or the debris might cover the sun for too long, and then we'll freeze to death," Riddick said.

"Blast!" Shaz cursed.

A low rumble emerged from the distance and Shaz cringed. The ground began to shake, and everyone scrambled to find something to hold onto. Riddick put his hands on the ground and sent his earth magic into the surface. The rusty-orange energy sank into the dirt and a hole opened a second before a blast of exhausted air shot out. Riddick controlled the fumes with his magic and encouraged the shake to release through the vent and the shaking settled. Riddick spoke softly to the earth's energy and Shaz understood he was speaking to the planet. He got the impression Riddick was apologizing for the explosions and asking the planet to be at peace.

"What in the world is going on?" Serin asked.

"Shaz made a mess and I had to clean it up," Riddick said.

Shaz shot him a sideways glare and Riddick smirked. Serin scowled and Amirra eyed them cautiously, so she wouldn't get sucked into their joke not knowing if they were kidding or not.

"You sure did make a mess," Serin said.

"Aye, but the party has started," Shaz said as he flashed his handsome smile hoping to smooth things over.

Serin tried to keep her smile under a scowl and shook her head. The Minca loaded more charges and pulled the pulley system to lift the massive balls into place and released another round of fireballs. The whizzing sound that happens a second before the whooshing sound sent shivers through them but exhilarated their excitement.

The Jaduuk neared close enough that the Ebassian's new hand cannon's would be accurate, and they stuck their long-shields into the ground and formed their wall. The archers and ballistas lowered their arrow tips into the canisters of burning tar igniting them and took aim. The soldiers with the hand-cannon's pulled the lever back and stuck the rounded tips of the small handheld cannons through the openings in the shield wall. Bowen held out his hand

and waited until the knot in his stomach was choking his breath. He released his hand in a downward strike and shouted his commands.

The archers let their arrows sizzle through the air and the soldiers flipped the latch that released the lever. The blasts from the hand-cannon's bit at their beings as the concussion in the air whiplashed back as it went down the long line of men. The compacted balls of ammunition pelted the Jaduuk with intensity, and they recoiled from the hits. A second later the balls heated up and exploded. The rip through their bodies struck fear through their faces as their insides turned to mush.

The ground shook as the explosives ripped through the beasts and slammed into the surface. Rock shards and debris shot into the air with the opposing forces. The archers reloaded quickly and continued their onslaught with speed and the hand-cannoneers reloaded with fresh ammunition. Crackling from the fire consuming it's victims filled the atmosphere and the sky began to cloud up with the smoke and debris. The shield wall picked up and advanced several paces as the arrows and ballista's launched overhead and the trebuchets let go of another round. Ebassian soldiers heaved the catapults several lengths behind the shield wall and loaded the buckets with the payloads and shifted the directions. Bowen stopped the shield wall, and the catapults released their ammunition. The bucket was loaded with smaller balls of the crackling explosives and the men heaved the lever to release the bucket.

The snap the thick cords made against the now soot-filled sky reverberated with an eerie slap. The balls tore through the company of Jaduuk which was dwindling but there was still an ample number left. Bowen signaled the ground forces, and the wall of shields broke into smaller units and moved into a zigzag pattern. Shaz and Riddick joined the ranks as did the Forrne. Serin and Amirra hung back but kept a solid eye on the guys. The front offense returned their shields to the wall formation and the soldiers gripped their swords.

Men shot out around the wall and ran toward the creatures. A soldier gripped his longblade and with both hands yanked the blade in an upward slice. The foul stink of the rancid blood raced to his brain a second after the splatter covered his armor. The beast fell with a thump, and he turned and raced his blade across the chest of another. Shaz blasted a Jaduuk with a torrent of flames and rounded the Honor Blade through another. Riddick rolled his battle-ax around his hand and sent a wave of his new rock shards into the masses and rolled out from the forward strike of a very large hoof and sank his blade into the beats back.

Shaz flipped up over a Jaduuk and stabbed the blade through the neck and back on his way down. The men slashed and sliced, and the second offence moved through the gaps between the forward offence. Serin and Amirra advanced enough to keep an eye on the guys and Serin blasted her wind shards into several beasts. Antorn sliced through the neck of a beast and Pillip yanked his blade out a chest and slammed his hind legs into the chest of a beast that was attacking from behind.

The new and fresh soldiers took their turn and the first unit returned to the cover of their shield wall for a breather. They found the effects of the nasty oily blood more alarming than the drain it took on their frames. The offensive repeated several times, and a new set of units took over continuing to attack the beasts while the trebuchets and catapults continued to fire overhead. Amirra focused on the enchantments of their armor and weapons and tried to include as many as possible with each casting, but she felt like there was something more she could do.

Amirra blinked and rubbed her eye as a flash of blackness shot across her vision. Her stomach lurched and her heart ripped open. The anguish she had tried so hard to heal was surging from the deepest part of her being and fear coursed through her. Serin read her energy and eased her calming magic over her. Amirra blinked and gave Serin a half-smile with the comfort it gave, but Serin cold tell there was still a high degree of struggle within her. Serin whipped a blast of air at Riddick and threw him out of the way of a battle-ax. Riddick rolled with the force and engaged his own geokinetic power. A deep vibration emerged from the depths and Riddick focused the inertia toward the Jaduuk.

The mid-day sun was becoming dimmer as the soot spread out over the savanna and Riddick released his hold. The power moved the earth under the packs feet, and they wobbled before the hardened surface softened and their large, clawed hooves sank several lengths before hardening backup. The Jaduuk's black eyes popped open with shock and horror as they found they could no longer move.

Riddick swayed and became light-headed as the energy left his being. Serin blasted him with a dose of healing magic, but it only partially helped. A Jaduuk reached out and hit him in the chest with the edge of the blade, but it caught the armor, and a transfer of health coursed into Riddick's frame. His body shuddered with the weirdness, but a satisfying eagerness calmed his nerves.

48-What Do You Think We've Been Doing?

Declan signaled for his men to move higher and further into the ravine as the catapults were unleashing their payloads. The ground shook and parts of the walls began to crumble. Men dodged the avalanche as they made their way higher in. The Jaduuk Captain growled his commands, but the horde didn't listen and raced into the ravine. The dimmed sky and the tallness of the walls left less light to see by and the Rangers had a hard time maneuvering over the dead bodies and uneven waterway. They reached their next mark as the echo of the chaos sank into their minds. At first, they wondered what was going on as the sounds were more like yips and whines instead of growls and drool breathing. Several Jaduuk were carrying their wounded and trying to find shelter from the blasts from the explosives. The dark-haired Ranger put his finger on his lip and signaled to the Ranger closest to him, and he repeated the signal.

Declan lowered from the middle of the ravine wall and listened. He couldn't make out the sounds he was detecting, and he leaped to the top of the ravine. He ran toward the drop-off where they had led them and lowered closed to the ground before he came to the edge. Declan crawled on his belly the last few lengths and found the horde was piling into the ravine. He spotted a Jaduuk, who was directing them into the ravine. The creatures face was somber with larger eyes and snout than the others. Declan internalized the marking on its shoulder and remembered the description Antorn and Tobis had given and understood him to be the smarter Jaduuk. It was larger than the rest, and they obeyed it, so he was certain it was the leader.

Declan raced back to the catapults and signaled for the trebuchets to load up. The gryphton's and Minca maneuvered the pulley's and loaded the sling. Declan called out the directions and the trebuchets launched the fireballs into the air. The rumble the crackling caused as they careened across the planet sank into their bones, and they held their breath and waited for the blasts. The large weapons rattled as the ground shook with the hit and Declan raced back to the drop-off.

Declan whistled and the archers sent another downpour of poisoned arrows. The paralysis stopped their bodies mid expressions and some of the men snickered at the almost comical sight before they beheaded them. Wandi sucked in and bellowed an ear screeching trumpet like sound and the Jaduuk covered their ears but continued toward them. The Minca alternated between the hand-cannons and darts and held on as the elephantines engaged the beasts. Wandi struck his immense trunk into the chest of a beast and the Jaduuk flew backward several lengths. Wandi gripped the battle-ax from the grip of one and swung it into the guts of another. The Minca blasted another round of charges and darts and another large bull stomped on the skull of a Jaduuk. Turkill tried not to let the sounds of the bones crushing under his foot make his skin crawl but there was something about that sound that made it difficult.

Declan moved the archers and catapults closer to the drop-off and began flooding the Jaduuk with their payloads. Declan searched the distance and found a small pack retreating. He gave instructions for one of the trebuchets to readjust and gave them their new coordinates. The sling whipped with a fierce speed as the bucket dropped and the fireball was propelled a substantial distance. The gryphton's had to pay attention to where the explosives were headed and made their attacks in between the hits.

They began to recognize the sounds the levers made and then the whipping of the cords as they released the loads and arranged their attacks accordingly. It was kind of nice to take a turn style approach to the attack, they decided it saved energy, and they were able to last longer.

It was remarkable at how far the machines could launch the ginormous bombs. Dirt and earth spewed upward as the bomb hit its mark and the fleeing pack disappeared under the earth with only bits and pieces of their former frames remaining. The Rangers and Ebassian's finished off the last of the company and shouts of victory ripped through the air.

They could still hear the distant echoes of the battle in the savanna, but they relaxed with a heavy sense of success and relief. Declan ordered several of his troops to inspect the carnage to make sure they found the Captain but after over an hour, they decided he had run off and perhaps was with the fleeing pack. A sick feeling in his gut settled in and Declan shouted orders to return to camp.

****

Shaz released a downpour of fireballs and Riddick sent more rock shards while Serin was busy healing the soldiers that here tiring or injured. Amirra was busy re-buffing armor and weapons while Bowen kept his zigzag wall formation moving around the battle-field. Even with the magic and respites they were beginning to tire, and overall, Shaz was quite pleased with how well the day had gone. Shaz sent out his energy and received an image that there wasn't many more and gave Bowen the signal to fall back.

Bowen ordered his men to fall back and the shield walls be-gan maneuvering backward. Shaz nodded to Riddick who hopped onto an earth-board and Shaz made one for himself. Shaz rounded the shield-wall he was behind and met Riddick on the far side.

"Let's end this," Shaz said.

"What do you think we've been doing?" Riddick asked.

Shaz heard the hint of annoyed sarcasm in his voice but also sensed Riddick too needed a break.

"You use your geokinetic-liquify while I use my combustion, I think we'll be able to finish this with one last hit," Shaz said.

Riddick nodded and followed Shaz to where the force would be moving away from their army. Shaz hovered gently and took in a deep breath. He nodded to Riddick who nodded and gripped the earth's energy. Riddick's rust-orange magic emerged from his being and mixed with the brown waves of the earth. Shaz focused on the fire elements combustion force and pictured the explosive nature. The bright red energy quickly merged into the vibrating force of Rid-dick's and Shaz counted down.

They released and the magnitude of the force shot across the distance like a solid band of light. The flash was so bright the soldiers flinched and covered their faces. The Jaduuk were incinerated with-out even having a chance to look toward the destructive power and then the boom came. Serin understood what Shaz was going to do and gripped Amirra's hand. She accessed Amirra's magic and whipped her hands around her head. The soft yellow of Amirra's magic was sucked from her frame and merged with Serin's light-blue air magic.

The wind whipped around them with ferocity and shielded the soldiers and the weapons from the impending concussion. The blast shredded the air and knocked everyone on their backsides, but the machines were untouched, and everyone was alright. Amirra and Serin sank to the ground and breathed in heavily.

"What happened?" Amirra asked.

"I hope you don't mind, but I borrowed some of your magic. I promise to ask next time, but there was no time," Serin said.

"That was my magic?" Amirra asked.

Serin smiled with the relief she wasn't angry with her. She was so much about choice that Serin figured she would be upset with her not asking first.

"Yes, it was, you're much stronger than you think," Serin said.

A flash of darkness crossed Amirra's vision, and she flinched. Serin interpreted her emotions and recognized the side of her magic she wasn't ready to see yet. Serin hoped it wouldn't take too much longer, she was certain Amirra could be a powerful Soul Mage, and they were going to need it.

The earth shook as the herd of rhino-moa made their way to where Shaz and the others were. Shaz started out to meet them and was impressed at their muscled features. There was a passive kindness in their eyes and Shaz wondered what Wandi had to do to get them to fight.

"Hello, I'm Shaz," Shaz said.

"Are you the Battle Mage?" the bull asked.

"Aye, what is your name?" Shaz asked.

"I am Makanaokeakua, you can call me Maka," Maka said.

Shaz was relieved, there was no way he was going to be able to say that name.

"Pleased to meet you, and thank you for your assistance," Shaz said.

"We will stay until these fiends are eliminated," Maka said.

Shaz was again impressed. He didn't expect the large animals to have an intellectual capacity, not that he thought that they would be unintelligent, well, maybe that's what he thought, and he chided himself for letting their appearance taint his first impression. After all, Helios was one of the smartest creatures he knew, and he was a ginormous lion-eagle-human. All of which were predators. Shaz cleared his ramblings and tried to remember what, if any, was the greeting for the rhino-moa. He came up empty, so he gave him the bow he used with grandfather. It somehow was fitting, and it warmed is heart.

"Thank you, Maka, we will be returning to our camp for rest and then planning the next assault. You are welcome to come," Shaz said.

"We will graze with Wandi and his herd," Maka said.

Shaz nodded.

"Do you have any wounded?" Shaz asked.

"A few scratches but nothing major," Maka said.

"Good, then we'll catch up to you later," Shaz said.

Maka flicked his head up and down a few times and then turned his herd and head out.

49- There's Something Wrong With Amirra

The armies returned to the camp and reported to Motavo and Asher and then drop off their gear before heading to the food tents. The aroma of hot food sank deep into their noses and the meal crews hustled with great speed. They were lucky that there weren't too many wounded and those that were had only minor injuries. Helios was correct, they only suffered mild stiffness and a stomachache. The Minca healers were effective and were able to get everyone treated within a few hours and Motavo and Asher were efficient at keeping the camp running smoothly.

Serin had already taken several draws from her raincloud water and was managing, but sleep was definitely on her mind. Serin and Amirra quickly ran through the wounded and praised the Minca and Traveler women, who had shown up while they were gone.

Shaz and Riddick made their way through the last of the inspections and then headed to the mess tent where they found Serin, Amirra, and the Minca. Shaz found himself experiencing an interesting sensation and wasn't sure what to think of it. It was similar to when he absorbed Semias' magic but different. His head was a little wobbly, and he struggled to keep his focus. Serin kept a close eye on him and examined his heartfire. She understood there was a higher level of shadow magic now burning along with his fire magic, but she didn't get a panicked or unsettling feeling like she had before.

The camp noise faded quickly as the days fatigue began to overtake the soldiers, now with full bellies, and it was hard for the crew to keep their eyes open. Even the Minca camp was quiet which was quite unusual. Riddick and Amirra turned off toward their tents and Shaz pulled the flap of their tent and let Serin in first. Serin pulled off her boots and moaned as her body started to relax into the effects of spent energy. Shaz unstrapped the Honor Blade and tucked the sword under the front corner of the mattress and pulled off his leather jerkin and gaters, then his tunic. Serin found a large purple bruise on his side and shook her head. He was going to go to bed without having her heal him again.

"If you weren't such a hottie, and I had fire, I would scald you right now," Serin said. Shaz gave her a sideways half 'huh?' look and Serin chuckled. "Come here," Serin said.

Shaz replayed her words in his mind and tried to figure out what she meant. Serin put her cool hands on his skin, and he twitched. The warmth the magic gave soothed the pain that now recognized in his brain.

"Hey, would you look at that, I had no idea that happened," Shaz said.

Serin looked at him with curiosity.

"It covers nearly half your body. You didn't feel that?" Serin asked.

Shaz shook his head and wondered why. Serin ran a diagnostics of magic and found his energy fluid as usual.

"Am I in hot water?" Shaz asked.

Serin snickered. She wondered how long he would take to figure out her tease.

"Very," Serin said.

Shaz dipped his hand in the washbowl and sent a wave of heat to warm the liquid.

"Speaking of hot water," Shaz took the washcloth from the dish and wrung out the liquid. Serin pulled off her leather armor and knife belt around her thigh. Shaz washed the grime from his arms, face and neck, and the sweat from his pits and returned the cloth to the basin. Serin took her turn at the bowl and scowled when the only thing she could see was brown muck.

She emptied the dish at the side of the entrance and snapped her finger. The bowl filled with clean water, and she held it out for Shaz to warm it up. He swooshed his hand in a circle and she put the bowl on the stool. Serin twirled her finger telling Shaz to turn around, and he complied. He pulled off his boots while Serin washed the grime from her body.

"Hey check this out," Shaz said.

Serin looked over her shoulder in a half turn to Shaz shooting a flame into a fireplace with a few logs propped on top of each other.

"Who put that there, and how did they know to do it, it's almost as if the Whispmother was here or something," Serin said.

Shaz looked around the tent for any signs of the Inugami and Serin turned in time for Shaz not to see her bare form. He turned back quickly and gazed into the fire. Serin pulled on a fresh tunic and walked up behind him. She ran her hand along his bare back and around to his chest. She rested on his back, and he squeezed her hand. His desire to take her was so hard to keep under control, he wanted romance, and he knew Serin did too, but he was so afraid that the shadow would find a way to destroy Serin as Sarud had told him that he didn't dare. He would have to settle with being able to be with her and the little physical affection they were able to show each other. Serin slipped under the covers and Shaz climbed in on his side.

****

Amirra stood in the center of the runecircle with her hands clenched tight. Sweat dripped down her hairline. The mountain temple she grew up in wafted in and out of view, and she struggled to make sense of what was happening. The tightness in her lungs gripped her nerves and her guts wrung together. A flash of darkness crossed in front of her, and she tried to find it but the smoke from the burning fires around the edges confused her vision. A set of dark eyes emerged from the rockface and her heart thumped against her ribs. She was certain her bones were about to crack with the heaviness.

Riddick's heart thumped, and he sat up with a start. He looked around but couldn't see anything. He laid back down but an itch at the back of his mind wouldn't let him relax. Riddick struggled to figure out what he was experiencing. Amirra's frantic emotions surged through her being at a rapid rate and the energy made her body tingle as well as shake. Riddick sat up and rubbed his face. His guts were twisting into knots, and he had no idea why he was feeling this way.

Riddick pulled on his tunic and boots and opened the flap of his tent. The night was calm and there was little noise coming from the surroundings. He put his hands on the soft dirt and sent his energy into the planet. Urgency spiked his nerves as the earth's image of Amirra trapped, shot to his brain. He spun on his toe and shot across the distance to Amirra's tent and threw open the flap. Amirra's frame was laying in her cot but her body was rigid, and Riddick could tell something was very wrong.

He dashed across the distance and stopped at Shaz and Serin's tent and threw open the flap.

"Serin, come quick, there's something wrong with Amirra!" Riddick said loudly.

Shaz and Serin sat up quickly and Serin shook her head from the daze of sleep.

"What's wrong?" Shaz asked.

"I don't know, but I can sense she's in real trouble," Riddick said.

His voice was shaky and Shaz and Serin hurried from the tent. They followed Riddick with eagerness, and he held open the flap. Serin did a full inspection of Amirra and sent a boost of calming energy into her rigid frame. Amirra relaxed but didn't wake up.

"What's wrong?" Shaz asked.

"She's having a dream-like interaction with someone or something," Serin said.

Shaz cringed. He understood what that was like and was sad now seeing how frightening it is from the outside.

"What do we do?" Riddick asked.

"Someone needs to go in after her and help her figure it out," Serin said.

"How do you do that?" Riddick said.

"You have to, you're the one bonded to her," Serin said.

Riddick's heart jumped and Serin could tell how nervous he was, but she got the impression it was a mix of Amirra's energy too.

"I'll help you," Serin motioned for Riddick to come to the side of the bed.

Riddick knelt next to the cot and Serin put his hands on the sides of Amirra's face.

"Now, close your eyes and imagine yourself moving through your hands and into Amirra's mind," Serin said.

Riddick received a clear picture of what to do as he had done it with the earth several times. He closed his eyes and made his way through the earth's energy until he found Amirra's essence. Amirra was spinning in circles trying to keep an eye on the flash of darkness as Riddick approached her.

"Amirra," Amirra stopped and turned toward him. Her eyes were dark and puffy, and he could tell she had been crying. "Are you alright?" Riddick asked.

"Riddick, where am I, what is going on?" Amirra asked.

"I don't know, but I'm here to help you figure it out," Riddick said.

Riddick stepped close enough to touch her, and he held out his hand. She reached out and touched his hand, and they absorbed the energy of the others touch.

"Can you tell me what you have been doing?" Riddick asked.

"There is a flash of blackness, I have to catch it but it's too fast," Amirra said.

"Do you know what it is?" Riddick asked.

"A soul," Amirra said.

"Why do you have to catch it?" Riddick asked.

Amirra looked at him with a confused face.

"I have no idea, I just need to do it," Amirra said.

"Have you tried your magic?" Riddick asked.

"No, how will that help?" Amirra asked.

"You're soul magic, so I would think your magic would be able to control the souls, ya?" Riddick said. Amirra thought about it and the art of Necromancy came into her mind. She understood how to call servitors, and even how to force them under her control and her yellow heartfire surged in her chest. "There ya go, like that. That is your heartfire, as Serin calls it. That's where your magic is inside, and how you access it," Riddick said.

"But I don't want to do Necromancy," Amirra said.

"You told me that Nitida told you, that you were raised by the Velshari for a reason, maybe that was to teach you how to use your soul magic when you were ready for it. Grandfather taught Shaz and I with stories and legends. He taught us how to fight, plan, strategize, and how to recognize things about our nature without having access to our heartfire. I think this was the same thing for you. You are a Necromancer, a Runecaster, a Soul Magic Mage. All of which have access to souls. The time has come for to you embrace the Necromancy as the way you were prepared for your magic of Soul," Riddick said.

Amirra contorted through a range of emotions and Riddick understood each one. He smiled as he was able to connect with her at such a deep level. He reached into his own heartfire and brought his rust-orange magic into his hand.

"Now you, bring your heartfire magic into your hand," Riddick said.

Amirra thought about how but her magic raced into her hand before she processed the decision. She frowned because she tried so hard to always make her own choices since learning she could. Riddick took her hand in his and his magic surrounded her. It was strong and powerful, but delicate and smooth. She could smell the fresh grass, a sea breeze, lilacs, and fresh sweet ginger. The impulse to command the soul breached her mental shield and Riddick gave her a gentle smile and a nod.

Amirra sighed and allowed her magic to command the entity. The flash of darkness immediately hovered toward her. The darkness stopped in front of her and bowed. Amirra thought she was going to cry because she refused to take the agency away from others as Semias had done to her, but a calmness sank into her chest, and she received its permission to be of service to her. Her chest heaved with the energy and Riddick held her from swaying. Riddick witnessed her yellow magic radiate from her being, and he understood the power of the soul magic.

It was astonishing and frightening, but he also was certain Amirra was the right one to have it. Her desire to have choice was her biggest ally in the magic of control and peace overcame them both. Amirra turned to see Riddick who was still gazing at her.

"Are you ready to wake up now?" Riddick asked.

Amirra nodded and Riddick faded from her mind. Riddick shook his head clear of the vision and Shaz and Serin waited with a bit of uneasiness as Amirra stirred. Amirra blinked and woke completely with a bit of a start. She sat up and Riddick pulled her into a tight squeeze.

"Did that really happen?" Amirra whispered.

"Aye," Riddick said.

"Do you hate me now," Amirra said.

"Goodness no, but do you hate yourself now?" Riddick asked.

Amirra pulled away and found Shaz and Serin near the end of the cot. Amirra burst into tears and Riddick held her.

"She'll be alright, but I'll stay with her for a while, and we can talk later," Riddick said.

Serin sent another surge of calming energy and Amirra smiled, then they left the tent.

"Do you think they'll be alright?" Serin asked.

"I'm sure they'll figure it out, just like we did," Shaz said.

Riddick scooched into the cot with Amirra, and she laid in his lap.

"I feel so bad," Amirra said.

"Why?" Riddick asked.

"Because I felt really good controlling the soul," Amirra said.

"Aye, and it should but I think that is a different kind of soul than the ones you have encountered before," Riddick said.

"How so?" Amirra asked.

"I don't think it belongs to anyone. I didn't get the impression that it had a life prior or that it was meant to have a life. I think it's just the essence of what souls are made of. Kind of like the energy of the planet, it's both the planet and its own entity," Riddick said.

"I see, I think your right," Amirra said.

"It said something to you, what did it say?" Riddick asked.

Amirra looked up at him with curious scrutiny.

"How do you know?" Amirra said.

"We are bonded now, I can sense a lot of things about you," Riddick said.

Amirra sucked in a deep breath. It was her worst fear and now he knew how horrible she was.

"Great," Amirra said with sad frustration.

Riddick stroked her hair.

"I love you, Necromancer and all. You are the most amazing woman I have ever met. Your strong and determined to do the right thing. You hide all of your darkness behind beautiful big hopeful eyes. You understand so much more than you think you do. You were raised to hate and yet you love so much about life. You are soul. You're determined, brave, patient, kind. You have integrity, you laugh and bring joy. You seek justice and virtue. You're brave, loyal, and honest. You're humble, you want to learn everything you can as fast as you can. You're smart and obedient to your truth. You understand greed, anger, hatred, cruelty, fear, and you seek to rid it from as much as you can. You are truly the absolute of soul," The images of the runes for these attributes came in and out of her mind as he spoke them. Her chest heaved with its truth, and she now understood why she was raised by the Velshari. "You understand the power of words and the cosmic nature they hold. You can create and change the forces of nature with them both for good and evil, but you choose good. You are so much more complete than anyone I know. I don't even have all that you do, and I can't imagine my life without you," Riddick said.

Tears streamed down her cheeks as she listened to everything he said. She understood why she had to suffer so much of the evil side of life. She now understood that everything had its opposite. Virtue and vice, good and evil, strength and weakness. She understood why the runes had picked her and how they are connected to the soul. Riddick held her tight as she processed all the rotations and training she had received. She now understood her soul magic and was ready to accept herself. She wiped the tears from her face and exhaled.

"On one hand I believe all that, but on the other I don't," Amirra said.

"That's because you are balanced. That's the best place for you to be. Grandfather always told us, that if you're not balanced then you're just a mess," Riddick said.

Amirra chuckled as she wiped her eyes again.

"Well, I'm certainly a mess, that's for sure," Amirra said.

"Well then, you're a beautiful mess," Riddick said.

Amirra blurted a ga-fa, but she loved the sound of it. Riddick smiled and kissed the top of her head. Amirra looked up and into his amazing brown eyes.

"I love you, Riddick," Amirra managed.

She had love for him since the beginning, but the words had never crossed her lips before. She had actually never uttered the words "I love you" at all, ever. It was terrifying, and she felt as though her stomach was going to lurch from her body. Riddick *listened* to her feelings and understood how hard that was for her to say out loud. He had heard it his whole life from his mother and was sad that Amirra hadn't. He decided he was going to tell her as often as he could from now on.

Riddick reached down and kissed Amirra. Amirra melted into his touch and kissed him back. The power of their shared magic, which was in complete balance with each other now, consumed them and their bodies sank with the comfort it gave.

50-I Smell The Blood Of The Lavari

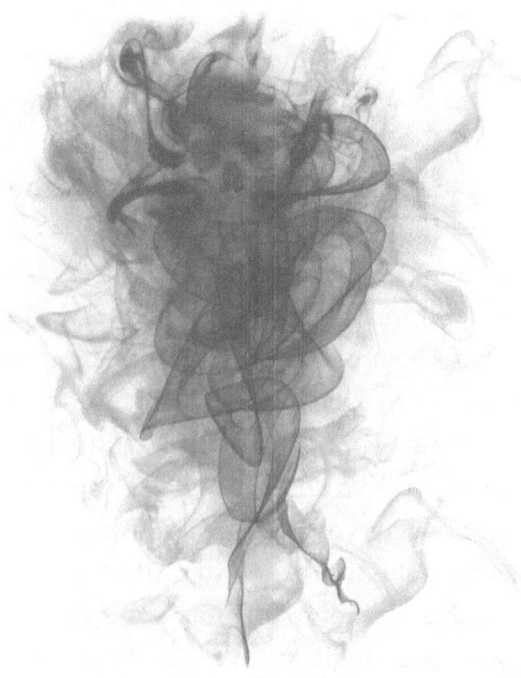

Antorn, Phillip, and Tobis headed· the small Forrne guard and galloped at a quick pace into the settlement. There was a feeling of vibrancy and excitement as they returned. A row of Forrne Fawns stood at the edge of the road into their section of the stronghold and Antorn wasn't sure what was going on. Stags began to line up next to the fawn and hold their heads high in their gesture of honor and respect. The Forrne Guard looked around with a bit of curiosity as they lined the street.

"What is going on?" Tobis asked.

"I have no idea," Antorn said.

"Antorn!" Mazen shouted.

Antorn turned as the panic in her voice ripped through his being. He leaped toward her at a fast gallop as she was running down the path.

"What's wrong?" Antorn asked his heart racing.

"It's Tissa, I can't find her, I've been searching all day, and I can't find her anywhere," Mazen said through heavy breaths.

"Come on," Antorn said.

Antorn took Mazen's hand, and they hurried back down the path. Tobis and Pillip nodded, letting him know they had things under control there and Antorn took Mazen into the camp. The settlement wasn't that far from the soldiers, but to Mazen it felt like forever. She had never planned on being a mother, at least not for a very long time, and especially not to a child already half grown, but Tissa won her heart, and she now understood how much one could mourn the loss of a child. She struggled to keep the horrible thoughts from eating at her nerves, but she had already had hours of worry, and she was sure she was going to hurl.

A twitch at the center of Shaz's chest bit at his understanding, and he allowed the magic to give him its report. He didn't have the details, but he was certain Antorn was coming at a fast pace, and he made his way toward them at a quick step.

Serin, there's trouble, meet me at the edge of the camp now, Shaz called in his mind.

Serin recognized his call and hurried from the healers tent and met Shaz as Antorn rounded the small bend.

"What's going on?" Serin asked.

"We're about to find out," Shaz said.

Antorn came to a quick stop and tried to suck in a few breaths before speaking.

"Tissa is missing," Mazen blurted.

Riddick, search for Tissa, Shaz said in his mind.

Riddick nearly jumped out of his socks and Amirra jumped from his start.

"What's the matter?" Amirra asked almost annoyed.

"It's Shaz, he spoke in my head," Riddick said.

An instant hint of urgency pricked at his mind, and he rubbed his hands together and put them on the cool dirt. His earth magic raced through the planets energy and gave him a mental picture of where Tissa was. He stood quickly and shot out of the tent and raced toward Shaz. His long legs leaped over the bits of camp life with a delicate ease. It was as if he wasn't running on the surface. Amirra jumped up and ran after him, but she was nowhere near as fast. She cursed and wished for an earth-board.

The ground ripped from its place and hovered in front of her. She smiled and hopped on and hurried after him. Riddick rounded the last tent and shoved his foot into the earth to stop himself. Dirt piled into a small heap as Riddick came to a stop.

"She's been," Riddick started but then noticed Antorn and Mazen. *She's been taken by Jaduuk,* Riddick said in his mind.

Shaz quickly told Serin and Antorn was sure they were talking in their minds.

"What is it, tell me," Antorn asked.

They could hear the panic and pleading in his voice, but they also didn't know how to handle it. Shaz always appreciated the knowledge even when the truth wasn't pleasant, so he figured Antorn would too.

"She's been taken by the Jaduuk," Shaz said.

"But, she's not hurt, yet, so we need to go now," Riddick said.

Mazen gasped, her heart thumped out of her chest, and she held back the lurch that desperately wanted to escape. Serin quickly sent her a boost of calming energy which helped, but she still sensed how much distress they were feeling. Shaz turned on his foot and Riddick followed.

"We'll get her, we know where she is," Serin said.

Antorn kissed Mazen and hurried after Shaz and Riddick.

"You're the healer, yes?" Mazen asked.

"I am, and I will be right there the whole time," Serin said.

Mazen smiled, and Serin understood it was about as much as she could do. Serin called an earth-board, and she and Amirra started after them. The late afternoon sun left a dingy orange and yellow cast on the fading blue sky, which in itself was pretty, but there was a silent attitude about it that was somehow unsettling. Riddick led the group through the bunches of acacia trees in the thickest part of the savanna. Large footprints sank in some places were the dirt was softer and in others the ground was so hard and dry that the heavy Jaduuk didn't leave prints. Riddick stuck his hand out and slowed to the speed of a brisk walk.

"Over that hill," Riddick said.

Shaz scanned the area and found she was in the center of a large horde. He ran through a few scenarios but couldn't decide on one.

"We need to move the horde away from her," Shaz said.

"I'll draw them out," Antorn said.

"We'll go together," Riddick said.

"Serin, after we take the horde, you get in and get her out," Shaz said.

Serin whipped her hands over her head and buffed them all with her wind-walk and Shaz gripped the hilt of the blade and lit his other hand on fire. He wasn't going to be quiet about it. The pit in his stomach that had been there for days was now hot in his chest, and he had a certain peace come to his mind. He thought about his father and how he barreled through the dungeons and a tiny glint tickled his eye. Riddick rolled his wrist and picked up a flurry of stone that sat in a wobbly force of vibration and pulled his battle-ax off his back with the other. Amirra didn't have a weapon yet. She was so focused on trying to keep herself from becoming everything she hated that she had yet to learn a weapon.

She wasn't sure what to do, but the darkness she had controlled hovered in front of her. The yellow magic in her chest eased down her arms and into her hands, and she allowed the magic to become part of her. Her hands glowed and Riddick nodded with a reassuring smile. Antorn gripped his spear and battle-ax and Shaz turned on his toe. The urge to shout overcame him, and he let out a holler so loud it startled even himself, but there was an enormous amount of power in it.

The Jaduuk jumped to alert and Shaz dug his toe into the ground and started into the masses. Riddick followed as did Antorn, but Amirra sent her darkness into the fray. Shaz dropped a plague of fireballs from the atmosphere and the consuming element sprang to life. Riddick unleashed a torrent of rock vortex's that unleashed shards that shot out and sped toward the beasts. The rocks pummeled the Jaduuk and the shards ripped through their skin and lodged deep into their beings. Howls and squeals of pain echoed around the now misty atmosphere. The debris from the destruction of the spawners still hung in the sky leaving a dingy mist hovering which gave Riddick an idea. Riddick organized the misty soot and debris particles around their beings creating a mirage-like effect as to where they really were. Shaz smiled with the added defense maneuver and was finding more joy then he had in a long time.

Amirra sent the darkness into the creatures and was horrified at the outcome. The darkness surged forward at an immense speed, sank into the beast, ripped its soul out of its being and consumed it as the body fell to the ground. The need to call the darkness back sat at the back of her mind but the words that Shaz had told her about using her anger for good came to the surface, and she allowed herself to be alright with the knowledge. It was time to let things be what they were, and she was confident that she would choose good. The darkness hovered and waited for her permission to continue, and she took hold of her strength in her choices and released the darkness on the Jaduuk.

The black mist surged through the beasts at great speed and consumed their souls as though it were ravaged with hunger. Shaz leaped over a beast in his usual fashion and sliced off its head and rounded into another strike throwing fire and slamming his combustion-liquify into another. Antorn slashed one, turned and kicked one, and speared another. Riddick allowed his earth's vibration to course through their frames leaving their insides like jellied berries. Serin kept a tight watch on their heartfire and Amirra's new heartfire was strong and even, and she smiled. Shaz directed them to move the attack so that Serin could get in, and she started around to the back side where she would have the easiest time getting to Tissa.

Serin sent out her air magic and it returned with Tissa's exact location. She was going to have to manage her way through the tents and things that the Jaduuk were now setting up and Serin cursed. Shaz sent another helping of fireballs and Riddick blasted more rock shards. Amirra continued to direct the darkness. Runes of the Necromancer came into her mind as did the runes of the Runecaster, and she blended them together in her mind to form a new language. She began her new chant and the magic of the two sides united.

The crew felt the new tingle of Amirra's mind shield as she created the Soulfire. It was hot but soothing and the crew's clarity was heightened. Riddick's vortex spun faster and hit with a bigger punch and Shaz's fire was hotter. Serin's wind went faster as she blasted a gust of wind-shards and Antorn had greater strength and speed. Riddick turned to see her encased in her sunrise-yellow magic and smiled. Her expression was that of complete peace, almost a bit of thrill. The darkness sank into a beast and then another and Serin amazed in wonder. She had no idea what Amirra's power-strike was going to be, and it was almost unsettling, but a comfortable reassurance came to her, and she refocused her attention on Tissa.

Serin's wind magic with Amirra's buff made her even lighter than air, and she had to focus on staying low to the ground, so she wouldn't fly away. It was almost comical and Serin chuckled to herself as she hopped a tent without any effort. She rounded some tents and caught a whiff of the smelly beasts. She slipped up against the poles of a structure that looked like it had been erected as a platform for speaking or giving orders. Serin re-examined her surroundings and found a handful of Jaduuk standing guard of Tissa, and she cursed.

Serin slipped out and peeked over the platform that was several lengths high. There were six Jaduuk and one of them was definitely a Captain. Her heart pounded the inside of her ribs and for a second she wondered if they would hear it. Serin's mind raced through what they knew of the Jaduuk, and so far it was apparent they were evolving, but how smart would they become. Her stomach churned with the thought, and she tried to steady her breathing. The Captain's nose flared, and he sniffed the air. The information sank into his brain, and he snarled a throaty sound.

"I smell the blood of a Lavari," the captain growled.

Serin gasped. One, she had never heard a Jaduuk ever utter words, and two, that it could smell what kind of lineage she was. Panic tainted her ideas, but she shoved it out and closed her eyes. She gripped her hands together tightly and the air around the Jaduuk thickened. They dropped their battle-ax's and grappled at their throats but there was no way they could fill their lungs. The anger at this whole mess eased into Serin's mind, and she too used it to fuel her attack. The first beast succumbed to the lack of oxygen and then another. She counted six thumps and continued to keep the air from their lungs.

She understood they were only unconscious at this point and waited until the thumps of their hearts weakened and then stopped, all but the one. Serin peeked over the platform and found the Captain, unconscious but alive. The image of his heart formed in her mind, and she realized it was different from the others. It was human. Her guts tightened again, and she shook out her hands to release the extra energy she was now experiencing. Her mind struggled against all the new questions, but she lifted herself up with her wind and landed on the platform. Serin walked to the Captain and gripped tighter. The beating finally stopped, and she waited another half minute.

Serin heard the bellowing and howling in the distance but it wasn't coming from the direction Shaz and the crew were, and she knew she needed to hurry. Serin stepped over the bodies and made her way toward Tissa who was tied to a large pole in the center of the platform. Shaz was starting to feel the same effect as when he was absorbing the energy from Semias, but it was different in that it was actual shadow magic. Semias' magic had shadow magic in it, but it wasn't raw like this. This was as though he was taking in the purest of elixirs instead of watered down.

Serin gripped the cords that were wrapped around Tissa's frame. She was small for a Forrne as she was a child, but she was nearly as big as Serin and probably twice her weight. The sting of the shadow magic bit at her skin. Serin winced and cursed but tried to untie the knots. The cords were very tight, and the knot was almost as big and her head. Serin called her light magic to her hands, then dropped it quickly and spun around in time to catch a glimpse of more Jaduuk running past.

Serin sucked in a breath and scooted close to Tissa. Her mind raced around what she was going to do. If she used her light magic to shrivel up the cords she would alert the new horde. She also needed to hurry, she had no idea how many of these beasts would come and how long the crew would have to fight. She ran a quick exam and found everyone doing fine and turned back to the cords.

The shadow magic bit at her skin to the point that it broke open her flesh, and she gritted her teeth through the pain. She didn't dare use her magic as the blue would emit a light as well and it was dark enough now that she feared that too would alert them. A twig snapped on the other side of the platform and she froze. Serin looked up and found a set of vivid black eyes staring at her. Her heart raced adrenaline through her, and she let lose her wind shards.

51-We're Out, Let's Go

The blades ripped through the Captain's flesh, but he hissed and Serin could now see his pack behind him. Pure panic hit her brain.

Shaz! Serin yelled.

Shaz turned and found the pack descending in on Serin. He was too far away, and panic raced through his being. The urge to shout surged through him like thunder, and he again let the force escape his being. The surge of shadow magic sent the force through his voice and hit the Jaduuk with an irritating itch that instantly made them angrier at Shaz, and they turned toward him. He looked the pack leader in the eye and said in his mind, *'come and get me?'* The beasts' turned and shot across the distance and an odd glee radiated within Shaz's chest.

Riddick on the other hand grimaced and Amirra called another darkness, then more. The black mists' crossed the distance with impeccable speed and Riddick got the impression they were ravished with a kind of hunger. Shaz's shadow magic vibrated and gave him a power that he usually kept deep. Serin turned to see the flash of 'evil' cross Shaz's face as though he was enjoying this a lot more than usual and her heartfire surged.

Serin started to pull against the restraints but struggled as they wouldn't release. Her mind raced to search Shaz's condition to make sure he was alright and finding that he had a calmness to his chaos gave her the comfort she needed. Tissa's limp body hung tightly against the cords and Serin sent a boost of air magic to lift her up. The bonds wriggled now, but she still couldn't get them off.

Shaz threw up his shield and braced for the impact. He wanted to find out how much of the Jaduuk's heath he absorbed with his new armor, as he usually killed them before they were able to make contact. The Jaduuk Captain slashed his clawed hoof at Shaz's chest, but the new armor, mixed with his shield, sent the beast flying backward. A small surge of energy tingled his being, and he was confident his armors new enchantment took some of the Jaduuk's strength, but it was the evil nature of the shadow magic which startled him at how good it was in his blood. The next Jaduuk struck and Shaz barely noticed the hit, and he again absorbed the Jaduuk's energy.

Riddick shielded himself and instructed Amirra on how to make herself a shield and sent another blast of earth-liquify into the oncoming Jaduuk. Nasty bluish bodies fell to the ground in droves as the crew continued to fight and Serin was growing more frustrated and her anger deepened the heat in her chest. Shaz on the other-hand felt like he could stand there all day and had a bit of joy in how angry his shadow magic made the beasts. Shaz whipped the Honor Blade through the arm of a Jaduuk and rolled the blade into a side-cut and sliced through the chest of another. The Jaduuk behind Shaz slammed its fist into the shield but the force shot it back-ward and hit its own face. The beast stumbled back from the force and Shaz stabbed another through the heart. Riddick, too felt the added strength the Jaduuk's hits gave him which was just in time because Amirra's new enchantment of 'Soulfire' was wearing off.

"I command you to release!" Serin shouted.

Serin squirmed as the prick of shadow magic she borrowed from Shaz trickled through her and the bonds released. She caught Tissa's weak body and wrapped her in her wind-walk. Serin gripped the earth-turf and started back toward the camp.

We're out, lets' go, Serin said in her mind.

Kinda busy, Shaz replied.

Serin turned to find that she couldn't see them in the pile of Jaduuk and her fearful rage surged. Serin stopped the turf and brought her hydro-light magic from her core and with immense power she blasted it toward the heap. The force shot her backward, and she had to catch Tissa and re balance before she fell. The light-beam incinerated the Jaduuk that surrounded him and ripped through those nearest leaving a hole in which Shaz gripped an earth-board and shot out of the pile with Riddick right behind. Antorn rounded the pile and darted toward Serin.

Shaz blasted the rest with a downpour of fireballs and Rid-dick swallowed the rest in the earth. Serin struggled to hold Tissa's dead weight as the blast took a substantial amount of her energy. Shaz caught up to her quickly and jumped off his turf-board and onto hers and wrapped his arms around the ladies and took over the steering. Serin relaxed into his energized frame, and they raced back to camp. Riddick swooped up Amirra and sent Antorn a new kind of inertia that acted like a propulsion effect. His already graceful leap lasted longer, and his lunges were intensified as the magic actually pushed him forward.

An Ebassian solder stood at the top of the land bank they had erected as their barrier and scanned the distance. Mazen paced back and forth and the soldier recognized the struggle she was in. He tried to offer kind words of encouragement, but he also understood the complexities of women, and was certain it wasn't really helping. He lifted the looking glass to his eye and squinted the other.

"Mam, they're coming," the soldier said excitedly.

The soldier handed her the looking glass and helped her locate their location. Tears escaped at a rapid rate, and she dashed toward the entrance they would be taking.

Mazen was at the entrance first but not by much, and she pranced nervously until they hurried through the gate. Antorn shoved his hoofs into the dirt and tried to stop, but he hopped a few times as he wrangled the earth's energy. Mazen wasn't sure what to think but at this point thinking wasn't really her option. The automatic endorphins had kicked in, and she was in panic mode. Antorn took her hand, and they followed Shaz, Serin, and Tissa to the healing tent where Serin did a full exam and sent a boost of healing magic.

"She's only unconscious, and she will be fine, but we don't want to wake her until her body has a chance to rid itself of the shadow magic from the bonds she was in," Serin said.

"Thank you, I can't begin to tell you how, well I don't even know what I feel," Mazen said.

Serin smiled, she did understand what she was going though.

"I would like to speak to her when she comes to. I want to find out how she got there and if she witnessed anything, is that alright?" Shaz asked.

"Yes, of course," Antorn said.

Mazen, however, wasn't sure and Serin understood her apprehension of having her have to re-live the terrible experience.

"I'll give her a small dose of the calming magic, which will make it, so she won't experience the pain or fright again," Serin said.

Mazen sighed with relief and Serin patted her hand.

Serin could barely keep her eyes open even after taking another drink of her concentrated magic water. Shati promised she would look after Tissa, and Mazen. Serin agreed and Shaz walked with her back to their tent. Shaz pulled the flap open and helped Serin to the bed. He pulled down the covers and pulled off her boots.

Serin was so tired she could hardly keep her eyes open but Shaz was still experiencing the heightened effects of the added shadow magic. He kissed Serin's forehead and waited a few lengths until her breathing deepened, then left the tent. The sun was setting quickly, and he needed to find out why the Jaduuk were now taking captives when they never had before. He was certain Serin would be angry if she knew what he wanted to do, but he needed to find out, and he needed a way to release the stored energy.

Shaz gripped an earth-board and hopped on. He started out at a smooth pace until the landscape opened then he sat forward, and the board increased in speed. He wasn't sure where he was going but the speed he was traveling gave him a fresh exhilaration. A recklessness overcame him, and he sped faster. A sudden mix of emotions sank into his awareness, and Grandfather returned to his mind. The image of his old and frail frame moving up the green conduit made his heart ache. The pain of the sorrow bit off a part of his being and his new energy was filled with angry rage.

Shaz wanted to rip something to shreds, he wanted to burn everything in sight. He turned the board around and spiraled several times before leveling out. An odor of pitch caught his nose, and he turned to see a vein of black earth. His anger took hold of his heart as the same flash of evil crossed his eyes, and he maneuvered the hovering earth toward the Jaduuk. It wasn't their fault exactly, but they did the bidding of the man whose fault it was, and he was going to make him pay. The closer he came to the Jaduuk camp the bigger his now green heartfire burned. Serin would be going nuts if she knew how much he was letting the shadow into his heart, and he was glad she wasn't there.

He usually kept his need to release the anger under wraps because he understood it wasn't anyone's fault he had to deal with it, but there was so much inside he had to do something. The sun crept the last few lengths below the horizon and Shaz's night vision took over. He sent out a search and it came back with their location, and he steered toward it. The Jaduuk camp came into view, and he gritted his teeth. He lit his hands and arms on fire and called the combustion forces to his being.

The fire had a hint of green in it, and he smiled. He liked the way the shadow magic added to his fire, his wizards fire. The mix between the red and green, it was the perfect balance of destruction. It was now more than just fire and it surged through him with fierce desire. The desire to kill. He lifted the earth-board a little higher above the ground and banked off a small group of trees and rolled. As he rounded the top of the circle he let out an enormous billowing of the orange-green fire. The ravaging force incinerated the Jaduuk who had barely recognized his presence. He shot over them so quickly the backlash of wind fed the inferno and it spread several lengths.

Shaz slammed his hands together and the force exploded sending several Jaduuk sprawling. He repeated it several times each time rolling and banking off the nearest tree or bush leaving it very difficult to spot him. He rounded the edge of the camp and flew back over. The flames had consumed an incredible amount of Jaduuk, but it wasn't enough. He clapped his hands and a torrent of fire balls fell from the sky encompassing more beasts.

Several Jaduuk had now woken to the stench of singed comrades and were looking around with shock and surprise. Shaz's joy jumped, and he blasted them with rapid-fire bursts of combustion. The force hit them with so much intensity, that they flew backward and hit the ground. Their bodies writhed with the pain and lack of function as most of their innards were now jelly. A small thought at the back of his head came to the surface and Shaz recognized it as Grandfather's voice.

Shaz pushed it away and sent another blast of green fire into the masses of Jaduuk that were still half-dazed. He raced over the top of their sleeping frames and the voice made its way forward again. A hint of shame bit at his heart, and he seized the anger. He sat forward more, and the hovering-earth blasted over the last of the camp back the way he came.

Tears now encased his eyes, and he struggled with the release of his anger. He hated crying, it was weak, it was stupid, it wasn't what a war wizard should do. He was such a mess and all for what, nothing he could change anyway. Shaz couldn't bring Grandfather back. He couldn't change the fact that an entire Jaduuk army, that is being created by a mad man, is hunting him and killing everything in their path. He couldn't change the fact that he can't protect everyone, and he can't even find the stupid man.

Shaz wiped the tears now flowing off his face and yelled at the top of his lungs. A sharp clap of thunder cracked open the night sky and the energy rippled through his being. He hated everything. He hated being him, he hated what he was having to do. He hated it all. Shaz was so angry, but nothing was going to change. Unless he did something. But what, incinerating the Jaduuk was only part of it. He had to think differently. He needed to think like the shadow. He needed to 'be ten steps ahead', as Grandfather would have said.

What would Grandfather do? What would his father do? He missed them so much and wished they were there with him, to tell him what he should do. He had no idea what he was doing. Why is he letting his emotions get the best of him? The camp came into view and he slowed his earth-turf. He decided he would walk the last little bit to try to compose himself and released the earth back into the ground.

52-What Does It Say?

It was quiet, only a handful of men and half spent fires were still left as he made his way to his tent. Shaz pulled the flap and listened, and sighed when he recognized Serin's deep breathing. He found the bed and pulled off his boots and slipped the Honor Blade under the top edge of his side of the bed, pulled his jerkin and tunic off, and climbed under the covers. He laid with his hands under his head and replayed the events at the Jaduuk camp in his mind.

Shaz wasn't sorry, but something told him he should be. He decided he would be sorry about letting himself become so angry, but he also decided that was part of the effects of so much shadow magic. He also decided he loved being able to control the beasts, but he needed to figure out a way to let the energy travel through his body perhaps. At any rate, he couldn't let himself get so worked up again. It was never wise to let anger be your driving force, and he wanted more now than ever to be what Grandfather wanted him to be. This was the only way to honor him.

"Are you going to sleep anytime soon?" Serin asked.

Shaz turned to find her propped on her elbow gazing at him. The faint hint of a fire outside their tent left a soft glow on her delicate features, not that his night vision didn't allow for him to make out her beautiful features even in the dark. Her beauty and love for him gripped his being, and he suddenly felt ashamed he let himself get so out of control.

"I thought you were asleep," Shaz said.

"I was, until all I could sense was your anger. Are you alright?" Serin said.

"I'm sorry, I thought I released all the energy before coming in," Shaz said.

Serin leaned over and kissed him, and he embraced her calming energy. He needed the soothing energy more now than ever. Serin kissed him with more vigor and sent a heavy dose into his frame. The euphoria pushed the anger from his being, and he shivered with the release. Serin pulled back and gazed into his now softened features.

"How many do you think you killed?" Serin asked.

"What?" Shaz asked.

"I know what happened," Serin said gently.

"How?" Shaz asked.

"Your emotions also give me a mental picture of what you've done in the past, I receive glimpses of your past as you remember it," Serin said.

"Oh," Shaz said.

Shaz didn't realize she could *experience* his *past* actions too and was now filled with a whole new set of worries to think about.

Serin smiled as she felt his new fears and ran her hand across his warmed bare skin.

"Your secrets are safe with me, I just wish there was something more I could do to help you with all this," Serin said.

"I have already put you through so much more than you deserve," Shaz said.

"Shazmpt Kallum O'Connon Nordvik, don't you dare, you know exactly how I feel about all this," Serin said sternly.

Shaz's brow raised.

"You called me by my whole name," Shaz said with a snarky interest.

Serin slugged him and he flinched and chuckled.

"There, now stop beating yourself up. You know there is nothing you can do to change the way things have worked out. You also know that Grandfather would say something like 'only a derp would beat himself up'," Serin said in her best old man voice.

Shaz cracked up blurting a hearty ga-fa, grabbed her and pulled her close.

"I don't deserve you," Shaz said.

"You won't if you don't go to sleep," Serin said.

Serin laid onto his chest and started counting heartbeats, he smiled and ran his fingers through her hair. She ran her fingers along his scar from when he saved William on board the Mirabella so long ago. Shaz wondered how he was doing and tried to figure out how old the lad would be now.

"We do need to figure out how to help you release all the shadow magic you absorb," Serin said.

"Aye, I never thought I would say this, but I really like the feeling I receive," Shaz admitted.

"I can see that, and I don't think that is a bad thing," Serin said.

"You don't?" Shaz asked.

"No, you are who you are, but I don't think you are strong enough yet to keep it from overcoming you, and that is what scares me," Serin said.

Shaz found he loved her even more than ever. She didn't judge him, she wasn't angry at his lack of control, she was always trying to help him be his best self, she never tried to change him. He has always been able to be himself with her, and he found his devotion to her deepen. Serin smiled at his improved feelings and listened quietly.

"I didn't figure out why the Jaduuk have gone to taking captives. That makes no sense. They have never acted this way," Shaz said.

"Well, Antorn did say that some of the Jaduuk are different than the ones we are used to, and they have more intelligence, and when Tissa wakes up we might gain some information from her," Serin said.

"True, but are the Jaduuk smarter, or is Gavin Rhill more present than before, or is there someone else?" Shaz said.

"I haven't a clue, maybe all three," Serin said.

"Aye, so what does that mean?" Shaz asked.

"And, I heard the Jaduuk Captain speak, it was eerie, I've never heard them speak before," Serin said.

Shaz lifted his head off the pillow and Serin looked up at him. Serin didn't have night vision, so she couldn't make out his features very well in the dark, but she understood his emotion, which was filled with curious dread.

"What did it say?" Shaz asked.

"That it could smell the blood of the Lavari," Serin said.

Shaz sat up and Serin sat up too.

"It said it could smell your blood, and it understood you are Lavari?" Shaz asked with a raised voice and a hint of horror in his tone.

"Umhum, just before I suffocated it," Serin said.

Shaz laid back down but his heart was pounding. She counted his heartrate and sure enough, it was beating faster than usual.

"It freaked me out too, what do you think this means?" Serin asked.

"That we are in big trouble," Shaz said.

"How so?" Serin asked.

"Part of the book we found in the dungeon alludes to something such as 'blood sniffing'. At first, I thought maybe it was related to the imprinting, but now I think this might be similar, but different,"

"You don't sound happy about that," Serin said.

"The thing is, that's all this says, I can't figure out the rest of anything, and I'm getting grumpy about it," Shaz said.

"Maybe I can help," Serin said.

"It's all in the ancient runes, but different, like the marks are the ancient runes, but they don't line up the right way and half the tik's are missing in some," Shaz said.

Serin sat up and crossed her legs.

"Maybe I can figure something out," Serin said.

Shaz wasn't sure if she would, but he was confident, she assumed he wouldn't find sleep anytime soon, so he scooched the covers off and pulled the book out of the pouch he kept them in. He made his hand glow and looked for a lantern and lit the wick.

Serin took the notebook and found most of the pages were blank, at least to her, but every few pages she viewed a small mark at the top inside corner that looked like there was only a partial mark. She found a writers tool and paper on the table and wondered if Shaz had noticed too. Shaz climbed in bed and put his hands under his head and closed his eyes. Serin was certain he wasn't asleep and that his mind was now racing with his 'if this, then that' mode of thinking.

Serin turned back to the front of the book and replicated the mark onto another piece of paper. She wrote the marks in a line across the page, but nothing came, so she reorganized them top to bottom and still nothing. She remembered the marks on her studies when she was with the wyverns and organized the marks in the circular pattern that the wyverns used and suddenly the marks joined together on the page and formed a symbol. She couldn't read the symbol but the fact that it put itself back together meant this was the wyverns language. Serin put the paper down and looked at Shaz who's brows were tight together at the center of his face, and she mused at how intent he was in his thinking.

"Do you want to see something," Serin asked.

Shaz lifted his head, and she held out the paper for him. He sat up and took the paper and then looked at her with wide eyes.

"What is this, I mean where did you get this?" Shaz asked.

"I found these marks in the notebook and figured out how this book is written," Serin said.

"How? I've been working on this for over a moon," Shaz said.

"Well, the marks didn't do anything in a line or top to bottom, so I tried the way the wyverns write, and the marks arranged themselves into this symbol," Serin said.

"You read the language of the wyverns?" Shaz asked his eyes wide.

"Well, some of it, I'm sure I don't know near all of it," Serin said.

Shaz propped himself next to Serin, and she handed him the notebook, and he leaned over and kissed her. Serin chuckled.

"These marks are all over this book," Shaz said.

"I only see these," Serin said and pointed to the ones in the corners.

"Humm, interesting, this mark is attached to another one, so I had no idea there was a separate mark," Shaz said pointing to the first tick-mark Serin had made. "You said the marks arranged themselves?" Shaz asked.

"Yes, the language of the wyverns is magical, and if you put the ticks in the proximity of the words or phrases, it will form itself based on what the writer wanted to say. Kind of like reading the writers thoughts at the time they wrote them down instead of what the ticks or marks actually mean," Serin said.

Shaz's lip puckered with partial understanding and Serin smiled.

"Here, you write all the marks you find on this page onto this one but write them in a circular pattern, like this," Serin said drawing the circular pattern on the page. Shaz opened the first page and began transferring the marks. Halfway through, the marks found the meaning and organized themselves into a group of symbols that made up the ancient language. Shaz's eyes sparkled with the delight of watching them move around the parchment.

"What does it say?" Serin asked, she already had her own understanding but wondered if the marks said the same thing to him, that was also something about the wyvern language, they could 'say' different things to different people.

"This is a history, but not sure what for yet," Shaz said.

Serin nodded, and Shaz continued to make the transcription. The marks continued to organize themselves onto the page as Shaz wrote them in the same circular pattern and Serin watched with both fond memories and not so fond. She hadn't remembered so much about her childhood in such a long time and the fact that she was able to understand the wyvern's language as a child committed her understanding of her being the Wyvern Priestess.

"Wait, you already understand what these symbols say," Shaz half-asked-half-stated.

"Once you write them from the notebook, then yes," Serin said.

Shaz tapped his finger on his chin and thought about how he could unlock the book to show her the language.

"Chento ma'ha vi say an'na marri she'late narata noshari sanate," Shaz said.

The notebook glowed a dingy gray and then a pop sounded, and the shadow charm disperses. Shaz opened the pages, and she now saw all the marks. She took the book, and her magic was accessed by the magical signature of the wyvern that left it and an image of a black wyvern appeared in front of her as did the white wyvern.

"Do you see the black wyvern?" Shaz asked.

"I do, and the white wyvern, do you?" Serin said.

"Aye, this book is more than just the secrets of the war wizards, but the key to the wyvern's," Shaz said.

Serin put her finger on one of the tics in the center of the page, and they jumped off and organized into a cohesive nature to form the words.

Shazmpt son of the Tooatha De Dannon and Serin daughter of the Lavari, I have waited many long rotations to speak to you again, for I saw you both in the begging and will meet you again at the end. This is the history of my people, the Tooatha De Dannon, Lavari, Bair Tiornecht and the Fir Bolg, the real history, not what you have learned. I have much I want to share with you and what we were unable to succeed at. Please only read this with all four of the descendants for there is information that will be given for all. This is of the utmost secret and requires your diligence in keeping these truths known only to you at this time.

The writing ended and Serin was sure it was because Riddick and Amirra weren't there.

"I guess we have to wait till morning to get the rest of the book," Serin said.

Shaz closed the book and repeated the words to return the shadow charm and tucked into his satchel.

53-In The Hollow

Shaz and Serin woke early and made their way to the healer's tents to check on Tissa. The nights were getting colder now with the layer of ash sitting above the wind currents and Shaz chided himself for being so careless. They had to deal with this in the Minca realm too, and he should have known better.

Serin patted his arm as she opened the flap. Tissa sat sitting in Antorn's lap eating a dish of morning porridge. Antorn smiled with a 'she's doing great' smile and Serin smiled back.

They rounded the edge of the cots and made their way over to them where they found Mazen asleep next to Antorn.

"How are you doing?" Serin asked quietly.

Tissa looked up and smiled but then her head dropped. Serin interpreted her emotions and understood that she hadn't been taken until she tried to follow Antorn and got lost. Serin relayed the information to Shaz who nodded. Serin pulled up a little stool and sat next to Tissa.

"May I check your heart to make sure there is no more yucky in your blood?" Serin asked.

Shaz smiled to himself at the use of the word 'yucky' as that was usually not a way to describe the ills of being wounded, but it was completely accurate at the same time. Serin brought her soft blue hues of color to her hands and Tissa's eyes widened with the beauty. She giggled at the tickle in her skin as the magic made its way around her frame. Serin received the report and nodded.

"All better, no more yucky," Serin said.

"Tissa, you need to tell them what you told me," Antorn said with a gentle but stern voice.

Tissa gulped but nodded.

"I was trying to be a warrior like Antorn, I am sorry I left the herd and made so much trouble," Tissa said softly.

Her voice was delicate and smooth and had the pitch of youth.

"Thank you, you actually helped us figure a few things out, but we still have a few questions. Would you be alright to answer them?" Shaz asked sitting onto his haunches as to be eye level with her. Tissa nodded and Antorn stirred Mazen. She had been strict about being present for the questioning, but they didn't fault her for that. Mazen stirred and rubbed her eyes and sat up when she realized Shaz and Serin sitting next to her.

"Oh, I'm sorry, I didn't hear you," Mazen blushed.

Serin smiled gently.

"Are you alright with us asking a few questions?" Serin asked.

Mazen nodded and understood that even if it was hard, it was necessary.

"Where were you when you were taken?" Shaz asked.

"In the Hollow," Tissa said.

Shaz turned to Antorn as he had no idea where that was.

"It's between the camp on the far side and the mountain pass," Antorn said.

"What mountain pass?" Shaz asked.

He tried to keep his tone neutral but Antorn understood the inflection. He would be irritated too, and he chided himself for not mentioning it sooner.

"I'm sorry I never thought to tell you, there's a pass that runs the side of the mountain along the ragged edges. We encountered a pack in the area back a rotation ago, but we led them out and killed them, so it never came to mind again." Antorn said.

Shaz reassured him he understood.

"Where does it lead?" Shaz asked.

"It's never been discovered before, as far as I'm aware," Antorn said.

"Did they hurt you?" Mazen asked.

"No, but the big one was arguing with another big one, and they were talking about one called Jaduuk'ai," Tissa said.

"Jaduuk'ai?" Shaz asked.

"The one wanted to take me to him, but the other one wanted to wait to see if you would come and fetch me," Tissa said.

"Did they say anything about what this Jaduuk'ai wanted?" Shaz asked.

"Only that he was going to kill all of the Tooatha De Dannon's," Tissa said.

"Thank you, you are very brave," Shaz said.

Tissa smiled and Antorn ran his hand over her head and gave her a squeeze. Shaz and Serin stood and walked to the edge of the tent.

"What are you thinking" Serin asked.

"We need to check out this mountain pass and what this Jaduuk'ai is. I have a feeling it is Baltair somehow, and I want to get another strike ready," Shaz said.

"I thought so," Serin said.

"We will go," Turkill said.

Shaz turned to see Turkill with his arms folded across his chest and Ladtwig with his best imitation of Turkill's harumph look on his face.

"Where's Jag, we're going to need stealth," Shaz asked.

"She's in your tent last I saw," Turkill said.

Shaz wasn't sure much anymore, she took turns sleeping with Shaz, the Minca, and Amirra.

"Alright, call a meeting and meet us in the war tent in twenty," Shaz said.

Turkill grunted and the Minca hurried away. Shaz returned to Antorn.

"We're going to need to borrow Antorn for a bit," Shaz said to Tissa and Mazen. Antorn looked up and found his earnest eyes and cleared his throat.

"I'll be back as soon as I can, and Tissa," Antorn started.

"I know, no running off," Tissa said.

Antorn nodded.

"And, I love you," Antorn said.

Tissa smiled and Antorn left the tent with Shaz and Serin. A prick at the back of Serin's mind made her stop and turn toward the portal as they passed the back half of the settlement.

"What's the matter?" Shaz asked.

"Probably nothing, I'll meet you there," Serin said.

Shaz agreed and he and Antorn continued toward the tent.

54-I Have Figured Out The Runecasting

Serin came into the tent and held open the flap for Tobis and Pillip, followed by a very large man. Shaz turned to see his father's soft brown eyes and his heart leaped.

"Father!" Shaz said.

He didn't expect the amount of emotion to fill his being but there was a certain comfort knowing he was not only alive, but there with him.

"Shaz," Merrick wrapped Shaz into a bear hug then pulled away. "You certainly know how to throw a party, son," Merrick said.

Shaz, Riddick, Amirra, and Bowen chuckled and Pillip stared. Humans were so weird but at the same time, he found a certain part of himself feeling the same way and wondered how much of himself was more human than he understood. He figured he half-looked like them and spoke like them, so there must be more to him than he knew. He examined Antorn and Tobis who were at ease with the exchange and figured they had already seen it since this was his first time at the table.

"So, what is the plan?" Merrick asked.

Helios, Phanes, and Declan came through the tent door and Shaz greeted Declan with the Rangers greeting. Merrick's strong brows raised, and he studied Declan. Declan's eyes popped out of his defined features and Merrick tried to hide the confusion on his face.

"It's absolute honorrr to meet you sirrr, I mean, I met you when I vas child, but zat doesn't kount," Declan said.

"You're Viktor's son," Merrick ask-stated.

"I am, Declan," Declan said holding his hand out in the Rangers greeting and Merrick returned the handshake.

"Then the honor is mine, your father saved my life a time or two, I owe you a great debt," Merrick said.

"Fatherrrs arrre so funny, he said same about you and zat he oves you grrreat debt, and if I ever have chance to pay his debt to you, I vas obligated," Declan said.

Merrick chuckled.

"You'll have to tell me everything when we can," Merrick said.

Motavo and Asher then came through the door followed by Jag, Turkill and Ladtwig who scurried in.

"Alright, we're all here. Father, you remember everyone, and this is Antorn, Tobis, and Pillip, the leaders of the Forrne," Shaz said.

Merrick nodded and the flap opened again and Shaz turned to find Nitida's small old Minca Runecaster's face full of dread and his heart sank.

"Nitida, what's wrong?" Shaz asked.

The room turned to see the small woman's gentle wrinkles and Amirra rounded the table toward her.

"I have figured out the runecasting," Nitida said.

"The Empyral one?" Amirra asked.

"Yes, come, this is quite complex," Nitida said.

Nitida made her way to the table. Riddick quickly made her a step stool, and she stepped up next to the surface. She pulled out her purple velvet pouch and opened the top. She reached in and pulled out all the stones and the cloth and set it out. Nitida placed each stone in the same places that they had originally fallen and ran her hand just above the surface. She mumbled her beginning chant and pointed to the first stone.

"This is the Hagalaz rune, this is in the placement of the past and is filled with loss, destruction, chaos, pain, suffering, torture, torment, affliction, passion, desire, and murder," Nitida pointed to the next stone.

"This is the Yanew rune and is in the North circle which means these horrific times have repeated for eons, this is no mistake, it will repeat again," Nitida's hand began to tremble slightly and the room was silent with the growing energy.

"This is the Caldean stone and is in the East circle. This is a powerful symbol as it leads to the future. It is the central point of all things and marks the beginning and the end. The power it has to unify the comic powers is unchangeable and indicates the war wizard and the turning of time," Nitida looked at Shaz, and he instantly understood what she meant, but the rest of the room had no idea.

"This is the Reiki stone and is next to the east circle in the mind and memory of time. This indicates the powers of the world sits in the palm of your hand, but heed it diligently for your own strength will be tested beyond your capabilities," Nitida looked into Riddick's eyes who shivered with its truth.

"The Pura is here in the depths of the hidden and connected to the deities, this one belongs to the essence of the soul and is utmost important, as this brings the needed elements for the completion of growth and spirituality, but will be faced with great adversity and pain before it blooms into its grandeur. It requires swiftness, migration to new grounds, teamwork and is supported by the immovability of the earth," Nitida made eye contact with Amirra, who nodded.

"This one is the Oneadi, and is also next to the east circle. Through the vibe of self, this is the tide of the great waters, a force that cannot be held back, but is pliable and movable. It encompasses the depths of the greatest meanings and has the power to cleans the world," Nitida gazed into Serin's eyes and a strange tickle of information eased into her awareness.

"This is the Teiwaz rune and is in the west circle. This is a very troubling indication, as the west circle is the place of decisions. The Teiwaz symbol is the infusion of masculine energy, bringing, as a result, anxiety to conquer. But to conquer is not the way, but unify. This is the struggle between the powers, and harness the option for great unity or great destruction." Nitida looked at all four the elementals and with a shaky voice continued.

"It is also the Rune of courage, dedication, and absolute trust in one's own resources and ultimate trust in one's friends. Teiwaz advises perseverance, at the same time reminding one that patience can sometimes be a kind of perseverance. The strength to analyze the foundation of one's life will allow the user to harness their deepest and most powerful resources," the nervous energy thickened, and people began to shift uneasily, "this stone is the stone for Forgiveness. This is placed in the center which means it is the center for all things to come to pass. One will never have the needed elements unless they have the capacity to forgive, even themselves for that is where the journey begins, deep within," Nitida said slowly.

Serin could see her fading energy and understood her time was coming to an end, and she turned to find Amirra with the same understanding. It wasn't fair, even with all of her healing powers, she couldn't keep them from leaving the realm of the living if they chose not to stay.

"This one is the Exception Rune. The symbol of Aesir, the Sun Goddess. This means the power of choice, as much as the past can affect the present and the future, choice will always supersede all things, nothing is ever written in stone as choice can change even the past if one so desires it," Nitida slowly moved her now shaky finger to the last two stones. Her voice cracked and she cleared her throat.

"These two are the Zed-Kal stones and mean 'Prime Power'," a dim light began to illuminate from the stones and connect with the others and the lines on the cloth started to glow.

The energy moved around the runecasting in the order of the stones as they appeared, and Nitida waited until the light beam completed its path, "this is the constellation of the Gods."

Nitida moved her finger to each stone. Shaz, Riddick, and Merrick had noticed it right away, but the others nodded with the new understanding. The light beam lifted from the casting cloth and a power radiated through Shaz, Serin, Amirra, and Riddick's frame as the same vision, that Nitida had seen, surged through their minds. The room watched with amazement and horror as they didn't understand what was going on, but the crews faces depicted the horrific scenes they were now seeing, and it was unsettling at best. The images faded and the crew gasped for air as they regained their composures.

Nitida sucked in a deep breath and everyone could see how much the casting had taken from her. A movement from the back caught their eye and Inelius moved toward the table. Shaz's heart thumped and fear eased over his awareness. Serin gripped his hand tightly and he looked at her. She gave him her kind smile, but he knew there was more, and his anger heated inside his chest. Inelius gave Nitida a flat square box, and she rested it on the table. She lifted the lid and revealed a gold neck collar that had gems in hues of yellows and oranges interwoven through the gold vine-like threads. A pair of earrings, a ring, and an armlet that matched. She motioned for Amirra to come around the table to her but Amirra shook her head.

Amirra's frame was shaking and the fear and dread paralyzed her. Riddick touched her arm, and she looked at him and shook her head, *No, if this is what I think it is, then no, I can't do it,* Amirra said in her mind. Riddick smiled as he heard her and gripped her hand tightly.

You'll be alright, its time, Riddick said in return.

Shaz and Serin understood exactly what was happening, and they smiled through their own shroud of emotions. Riddick helped Amirra to Nitida who pulled the neck collar out of the box and fastened it around Amirra's neck. She took the earrings and Amirra tried to put them on, but her hands were shaking so much that she just wrapped them in her palm instead and Nitida gave her the armlet and the ring. Riddick helped her put the armlet on, and she slipped the ring onto a finger. She smiled as the ring sized itself to be the best fit for the finger she chose.

"Amirra, this is the Set of Soul, Turkill and Ladtwig have been on mission to gather all the pieces that have been separated as their union holds great power and is for you, and you alone. This will help you connect your magics until you understand it on your own. This will also shield you from your father who became a powerful necromancer in the Velshari and only found out about you after your mother died, they search for you, not to destroy you but to bring you home," Amirra shook her head, she didn't want to hear anymore, "You are now the Runecaster and my time has come to an end here. The universe picked you long before your birth. You are enough and you will become the force you were meant to be," Nitida said.

"No, you can't. I'm not ready to lose you," Amirra said.

"Yes, you are, and I am ready to go, it is time, and I am tired," Nitida said.

Amirra pulled her into a tight embrace and everyone found a knot form in their throats. Amirra's heart leaped with shock and dread as she found the once delicate tattoos of the *Runecaster* were no longer visible on Nitida's aged skin. Riddick's heart skipped as he internalized her emotions. He felt her emotions and *her* sick dread hit the bottom of *his* stomach. The scar on the back of Amirra's neck heated up, and she could feel it sink deep into her soul.

Inelius smiled at Shaz and Serin who embraced him tightly.

"Mathieu did well, I am honored to have been able to know you," Inelius said.

"Good-by dear friend, be at peace," Shaz said.

"I'm going to miss you," Serin managed.

Amirra hugged Inelius but couldn't manage any words through her tight throat and teary eyes. Inelius embraced the rest of everyone and Turkill choked back the forming tears but Ladtwig sobbed into Turkill's shoulder. Jagwynn rubbed against his leg gently, and he rubbed her chin and face.

"Until we meet again my friends," Inelius said.

Inelius took Nitida's hand and a light began to grow around their bodies. The energy formed a sphere around the two and then disappeared quickly and the tent was left dark. Amirra broke down and sobbed into Riddick's chest who found it hard to keep his own emotions under wraps. Riddick led Amirra toward the door and gave Shaz the 'go ahead' look and Shaz cleared his throat. He found it harder than he had expected so Motavo, Asher, Declan, and Bowen all jumped into gear and started discussing the next attack.

Shaz and Serin left to find Riddick and Amirra and took several lengths to allow their emotions to overcome them. Amirra ran her fingers on the earring's nervously and Serin helped her put them on. The set was beautiful and Amirra experienced a calming strength and was able to steady her emotions.

"Let's get this done," Amirra said with a new resolve that had a hint of anger in it.

The crew understood the tone and agreed as they all were of the same opinion.

"Are you good then?" Shaz asked.

"No, but I will be, and I want to hurt something, so it better be a stupid Jaduuk," Amirra said.

"As opposed to a smart one," Riddick teased.

Riddick flashed her his smile, and she blurted a teary ga-fa, and they all chuckled. They returned to the tent to learn the plans and for the most part Shaz agreed with them all. Shaz rehearsed the news from Tissa and organized the scouting party putting Jag and the Minca on the task while they begin another round of attacks. The idea was that if they were distracted with fighting, Jag and the Minca could sneak in.

"I think the plants to make the Elixir of the Undetected are about ready, but I'm not sure how much it will make," Riddick said.

"Then whatever we are able to make will be for the Minca and Jag," Shaz said.

55-This Makes Things A Bit More Interesting

They spent a lot of the day working out new plans for the attacks, how to get the Minca into the mountain pass and the notebook continued to eat at Shaz's mind. He was getting more and more anxious to find out what Alisdair had to say and the inkling he needed a part of the information ate at his being. Serin too kept thinking about the notebook and the image of the white wyvern came to her mind several times throughout the morning. The heat of the day, as much as was possible eased the coolness, and their stomachs began to grumble. They broke for lunch and Shaz held Riddick and Amirra back.

"What's the trouble?" Riddick asked.

"Why do you ask that?" Shaz asked.

"Come on mate, you can't fool me," Riddick said. Shaz knew that, and he did expect it, but he enjoyed giving him a bit of his own torment from time to time. Shaz pulled out the notebook. "Is that the book from the dungeon?" Riddick asked.

"Aye," Shaz said.

Shaz repeated the ancient words to de-crypt the shadow charm and opened the front cover. The pages flipped on their own and Amirra jumped with the start. The words organized off the pages and hovered in front of them.

Shazmpt son of the Tooatha De Dannon, and Serin daughter of the Lavari, I have waited many long rotations to speak to you again, for I saw you both in the begging and will see you again at the end.

The glyphs illuminated as the voice of the author sounded in their minds.

Riddick son of the Bair Tiornecht and Amirra daughter of the Fir Bolg, I am pleased to meet you. You come from the most noble of lineage, but it comes with a price I wish you did not have to pay. This is the history of my people, the Tooatha De Dannon, Lavari, Bair Tiornecht, and the Fir Bolg, the real history, not what you have learned. I see the Runecaster has shared with you our history, so I will spare that for now.

Your battle in the Timeless Plains is only the beginning as you are soon to meet the real force which plagues this world. I and my sister Malita, the mother of the Lavari and brother Todan, father of the Bair, were unable to defeat our brother Baltair, father of the Fir, who has chosen to serve the Shadow, but worse, for he is already a God and with his immortality, he has taken on the form of the Jaduuk'ai and forged an eternal alliance with the Shadow. Evil is his only course as he detests me the most, for I am who he blames for his being rejected by our father. You must keep the Sev-Rin-Ac-Lavah out of his possession, for if he even has one of the artifacts he will have enough power to destroy this planet, not only the inhabitants, but the planet itself. Not only the Sev-Rin-Ac-Lavah, but there is yet another arti-fact that you must secure.

The Astronomers Armillary ring holds the secrets of the universe, the Cordelia Tari Nebula, all of her galaxies, and the cosmic powers that dictate their existence. This is the missing part I did not understand and in order to banish a God into outer-darkness, one must understand where outer-darkness is. The ring was last known to be held by the astronomer Leonid in the Room of Thrones. Descendants, make haste and be steady in your purpose, I will come again, but for now, unite in strength.

The words disappeared and the four stood with wide eyes and a new weight on their shoulders. The clanging of weapons and armor sounded in the distance as the armies were getting ready to deploy once again. No one wanted to be the one to break the austere silence from what they had just heard but Shaz cleared his throat. He closed the book and placed the charm back on the book and tucked it into his jerkin.

"I guess this makes things a bit more interesting," Riddick said.

"As soon as we check one thing off our to-do list, we find another one," Shaz said with a heaviness in his words. Serin and Amirra nodded but had no words. "Come on, let's get inside that mountain," Shaz said.

The four dispersed quietly to make their last-minute checks and still deep in thought of the implications now looming over their heads. Merrick studied Shaz and recognized his expression as the one he used when he was running through his system of battle tactics and outcomes. Merrick understood the best, that Shaz needed time to work things out on his own, and he was always fascinated with what he came up with. Shaz had such passion for the details and ran through them until he understood them. Shaz kept getting the feeling he was being watched, and he examined the surroundings with his magic as he heaved a large box of ammunition and shoved it onto the back of a cart tied to an elephantine. His magic reported it was Merrick and Shaz sighed. He shook his head and dispelled the thoughts someone or something else was 'watching' him, which was a sure way to creep oneself out. Shaz stepped over a smaller box and found Merrick trying to look busy.

"Father, I can tell you're worried, what is it?" Shaz said.

"Are you alright?" Merrick asked.

"Aye, why?" Shaz asked.

"I'm your father, I've been watching you since you were in nappy's. I know when your working things through, but you have more, well that's the part I don't have a clue. Sadly, I don't see what you do or hear what you do, and that leaves me at a disadvantage," Merrick said.

"Come with me," Shaz said.

Merrick put the sack of supplies next to a tent and followed Shaz away from the camp. When Shaz was confident they were far enough away he stopped, took out the notebook and handed it to Merrick. Merrick took the book and turned it over and looked at Shaz with a questioning eye.

"What's this?" Merrick asked.

"It's a book written by Alisdair, the God of the Tooatha De Dannon, it has the entire history of my people. It contains the events which led up to and after the destruction of my people. I haven't been able to read it all, it's written in the language of the wyverns, which Serin actually knows how to read. Anyway, this is just the beginning and Gavin Rhill is nowhere close to being the worst thing we have to worry about. The histories the Dodjen have are only the recent ones, and it doesn't include any of this. I have been instructed to find the Room of Thrones and secure the Astronomer's ring," Shaz said.

Merrick listened with intensity. He too was excellent with the details, but he found he had nothing to offer.

"Do you know where this Room of Thrones is?" Merrick asked.

Shaz shook his head.

"It might tell me in the book, but I haven't had a chance to read it all yet, I'm still trying to process everything from the casting, and I have to get these Jaduuk under control. Baltair, the God of the Fir, is the Jaduuk'ai, which means defeating him isn't going to happen this time. That's what I am trying to figure out. How to end this war with the Jaduuk and secure this realm for the Forrne, because I am certain Baltair isn't going to go away anytime soon. If anything, he'll retreat like a coward until he finds a new way to destroy me," Shaz said.

"Why you?" Merrick asked.

"I am the only Tooatha De left, and he swore in his wrath to destroy every single Tooatha De," Shaz said.

"Maybe he won't," Merrick said in a dreaded tone disguised in fake hope.

"Revenge doesn't work like that, at least not to the Shadow. Swearing revenge is a binding contract he can't be released from, even being a God doesn't keep him from the powers of evil, it's either him or me," Shaz said.

Merrick internalized his words and acknowledged his sons maturity since the last time he spoke to him at length.

"So, what is your plan then?" Merrick asked.

"Get the Minca in the mountain and find the Jaduuk'ai," Shaz said.

"What will that do?" Merrick asked.

"I believe there is a mountain temple there which is why Baltair is able to access this realm, and any mountain temple for that matter, and I need to close the access," Shaz said.

Shaz was assured the Minca realm was safe and the Ebassian's as he just closed that one too, but there's still many more. His stomach churned as he thought of Turob and his hands burned hot. Merrick gazed with eager eyes as he noted Shaz's fire element come to the surface. Even though he had seen Shaz fight with fire and magic, it was still an awesome thing to behold, and he realized there was so much about his son he had no idea about.

"As well as I know you, I don't actually know you, son," Merrick said.

Shaz turned with a surprised glance and realized his hands were still glowing red-hot. He squelched the heat and the exhausted steam dissipated into the atmosphere.

"Oh, I'm the same obnoxious, irritating, and snarky kid you've always known, just ask Serin, just now I play with fire instead of dirt," Shaz said with sassy eyes.

Merrick boomed a hearty ga-fa and pulled Shaz into a tight grip. That was one thing Shaz missed, getting the big squeezes from a man that could squish him like a bug. A peace radiated around Shaz, and he was thankful for the man who taught him how to be.

"Come on, let's go kill some Jaduuk," Merrick said.

Shaz chuckled and they began discussing the impending details. They found Jag who was quietly stalking the boxes of ammo as if she were lecturing them on how to behave. Shaz ran his hand along her head and down her back, and she raised into his touch. With everything going on they hadn't spent as much time together and Shaz had a bit of homesickness hit his heart. Jagwynn purred and rubbed against him, and she licked his hand. It was an interesting thing to undergo the transformation he had. The complexity of his magical nature and his human nature, then you add all the people in his life on top of that, plus the bond he had with Serin which then gave him all of her nature to include into his. He mused that he hadn't gone mad yet, then shoved the thought out of his mind as he feared that was a possibility, and he didn't think Serin could heal a mad mind.

"Shaz, are you ready?" Shaz looked up and into Serin's gentle eyes. "The Minca are ready," Serin said.

Serin hadn't been listening to his feelings as she was preoccupied with the details of the rainstorm near the food tents which was getting a little out of control, and she had to have a stern talk with the energies. She had learned the cloud wouldn't let anyone get close enough to draw water and would shoot little sprigs of lightning to keep anyone away. She found it both comical and irritating, but she understood how unpredictable lightning was, and she remembered when Riddick spanked the earth like a little child, which she found was exactly the same thing she had to do.

"Of course," Shaz said.

Shaz didn't want to admit he didn't have the faintest idea what he was 'ready' for, but Jagwynn let him up, and he followed Serin.

"You don't have a clue where we are going do you?" Serin teased.

"Yes, I do," Shaz said, but he did understand she knew better, and he shook his head. "No, what are we doing?"

Serin smiled.

"We're helping Riddick and Amirra finish the Elixir of the Undetected," Serin said.

Shaz nodded with the understanding of where they were in the planning, but his mind was still far away. Serin squeezed his hand, and they walked hand in hand to the healer's tents. Riddick was carefully lifting the delicate plant from the pot it had been in and his movements were slow. Shaz wondered what was so sensitive about the large bulb at the bottom of the green fern-like leaves at the top. Riddick set the round bulb on the table and stood back and exhaled the breath he was holding. Riddick turned and waved Shaz and Serin to come in, and they made their way to the table.

"Shhhh," Riddick said.

"Why?" Shaz asked in a whisper.

"You haven't charmed the root yet, and I'm not about to be sucked into a void of nothingness," Riddick whispered back.

"I have to charm it?" Shaz asked.

Amirra gave him the notes from when they decrypted the recipe and Shaz scanned the marks.

"Teo latta chi chada'rrha, machina, noah la tenta. No, me 'tay tarren menin," Shaz said.

The root shriveled into a dried version of its former shape and the fern leaves withered and fell into dust.

"That should to it," Riddick said.

"Oh, and one more thing," Amirra said.

Amirra held out a set of stones and gave him the notes again, and he enchanted the stones with the needed magic. Amirra took the stones and set one on the table and sliced a wedge of the root and began to grind it into powder. The powder glimmered a soft sparkle as it was infused with the magical components. Riddick prepared the other ingredients, then carefully added them in order and swirled them around a medium-sized bowl. Amirra scooped the powder in her hand and dumped it into the bowl and continued to grind the rest of the root. It took several lengths to finish all of the grinding and each time she poured more of the powder the concoction deepened in color and thickness. The room was silent as no one dared speak until the mixture was complete and Amirra poured the contents into several palm-sized jars that Riddick enchanted to be quite strong.

"There, all done," Amirra said.

Amirra handed one to each person and put the rest in her pocket, so she could give them to the Minca.

56-We Need To Get To The Ground Now

Turkill took the bottle, opened the stopper, and the thick potion oozed into his mouth. His lips peeled back as the strong odor hit his nose a second before the taste buds reflected the sentiment. He swallowed hard before his mouth decided to try to chew the goobery stuff. Ladtwig tipped his jar into his mouth and swallowed quickly but the major rankness bit at his being, and he shivered.

"This is the most horrific thing I have ever had to endure," Turkill said.

"Oh, come on, it's not that bad," Riddick said.

Turkill's dark-bronzed skin turned a shade of green and his usual hurmpf scowl was replace with an expression of panic, almost terror. The one that says, 'I think I'm going to hurl' and Riddick's brows hit the top of his hairline.

"Maybe we should have added the sweet root after all," Riddick said.

Turkill gave him the 'are you kidding' look and slammed his fist into his chest to keep himself from spewing. Ladtwig sat down and ran his hands over his now sweaty face. Jagwynn let a deep growl escape and Riddick took a step behind Shaz who gave him a 'don't bring me into this' look.

"You're going to have to take it Jag," Riddick said still standing behind Shaz.

"Before or after I eat you," Jagwynn said with her grumbling purr.

Riddick's hands instantly went clammy, and he gave the bottle to Shaz to deal with her. Shaz chuckled and ran his hand along the scruff of her neck.

"You can eat him later," Shaz said.

Jagwynn licked his face, and he put his forehead on hers. The connection was the same as when they met as younglings, and they relished in the old memories. Jagwynn lifted her immense head and stuck out her gritty tongue. Shaz poured the goop into her mouth, and she swallowed the tincture. Jagwynn's face drained of color, as if a black as night jaguar could, and she hissed. Riddick stepped back again and Serin came around the corner. Serin internalized their distress and sent a round of soothing energy into their beings. They all sagged with the relief and Jag rubbed up against her.

"Is everyone ready," Serin asked.

"So, how does this work?" Ladtwig asked.

Ladtwig screeched as he watched his skin fade in and out of the mirage-like effects of his surroundings. Turkill examined his hands and found they too were changing to become a reflection.

"That's very cleaver," Turkill said with new excitement.

"Alright, we'll take you as far as the Hollow, then you're on your own. Remember, get in and find out what you can, but you only have a few days' time, or less," Shaz said.

"Who do you think you are talking to," Turkill barked.

Shaz smiled, it was exactly what he figured he would say, and he liked it. Jagwynn lowered and the Minca climbed onto her back. With their new disguise it was nearly impossible to see them as she took her long powerful strides. Turkill laid closely to Jag's neck and Ladtwig leaned closely to Turkill. Jagwynn slowed her pace as she came to the edge of the first Jaduuk settlement. The grass under her paws was dry and hard, and she cringed as she tried to navigate quietly. It didn't take long for a Jaduuk to hear the noise and it's ears twitched. The Jaduuk's beefy head turned slowly as it interpreted the sound and Jag slowed to a stop, mid-step. She scanned the surroundings and eyed the beasts looking in her direction.

Her heart skipped a beat, and she held her breath, as did the Minca. The Jaduuk finished its inspection and went back to polishing the bone it was eating from. Jag took another step and estimated how many more there would be until she reached the next patch of black earth. She lunged toward the scorched dirt and with a few long strides was back onto the soft quiet surface. The Jaduuk searched again, but they were now out of earshot. Jagwynn made her way quickly through the blackness and was thankful that they all blended in. The Minca with their dark skin, and she herself was black as night.

The rest of the travel went smoothly as there was a significant amount of the black veins that lead directly to the mountain path. The ridge of the jagged peaks that protruded from the hardened rock came into view as they crept over the ridge. Turkill pointed to Ladtwig that they should move along the edge on the far side, he nodded and Turkill explained his thoughts to Jag, who agreed. It wasn't a path exactly, but she could navigate the terrain easy enough and it would leave them on higher ground. Turkill took out his dart-gun and gripped it between his teeth. Ladtwig pulled his, and they hunkered low to Jag as she leaped onto the first protrusion.

The Minca's guts tightened as they neared the rounded bowl-like structure that they weren't sure if it had been creature made or was the remains of a long-ago lake. Turkill took in as much of the details as he found while they stalked the ridge. Jagwynn examined her exit strategy and made her heading. The valley was covered in the massive beasts and the Minca wondered if there was even enough room to move around. The sun was out but the dimness of the atmosphere left a shadow over the landscape, which was also a plus. Jagwynn slowed and lowered to the ground quickly. The Minca slowed their breathing and tried to keep their hearts from beating out of their chests.

Long shadow's crept across the path as a Jaduuk Captain strode with heavy steps toward the opening. The mountain's cave entrance was tucked between two enormous slabs of black rock and the warmth that surged from the depths left the atmosphere with a hint of irritation. The bowl-like formation made for the perfect training area for the new Jaduuk Captains, and the Minca eyed the new contraptions and weapons, like their own, and swallowed hard.

"Jaduuk'ai, our forces are growing, but we have a new problem," the Captain said.

"What is it?" Jaduuk'ai said.

The Minca's dark skin faded of color as they tried to assimilate the extremely humongous Jaduuk thing. It was most definitely a Jaduuk, but it also had the likeness of a human in some of the features of the face and torso.

"I got reports that the blood of the Lavari was detected," the Captain said.

"Blood of the Lavari? Where?" the monstrosity asked.

"In the place the locals call the Hollow, after we took the prisoner," the Captain said.

"Why did you take a prisoner?" Jaduuk'ai asked.

"We were hoping to lure the armies to us, but we were ambushed instead, and the prisoner escaped," the Captain said.

****

The armies were nearing their places of attacks and it wouldn't be long before the next show began. The first theater was organized much the same as the last one, but this time they were attacking in the Hollow instead of the ravine, and the second theater was in the savanna again. They had made quite the impact on their last attack and gained a great deal of ground, so they divided the second theater into two and added a third.

The Jaduuk's settlements were organized in a circular fashion which would make surrounding them a bit harder if they wanted to keep their strongholds. They devised a plan to strike down the center and divide the groups into halves with two companies on each side. The trebuchets kept their distance, but as the Jaduuk were divided, the catapults moved down the center to aid in the attacks at the back. The cannons were also moved about with smaller groupings on each side and down the middle. The Forrne Guard was organized into smaller troops and stationed with each battalion. They aided in the mid-level attacks and used the cannons as protection.

Shaz took lead with Bowen in the first theater, and Riddick headed out with Declan who was commanding the second theater. Serin took flight with Brigdon hoping that she could have a birds-eye view of the wounded. They found a section of sky that she was able to stay in and see both operations. It wasn't as ideal as she had hoped, but she was able to reserve most of her strength for healing, which she found she did more of this time. Amirra went with Merrick to the third theater.

****

The wind was strong and the gryphton's had a hard time flying against the force. Phanes signaled for the flight on the left to round and drop their powder and began to bank towards the other side. An up-draft snagged his wing, and he allowed it to spin him into a twist and leveled off as he snagged another and lifted higher. The air was colder the higher he went, which was actually a nice reprieve, and he scanned the distance. He found a large horde and signaled for his last flight to drop their powder. He fell into the formation as the gryphton's descended in a spiraling movement and each lion-bird opened their pouches and let the granules fall over the Jaduuk.

It was a calculated effort as they had to judge the wind speed and direction to get the best coverage and make note so the Minca would be able to launch their trebuchet's with the fire to light it up. The flights stayed high enough to stay out of direct vision of the Jaduuk, but they didn't actually know how far the beasts could see with their eyes. They used their nose most often which was a nice advantage for the gryphtons. Phanes caught a glimpse of an odd formation at the edge of the Jaduuk camp. He signaled for the flights to return, and he banked to one side. He made his way closer, but the details were still too blurry, and he dropped several lengths.

His heart jumped as he realized it was a kind of catapult of their own and had a sizable spear that rested in the sling. He began to twist but not before the catapult was released. The spear shot through the sky with fierce speed and Phanes didn't see it hit his chest before he felt the instant pain. His body immediately fell numb and his breath ripped from his lungs. His mind faded in and out and all he could see was the top of the sky and the clouds fall from his vision as he plummeted to the earth.

Serin's stomach churned, and she turned to see Phanes' body surging to the ground. She shouted with instant panic and ripped the wind around his falling frame. The wind instantly obeyed and carried him at a fast rate toward her.

"Get to the ground now!" Serin called.

Brigdon obeyed and Serin gripped his copper feathers as his body turned to a headfirst dead-fall. He opened his wings a second before hitting the ground and threw his legs out to snag the ground and ran through the motion until he reached Phanes. Serin leaped off his large body and darted to the crumpled figure. Serin tried to keep her heartfire in check but her eyes teared anyway. She started to exam his body before she even reached him, and she barely detected a heartbeat. Pure raw magic surged from her core and Shaz acknowledged the disturbance, gripped an earth-board, and shot toward her. Riddick and Amirra too felt the energy shift and raced toward Serin.

Serin blasted Phanes' armor off his fading chest and gripped the water in the air. A small raincloud popped into existence and started to drizzle its contents onto the spear that was protruding from his chest. An image entered Serin's mind, and she knew that she wasn't going to be able to heal his heart unless she removed the spear, but she couldn't do it here and would need more than magic at this point. Shaz shoved the earth-board to a halt and hopped off and hurried the last length to Serin.

"We need to get him to the tents as fast as possible, I don't know if I'm going to be able to heal him," Serin's voice choked on the lump in her throat and Riddick gripped the earth Phanes and Serin were on and blasted it with a hefty dose of energy. The ground shot across the surface, and they raced back to camp. Shaz hurried in front and hollered for everyone to make room and Leeta came out from one of the tents. They didn't know that she was coming and wondered what was wrong.

Her guts churned as she internalized what her eyes were seeing, and the tears escaped at a sudden force. She lunged into a dead run, but Shar launched toward her. Shar lifted off the ground and caught Leeta in the air as she was going to fly over her. She gripped her tightly and they tumbled to the ground.

"Leeta, let her do her thing, there is nothing you can do right now," Shar said.

Leeta squirmed and put up a good struggle before the energy left her being, and she sagged into the ground. The earth moved into place and the Minca women hurried over. They were excellent now at helping Serin, after all of the healing they had done during the first Jaduuk war, and Serin barely had to tell them what to do. Fionte pulled several cloths from the bin and Babbesh grabbed the small blade and implements that Serin had come up with to teach the ladies how to sew wounds properly as she was unable to be there all the time.

****

Jagwynn stayed low to the ground but moved the last few lengths until she was near enough to the entrance that she could leap over the drainage ditch of the green ooze. The acrid odor left a metallic taste in their mouths as they tried to keep their breathing silent. The Captain moved away from the entrance as the enormous behemoth of a Jaduuk man crawled out. Jagwynn waited another half-second and then leaped across the ditch and into the Jaduuk'ai's lair. They shot into the darkness and toward the small flame several lengths into the cavern. It was just large enough for the Jaduuk'ai to crawl through, and they wondered where the creature lived. Jagwynn kept to the right side of the cave wall as the first corridor broke off the main trunk.

The hallways were rough but there was a human aspect to their construction. The hall ended with a bright green light emanated from the opening. Jagwynn slowly crept to the edge of the room, and they examined the contents. In the center was a large egg surrounded by the lava pools and the vein-like tubes that secured the egg to the ground. They got the impression by the shimmering heartbeats inside and the pulsing of the veins that the egg was feeding the entities inside with the nutrients coming from the lava. Jagwynn made a quick sweep around the room and then returned the way they came. At the return to the main trunk of passageways, they continued on their 'keeping to the right' method and inspected the lair.

****

Babbesh set fresh cloths onto a table and Serin gripped the blade as Fionte wrapped the cloth around the spear. The raincloud drizzled its contents, and the fibers infused the magic into the surrounding skin as well as absorbed the blood now seeping from around the wood shaft. Shaz watched with wonder and awe as Serin took the blade and cut the skin deep. Fionte consistently wiped the blood and wrapped more cloth as Babbesh handed them to her. Serin made another cut into the skin and when she reached the rib cage she took her clenched fist and hit the sternum hard and fast. A pop echoed off the cavity of his chest and two rib bones lifted off the center bone.

Serin reached into the cavity and searched around the tip of the spear and determined it was lodged deep.

"Shaz I need your help," Serin said. Shaz gulped but hurried to the side of the massive lion-eagle and stood ready, for what, he had no idea. "When I say, you have to pull this out as hard and fast as you can," Serin said. Shaz nodded and Serin took another swipe around the spear tip with her fingers and Shaz gripped the shaft. It was larger than the average spear, and he was both impressed and terrified. "Now," Serin said.

Shaz yanked with all his might. A ripping sound lodged into their brains as the spear released its hold and was followed by a sucking sound. Serin immediately launched her full magic into the opening throwing every bit of energy she had at the sewing and mending of the intricate details of his human heart. The blue magic raced around as her hands instructed it. Fionte kept wiping and dabbing the wound and the rain kept it washed and clean. Babbesh brought more cloth and helped Fionte with the compresses. They eagerly applied Mrs. Bailey's pain relief ointment around the wound and over his bare skin to help keep him as comfortable as possible.

Shaz stepped back and let the women work and was so impressed at how focused and speedy they were. Shaz could hear Leeta's soft sobs from outside the tent and Amirra and Shar trying to comfort her. Riddick was barking orders to investigate the new spear launcher and re-fit their own with more ammunition. He organized a hunting party to go after the horde responsible for this and Shaz eased into the comfort of his capable crew. Fionte dabbed the sweat that dripped from Serin's brows as the heat of her energy radiated around them. Phanes' heart started to take shape again and the dark red seeped into the new vascular tissues that were growing at an impeccable rate.

The heart was soon in full shape and Serin started working on the surrounding tissues. The blood began to ease as the vessels mended shut, and she was ready to start the heart back up.

"Stand back," Serin said.

Serin gripped her hydro-light magic and focused it into her finger. The energy sizzled and popped off the tip, and she zapped the heart with three quick bursts. The organ jumped in its place but didn't start beating on its own. Serin repeated the process which took three tries, but the heart finally began to beat on its own. Phanes gasped and his lungs filled with air as his reflexes initiated its life mode. Serin listened carefully but noticed there was fluid in his lungs.

"There's blood in his lungs, I need to look to find it," Serin said.

Fionte removed the old cloth and added more but slipped out of the way as Serin moved closer to the lung. She ran her hand over the breathing lung with her magic and found the hole and sent her magic stitches. The lung filled with more air and Serin nodded with acceptance. Shaz stunned, was still holding the spear as Serin began to stitch up the incision. Shaz remembered back to the forest when she stitched him up for the first time and understood that was nothing compared to this and his heart swelled.

Several lengths later Serin smoothed out the top skin and took extra care to leave as little scar as possible. She learned that she couldn't keep every scar from disappearing as it depended on how deep the wound was in the first place. She ran through her detailed exam and found his body was in full repair. Fionte reached onto her tiptoes and dabbed the sweat from Serin's brow again and Serin smiled.

"He's going to be alright, but he lost a lot of blood and will take time to make more," Serin declared taking in a deep breath.

Screeches and roars sounded from outside as the last flight to leave expressed their salute to their leader. The sound was deafening but also magnificent. Shaz shoved the spear under the cot behind him and then let Leeta into the tent. She hurried to his side and started to cry tears of relief.

"He's going to need to sleep for a while," Serin said patting her shoulder and nodded to the Minca, and they started to clean up the soiled cloth.

"I don't know what to say, that was simply the most remarkable thing I have ever seen. How did you know how to do all that?" Shaz asked.

Serin smiled but her knees wobbled and Shaz steadied her.

"I really don't know myself, it's like you I guess, and it comes to me when I need it," Serin said.

"I'm sure you're exhausted, let me help you to the tent," Shaz said.

Shaz pulled the flap open and the Armada of gryphton's, that had yet to be deployed, stood at immaculate attention with full salutes. Serin looked around at the awe-inspiring features and blushed. She was just doing what she would do for anyone, but it was clear they felt differently. Shaz led her into the crowd, and they parted and bowed reverently as she passed. She smiled and nodded at them as they made eye contact with her, and she could see how much devotion they held for their leader.

A distant rumble echoed as the Minca's catapults launched their fireballs. It would only be a few tiny lengths before the explosive granules would ignite setting the Jaduuk ablaze. Sparks of shooting funnels from the explosives lit up the distance and the horizon was now dancing in reds and oranges mixed with gaps of dark black smoke.

"Riddick sure knows how to throw a party," Shaz said.

The flashes of the hand canons, now carried by the Ebassian's, flickered against the fading light and howls and cries encompassed the distance. Cluck shouted deployment commands and the reverent soldiers leaped into the sky. They shot into the distance with their slings and ballista's that had been fashioned for their size. It was one of the favorite weapons and it had become part of the regular weaponry for every unit, troop, and flight. Finlo had become the expert ballista maker and had earned the respect from the entirety of the three armies. Shaz lifted the flap and Serin crossed the threshold as a troop of Forrne thudded behind them.

"I'm surprised everyone has taken this so personally," Serin said.

"I'm not. We've been lucky so far that we haven't lost any men yet and this is a bit of a wake-up call, 'you mess with our leader, you mess with us all," Shaz said.

"I know, but, I guess you're right," Serin said.

"I have a feeling this attack will go on for a few days. Maybe it was a good thing, we might be able to gain some more ground and get closer to getting the rest of those spawners," Shaz said.

"That would be nice," Serin said through a big yawn.

Shaz pulled the covers down, and she slipped inside, and he kissed her.

"I'm going to kill me some Jaduuk, I'll be back," Shaz said.

Serin barely managed a muffled agreement before she was out.

****

Jag stopped as the ground rumbled. She scurried up against the wall and the cold bit at her fur. She shivered as the tingle of shadow magic ticked her skin. Turkill and Ladtwig too tried to keep away from the sting of the magic but also keep to the protection the wall offered. They determined the battle had begun in which they weren't sure if the Jaduuk'ai would return to the caves or stay in the valley giving orders. A second kind of rumble crossed their minds, and they determined it was coming back inside.

Jagwynn hurried to another corridor and slunk as far into the darkness as was possible. There were no green lights at the end of this corridor to indicate they should investigate but Jag found a tickle at the back of her mind, and she moved backward at a slow and steady pace. Turkill wanted to chide her, but he stuck his foot into her side instead in which she nipped at his leg. Turkill clicked his tongue at her but decided not to push it. The corridor opened into another room and Jagwynn sniffed around. There was absolutely no light, but Jag's nose gave her a rough image of what it was, and she determined it was a lodging for a human at one point.

"Use your flick-stick," Jagwynn purred quietly.

Ladtwig fumbled in his pouch for a second and found his flick-stick. He struck the end on the plate and a flame flickered. He repeated the process a few times, each time quickly searching for a torch or anything to hold a small flame. A torch on the floor near the opening was spotted and Ladtwig hopped down and fumbled his way to the stick. He lit the torch and Turkill slipped off her back. She was right, it was a living quarters for a human at one point. Jagwynn sniffed the items and the Minca investigated quickly. The rumbles in the distance were soft but steady and there was a kind of comfort in it.

"Take these books," Jagwynn said.

The Minca quickly shoved the books from the shelf into their packs and were about to climb back onto her back when Turkill spotted the time-ticker. He scurried across the room and shoved it into his pack but stopped as a breath of stinky animal breath crossed his nose. Jaduuk'ai peered into the room and inspected the odd flame sitting in a holder at the side of his table. Ladtwig's face was getting red with the breath he was holding and Jagwynn was crouched low to the ground partially under the table. Turkill cursed to himself as sweat dripped down the side of his face. His long black hair was braided into tiny rows of intricate details that were grouped together at the back of his head, and he wondered if he was about to become Jaduuk'ai food.

Jaduuk'ai squeezed into the room and Ladtwig scooched against the wall and slunk to the ground. Their small frames made it easier to find hiding places as the Jaduuk'ai sniffed but found no scent of anything. He tried again coming within a few tiny lengths from the top of Ladtwig's head and Turkill was certain he was about to swallow him up. Ladtwig's shorter hair was also braided into rows of braids, but they weren't quite long enough to pull back like Turkill's, and was a little poufy at the back. Ladtwig didn't want to move, but he was certain his hair was about to make the beast sneeze which would alert his whereabouts for sure.

Turkill spied a pebble near his toe, and he slowly moved his foot until he could kick it down the corridor. The rock shot under the beasts legs and Jaduuk'ai turned and darted away. They let out their breaths and Turkill raced back to Jag and Ladtwig.

57-I Have An Idea

The blasts continued into the late afternoon and Shaz signaled for the troops to switch positions. The new and fresh troops came into the battle as the tired troops retreated back to camp. They had arranged three sets for each theater. The food, healers, and cleanup crews were also set into shifts and Motavo and Asher kept a tight schedule. The warriors returned to camp and ate and quickly found sleep as to be ready for their next shift. The day turned to night and back into day and Shaz was getting nervous since he hadn't heard any news from the Minca.

To make things worse, things only marginally improved as Shaz tried to focus on a way to let out the shadow magic he was gaining each time they fought the Jaduuk. He was nearly resigned to giving up his armor and having Amirra enchant something else. Shaz was so angry that he couldn't see straight and Serin was shocked at his sudden burst of rage. She sent a burst of calming energy which he shot back at her. She stomped her foot and gritted her teeth. She was certain the shadow magic was becoming unstable within him, but she had no idea what to do about it.

"What is wrong with you?" Serin demanded.

"Nothing, leave me alone," Shaz demanded back.

"Are you serious," Serin said.

Shaz glared at her with a fierce eye and for the first time Serin was truly scared. She had no idea what the matter was and Shaz was not acting like himself at all.

"You are so stubborn," Shaz said through gritted teeth.

"Just stubborn enough to put up with you," Serin called as Shaz started to storm off.

Serin sulked as the flicker of flames emanated from his body, and he ignited a stack of wood and she was certain she had to do something. Serin started to call the water element but a hot flame emerged from his body and shot a fire ball at her. Serin gripped the ball of flames and wrapped it in an air bubble which sucked the air from the flames, and the ball fizzled away. Her own rage surface, and she gripped her water magic and blew out an icy breath. The freezing cold wind encompassed the water and a billowing blizzard surrounded Shaz's entire body. The blizzard fizzled to the ground leaving a patch of white powdery snow and Serin examined Shaz's energy. Shaz was shocked out of his rage with the instant chill that encompassed his entire body and his mind raced to find a reason. He quickly figured out he couldn't move, and he was entombed in a block of ice.

"I don't think you need to worry about her, she certainly knows how to handle him," Merrick said in a near booming laughter.

"So, it would it seem," Motavo said.

"She is so much like her mother," Asher said.

Shaz heated his inner core, and the ice began to melt at a rapid rate. Shaz turned as the last bit of ice fell off his legs to find Serin with her hip cocked to one side, her arms across her chest, her thin brows scrunched in the center of her fierce green eyes and her lips puckered tightly in the center. Shaz shook his now drenched hair from his face and amused at the steam radiate from his being. Shaz realized the entire, and he wasn't kidding, the entire army was staring at them. Shaz flashed his dashing smile hoping it would, in part, get him out of whatever mess he had gotten himself into. Serin shook her head giving him that 'don't you dare,' look, and he quickly made his way to her. Serin determined he was now diffused of the built-up energy, but she was still non the less irritated at best.

"You entombed me in a block of ice, which is crazy sexy by the way," Shaz said.

"Are you serious?" Serin asked.

Serin peered into his blue eyes and found he really was sorry, and his behavior was a result of the shadow magic. She even understood he didn't actually know what had happened.

"I'm sorry, I don't know how to control all this raw energy," Shaz said.

"You threw a fire ball at me," Serin said.

Shaz's eyes filled with understanding and his heart raced into 'oh crap' mode.

"And, I will never live that down, that's for sure," Shaz said.

Serin snorted but then pushed away.

"The entire camp is staring at us," Serin said.

"Aye, I'm in big trouble aren't I?" Shaz said.

"Well, kind of, we certainly need to figure out what to do," Serin said.

Riddick and Amirra came from around the tent and hesitated and the armies peeled their eyes from the spectacle and returned to their business. It was quite the sight to witness steam radiate off the top of someone's actual head, let alone their whole body. Riddick smirked but a pit in his stomach told him there was something wrong. He didn't want to intrude because if Shaz and Serin were at odds for some reason, which they rarely were, he didn't want to be *that* friend.

"Oh, there you are, I was just looking for you," Riddick said.

Amirra shook her head and rolled her eyes. Riddick figured he might be able to gain some intel without being obvious. Serin looked at Riddick and an instant panic surged through his frame as he was suddenly afraid Serin could 'read' in intentions, and he swallowed hard. Serin gave him a 'yes I can read you' look, and he gave up, but she realized he didn't know what was going on, so they needed to fill him in. Riddick shuddered with the tingle that was definitely radiating from his being.

"Shaz's armor takes shadow magic from the Jaduuk when he fights them, instead of like the rest of us which only takes their health. He absorbs the shadow magic and after a while he is so charged up he nearly explodes, literally. We've been trying a few different things, but nothing seems to help," Serin said.

"Wow, I had no idea. How can I help?" Riddick asked.

"We've tried to meditate, burn things, and going real fast on the earth-turfs. It's as though there is a different kind of energy to it. Almost like the tingle you feel before lightning strikes," Serin said.

"Maybe that's what it is then," Amirra said.

Serin's brows scrunched, and she cocked her head to one side, but it did make sense. Lightning was the kind of force that built up and then releases, at least that's how the mini-rain storm acts when she calls it.

"Maybe all this raw energy is accessing your lightning magic, and letting it out with your fire isn't going to work," Serin said.

Shaz's face scrunched through the notion and settled on a comfortable acceptance.

"Alright, so what do you suggest," Shaz asked.

"Instead of trying to keep it under control, channel it the way a lightning bolt would," Serin said with a shrug.

"I'm all over the place, I can't even think there's so much noise in my head," Shaz said.

"I have an idea, come on mate," Riddick said.

"Where?" Shaz asked.

"Just come on," Riddick said and motioned for him to follow.

Shaz sucked in a deep breath and followed Riddick. He wasn't sure what he was going to make him do, but he needed something to help him figure out the chaos in his mind. The heavy shame from the fact he shot a fire ball at Serin, ate at his awareness. Riddick walked a good distance away and then put his hands on the ground and asked the earth to move the stickery weeds and grasses. The weeds dried up and sucked into the ground.

"What are you doing?" Shaz asked.

"Take off your shoes," Riddick said.

"Why?" Shaz asked.

"Because I told you to, and I *am* bigger than you," Riddick started to unlace his boots and Shaz stared at him, "Do it," Riddick said.

Riddick stood up tall and kicked his boots off, Shaz now had an idea what he was going to do. Shaz smiled a sly but thankful grin, but it was also mixed with a dread he didn't expect. Shaz unlaced his boots and Riddick pulled his tunic over his head and tossed it on his slumped-over boots. Shaz pulled his tunic off and tossed it on his and Riddick wriggled his toes into the now soft dirt. Riddick stepped into the clearing and Shaz moved to the other side.

Riddick put his hands together over his head and brought them down in front of his chest and bowed his head. Shaz mimicked the bow with his own and pulled in a deep breath. Riddick took a long step to the side in a slow and calculated movement to show Shaz which Kata he was going to do. Shaz followed and they moved together in near perfection through the relaxation Kata that Grandfather had taught them.

The movements were so natural neither of them had to think about it, their muscular and trim bodies just did it. They pulled in deep cleansing breaths and slowly, but deliberately maneuvered from hand strikes to kicks, back to strikes and blocks. The fading sun behind them left a soothing caress against the soft sky as Serin and Amirra amazed at how elegantly powerful the dance-like movements were. Serin found herself even more attracted to him but a sadness for *her* father crept in. He had taught her similar Kata's but now she couldn't help feeling he was gone forever.

Shaz and Riddick finished the first Kata and moved into the second one and again the movements were strong and powerful, exact, and deliberate. Serin watched Shaz's body move but what she felt was his pain inside. His memories raced from when he was small and his father and Grandfather were so excited when he mastered the first Kata, to the many hours learning them all and doing them with Grandfather, father, and Riddick. Shaz's heart swelled as he now saw Riddick as his brother and not just his best mate. When he would find Grandfather in the middle of the forest going through the Kata's and how elegant he was. How strong and powerful his body moved.

The gentle glint he always had in his eye and his kind scowl and stern look. Shaz always knew he was as soft as they came, but he respected every single thing Grandfather stood for. His heart swelled with a kind of thankful grief he had never known, and Serin could see the tears streaming down his face as he executed his movements with determination, as if he was performing them in front of

Grandfather once again. Serin's heart broke, and she found the lump in her throat hard to control. Amirra wrapped her arm around Serin and gave her a squeeze. Serin smiled and wiped the tear from her eye.

"He really misses him," Serin said.

"Like, you say, grief is the hardest thing in the world," Amirra said.

"I do believe that," Serin said.

"But you also say, if you keep it safe and protected, it becomes part of the strength of your soul, and I know about the soul," Amirra said.

"I do believe that too," Serin said.

"But how long does that take?" Amirra asked.

"I have no answer, I think it takes a lifetime and maybe longer," Serin said.

"Me too. How long do you think they will be?" Amirra asked.

"I can't say, Shaz's energy is still pretty raw, he might be at it a while," Serin said.

Serin turned her attention back to Shaz and found they were now sparing with each other. Serin kept a close eye on his heartfire and understood how much he needed this. It wasn't to show who was best, but to return to the happy moments of their youth when things were nowhere close to as complicated as they now were.

The sun dipped a little bit lower and the deep oranges of the Timeless Plains began to illuminate their efflorescent glow on the savanna, and Serin sensed Shaz's energy shift from the chaotic sadness to a focused determination. Serin did a quick scan on Riddick and found he was nowhere close to finished either, and she noticed they were sharing their magic and wondered if they even realized it. Serin also wasn't sure if this was the kind of magic that the sqwalls could track and or if they would come to this realm. They never did in the

Minca realm, and so far, they hadn't seen any and wondered what realms they were able to go to.

"I think they'll be a while, let's go see what we can do to help somewhere," Serin said.

"Do we have to," Amirra said.

Serin looked at Amirra who was quite happy to be watching Riddick and chuckled.

"Come on, they need us in the medic tents," Serin said.

58-You Need To Teach Me How To Do That

Jagwynn lowered close to the ground and found the heat radiate more than she thought it should. Turkill gripped his dart gun between his teeth and Ladtwig slowly slipped off Jag's back. Ladtwig scooted up against the wall and steadied his breathing. Jagwynn crawled slowly until she reached the doorway, and she peeked around the corner. The horde of Jaduuk Captains filled the vast cavern and Jag internalized the number and locations. Most of them were sleeping or lying about which would come in handy. It didn't really matter though as there were more than she wanted to count, and they nearly covered the floor. The stench was so hefty that she had a hard time breathing. Turkill climbed down and peeked around the corner. Turkill figured if he started hitting the Jaduuk at the side of the cave they could creep along the outer perimeter with the hope of not disturbing the rest of the Captains.

Turkill sucked in a deep breath and aimed his darts. Ladtwig slipped along the other side of the opening and peeked around the corner. Ladtwig bit his dart gun and let loose nearly at the same time as Turkill. The paralyzing darts hit their marks with exactness and the beasts slumped deeper onto the floor. The Minca continued to hit as many as they could without having to leave the corridor, but that wouldn't cover the entire group, nor did they have enough darts to do that either. Turkill gave Ladtwig the signal, and they hoped onto Jag's back and laid closely to her warmed hide.

Jagwynn crept one paw out of the darkness and waited and then another. She took slow and calculated steps across the cold stone until she came to the first dead beast. Jagwynn stepped over its foul-smelling body and then another and tip-toed the best a ginormous jungle cat could. Jagwynn started over another about halfway through the throng and stopped mid-step. The beast wasn't one of the ones which had been poisoned, and she froze as the creature stirred, snuffed its nose, and returned to his drowsy sleep. Turkill and Ladtwig held their breaths and Jagwynn quickly hopped over the beast and the next few that were also not dead.

They made their way to the other side and Jagwynn's flawless and sleek swagger disappeared into the corridor on the other side. After several more corridors and egg-spawners they reached the deepest part of the Mountain Temple.

"What do you want to do, we haven't found the portal room yet," Turkill asked.

"I think we should return to Shaz, I am sure he will be able to find it, it may be hidden from our view," Jagwynn said.

"Let's go then," Turkill said.

"Now to find a way out of here," Ladtwig said.

"Look, a tiny bit of daylight," Turkill said.

Jagwynn padded down the corridor and toward the light which grew the closer they came. The cavern opened onto a small terrace which overlooked the realm of the Timeless Plains. The three gazed about the landscape with a sickening sensation ripping through their guts. The destruction was incredible, and the carnage of dead beasts mixed with the horrid conditions of the living left a stain on their minds. One in which they weren't sure if they would ever be able to forget.

Turkill noticed a small trail and indicated to Jagwynn who agreed she would be able to climb. They took a moment to study their return route and how they would avoid the Jaduuk but have the most direct path back and Jagwynn began her climb down the mountain side. The trek was uncomfortable, but she made good time considering the narrowness of the trail. The sun was shifting in the sky behind the debris covered atmosphere and even though they couldn't see the sun rays the light was enough to manage.

Jagwynn finished the last several lengths on the mountain trail, and they reexamined their position and shot across the savanna. They returned to camp as the last bit of night pushed the day from existence and the three sighed a huge sense of relief. Jagwynn darted through the soldiers and made her way to the war tent, but she didn't find anyone. They hurried to Shaz's tent, but no one was there either.

****

Amirra sat at the back of the tent with her arms folded and a scrunched face. Serin made her way around a few of the empty cots and sat down next to her.

"I can tell there is something bothering you," Serin said.

Amirra looked up and tried to relax her tight brows but her eyes shifted around like she was looking for some kind of information in her head.

"I wish I had what you and Shaz have, with Riddick," Amirra said.

Serin turned to find Amirra's gaze, her admiration for Riddick was evident, but Serin understood her desire to be connected to him like she was with Shaz. Serin gripped her hand and gave a squeeze. Serin wondered what might have happened to be causing Amirra to experience these feelings now, but figured she would tell her when she was ready.

"I think you do. Remember when you came up with the idea to strengthen the glass for the raincloud," Amirra nodded, "that was you understanding Riddick's abilities," Amirra cocked her head to the side in the reexamination of the memory. "And how long it didn't take for you two to enchant all the armor and weapons. You were in complete sync with each other and you didn't even realize it," Amirra smiled but scrunched her nose in the way she did when she was fighting the old thoughts, "but maybe there are some things you have to do before you can accept the knowledge for yourself," Serin said.

"Like what?" Amirra asked.

"Accept yourself for who *you* are, every bit of it, if you don't want to see it in yourself, then you'll never be able to let Riddick see it, and that will hold you back from being complete with each other, all the time," Serin said.

"Is that what you two have?" Amirra asked.

Serin nodded.

"Shaz can hear my thoughts and I can feel his, so it doesn't do any good hiding anything," Amirra nodded and wondered how she might be able to figure out how to accept all of herself. "Maybe you could ask Riddick to teach you those movements, maybe that could be a kind of meditation to help you figure out those parts of yourself that are so complicated," Serin said.

"Do you think he would?" Amirra asked.

"Of course, he loves you, and he likes you," Serin said.

Are they different? Liking someone and loving them. *I guess there would be a difference, you can have love for a person and not like the things they do.* Amirra thought. Amirra was certain he loved her, he said so all the time now, she loved him, and she liked being with him, so it did make sense they would be different, because when he did something she didn't like, it didn't change that she still loved him. But then was the question, did she love herself enough to fully let him love her, that was the real problem. The heat inside her chest surged, and she understood the power of its truth. Serin watched as Amirra worked through her understandings.

"Ask him, I bet you'll be surprised what happens," Serin said.

Serin sent a cooling dose of her light magic into Amirra's hand and smiled. Amirra soaked in the brightness, and let the magic lighten the darkness of her soul and make her not so afraid.

"Come on, let's do some now, I'll teach you a few," Serin said.

Serin pulled Amirra through the tent and outside. The dimmed sky was cooling off and Serin rounded the last of the tents toward the training grounds. Serin pulled her tunic off and draped if over a log pole and Amirra's eyes popped out of her head. Serin's under shirt was tight to her form which would make it easier to show Amirra the movements.

"Take your tunic off," Serin said.

"Are you sure, there are a lot of men around," Amirra said.

"You do have underclothes on don't you," Serin said.

"Yes, but-" Amirra started.

"You'll be fine," Serin said.

"Alright," Amirra said.

Amirra wasn't sure what to think about it, but she swallowed and pulled off her over tunic. Serin moved her into the center of the flat ground which had been made to teach and practice different fighting techniques and put her hands in high position.

"This is called high position, from here you have the advantage to either strike or block," Serin said.

Amirra put her hands in the same position and looked at Serin who adjusted her fists and elbows a tiny bit. Amirra sucked in a deep breath and Serin took a step toward her and shot her hand out in a shuto side-strike and Amirra flinched and recoiled.

"What I want you to do, is hit my hand away," Serin said.

"How?" Amirra said.

Serin took Amirra's hand and moved it toward hers and blocked with the other hand to show her what to do and Amirra nodded. Serin tried again and Amirra blocked.

"Good, now I'm going to show you a few more, but I think we need to start with learning the Kata's," Serin said.

"What are those?" Amirra asked.

"They're the movements that make up the strikes and blocks," Serin said.

"Oh," Amirra said.

Serin took Amirra's hand and moved it into the position to show her the next move, and she slowly went through the motions with her. Amirra paid as close attention and tried to remember everything Serin was showing her. Shaz rounded the tent and found the girls working through a side-strike-block and his heart skipped. Serin was the most amazing woman to him, but seeing her able to fight was super attractive, no, she was plain sexy. He leaned against the pole of the tent, shoved his hands in his pockets and beheld her lean frame execute the movements with precision. It did clear up the fact she knew about the box, but left the question as to where she learned about it. Riddick came around the corner and stopped, seeing Shaz leaned up against the pole.

"What are you doing?" Riddick asked.

Shaz nodded and Riddick turned to find the girls now working through an upper-hand-block and elbow strike combination.

"Oh," Riddick said as the blood rushed to his cheeks.

Shaz smiled and nodded, he agreed totally. Riddick flicked his hair from his face and stuck his thumbs in the loopholes of his waistband and gazed at them. A heat filled his being and he blushed again.

"Is it totally weird that I find that incredibly sexy," Riddick asked.

"Nope," Shaz said.

"Good," Riddick said.

Serin smiled as she sensed Shaz and Riddick watching them. Serin steadied her breathing and the guys could see the gentle hint of sweat on their trim features.

Are you going to stand and stare all night? Serin asked in her mind.

As long as you'll let me, Shaz replied.

You're such a derp, Serin thought.

And you're beautiful, and sexy, and tough, and-

And you're distracting, Serin thought.

Serin shook her head and blocked a direct punch from Amirra and rounded her, scooped her leg out from under her and threw her onto the ground but caught her with an air cushion, so she wouldn't hit the ground. Amirra stunned, looked up with total confusion and Serin helped her up.

"You need to teach me how you did that," Amirra said.

"I think someone else wants to teach you," Serin said with a small grin.

"Who?" Amirra asked.

Serin motioned to where Shaz and Riddick were still staring. Amirra looked over and instantly turned pink.

"Oh my, I don't know what to say," Amirra whispered.

Serin chuckled and patted her shoulder, and they retrieved their tunics and slipped them on as they walked to the guys who quickly tried to look busy.

"You don't have to pretend you weren't watching," Serin said.

Riddick blushed and Shaz pulled Serin into him.

"That was fantastic," Riddick said.

"Thanks, but I'm nowhere good enough yet," Amirra said.

"Aye, but you have to start somewhere don't you?" Riddick said.

"I guess," Amirra said.

"Come on, let's get some supper, and then you can show me what you learned," Riddick said as he pulled her into a side squeeze.

"There you are, we have been looking all over for you," Turkill grunted.

"Turkill, Ladtwig, Jag, your back. How did everything go?" Shaz said with a huge sigh of his own.

"Not good, we are in big trouble," Turkill said.

Shaz's guts twinged and Serin's heart skipped. Riddick and Amirra too studied their faces as the news sank in. Turkill pulled off his satchel which held the books they had found and handed it to Shaz who took it with curious hesitation.

"How so?" Shaz asked.

"We searched every inch of the temple and found over forty spawners, but we couldn't find the portal room," Turkill said.

Shaz ran his hand through his hair. Forty spawners, how were they going to take out that many without blowing up the mountain.

"We also found the original lair of the Jaduuk'ai, we brought his books and a thingy," Ladtwig said.

"They have their own weapons, catapults, ballistas, and one I have never seen before," Turkill said.

"Aye, we almost lost Phanes to a ballista," Shaz said.

"I hate these things," Ladtwig snarled.

Serin and Amirra agreed, but the fact Ladtwig snarled gave it a slight comical nature.

"What did the other weapon look like," Shaz asked.

"It was a steel box on wheels and shot flames from a cannon," Turkill said.

"They have a flame thrower?" Shaz asked his tone higher and filled with panic and anger.

"That is what it looked like. They were pouring in the green goo and igniting it. It shot green flames a far distance too," Turkill said.

"They certainly aren't the same Jaduuk we met rotations ago that's for sure," Serin said.

"No, they are gaining intelligence from the Jaduuk'ai, I'm sure of it," Shaz said.

"Blast," Serin said.

"We need to end this. Riddick, Amirra you need to get the next battalions shields to include resist-heat. We need to inform the trebuchets to make sure they take those out as fast as possible. Turkill, could you tell how many they had?" Shaz asked.

"No, but what we could tell, they had a lot of them," Turkill said.

"And with all those eggs making the green goo, they can keep them fueled for a long time," Riddick said. Shaz ran his hands through his hair and breathed out a heavy sigh. "We'll get started on the heat shields, I have a good idea as to how I'm going to do it."

"I'll send Frebin out with the new instructions," Serin said.

Shaz nodded, but the pit in his stomach lurched and Merrick came around the corner in time to spot Shaz slam his fist into a pole of the tent.

"What's wrong son?" Merrick asked.

Shaz filled him in on the details of what the Minca found and how he gets when he gets charged up, what Serin and the others think, and Merrick scratched his scruffy chin.

"Do you remember when you were little, and we were out on the Mirabella, and we watched the lightning storms," Shaz nodded, "you asked me how does the lightning know where to go next," Shaz gazed into his father's warm eyes, "and I told you I didn't know, but I was certain that one day you would figure it out," Shaz gave him a perplexed side-eye tilt, "I think this is the time you figure out where the lightning goes next," Merrick said.

"So, you're saying I can direct the lightning where I want it to go," Shaz ask-stated.

"Well, I'm only suggesting you could try, I don't know if you can, but like Grandfather would say, 'you won't know until you try,'" Merrick said.

Shaz smiled, the thought had been running around in his mind for hours now, and to have his father bring it up too. Shaz took several steps from the tent and felt the organized chaos in his chest. He searched for the lightning and imagined what he remembered from when they were on the ship and his hand tingled with the hot energy of the bright sparking force. Merrick took a few steps back and Serin came back around the tent. She examined his heartfire and found that it radiated a bright white color now instead of the fire red. Shaz held out his hand a released the crackle. The bolt shot across the sky and hit a tree several lengths away. The tree split in half and caught on fire, which Shaz quickly stifled, and he turned to find Serin and Merrick with pleased smiles.

"There ya go, does that help release the buildup of the shadow magic?" Serin asked.

"No, but I think I know what to do now," Shaz said.

Shaz returned to them. He couldn't believe he threw a fireball at her. His shame wrapped around his heart, and he stifled the ache in his chest. Serin gave him a squeeze and tried to reassure him she wasn't angry, *but the next time it happens, I won't just freeze you in a block of ice,* Serin said in her mind, Shaz smiled at her thoughts and Merrick beamed with pride.

"Come on, let's go kill some Jaduuk," Shaz said.

59-I'm Ready To Kill Them All

Shaz called a meeting with the leaders, and they spent most of the evening strategizing their efforts to take out the spawners and infiltrate the temple.

"Alright, so far, what we know is we can't use the bombs as they are to destroy the spawners. The Minca can refit the bombs with less explosives, but we will need more than one per egg. Once the first bomb goes off, we will only have seconds to ignite the rest before signaling the Jaduuk of our whereabouts. There are over forty eggs, and the temple is filled with Jaduuk. They now have flame throwers, and launching weapons. The gryphton's are going to have be extra careful and keep a low profile to avoid them. Riddick and Amirra have refitted the shields to include the resist-fire, but we don't know how hot the green goo burns," Shaz said.

"I'm worried about the lava. If we start blowing up the ground it's going to become very unstable. The lava will begin to flow at a rate we can't predict. How fast and how far a lava flow can travel from the vent depends on its viscosity, which is determined by temperature, chemical composition, gas content, and crystallinity. Eruption rate, and ground slope is also a problem," Riddick said. The group stared at him with blank stares and Riddick shook his head trying to figure out a way to explain what his mind was telling them. "Lava has a mind of its own, and there is no way to predict what it's going to do especially if we blow it up," Riddick said.

"Alright, so what do you suppose?" Shaz asked.

Riddick tapped his finger on his chin for a few minutes.

"The only thing I can think, is to use my magic and ask it to cooperate, but you don't just tell the earth what to do. It likes to be part of the solution, not be bossed around, still there's no guarantee it will cooperate," Riddick said.

"Where do you think you'll need to be to communicate with the earth?" Shaz asked.

"I'll need to be at the first one that was started, hopefully if I can ask it to change course, I can redirect it from the eggs," Riddick said.

"How will we know which one that is?" Amirra asked.

"Turkill, Ladtwig, was there any of the spawners that had lava flowing from only one direction?" Riddick asked.

The Minca thought a moment.

"The very farthest one, by the cliffs we climbed down from, that one only had one vein of lava that came off of it," Ladtwig said.

Ladtwig pointed on the map where they found their exit.

"How hard will it be to get back up there? "Riddick asked.

"Not hard if you're on a gryphton," Turkill said.

Phanes opened the flap and crawled in. The group turned to find his large frame full and vigorous. Serin smiled and went over to him, and he wrapped his arms around her in a huge hug. Gryphton's by nature were not an affectionate race, but the humans had won their hearts on so many occasions that it was hard to deny their love and devotion to them.

"How are you feeling?" Serin asked.

"I'm ready to kill them all," Phanes growled.

Serin perceived his maturity had reached a new level, and she patted his arm.

"Good, because we're going to need your can of whoop-ass," Helios said.

Phanes looked at him and now understood what that meant and nodded with the accepted challenge.

"You two figure out your strategy, we need Riddick here," Shaz said to Helios and Phanes as he pointed to the map, "I need to get to the portal room, but I have to find it first. How can we mobilize the horde inside the mountain?" Shaz asked.

"I have an idea," Ladtwig said.

A flash of evil glee crossed his face and Turkill peered at his brother. Turkill was about to give him a piece of his mind, but Ladtwig gave him a 'remember' look, and a flash of evil glee too crossed his expression, and they slapped hands. The crew waited eagerly for their details but the Minca brothers chuckled an eerie throaty laughter and hurried from the tent.

"Well, I guess we'll find out what that is all about later," Shaz said with a grin of his own.

"I think I'm a little frightened now," Serin said.

"Me too," Asher said.

The men chuckled and Declan, Bowen, Asher, and Merrick began moving through their detailed attacks. Shaz listened to their ideas and agreed with everything, it was nice to have such capable men who could handle that part, letting him focus on how he was going to defeat the Jaduuk'ai. Shaz remembered the books Turkill had given him, and he motioned for everyone to keep working through what they needed. Shaz found a chair in the corner and picked up the satchel. He pulled a book and read the title and pulled a few more. The last one had a large symbol that indicated it had information on transformations. He ran his finger along the binding and interpreted the nature of the book. After Serin taught him how to understand the language of the wyvern's, which he learned was really the language of the Gods, he knew he needed to bond with the book so the original author could illustrate what they wanted to provide in the way the reader would understand.

Shaz lifted the cover and inhaled the aroma of the Creeping Dewberry of the Minca realm mixed with the sweet ginger from the Ebassian realm and he wondered if there was a place that had both or if at the time the author wrote this book there was. His mind filled with images of the gentle plants blowing in the breeze and was intrigued as he had yet to read any of the symbols to give him the imagined ideas. Serin smiled as she related to his feelings and came around the table. Shaz skimmed the first page and understood the complexity of the details.

What is that? Serin asked in her mind.

A book on transformations, I think this is what Baltair used to become the Jaduuk'ai. In fact, I think they all used it to become their chosen entities, Shaz returned.

What does it say?

Shaz flipped through a few of the pages and the book stopped on one.

This is very complex and similar to the scroll and is very dangerous. I need to get these books into the wizards keep as soon as we can, Shaz said in his head.

Will it help us now?

Aye, I don't think we will be able to defeat Jaduuk'ai. The best we can do is to banish him, either to another realm, preferably the shadow realm, but we might be able to capture him in an orb or something, like the Shadow Selket, Shaz said.

How hard is that going to be?

I have no idea, the Selket was a pain as it was and it was just a scorpion, not a God, and there are still several temples and who knows how many are open or have been sealed properly. This is only going to delay his return and next time I don't think he's going to be as nice, Shaz replied.

Blast, Serin said in her mind.

Give me some time to read through this and see what I can find,

Alright,

Riddick cleared his throat and the two turned to find the company staring at them.

"Sorry, I guess we missed something," Shaz said.

"Some leader you are," Riddick teased.

Shaz rolled his eyes and tucked the book into his heavy-leather jerkin.

"We will leave for the temple as the next shift returns, does that give you the time you need?" Bowen said.

"Aye," Shaz said.

The company left the tent and Shaz filled Riddick and Amirra in on the book and his thoughts.

"Oiy mate, you certainly don't like doing things the easy way do you?" Riddick said as he ran his hands over his face.

"Is there an easy way?" Amirra asked.

Riddick peeked from his hands covering his face and noted the edge of her lip twitch, and he smiled.

"You're not helping," Riddick said.

Amirra snickered and it was refreshing that they still had the ability to laugh in hard times. Shaz was eager to make it to the battlefield. He wanted to see what would happen when he gets charged up from the shadow magic. They quickly gathered their gear and ate a fast meal, but their nerves were both excited and filled with dread.

They found the Minca, but the brothers refused to give up their secret plan which fueled Shaz and Riddick's curiosity but set in motion the need to puke for Serin. She usually didn't have such notions, but with the unknown of what is happening, she couldn't help fear they were getting in over their heads.

Turkill took the bottle and opened the stopper and handed it to Riddick. Riddick caught a glimpse of the evil twitch in Turkill's eye as though he was certain they had spiked it with something worse. He quickly poured the thick potion into his mouth. Riddick's lips peeled back as the strong odor hit his nose a second before his taste buds were set on fire. He swallowed hard before his gag reflex initiated its full assault mode.

"This is the most horrific thing I have ever tasted," Riddick admitted.

"Oh, come on, it's not that bad," Turkill said.

Riddick's pale skin turned a shade of green and his usual playful expression was replaced with an expression of panic, almost terror. The one that says, 'I think I'm going to hurl' and Shaz hesitated.

"We most certainly should have added the sweet root after all," Riddick managed as his lungs expelled their last-ditch effort to stay full. "Now, your turn," Riddick said.

Shaz gave him a sideways glare and Turkill snickered. Turkill smiled as much of grin as he could muster at the payback. Riddick threw out his tongue and gasped for clean air, but his body couldn't figure out what was happening to it. His muscles tightened and his nerves tingled as the magic ran its course through his body.

Shaz closed his eyes and sucked in a deep breath. The sensation of dread sat at the back of his mind, but he had to do it. He pulled the stopper and quickly dripped the elixir into his mouth. The fire in his throat hit his brain, and he gagged through the swallow. A heat radiated from his bowels and surged up his core. His lightly tanned skin reddened like Riddick's did as the magic took hold. Serin and Amirra gave each other a look of horror and sweat formed at their hairline. If the guys could barely handle the stuff, what was going to happen to them.

"Maybe we'll just wait out here," Serin said.

"Oh, no, you're not getting out of this," Turkill grunted.

Serin opened her jar and Amirra followed. They poured the jar into their mouths and the cold goop sank into their tongues. The flavor was delicate and smooth, with a light minty flavor. They looked at each other with perplexed expressions. They swallowed and a caressing tingle moved about their frames. The guys examined them as they didn't show a single sign of distress.

"I don't know what you guys are complaining about," Serin said.

Shaz, Riddick, and Turkill gaped in disbelief.

"Is that the same stuff?" Riddick asked moving to take the jar to examine it himself.

"Yes," Amirra said with a hint of annoyance as she kept the jar from Riddick's reach.

"Why didn't it taste nasty to you two?" Shaz asked will full distress.

Serin was not about to explain how she had given herself and Amirra a dose of her pain relief magic first as that would for sure make things more, well, we'll go with 'interesting' for sure, but Shaz had a look in his eye as though he was certain he knew what she had done and Serin played if off as 'it's a girl thing', which only fueled his energy.

"How long does this last?" Serin asked.

"About a days' worth, and we have enough for a second dose," Amirra said.

"I am not drinking that again," Riddick said.

"Then I suppose you hurry," Serin said.

She had to admit she was having too much fun at the guys expense and figured she better cool it. Then she chuckled at her own joke and Shaz gave her the 'stink eye'. Shaz checked his hand and it was starting to become a mirage now too.

"How are we going to communicate if we can't see each other, and we have to be quiet, and what if we run into each other," Amirra asked.

"Blast," Shaz said.

Shaz's whole body was now becoming the mirrored reflection of the surroundings.

Can everyone hear me? Shaz asked with his mind conference.

Yes, they all replied. Shaz was going to regret opening his mind conference with the Minca, but to his surprise they were quite still and focused. He hadn't noticed them take the serum, but he couldn't find them, so he figured they had, then he wondered if Serin had buffed them too, and he scowled.

Alright, everyone put up your shields, Shaz said.

We don't have magic shields, Ladtwig said.

Activate your head pieces I gave you, I enchanted them with magic shields, Amirra said.

The Minca tested it out and were quite excited about their new adaptions.

"Let's go," Shaz said with a scowl.

60-Now, You Behave

Turkill and Ladtwig made their way to the elephantines where they had left their stash and started to leave when a baby elephantine snagged Ladtwig's satchel. Ladtwig jumped with the shock and turned to find the inquisitive baby rummaging through it.

"Hey, get out of there," Ladtwig said.

The baby didn't seem to listen and dumped the whole of the contents onto the ground. Ladtwig screeched with the horror of seeing all of his food now on the ground and Turkill turned to shoosh him, but snickered at his brothers distress. Ladtwig was now in a hand war over the jar of potion with the elephantines strong trunk. For a baby it was quite strong, but then again he was fighting a miniature human. Even though it was a baby elephantine, the mammal was nearly three times the height of the Minca, which added to Ladtwig distress. Ladtwig struggled the jar out of the reach of the baby and started to put it back in the pouch along with everything else. The baby however was determined to get the jar and waited until Ladtwig had secured most of the items.

"Now, you behave," Ladtwig said.

The baby pachyderm nodded but Ladtwig was convinced he was not going to obey.

"Is that the same baby you had trouble steeling your stuff as before?" Turkill asked with a slight laugh under his gruffness.

"Yes," Ladtwig managed as the elephantine wrapped his trunk around Ladtwig's waist and lifted him off the ground.

"Come on you twerp, let me go," Ladtwig said trying to dislodge himself from its clutches.

Turkill pulled out a fresh stick of sweet root and waved it at the baby. The animal put Ladtwig down and hurried over to the root and Turkill gave it to the baby. Ladtwig grabbed his pack quickly and hurried away, but didn't see the baby snag the jar from his pouch as he rushed away. Ladtwig and Turkill found Frebin, Drager, Harmus, and Tomos, gave them the potion and waited with glee as they all gagged and cursed. Harmus was about to pelt Turkill, but he ducked out of the swing and quickly left camp.

They needed to get there before anyone else if their plan was going to work, so they secretly asked a troop of Forrne to take them, who accepted happily. They reached the mountain pass and the Forrne Guard returned leaving Turkill to lead the men over the path they used last time. As they neared the cave entrance they slowed to a crawl. They listened for a moment and leaped across the gurgling goo. The other Minca were shocked at the masses of Jaduuk and a few times Turkill had to give them the glare of death, but it was a little lacking in conviction as they were hard to see each other with their disguised features.

****

Riddick had the satisfied reward of heightened energy, but Amirra gripped Shar's neck with a white-knuckle death grip. Amirra struggled against the wind in her face and images of her dream of her mother flying on a wyvern surfaced, and she tried to make a connection to Shar. Amirra closed her eyes and tried to think of how her soul magic would, or could connect to Shar's soul, and an interesting thought came to her mind. Amirra perceived Shar's thoughts as she realized how much she had begun to really like Amirra as they had spent a lot of time together in the off hours.

Shar had never thought she would learn so much about herself from a human, well, she didn't even know about humans, but when she did find out about them, she had no idea how much this little cinnamon haired girl would mean to her. Amirra smiled as she internalized Shar's connection to herself, and she imagined herself face to face with Shar. Amirra looked into her deep green-brown eyes. Shar looked back at her, and she found her reflection in them. Amirra's magic eased into the gryphton, and she relaxed when she saw a mental image of her soul. It was strong, honest, loyal, determined, and friendly. Amirra asked her yellow magic to surround her face so that she was able to breathe and the force obeyed.

The softness surrounded her frame, and she sat up a bit and examined the distance. An odd peace overcame her, and her heart leaped with acceptance and excitement. It wasn't that different from the earth-board when Riddick was steering, and she eased into the gryphton's movements. Shar smiled as she too interpreted Amirra's energy and found her to be loyal, determined, and honest.

Riddick noted the veins and studied the way they moved across the savanna to gain an idea of how to heal the earth when it was time. They raced toward the far side of the mountain and the gryphton's let them off on the small terrace like formation at the edge of the opening. Amirra gripped Shar around the neck and gave her a tight squeeze and Shar returned the hug.

****

Shaz and Serin used an earth-board to maneuver over the terrain of the now battered grounds of the savanna. Shaz sent out his energy and examined the image he received. They used the hover-turfs until they reached the first settlements, and then they would have to go in on foot. He steered around the outer edge and slowed as they came to where the moving earth could be spotted. Shaz hopped off the hovering dirt and sent it in the opposite direction and Serin buffed them. Turkill had explained where the human lair was and Shaz figured that would be close to where the portal room would be, which was on the closer side of the mountain. They made good time up the path and came to the part where Jag had climbed over the ring of the bowl-like structure. Shaz hopped the ridge and Serin followed. Shaz's guts sank as the bowl was filled with the Captains. Serin's heart thudded in her chest as she remembered how the Captain smelled her blood, and she feared if the potion would hide that.

Do you think they will be able to detect our blood through the potion? Serin asked in her mind.

Blast, let's hope not, but if they do, we'll need to move very fast,

That's not reassuring,

It's the best I got, love,

Sure enough, the Captain's in the group, which ended up being most of them started to perk up with the scent and Shaz and

Serin's hearts nearly ripped through their beings. He hadn't had a chance to experiment with his lightning yet and figured this was as good a chance as any.

I have an idea, Shaz said in his mind.

Get eaten? Serin returned.

Close, follow me,

I figured,

Shaz jumped down from the ledge. A Captain nearby turned, and his nose registered the scent of Shaz's blood, but it couldn't see him with his eyes and his nose couldn't pick out an exact location either.

"The blood of the Tooatha De Dannon, now that is what we are searching for," the Jaduuk said as it sniffed through its huge nostrils.

"So how does it feel to never have found me, I had to come to you?" Shaz said.

Serin rolled her eyes and the Captain's brow flickered with the question. Shaz pulled the blade from its sheath and the ring of steel against steel rippled over the air. The masses of Jaduuk lurched to alert and Shaz's heart pumped blood to his whole body. Shaz slashed through the heart of a nearby Jaduuk and turned and pulled the blades sharp edge through the neck of another. The Captain took a few long strides toward the fallen beasts and Serin sidestepped the oncoming animal. It turned its head, caught a whiff of her blood and the confusion ran over its face.

"Yes, the Lavari are there too, and the Bair, and the Fir, so why don't you go tell your boss we're here and want to give him his eviction notice," Shaz said.

The Captain roared and drool dripped form its upright fang. The whole of the horde was on alert and Shaz understood, he did in fact just send the signal to Jaduuk'ai. Shaz slammed his combustion forces into some Jaduuk, who flew backward and hit the ground hard. Serin blasted her wind shards into the masses and howls rang through the atmosphere. Serin leaped out of the way of a beast who had tracked her blood and ripped the air from its lungs. She rolled into a flying somersault and her air magic carried her over several others while she sent another blast of wind shards.

Shaz yanked his blade from the chest of one and decided he needed to speed things up. He lit his body on fire, so they would be able to see him better and called his shield. The masses descended on him, and he began to feel the effects of the shadow magic his armor gave him. The sensation was exhilarating and with his new understanding of it, a clear picture of the lightning storm came to his mind. He continued to hack and slash at the beasts as they hit his shield. Shaz soaked in the new rawness and at the last minute shifted his fire element to the lightning element. Serin braced herself as she felt the tingle of the lightning she was so familiar with. Shaz let the sizzling element form in his hand and focused on where he wanted the bolts to go.

A blast of white light flashed blinding the horde as the bolts shot through their bodies. The Jaduuk flailed away like rag dolls but were in pieces as the bolts took out the next target behind them. Serin smiled at his understanding of the new power and took a quick glance around them. Half the bowl was laying on the ground, some were still jerking from their last movements instructions. Shaz smiled to himself and was ready for another dose of the new euphoria.

****

The Minca men found the small hole that was above the caverns and Turkill pulled out his hook and rope. He stepped back enough to swing the hook and launched it into the ceiling. The hook grabbed hold of the bottom of the opening and Turkill lifted Ladtwig onto the rope, and then the others. Turkill sent up the satchels and climbed up. The Minca crawled into the air duct and was pleased to see that they were correct, it was a system of vents that allowed for the air to move around the temple. These vents were also in the Mountain Temple back home and Semias' temple. Ladtwig shifted his pack as he rounded a corner.

It was pitch black, and they had a hard time knowing where they were going, but as one could imagine, it didn't take much to figure out where the highest concentration of Jaduuk was based on the odor they emitted, and being in the air ducts, made it even easier. They had learned on their first trip through that the green eggs gave off a glow which helped give some light to the tunnels so at each intersection they checked to see how much light they found and finally found the location they wanted. The intersection was big enough for them to set up their contraption they had devised. Harmus and Drager continued down another tunnel until they found another intersection and Tomos headed to the next one. Ladtwig pulled out a set of coconut shells and strapped them onto a pair of handles at the end of the contraption and Turkill secured a long horn-like object that had a series of papers in the tubular structure.

The contraption was propelled by moving a lever up and down which made the connecting parts move together in a rhythmic pattern like a musical instrument, only this didn't make nice sounds. Turkill scooched it to the center and sucked in a deep breath and blew into the horn. A loud obnoxious sound radiated from the cone and echoed off the small tunnels as it coursed through the caverns. The deep rattle of the horn and whooshing of the papers made an eerie crackle that could have been from something dying or coming to life. Harmus and Drager made their noises come to life and Tomos soon joined in.

The sounds came out of the vents high above the Jaduuk in the main cavern, and they shielded their ears as they cringed and looked around. Ladtwig pulled the lever and the coconut shells clopped together in an offbeat pattern that ricocheted through the small openings. The Jaduuk came to an alertness and Turkill blew in the horn again, followed by Tomos and Harmus. Drager frantically hit a stone against the wall letting the high pitch of the clicking penetrate the distance. The mixture of the sounds really did sound dreadful and it was hard not to laugh, but the Minca repeated their music again. The Jaduuk searched again but couldn't find anything to explain the noise and couldn't decide if they were going to fight or flee.

Turkill moved to the edge of the vent and pulled his sling. He loaded a stone and flicked it with a snap of his wrist and the stone shot out and hit a Jaduuk in the head. The beast jumped to his claws and snarled at the beast next to him, who jumped in his face in return. Turkill flicked another stone and Ladtwig blew in the horn. The deep breathy gurgley sound radiated around the corridor and the Jaduuk cowered. Turkill flicked another stone and another beast yelped, and the masses began to whimper with the uneasiness. The irritation in the group began to grow but there were no Captains to bark orders, so the horde didn't know what to do.

Turkill returned to the contraption and added the tambourine-like instrument to the lever system and the high pitch of the symbols clanging together sent a new sound of irritation though the tunnels. Turkill returned to the opening and noticed a commotion on the other side. He squinted to see what it was and caught a glimmer of the outline of the baby pachyderm. Turkill cursed and darted back to Ladtwig and the contraption.

"What is the matter?" Ladtwig asked.

"That blasted baby pachyderm followed us, it must have gotten your potion, it's disguised as well," Turkill huffed.

"Blast," Ladtwig said.

"What are we going to do now?" Turkill barked.

"I have an idea," Ladtwig said.

Ladtwig handed the levers to Turkill and searched through his pouch.

"When I signal, blow on the horn as loud and long as you can," Ladtwig found the sweet root and shot off toward the opening Turkill had used to hit the Jaduuk. Ladtwig bit into the sweet root and yanked the outer casing with his teeth. The fibrous sheath peeled away, and a sweet aroma wafted into the air. The baby lifted its trunk, recognized the scent, and started toward the root. The problem was that it had to cross the entire cave. Ladtwig clicked his tongue and Turkill blasted the horn. The sound accompanied by the sudden trampling of the baby elephantine, which was nearly as large as the smaller Jaduuk startled them, but it was what was about to come next that Ladtwig was so looking forward to.

The sweet root that Turkill had given the animal before they left was about to make the farts of this little creature near deadly, and sure enough with each step the baby crop-dusted the surroundings as it went. Jaduuk began to gag on the odor and the horn created an irritation in their guts. Ladtwig shot his dart gun which was loaded with the paralytic poison. Jaduuk's began falling and running around in total confusion as their noses became encased in the stench of the baby's exodus of odors and the noise echoed discord in their brains. Turkill slapped the levers at a fast rate and slammed another into the stone wall. Tomos blew through his horn and Drager clapped his coconut shells with eagerness.

The Jaduuk had had enough confusion and began dodging the unseeable pachyderm as it barreled through them. The claps of their clawed hoofs created more clatter and the Jaduuk darted out of the cavern. Ladtwig was trying so hard not to laugh, but he couldn't help it. The baby made his way to where the root was sticking out of the vent and snagged it nearly pulling him out. Ladtwig turned to find a gleeful half grin on Turkill face, and they and the rest of the Minca climbed out of the vent and onto the elephantine's back.

61-I Hope Everyone Is Ready For This

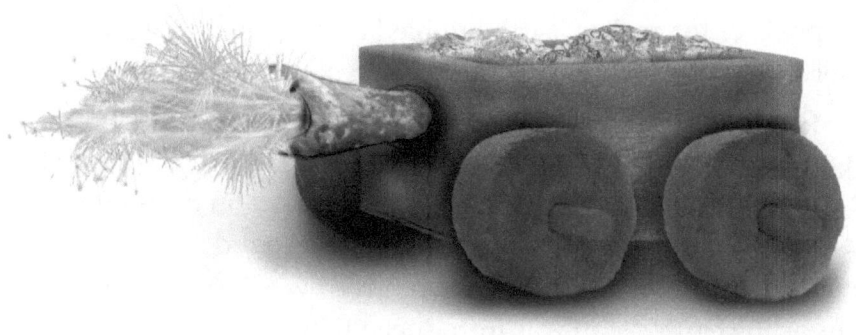

Riddick and Amirra hurried into the cave and Riddick called his earth's energy to his hand. It wasn't as bright as Shaz's fire, but it called the elements in the stone and small veins in the walls lit up. Riddick sent out his energy to gain an image of where the passageways were, and they headed toward the room the Minca had told him about. They rounded a few corners and found the room. The egg was bulging on one side and Amirra puckered at the rancid odor. Riddick pulled Amirra back behind the wall and put his finger on his lips. He snuffed his magic, and the hallway went black.

The cold of the stone bit at their skin, and they scooted away from the entrance as a Jaduuk emerged from the egg with a gross sucking and sloshy sound. Riddick peeked around the corner and found the beast licking itself clean of the green goo and had to shove his hand over his mouth to keep from vomiting all over. Riddick shook his mind clear of the nasty image, gripped the earth element and slammed his liquefy into the fresh Jaduuk. The bluish skin of the Jaduuk radiated the green glow from the egg as its eyes bulged from its head as it crumpled to the floor. Riddick wanted to bury the beast, but he feared it would alarm the rest, so he shoved it into the farthest part of the small cave with his magic, there was no way he was going to physically touch it.

Riddick cleared his mind and reached out to the lava. The little pools of the melted earth bubbled and popped as it simmered under the egg and Riddick started to speak to the earth. The planet moved at a very slow rate, and he was certain it was going to take some time to get its attention, and then its permission, and then its cooperation. Amirra closed her eyes and focused on her soul magic. The yellow energy moved from her core and found its way into the crevices of the floor. The image she received was beautiful and won-drous as the earth's soul was introduced to her.

"Shh, do hear that?" Riddick asked.

An irritating pitch of deep vibration rippled into their hear-ing and Amirra nodded. Riddick put his hand on the wall and sent his magic out to determine if he could detect what it was. Riddick shook his head and smiled as the image of the Minca came to his mind.

"What is it?" Amirra asked in a whisper.

"The Minca," Riddick said with a snicker.

"Doing what?" Amirra asked.

"I have no idea," Riddick said.

****

Shaz gripped the blade and shouted his aggression shout. The horde lowered their heads and lunged toward him at a dead run. Serin moved around them on the outer edge of the bowl while Shaz was becoming charged again. It didn't take long with all the creatures and Shaz unleashed another infinite-charged lightning at-tack. The bolts shot out from every direction penetrating right through the Jaduuk's beings and surging into the creatures behind them. The charge was magnificent, and a new set of bolts emerged from the sky aiding to his attack.

The masses fell quickly and only a few remained, until they detected a thundering of clawed hooves barreling toward them. The fleeing Jaduuk rounded the corner on all fours and were running at full speed. Serin yanked him with her wind carrying him out of the way of the oncoming stampede. Horde after horde filed out of the cave and Shaz and Serin watched with amusement and wonder. Shaz was so intrigued on how the Minca managed this exodus and Serin too found herself wanting to know, but not wanting to know at the same time. The Jaduuk clambered over each other as they funneled down the mountain pass.

"It's a good thing we weren't in the way," Shaz said.

"That's for sure," Serin said.

"Send our scents in the breeze, so they keep going," Shaz said.

Serin wrapped her wind blanket around them and shot it into the distance.

"I hope everyone is ready for this," Serin said.

The screech of the gryphton lookout echoed over the mountain.

"Aye, me too, come on," Shaz said.

They waited a few lengths as the stragglers made their way out of the tunnel and hurried inside. Shaz's night vision took over but Serin couldn't make out a thing. Shaz took her hand and guided her with him. He touched the wall every so many lengths trying to get a read on where the portal room might be, but nothing came. He continued down the corridor and stopped quickly guiding Serin up against the wall.

We found the Jaduuk'ai didn't we? Serin asked in her mind.

Aye,

****

Turkill took out his glow stone Riddick had made for them, picked up the rest of the Minca and gave them their directions. The men picked up their satchels and pulled out their time-tickers.

"We have exactly," Turkill examined the time-ticker, "twenty lengths to secure these bombs into place and armed," Turkill said.

The Minca clicked the button that started the countdown and raced away, each in their directions. Turkill and Ladtwig climbed onto the baby pachyderm and directed him to the first egg room. The green glow illuminated the surroundings, and the heartbeat-like pulsing sent a weird shadow on the ground. Turkill jumped off and ran into the room while Ladtwig moved the animal to the next room. Harmus found his first mark and Tomos his. Drager rounded the corner and found his first mark. Turkill stuffed his first bomb under the largest root-like vine and then shoved the next one under the next largest root. The third bomb, he tucked under the root on the side that would make a circle and stuck the wick into the top of each canister.

Each Minca organized their bombs and connected them together and attached it to another time-ticker, clicked the button and raced toward the next room.

****

Declan watched through his looking glass and saw the massive train of Jaduuk nearly falling out of the mountain pass and lifted his hand. The trebuchet operators gripped the lever and readied themselves for the drop of the bucket. Declan waited and was surprised to see how many of the beasts there was in the mountain. His heart began to sink, and the men's guts started to ache as it was taking forever for him to give the signal. They had to wait for the last of the Jaduuk to make it out of the pass before they blew it up to keep them from returning. Declan scanned the Jaduuk settlements and found several of the ballista launchers and flame throwers.

He scanned back to the mountain pass and noted there were only a few stragglers and dropped his arm. The men heaved the lever and jumped out of the way of the ginormous machine. The strap released the bucket and it plummeted to the ground sending the impending fireball soaring into the atmosphere. The second trebuchet noted the first and released its load as did the third and the fourth.

The first fireball sizzled through the air and landed its mark, and the path was blown to bits sending a heap of falling stone from above clamoring to the ground. A second ball hit its mark as did the other two each taking out the Jaduuk's machines. The Jaduuk had been busy improving their machines since they hit Phanes, and their numbers had been nearly decimated by their retaliation, but Jaduuk'ai increased the eggs production and the army was nearly as large as it was before. Bowen looked through his looking glass and found the flame throwers and called out their locations. The second theater shifted their trebuchets to the degree needed but the massive machines didn't move easily. A burly soldier in charge of the coordinates examined their mark and whistled his findings and Bowen dropped his arm.

All the trebuchets launched their payloads and the atmosphere surged with the stink of burning minerals. The fire balls hit their marks and the explosives ignited the green goo. Blasts shot out and sent the surrounding Jaduuk flying and landed on the ground with splattered and singed bodies. The green fire shot so many lengths into the sky the gryphton's were nearly eye level with the funnels. A loud deep buzzing horn echoed over the landscape which signaled for the Jaduuk armies to attack.

Bowen gave his signal and his Ebassian's and the rhino-moa attacked. Declan gave his and the Rangers and the elephantines attacked. Phanes' roar blasted across the sky and the gryphton's attacked.

****

Riddick's brows cinched tight in the center of his face as he focused on the pathway the lava was moving. The strength of the planets forces was incredible, and he found it harder than he had expected. A bit of panic crested Amirra's guts as she watched him struggle, then a thought came to mind. Amirra took Riddick's hand and closed her eyes. She imagined standing next to Riddick in the Teorran Belt back on the island and Riddick felt the tug at his mind. He allowed her thoughts to ease into his awareness and examined the room. The sifting particles of the void wrapped around them and Amirra send her soul magic into Riddick's hands. Riddick took the magic and wrapped it around his and the vibrations evened out and sank into the darkness of the void.

The planets desire came to his mind, and he understood that it wanted to be at peace.

"I'm here to help, but you have to help me help you, I'm sorry for the way you have been treated," Riddick said.

Amirra began the apology chant she and Nitida used when they closed the rip in time and tears she didn't expect flooded out. The earth shook gently, and Riddick understood it had accepted the apology. Riddick nodded and began to harden the surface of the lava closing off the flow to the egg. He asked for the earth to cover the surface closing the rest of the lava openings and the earth grumbled.

Turkill came around the corner and stopped when he found Riddick and Amirra hovering in a ball of radiating earth energy.

He rounded the other side and shoved his bombs under the roots and set the clicker. Riddick perceived is presence and opened his eyes.

"We're all set, and heading out," Turkill said.

"Aye," Riddick said.

Turkill hopped up and darted out of the room and met up with the rest of the Minca. He led them to the outside terrace where a few gryphton's were waiting. They hadn't planned on the baby elephantine and didn't know what to do.

"Go, I'll get him out," Ladtwig said.

"Not without me," Turkill said.

Riddick came out of the tunnel and ripped a large slab of rock from the side of the mountain.

"Climb on and I'll send you back to camp," Riddick said.

Turkill gripped the babies trunk and Riddick shoved them down the slope of the mountain. The pachyderm's trunk sounded the most amazing blaring of terror which matched the instant surge in Turkill's guts. Ladtwig hooted and hollered with the exhilaration of the near fall and Turkill and the baby gripped each other for dear life. The babies frantic mother heard the cry and blasted through the oncoming Jaduuk like a mad hornet. Jaduuk went flying and flailing as the mother bowled them over.

Riddick returned to his work and the gryphtons flew the Minca to their stations. Riddick listened to the ticking of the time-tickers and tried to concentrate, but he found the noise irritating. Amirra too found it a nuisance but was more concerned about how much time they had. Riddick gripped his magic even harder and the earth began to solidify under the eggs. Over half were covered and the temperature dropped several degrees, which was a good sign.

Riddick searched for the original path the lava took to the surface and when he found it, he doubled his focus on getting the lava to return and follow its path back to the depths where it belonged.

62-Shaz, Don't You DARE!

So, what is your plan? Serin asked in her mind.

Her heart was beating heavily, and she feared the beast on the other side of the cavern would hear her.

Riddick as soon as your finished meet us here, Shaz said in his mind conference.

Aye, Riddick replied both in his mind and out loud.

He wasn't used to the 'not speaking out loud' part yet, and wasn't actually sure how to do it. Riddick opened his eyes and motioned for Amirra to leave the room.

"Let's check each one as we head toward Shaz and Serin, but we have to hurry," Riddick said.

Amirra nodded and they hurried from the room. They checked the rooms they found as Riddick guided them toward the location Shaz had given him and so far each of the openings had been closed. A sudden burst of three mini-blasts echoed from the chambers ahead and Riddick determined they were heading their way. He raced down a corridor and threw up his shield as they ran past one of the next rooms which was igniting the charges.

The explosions were mild in comparison, but the severed egg was now unstable, and it rolled off the mound and began to shrivel. An ear-splitting sound rang through the room as the power was sucked from its once vibrance and fizzled into the dimness of its demise. Riddick and Amirra rounded the corner and found Shaz and Serin on the other side of an opening. Shaz held his finger to his lip and Riddick slowed and scooted up against the wall.

The coolness was good on his warmed skin. Riddick felt something brush his leg and his heart skipped a beat. He looked down to find the Minca, and he breathed out.

"I thought I sent you back to camp," Riddick said.

"And let you have all the fun, no way," Turkill said.

"Me too," Ladtwig said in his best Turkill voice.

Riddick shook his head but smiled. Amirra began her mind shield, extra strength, agility, and divergence casting and Serin buffed with wind-walk, pain-block, resist-damage, and internal-repair. Shaz stepped around the corner with his thumbs in his belt loops and flicked his hair out of his eyes.

"Hey there," Shaz said.

"Oh look, children," Jaduuk'ai said.

"Yeah, I guess you're right, you are a bit immature for your age," Shaz said.

Jaduuk'ai snarled a throaty chuckle.

"Aren't you a funny one," Jaduuk'ai said.

"Naw, I'm the grumpy one, but you should meet my friend Riddick, he's the funny one," Shaz said.

Shaz called the fire element to his hand and the flame burst into existence and Shaz looked around the room for any torches. He found a few on the side and ignited them. Shaz gripped the Honor Blades hilt out of habit and comfort and side stepped a few steps toward the middle of the room. Jaduuk'ai emerged from the blackness of the cave and Shaz stopped mid-step.

"Ouch, what happened to your face?" Shaz asked. Jaduuk'ai caught the scent of Shaz's bloodline and the corner of his lip peeled. "Yes, I am a Tooatha De Dannon," Shaz said.

"You are not just a Tooatha De, you are Alisdair's descendant," Jaduuk'ai said but wondered how Shaz knew what he was thinking.

"Aye, and you Baltair have made a huge mess, it's time you clean up and go home now," Shaz said.

"You Tooatha De are all alike, arrogant, pompous and snarky," Jaduuk'ai said.

"I'm usually called grumpy, cocky, and, alright you got me on snarky," Shaz said.

Serin rolled her eyes, Riddick covered his mouth, Amirra tapped her foot, Turkill hurmpfed and Ladtwig snorted.

"I didn't think there would be any Tooatha De's left, tell me, how many are there. I should have the most satisfying time killing you all," Jaduuk'ai asked.

"It's just me," Shaz said.

"That's a pity, but at least there is still one of you. I would have loved to see my brothers face when I suck your soul from your little body," Jaduuk'ai said.

"There's just one problem, I don't feel like dying today," Shaz said.

Jaduuk'ai's brow raised, he wasn't sure what to think of Shaz's attitude. He couldn't smell an ounce of fear on the, in his opinion, boy and he was certain it wouldn't be hard to kill him, but with how he was just standing there, it made him wonder if there was something he had missed. A deep heat radiated to the center of his being and Jaduuk'ai's rage surfaced. That was the same tactic Alisdair would use on him. Shaz studied Jaduuk'ai's energy as he witnessed his black eyes turn red. Shaz used the same tactic as he had with Tristan and wanted figure out what it would take to make him angry.

"I've had enough of this nonsense, you can either bow to me or die," Jaduuk'ai said.

Shaz lifted his hands from side to side as though he were balancing the two ideas between each other and shrugged.

"I got nothin'," Shaz said.

Shaz interpreted the beasts notion and gripped the hilt of the blade and pulled it from the sheath.

"So, you have the Honor Blade too," Jaduuk'ai snarled.

Jaduuk'ai gripped his hefty claws into the stone floor.

"And a few friends," Shaz said.

The crew stepped out from around the corner and Jaduuk'ai caught their scents as Jagwynn too made her way into the cavern.

"The Lavari, Bair, Fir, and a Daughter of the Light. Oh, and Minca too, how nice. So, you think you can banish me like my dear 'ol family did? Just so you know," Jaduuk'ai sniffed to determine which one was the Fir, and made eye contact with Amirra, who glared at him, "I am you're relative, you are going to try and kill me?" Jaduuk'ai laughed a throaty gurgling laugh and the irritation of the shadow magic ate at their nerves, but Shaz soaked it in.

Serin examined Shaz's heartfire and amazed that his fire element was now united with the green of the shadow magic and the bright-white of the electricity. Serin kept her distance in the back with Amirra but Riddick, the Minca, and Jag made their way to Shaz. Jaduuk'ai snarled and laughed a cackling growl.

"You know, that is the worst sound ever, are you sick?" Shaz asked.

Riddick snorted as the Jaduuk'ai gripped his front claws into the stone floor and launched himself at the crew. Shaz raced underneath his large frame sliding onto his knee with one leg outstretched and ran his blade along the center of his body while Riddick rounded his battle-ax into the side of his massive shoulder muscle. Turkill and Ladtwig both launched several rounds of darts. The darts hit the Jaduuk'ai but only stuck in the extra thick hide a tiny bit. Jaduuk'ai felt the tingle of his chest muscles going numb and a flash of curious irritation crossed his mind. Jagwynn lunged and sank her sharp long canine teeth into his haunches. Serin sent a blast of wind-shards and the force ripped through the beast. Blood oozed from the lashing and Jaduuk'ai snarled with the pain from all angles.

Amirra let her yellow magic encompass her frame, and she called the darkness into existence. The black mist emerged and hovered waiting for permission to attack. Amirra gave it the needed allowance and the mist shot across the cave. The darkness sank into Jaduuk'ai, and he reared back with the sensation of the force eating it from the inside. Shaz continued through his slide and shoved himself up with the last bit of movement. He spun on his foot and brought the blade down in a side-slice and slashed through the Jaduuk'ai's achilles tendon. The blade severed the beasts' movement of his foot and Jaduuk'ai roared with pain. His enormous frame fell to his knees as his foot no longer was able to hold himself up.

Riddick jumped into a roll as he dodged the huge beasts fist. Riddick gripped the rocks on the wall of the cavern and yanked. The shards grouped together, and Riddick thrust them toward the Jaduuk'ai. The rocks embedded into his thick skin, and he snarled and hissed. Blood oozed from the intrusions and Jaduuk'ai slammed his fist into the ground. The ricochet knocked everyone off balance, and they tried to stay standing. A thudding outside the cavern ate at

Riddick's senses, and he searched with his magic. Riddick whistled and Shaz turned to find him pointing to the opening.

We're about to have company, Riddick said in the mind conference.

Blast, Serin said.

Turkill and Ladtwig turned to the door and readied their darts. The first Captain barreled around the corner and the Minca let their darts go. The paralytic infused into the creatures blood and it fell with a thud. The next beast came in and the Minca again shot their darts. The beast fell on top of the other and Shaz gripped the fire element and doused the Jaduuk'ai with a torrent of fiery ooze. Serin sent her wind to accelerate the flames, and they bit into his flesh.

Jaduuk'ai's red-hot body shook violently and a thick layer of hardened rock-like material emerged and embedded itself onto his skin. Shaz stepped back in shock as he understood that Jaduuk'ai just created a rock shield and his fire and Serin's wind would no longer be effective. Jagwynn searched for an exposed piece of skin and sank her teeth into Jaduuk'ai's hind leg. Jaduuk'ai pulled his leg in but Jag bit harder. He tried to wriggle her off, but she wouldn't let go.

Turkill leaped out of the way as a Jaduuk jumped over the dead carcasses toward him. He rolled into a dead run and gained enough distance to send another blast of darts. Amirra called more darkness' and they ripped the souls of the Jaduuk from their frames. Riddick didn't see the Jaduuk'ai's fist round him, and he coughed as the force of the sudden hit to his chest lifted him off the ground sending him flying backward against the wall. Serin shot a surge of healing magic and his bones quickly realigned before he hit the ground. The pain was immediately dissipated, and he let his legs shove himself into a leaping somersault. Riddick pulled his ax through the Jaduuk'ai's now rock-like armor, but the ax bounced off.

Jaduuk'ai slammed his clawed hoof into the wall behind him and Jagwynn was thrown off by the thrust. She flew through the air and slammed into a jagged shard of rock at the back of the cavern and fell to the floor.

Riddick gripped his earth energy and slammed his hand on the armor before he returned to the ground. The kinetic energy gripped the minerals of the armor and it started to tighten around Jaduuk'ai's body. Jaduuk'ai sucked in a breath, but he struggled to fill his lungs as the armor continued to tighten around his frame. The strength of the rocks began to put pressure on Jaduuk'ai's bones and Riddick shuddered with the cracking sounds. Serin gripped the air he was trying to suck in and yanked it away as she sent a wave of healing magic into Jagwynn. Shaz ran to the opening where a fresh wave a Jaduuk and Jaduuk Captains were making their way back down the corridor. Shaz shielded himself and let the animals attack. His armor did what he needed it to, and he began to absorb their shadow magic. Serin continued to squelch the air Jaduuk'ai was trying to suck in and his eyes bulged from his hefty skull. The Minca shot darts at the oncoming Jaduuk to keep the pile from getting to big on top of Shaz and Serin blasted them away with her wind-slam.

Jaduuk'ai struggled against the forces and pulled the fire element to his grip. He sent a blast at Serin who recoiled as the heat wrapped around her frame. She called out in horror as the inferno terrorized her thoughts. She gripped the water element within herself and a huge wave doused the flames. Her body steamed from the combination and she growled. Jaduuk'ai sucked in a heavy breath as Serin was busy dousing the flames and sent a blast of fire at Riddick. Riddick threw up a wall of earth around him and the fire slammed into the wall of rocks. Riddick gripped the heated ore and wrapped his hands around in the motion of making a snowball. The hot ore formed into tight balls and Riddick launched them back toward the Jaduuk'ai.

The mineral orbs slugged Jaduuk'ai in the guts and his body was thrust backward with the force. Riddick thought he might have heard more bones break and stomped on the ground. The earth threw up several stones that he whipped around his head creating his vortex. Amirra sent her darkness' again through the center of the Jaduuk'ai and his body wriggled and writhed with the weirdness that he felt as his insides were eaten by the darkness. Jaduuk'ai blasted Amirra with a torrent of fireballs, and she recoiled but a second before the flames bit at her skin, her servitor's encompassed the fire element and fizzled into black mist. Amirra cursed and made her shield radiate from around her. Shaz was finally charged with the max effects of the build-up and he readied his mind to call on the lightning.

When I say, everyone attack the Jaduuk'ai, Serin, I need you to try and keep him suspended in the air while I open the portal, Amirra, I need you to take out all of these Jaduuk, and Riddick I need you to use your forces to shove the Jaduuk'ai toward the portal, Shaz instructed.

They affirmed the instructions and made ready to advance. Shaz closed the mind conference to the others and spoke only to Serin.

I'm going to have to use a great deal of shadow magic, and I might not be able to separate myself from the Jaduuk'ai, Shaz said in a near whisper.

What are you talking about? Serin's thoughts were clouded with the rush of elemental powers coursing through the cave.

I love you,

Shaz, don't you dare, Serin wasn't sure what that meant, and panic filled dread hit her chest.

"Now," Shaz yelled both out loud and in his mind. Shaz allowed the crackling energy to radiate from his being and Amirra called her servitors again and thrashed them through the pile of Jaduuk. Riddick slammed his forces creating a wall-like form of pulsating energy. Serin whipped her wind around the beast who lifted off the ground a few lengths, and Shaz let go of the bolt. The light beam hit Jaduuk'ai straight in the chest and the beast reared back with the sudden shift of powers.

"Teri nara shento mea'aha ano me'eari, lataya narra anoto chari ha' no soma menin. Potenta stoma nome," Shaz said.

The portal on the other side of Jaduuk'ai opened and Riddick slammed his forces toward the enormous beast. Sweat dripped down his face and chest as the heavy force resisted the strength of the Jaduuk'ai. Serin gripped her wind element and flung it toward Jaduuk'ai and his body began to shift. Shaz focused his continual lightning beam toward the God and moved closer to the portal. Serin's heart raced as she now understood what Shaz meant. A green glow began to emerge from Shaz's core, and the bolt increased. Amirra finished off the Jaduuk and turned her blackness' onto the Jaduuk'ai.

The soul eaters feasted again on the giants energy and Jaduuk'ai roared and snarled, but he couldn't manage the needed strength to penetrate the forces. Riddick doubled his energy and another wall of energy shot up behind him. He pushed his feet against the force to give him the support he needed to continue pushing the Jaduuk'ai. Shaz sheathed the sword and gripped a new form of raw energy. A green energy similar to the fire element came to life in his palm. The force wobbled and danced with a static kind of movement and Serin understood it was his shadow magic. She had never seen it as an element, and found it perplexingly beautiful.

Shaz let go of the green crackle and the jagged force ripped across the atmosphere. The Jaduuk'ai howled a deafening noise and tried to speak but the sound was muffled under the heavy vibrations of the earth pulsing, but Shaz understood what he was saying. It was, exactly what he figured would happen. Jaduuk'ai stopped resisting and allowed the forces to carry him into the portal, and he sucked Shaz with him. Serin screamed as Shaz's body was about to be swallowed up by the green mist of the shadow realm.

"Ste namari sheltet narata noshari, nada' no'halla toma nosh vi say na moha," Serin yelled as Jagwynn leaped into the forces.

Jagwynn wrapped her massive paws around Shaz's body and let her lunges force take her and Shaz to the ground as the portal closed with a slam. Riddick released his forces as did Amirra and Serin shot across to Shaz who was laying inside Jagwynn's limp bodies grip. Serin called her hydro-light magic and wrapped it with her love magic and placed her hands on his chest, and Jagwynn's heart. The magic shot into their body and began its full accounting of injuries with the instructions to mend everything. There were only minor injuries, but they were unconscious. Serin wrapped them into her arms, as best as she could muster the enormous cat, and tried not to panic. She knew they weren't dead, and their bodies were in full repair, but she didn't know what was happening. She focused on using their shared magic to see what he was seeing but it was pitch black inside his mind.

"Is he alright?" Riddick asked.

"I don't know," Serin said through a thick knot in her throat.

Amirra gave Riddick a look of panic and Riddick tried not to show his own fear. Shaz gasped and his lungs expelled the fumes his body had absorbed from the infinite-charge. Serin pulled the hair from his face and ran her fingers through his hair. Her armlet rearranged giving her the instruction she needed, and a reassurance eased her mind as she understood what had happened, and that she needed to just wait a bit.

"He'll be alright, he just needs a few minutes to initiate his normal function mode," The crew looked at her with perplexed glances, but she smiled and nodded. "Go, they need your help outside," Serin said.

"Are you sure," Turkill grumbled.

"Yes, we'll be out shortly," Serin said.

"Alright," Riddick said.

Riddick ushered the crew out of the cavern, and they made their way out to the battlefield. Serin stroked Jagwynn's long sleek body and settled into her warmth. Not only from her body heat, but her love for Shaz and her willingness to risk herself for him too. Serin held Shaz in her lap and continued to receive updates as his energies aligned and restructured his levels of operation. It was quite remarkable really, and she tried to make as many notes as possible so that she could remember what to do next time. She was certain there would be a next time and a hefty dose of dread settled on her mind. Jagwynn stirred and Serin sent her a boost of her soothing magic, and she blinked. Jagwynn lifted her large head and Serin stroked her chin. Jagwynn licked her gently and Serin smiled.

"How are you? Serin asked.

"Not dead," Jagwynn said.

Shaz blinked and stirred and Serin ran her hand over his chest. Her cool touch mixed with her pain and calming energy sank into his flesh, and he sighed.

"I love you," Shaz said.

Serin looked into his eyes and found he was gazing into hers.

"I love you, you big derp," Serin said.

Shaz smiled.

"My best mate said I was stupid, so I'll take being a derp over stupid," Shaz said with a sly grin.

Serin chuckled and kissed him. His lips were warm, and his energy was smooth and strong.

"How are you feeling?" Serin asked through the kisses.

"Amazing," Shaz said.

"Good, because we still have a war to end," Serin said.

63-We Better Get Down There And Help

Riddick and the others made their way to the landslide and Riddick ordered the rocks to shift creating a new pathway over the top of the fallen slabs. They hurried over the rubble and Riddick stopped as the scene unfolded before his eyes. The sun hadn't quite set yet and left a dim cast of light on the landscape. The armies were in full swing and the noise and chaos of weapons against shields was deafening. Blasts of fireballs careened through the air as the trebuchets and catapults released their loads. Howls and yelps mixed with the shouts and cries of the soldiers was nerving, and they found their skin itched with its realization.

"I can't believe this," Amirra said.

"Aye, we better get down there and help," Riddick said.

Riddick called an earth-board for everyone, and they raced around the edges. Riddick slowed his board and hovered near the Hollow where he and Amirra had first seen the Jaduuk over a moon ago and hopped off the board. He sucked in a deep breath and put his hands on the planet's surface. The energy radiated into his core and his heart broke for the pain it was suffering. Anger hit his nerve endings, and he slammed his hands together. The clap radiated around the atmosphere like thunder and a grumbling vibration shot away from him. The force peeled the skin off the Jaduuk and jellied their innards as it pelted the distance. Amirra called her servitors and this time fifteen black mists emerged. She commanded them to attack and the ravaging soul eaters consumed the beasts.

The Minca maneuvered their hover-boards into a position where they could launch their darts and began unleashing them at a fast rate.

Bowen signaled another advance and the shield wall picked up and started to move forward. A Captain signaled for his flame thrower to be ignited and the Jaduuk struck the wick with a flick stick. The cord caught on fire and raced to the inlet dish that operated the ignition. Green flames blasted from the long skinny tube and the soldiers braced for the hit. The shields did quite well, but they were wearing out and would either need to be replaced or repaired soon. The bowl of fluid fizzled out and the flame thrower stopped. Bowen's men raced around the shield-wall and attacked the beasts. The Jaduuk had learned so much in the time fighting, and they were harder to take down as they began to evade and use a more calculated attack. Riddick stomped on the ground and holes all around the flame thrower opened right underneath the creatures, and they fell through with a holler.

Bowen's men seized the machine and began to turn the heavy stone box that was on small stone wheels toward another flame thrower. Amirra started a chant to rebuff the shields and give the men a boost of energy while Riddick finished off burying the beasts.

"Where is Shaz?" Bowen asked.

"He's coming," Riddick said.

Riddick's chest heated with its truth and was certain he was. It was a curious emotion for him to have a different kind of connection, and he decided he liked it.

"Did you defeat the Jaduuk'ai?" Bowen asked.

"For, now, but this won't be the last time we'll meet him," Riddick said.

Bowen cringed but nodded and barked orders for his next assault. The crew continued to make headway, and they met up with Declan and the Rangers theater. Shaz secured the portal locking it shut and creating an alarm notice to notify him at his castle if anything ever tries to access it with the same identifiers as the others, which would allow the crew to use as an emergency to his castle if needed. Shaz, Serin, and Jagwynn came out of the tunnel and Shaz stopped to seal it off. He made the same disguise on each entrance as the other mountain temple and the face of the mountain became as the same structure as the rest of it.

They made their way to the rubble and crossed over Riddick's pathway. Their hearts sank as they internalized the amount of destruction. There was some solace in the fact that there were very little of any of their soldiers wounded or dead, but they couldn't believe how many Jaduuk there were.

"And I thought there was a lot in the Minca realm," Serin said.

"Aye,"

Shaz wasted no time, and called an earth-board and Serin buffed it. Jagwynn allowed herself to use the kinetic energy that Riddick had organized for her, and they dashed over the fallen creatures and destroyed landscape. Shaz's new green and red heartfire burned at a comfortable equality and his heartache for Grandfather was minimal. A smile formed, and he was thankful for the relief of the grief and anger.

"There's a horde over there with a flame thrower, I'll let you off here," Shaz said.

Shaz slowed the board and Serin jumped off. She began searching for any soldiers that might need her, and she hurried to a small group of men that were huddled under the remains of a catapult. Serin quickly assessed the needed mending, and she sent her pain magic into their tired bodies. The men relaxed with the releases on their frames, and she began to sew and heal their wounds. Shaz pulled the blade from the sheath and slashed through the neck of a beast and rolled his wrist and brought the blade down through the arm of another as he raced by. A prick at Shaz's mind made him turn in time to watch a giant spear let loose heading straight for him. Shaz gripped the lightning element and released the bolt from his palm. The speed in which the bolt hit the tip of the spear was incredible as no one even saw it before the spear was incinerated with a blinding shot of light.

Shaz turned back around to the green flames of the flame launcher being ignited. He smiled as he awaited the new euphoria the shadow magic inside him gave. The flames erupted from the tube but instead of incinerating him, the force wrapped around his body. Shaz soaked up the energy and felt his infinite-charge rising. The rush of the fire conduit reminded him of the conduit that took Grandfather, and he flicked his fingers. The heavy stone box shattered and shot out in all directions as his combustion ignited the goo inside.

Declan ordered his advance and Riddick and Amirra continued to annihilate the Jaduuk and even with the added health that their armor gave, they were starting to tire of the war. Serin finished her mending and the men jumped up with new vigor. They hurried through the carcass' and met up with their platoons, troops, and or battalions and regained the fight. Serin continued to search for any wounded but kept her search path close enough to Shaz that she could heal him if needed, but she was certain his new multi-dimensional magic gave him the needed protection, which then led her to wonder if she was going to need additional forces to keep up with him.

The Minca caught up with the rest of the Minca and joined the barrage of darts. The Minca warriors had taken to riding the elephantines and the rhino-moa and Turkill was the first to mount one of the largest bulls of the rhino-moa. Turkill hollered a war cry and the rhino-moa charged into the fray. The sharp and sturdy horn at the tip of his square nose pierced a Jaduuk and flung it and Turkill shot a dart into another. The beast lost its function to move and Turkill cringed as the rhino-moa's hefty foot crushed its skull. Ladtwig jumped onto the trunk of an elephantine, and she lifted him onto her back. The mammal thundered into the Jaduuk and swung her trunk flinging the Jaduuk into the air. Ladtwig arranged his darts to take out the next several Jaduuk as she grabbed one by the waist and used it to knock out a row of Jaduuk coming right at her.

The Forrne Fawn of the Guard kept their distance and launched their arrows in a steady pattern. The paralytic worked wonderfully and the Minca's poison did the rest. The stags advanced with their ballista's and spears. Antorn took his troop with Bowen, Tobis went with Declan, and Pillip went with Merrick. The Forrne, even though they were the most tired, fought with fierceness and determination. The gryphtons attacked at a stronger and calculated manner now that the spear and fire launchers were gone. Phanes fought with a deeper kind of fierceness. Vengeance has a way of changing how a creature decides what fierce is. Phanes nosedived toward a large Captain and pulled up at the last second. He threw out his talons and gripped the Captain by the throat. He caught the

Jaduuk's arm with his and yanked the battle-ax from his grip, then snapped its neck with his clawed paws. The Jaduuk fell to the ground with a thud. Brigdon raked his talons across the face of a Jaduuk as he twirled into the air, bent at the waist, and dipped back toward the beast. Brigdon pulled his sword and slashed it through the beasts' spine severing its spinal cord and it hit the ground. Jaxton released his ballista, and the spear-like arrow sank deep into the Jaduuk's neck.

Shar swung her slender gryphtoness figure into an upward thrust and caught a wind current that carried her away from the bomb she just dropped. The combustible material landed on the last spear thrower and sent the machine into shards all over the ground.

The Jaduuk's numbers began to decrease rapidly now that the spawners were gone, and the mountain was sealed. Shaz took on another pile of beasts until his infinite-charge was at max and focused on where he wanted the lightning to go. The bolts ripped across the landscape and rained down from the sky incinerating the bodies of the animals. Serin found and healed more soldiers and a few gryphton's while Bowen and Declan caught up with Merrick and his forces. The night was about to shift back into day when the last of the beasts fell and the armies shouted with an enormous cheer. The sound cascaded over the landscape and bounced off the mountain returning with a powerful affirmative which sank into the hearts of the men.

64-We Can Handle Things From Here

Congratulations were given all around and a huge weight left Shaz's being but was replaced with a new one. He was certain that Jaduuk'ai was not gone, nor was he going to be as nice the next time. His few minutes being connected to the Jaduuk'ai gave him the understanding of how he thought, at least in part, and his guts ached. Evil didn't have regard for life, nor did it care for equality or justice. Serin too understood the complexity of their new situation. Dread sat heavily on her emotions, and she struggled with the urge to wretch. Things had definitely changed for the good, and the bad, and the scariest part is just how bad will bad become before they figure things out.

Bowen signaled for the armies to retreat back to camp and the march was filled with renewed energy. The last moon cycle was one of personal growth for many, as well as a new acceptance of their universe.

"Riddick, let's make a sweep over the land to make sure we didn't miss any," Shaz said.

"Aye," Riddick said.

The two made their way to the gryphton's and found Brigdon and Phanes.

"Brigdon, can you take us around the savanna, we want to make sure we've taken care of everything," Shaz asked.

"Of course," Brigdon said.

Shaz and Riddick climbed onto the massive gryphton's, and they launched into the atmosphere. The image sank into their awareness and sadness plagued their hearts. The destruction was incomprehensible, and the earth was in ruins. The once flatlands were pocketed with holes the size of homes and buildings. The black earth covered nearly the entire surface, the trees that were left were dead or half-dead. Anger surged through Riddick's frame as he internalized the damage. Shaz sent out his radar-like energy and waited for the image to return. Brigdon and Phanes flew in a grid-like pattern and examined the surface with their eagle vision.

It took most of the day, but they were glad to find that there were no stragglers, and they headed back to camp. Shaz opened his mind conference with Riddick, and they discussed their options on how to heal the earth. Riddick was positive he could start the process, but he understood time would still be required to finalize the details. Shaz was most concerned about how to get rid of the shadow element that was now a part of the Jaduuk Captain's bodies. They had discovered that the green goo was toxic to the land and burning them and burying them might not be enough. To make things worse, they no longer had Inelius and Nitida to consult with and the uneasiness of figuring things out on their own was becoming real.

Camp came into view as they left the battlefield and the gryphton's landed near the war tent.

"Thank you," Shaz said as he climbed off Brigdon.

"Shaz, is everything alright?" Serin asked.

Shaz turned to find Serin gazing at him with concern on her features.

"Aye, why?" Shaz asked.

He was experiencing a host of emotions, so he wasn't sure which ones had caused her concern.

"Never mind, we can talk later," Serin said.

She pulled the flap open to the war tent, and they made their way inside. The leaders were there for the debriefing, and the rest of the afternoon was filled with plans to return the armies and help the Forrne and other animals rebuild their lands. Shaz had a hard time staying focused and Serin tried to boost him with her calming energy which only made him sleepier.

"Why don't you go get some sleep, we can handle things from here," Merrick said.

Shaz lifted his head off his palms and nodded. Serin went with him, and they walked quietly back to their tent.

"So, what is on your mind?" Shaz asked when she closed the flap.

"I sense a different kind of emotion in you I haven't seen before, and I have no idea what it is," Serin said.

Serin pulled her hair from the tie at the back of her head and let her soft waves fall. Shaz wrapped her in a hug.

"I have no clue," Shaz said.

"Well, we'll figure it out, this doesn't mean it's a bad thing, I just haven't seen it in you before that's all," Serin said.

Shaz nodded but his tired frame began to feel heavy on hers.

"Let me help you out of your armor, I need to inspect you anyway," Serin said.

Serin unlatched the buckles that secured the heavy leather chest armor. Shaz didn't like how restrictive the steel armor left him, so he opted for the beefed-up leather armor which allowed him to do all of his acrobatics and evade tactics he was fond of. Shaz removed the pauldrons and bracers as Serin set the armor on the table then she unlatched the buckle at the back to remove the gaters.

Serin ran a diagnostic on his body as he removed his tunic and found he was fine. The Binding of the Crypt scrolls mark was now outlined with a green glow. Serin touched one of the symbols in the center, and she understood his new emotion. Shadow Pathokinesis which Serin now understood as the ability to manipulate and control others emotions. Shaz's new shout which controlled the Jaduuk's emotions came in handy, but she now understood how incredible the power is, and how frightening it is. Shaz shivered with her cool touch and the image of the symbol came into his mind. Serin closed her eyes and read the markings. The intricate details of the scroll which sealed the grave was now tied to the cosmic powers of the Gods. Shaz read the same markings and understood how he was now connected to the realm of the living, the realm of the dead and the realm of the Gods, but what it all meant exactly was still a mystery.

"This changes things," Serin said softly.

"How so?" Shaz asked turning to face her.

"Our big world just got a lot bigger," Serin said.

Shaz nodded. The pieces were still floating around in his head, and he was sure it would take some time for him to sort it out. Shaz was thankful for Serin's affection as she tucked him into bed and sat next to him quietly. Serin drifted in and out of sleep but wasn't able to find a deep sleep. The voice of her father came in and out of her mind several times but now it was accompanied by images of Medrith and other wyverns and ruins of a beautiful city high in the sky. She couldn't figure out where she was, but the consensus of thoughts was that she was in one of the cities of the wyvern realm.

It was familiar as though she had been there, but it was different in that she didn't actually recognize the details.

Serin woke to the clanging of armor and shields and rolled over to find Shaz still sleeping. She closed her eyes and replayed the images in her mind, but her stomach wanted food, so she got up and went to the food tents. She found Riddick, Amirra, and the Minca and finished getting her breakfast. It wasn't terrible, in fact it was quite good considering it was travel food, but she missed the meals the Whispmother prepared and was looking forward to getting back to the castle. She understood that it wouldn't last long before something else took them somewhere, that's what seemed to be the new normal now.

She took a seat next to Amirra who was in a 'discussion' with the Minca on the technicalities of some issue Serin couldn't tell what. Riddick was in his own thoughts and Serin cut the meat and put a bite in her mouth. Merrick, Motavo, and Asher came into the tent and made their way toward them. Serin peered into concerned faces.

"What's wrong?" Serin asked.

"We found something," Merrick started. He hesitated and Serin gave him the 'stink eye', "we encountered more black earth, but there's something different," Merrick said.

"What do you mean different?" Riddick asked.

"You'll have to come see for yourself," Asher said.

The crew followed them out of the tent in a hurry and stopped at the black marks. Dark green veins now etched in the blackness glowed the eerie green from the shadow world.

"I'll go get Shaz," Serin said.

Serin grabbed an earth-board and hustled back to the tent. She jumped off and ducked in under the flap. She found Shaz still in bed, and she felt bad for having to wake him, especially since his war wizard brain had kept him awake so much lately. Serin rested her hand on his shoulder and then shook him gently. Shaz stirred and then sat up with a start.

"What's wrong?" Shaz asked shaking the sleep from his mind.

"Shadow magic is seeping into the veins of the black earth," Serin said.

"Blast, I wondered how long it would take to try to find me," Shaz said.

"What do you mean?" Serin asked.

"Unfortunately, the Jaduuk and Sqwall are not the only thing that will hunt me," Shaz said rubbing his hands through his disheveled hair.

"What is it now?" Serin asked.

"I'm not sure yet, but it doesn't make me eager to find out," Shaz said.

He quickly dressed and followed Serin to the green shadow veins. They dismissed the earth-boards and Shaz squatted down, touched the goo, and rubbed it between his fingers. It was indeed shadow magic in its liquid state.

"What are we going to do?" Riddick asked.

"We need to find the source of the goo, close it and heal the earth," Shaz said.

"How are we going to do that?" Amirra asked.

Shaz gazed around and the training ground they had used crossed his vision.

"I have an idea. Follow me," Shaz said.

He started toward the soft dirt and began to unlace his boots. Riddick took his off and the girls followed. The Minca came from their camp and took their shoes off too. Shaz smiled at their determination to always be a part of the solution. Shaz put his foot out to show which of the Kata's he was going to start, and the others followed. Their movements where strong and deliberate as their bodies executed the strikes, blocks, and kicks which were mixed with stretch-like movements. Amirra still hadn't learned them all but with her growing synergy with Riddick she was able to draw on his knowledge and found a strength in the movements. Merrick, Motavo, and Asher amazed at their exactness and even more so as their magic elements emerged from their bodies.

The forces wrapped around each other and began to make their way to their destinations. Riddick's deep orange mist began a conversation with the earth as Amirra began the apology chant. Her soft yellow aura seeped from her curvy but trim frame and dissipated into the earth and sky. Serin's blue magic wafted from her frame in waves like the sea and caressed the earth's surface for a time and then her wind gusts took it into the atmosphere. Shaz's multi-colored hues danced and swayed around the others and reinforced their efforts. The magic found the Minca following in the Kata's and even though they don't possess magic, their love for their friends both old and new was powerful enough that Shaz's magic picked it up and took it into the world.

"Have you ever seen anything like it?" Motavo asked.

"No, never," Merrick said.

Antorn, Mazen, Tobis, and Pillip, came up behind them and stopped to take in the amazingness of the magic. Brigdon, Jaxton, Helios, Phanes, and Leeta too made their way and stopped next to the Forrne. The silence was evident of their awe in absorbing the breath-taking light show. Shaz began another Kata and the group followed. The energy grew as they focused on their goal. Shaz's mind was clear and energized and his chest heaved with the relaxed sensations of acceptance. He had be struggling with the grief of losing Grandfather in the midst of fighting a war and peace finally overcame him. His energy surged with approval and the strength of his trial etched in his mind.

Riddick focused on the black earth and it began to fade away. The brown dirt emerged, and new blades of the tall grasses wriggled to the surface. A heavy pulsing vibrated from Riddick's magic and the earth shivered. The wobbling alerted the armies and they searched for the cause. Serin's wind pushed and pulled against the debris hanging over the landscape and her water magic broke through to the atmosphere above. The particles in the sky arranged into rainclouds and a deep rumble crossed the sky as thunder signaled the beginning of the rains. Amirra's yellow moved into the shape of a delicate dancer and made its way around the soul of the planet, tickling the plants and stroking the trees to give back the soul of the vegetation and animal life. Sweat formed on their skin with the heat of their magic and their bodies in motion with the Kata's.

The clouds overhead opened, and rain fell from the sky. The cool clean moisture hit the dark ground and at first bounced off. Shouts of joy rang from the Forrne settlements as they hadn't seen rain in over a rotation and Serin's heart swelled. The notion that she was healing the planet was invigorating, and she understood a new element to her magic. The rain was comforting on their warmed bodies, but they continued through the motions. The group grew larger as more soldiers, Forrne, and Gryphton's came to watch.

Rain soon began to sink into the dirt and the blackness faded even more. Shaz turned his focus to the shadow magic and began to search for the cause. His mind followed the veins back to the mountain, and he realized the shadow magic was seeping from all the carcasses. He had wondered if that was going to cause an issue, and he was right. Shaz's bright white lighting magic came to the surface and seeped into the cracks of the veins. The energy crackled and popped as it sizzled along the veins incinerating the green goo. The water of the rain acted as a conduit and helped the lightning cross the vastness of the savanna incinerating the dead Captains and dissipating the shadow magic. The light show increased in magnitude that everyone shielded their eyes from the brightness.

Soft tufts of beige grasses surged to full height and the living acacia trees sprouted new growth. The group flowed into another Kata and the vibrant colors of the savanna at night emerged as the brightness moved farther away. The earth transformed into the beauty it once was and Antorn bowed reverently to the crew. Mazen bowed, lowering one leg reverently. Tobis followed and then Pillip and the rest of the survivors.

The lightning finished its path through the land and dispersed leaving the rain to continue cleaning the world. Serin focused on her light magic and the clouds parted to let the sunshine though. The rays bounced off the raindrops and sent a new cascading glimmer across the distance. Sun rays coursed over the land and the elephantines horn-like trunks sounded a mighty tune followed by the roaring billows of the rhino-moa and the birds chirped and sung from the protection of the acacia trees. The crew understood the planet would now take over, and they released the holds on their elements.

65-I Made Nama A Promise

The rains drizzled outside the pavilion, but the air was clear and fresh. Antorn took Mazen's hand and gave it a squeeze, and she gazed at him. Antorn's heart thumped against his ribs as it thrust endorphins through his body at lightning speed. Nama smiled her gentle grin and the wrinkles on her old frame showed years of experience which was somehow soothing. He turned to face Mazen and took in the depth and beauty of her amber eyes.

"Mazen, I made Nama a promise and I meant every word," Antorn started. Mazen's heart skipped, and she put her hand over her mouth. "Will you be mine forever?" Antorn asked.

Mazen struggled with the emotions which were surging to her throat but managed to say, "Yes."

The crowd erupted with cheers and Tissa squeezed in between them. Antorn leaned down and looked Tissa in the eye. His warm eyes glinted in the new daylight.

"Tissa will you be ours?" Antorn asked.

Tissa's eyes filled with tears and escaped her small delicate face. She threw her arms around his neck and hugged him tightly as Mazen ran her fingers through her hair. Tissa pulled back and Mazen gripped her tight. The crew smiled with warmed hearts and was happy for the renewed energy which seemed to radiate from the savanna.

"Congratulations, I'm happy for you," Shaz said.

Serin gave them all a hug and Riddick slapped hands. Amirra hugged them all and the Minca tried to slap hands, but they found it harder to reach their tall grips. Pillip came up to them and lowered into a bent knee bow and then Tobis. The rest of the Forrne followed and Antorn suddenly was full of uneasiness. Pillip rose and held his hand in the Guard Salute and the rest followed. Shaz also saluted and the rest of the army followed. Phanes moved his sleek and powerful frame through the Forrne who moved to the side. Phanes rose to his hind legs and held out his paw.

"It is the honor of the Gryphton nation to call you an ally and a friend," Phanes said.

Antorn took his paw and shook it the best he could. The Gryphton's screeched and roared into the atmosphere. The sound was deafening and inspiring. Bowen made his way to Antorn and saluted. The Ebassian's slammed their fists to their hearts in unison sending a rippling of thudding through the masses.

"Ebassia is honored to be your allies, and friends. If you are ever in need, we swear an oath to help," Bowen said.

"It is I Antorn and the Forrne who swear our allegiance to your great nations, we owe you a debt we can never repay," Antorn said.

"Now let's party!" Ladtwig shouted.

The crowd broke into cheers and laughter. Shaz couldn't deny the ache in his stomach.

"I'm starved," Shaz said.

It had been over a day since he had eaten and the smell of the roasting meats that came from the food tents sank into his being. They made their way to the serving lines and festivities broke out all over camp. Motavo and Asher introduced the Forrne to their custom of a large bon-fire and the Minca brought their music in which the Forrne added their drums and rain-sticks to the mix. The night was filled with impressive celebrations and Shaz found Serin listening to the fiddler.

Shaz took her hand and she smiled. Serin loved dancing with him, it was the time they had to celebrate their small wins and re-connect with each other. Shaz's new powers gave his features a brighter appearance and Serin escaped into his deep blue eyes. Motavo and Asher even joined the dancing with some of the Traveler ladies who had come to help and Riddick and Amirra joined the festivities. The gryphton's curled up near the fire and gazed at the different celebrations.

Phanes and Leeta cuddled close and Jaxton and Brigdon chuckled to themselves thinking about how Ralti was going to handle the news. They were certain he would be grumpy on the outside and profusely proud on the inside. Phanes had certainly become the lion natured aggressor with the ability to have the compassion needed to lead a pack properly. Shar came into the circle and Brigdon motioned for her to sit next to him. Shaz eyed the two and pointed it out to Serin who smiled. Serin caught the glint in Brigdon's eye, and she was certain things would work out for them.

The evening passed quickly and Serin turned in for the night and Shaz stayed up to tend the fire for a bit. The night was cool, and he was certain things would return to normal for the Timeless Plains, especially with Antorn and Mazen as the leaders. Shaz was also certain Baltair would make his presence again. Which made him wonder what kind of threat Gavin Rhill really was, and if he even knew about Baltair. Shaz guessed he didn't, and he was still under the notion he was the one to gain the Sev-Rin-Ac-Lavah and become a God.

Shaz now understood that would be a very bad thing and would make two gods he would have to battle. At least he has the sword and the scroll, but he wondered if there would be enough magic in two of the relics to make him more powerful. A nagging feeling at the back of his mind he had learned to recognize as cosmic intuition kept telling him he needed to secure the spear and fast. He hadn't had much time to think about the spear and what it's implications were.

He understood whoever held it would never lose the battle, and it was made from the horn of the Kar-ka-dannon's which had healing powers, but what did that mean exactly. The crackle of the fire aided in his thinking, and he found his mind wander around all the details he had learned. Serin stirred and Shaz's thoughts were interrupted by a sense of panic, and he darted toward their tent.

A dim light emerged and Serin looked around but couldn't make anything out. She was certain she had been asleep, but she wasn't in her bed in the tent. The light grew, and she covered her eyes as it became too much for her to watch. The bright light disappeared with a pop and darkness crept into the room she was now in. The rank odor of the dungeons of Ebassia sank into her senses, and she puckered with the stink. Serin saw her reflection in the small puddle on the ground. Sounds of the other prisoners filled her head while she stood shackled to the wall.

She had not slept or eaten, and she was exhausted and starving. She wondered what would happen to her. Serin didn't have any idea why she was there, what she had done or not done to have been cast into the dungeons. Rats scurried to and from all around her, her body quivered with fear as they nibbled at the laces of her boots. A loud thud echoed from outside the cell door and the door opened. A nasty old haggy witch stood in the doorway and cackled at her while pointing a crooked finger. Shaz's face surfaced, and she could tell his lips were moving but there was no sound.

"You will die this day," the witch cackled.

The door slammed shut and darkness carried her away from the dungeon cell and left her surrounded by a wall of fire. Deep gurgling growls rang in circles around her as she felt the hot putrid breadth of the Jaduuk surrounding her. Shaz's face surfaced again, she could see his lips moving again but there was still no sound. The leader of the Jaduuk pack laughed an evil roar and lunged at her. She suddenly began to fall down the cliffs that lead to the Minca realm. Serin hit the ground and a sharp pain stabbed her in the side. The pain raced to her brain, and she sucked in a deep breath as tears raced down her cheeks. She rolled over to find Tukill's dead body laying mangled next to her and her heart thumped against her ribs.

A jarring sensation gripped at her arms, and she struggled against the forces. She tried to stand up and run, but she couldn't. Her whole body wouldn't move. She tried and tried but nothing, she was trapped. Shaz's face surfaced again, and she saw his cheeks red with frustration which bordered on panic, and this time his faint voice sat at the back of her mind. She blinked but still couldn't make her body respond.

"Serin, Serin, wake up. You have to wake up, please wake up," Shaz's tone was filled with fear and panic and Serin struggled against the forces on her body and then realized it was Shaz who was trying to move her. Serin jumped with a start and sat straight up. Tears ran down her face as she realized where she was. She fell into Shaz's shoulder and sobbed.

"It's alright, your safe, your safe," Shaz said trying to console her, not sure himself.

Serin's frame shook from the energy it took to experience the nightmare, and she was convinced there was more to it than just a nightfright. Shaz stroked her hair and tried to calm his heartfire. The heat in the room was getting overwhelming, and he knew it was his magic in panic mode that created the heat.

"I'm sorry," Serin managed.

"I tried to come after you, but you couldn't see me," Shaz said.

"I was in the dungeons, the witch, there was fire and Jaduuk, then I fell and saw Turkill dead. I couldn't get away," Serin said still crying.

"I know, I saw it all," Shaz said.

Serin wiped away the tears and pulled in a deep breath.

"You must think I am a child," Serin said now embarrassed.

"No, the shadow is trying to overcome you through night-mares now." Shaz said softly, but Serin heard the hint of anger under his tone. "You have been through more than what is fair and most of it because of me. Now if it were me, you would think I was the baby," he said with a grin.

Serin laughed through the tears.

"Yeah your right I would," Serin said.

Shaz pulled her into him, and he wrapped his arms around her.

"We'll have Amirra enchant you a dream ring, and I can give you a ring this time," Shaz said.

Serin liked the sound of that, and she listened to his heart beating in his chest and tried to listen to her own. She was always paying attention to his that she never thought about hers.

I always listen to your heart, both its beating and its wisdom, Shaz said in his mind. Serin smiled but noticed he was trying really hard not to let her sense his urgency to leave.

"We are on the move again aren't we?" Serin asked.

Shaz slid his hand under her hair at the side of her head and gazed into her eyes. What he wanted to do was to make a timeless realm of their own and take her away. To give her a family, happiness, joy, and live for the rest of ever without the evils, but he also loved the world and wanted the same for everyone. Serin read his emotions and her heart swelled with love for him. She put her hand on his arm and leaned into his grip. His skin was warm and sent a coursing sensation through her. She looked into his deep blue eyes and was certain with more than any other power, she belonged to him.

"Baltair isn't gone, so we really need to find your mother and Gavin Rhill and remove him from the picture. I don't think he is even half the trouble that Baltair is going to be, but I would rather only fight one thing at a time," Shaz said.

"Where are we headed then?" Serin asked still trying to control her tears.

"We need to head to Turob and find the staff, Riddick is fairly certain he knows where it is, and then we start searching for your mother and figure out what your fathers warning means," Shaz said.

Serin didn't expect the emotions race through her frame and Shaz watched as she processed the information. He could tell she was both eager but completely terrified, and he pulled her into his tight embrace. Serin sank into his grip and soaked in his magic. He had the most amazing way of making her feel better, feel complete, feel invincible, powerful, and his kindness and empathy was incredibly attractive, but it was his love for her that made her feel perfect.

The days passed quickly as Shaz remade the portals and the armies began their return march. They dismantled the trebuchets, catapults, and carried back the flame throwers that were still operable and the elephantines returned them to the castle. Motavo and

Asher had become so good at keeping things moving it didn't take long before they were saying their good-byes to the Forrne.

Shaz packed the last of his pack and Serin pulled the flap of hers.

"Ready?" Shaz asked.

"Not really, but hey I'm with you," Serin said.

Shaz smiled and they left the tent.